THESE

TANGLED ROOTS

INTO THE STAINED-GLASS FOREST:
BOOK ONE

DAPHNE TATUM

For Mom,
who began my story.

Nathan,
who added the friends-to-lovers trope,

and my kids,
who keep the plot twists coming.

My chapters would be
meaningless without you.

AUTHOR'S NOTE

As you enter the Fold, please be aware that some things lurking within this world are scarier than any goblin. Though good ultimately triumphs over darkness, darkness does exist.

Content warnings can be found at the back of the book for readers who may be sensitive to particular subjects (on page 408 for physical copies & under Content Warnings in eBook versions). They may also be found on my website: daphnetatum.com.

All material is intended to be suitable for YA readers. If *These Tangled Roots* was a movie, the rating would be no higher than PG-13.

SHADOW

$\blacklozenge$

He waited beneath a gnarled fey tree, shrouding himself with its shadows. Three girls strolled past. Their scent teased him, made his mouth water. His shaking hands curled around a branch, obsidian claws slicing through the bark with a thin crackle.

Patience. He needed to see if she was the right one.

Two of the girls skipped up the steps to the female dorms. A peal of thunder drowned out their goodbyes. The third—the fair-haired one—smiled with anticipation. She turned towards the river, as he had known she would. He'd been watching her for weeks.

He crept soundlessly through the darkest patches, which seemed to bend and follow him, as befit a shadow. Perhaps it was time to choose a new name. However, the banality of Shadow for a creature of the night amused him, and it worked as well as any.

A cool breeze slid under his hooded cloak. It sent the hem dancing across a patch of dry leaves. They rustled, whispering warnings to the girl—now perched on the rocks at the water's edge, her blonde hair transformed to a rippling white curtain in the moonlight. But another peal of thunder overwhelmed their papery voices.

The girl stretched her arms out to catch the first raindrops as the wind picked up speed, chasing roiling steel clouds across an ebony sky.

Darkness over darkness.

Like blood dripping into blood.

Now was the time, while she glowed with new energy, before she drew too much strength from the oncoming storm. He ran, a swift black night-wraith. The girl barely had time to turn. Shadow bore her to the ground, his heavy cloak settling over them both. Delicious fear widened her eyes.

She lifted one hand, a pale point of energy building in her palm.

He whispered to the nearby trees, syllables of the ancient language slippery on his tongue. Roots crashed upwards through the rocky earth. One whipped around the girl's wrist and yanked it down. Her bolt of power blasted into the soil, sending up a shower of pebbles and dirt. The wind chased grit over Shadow's skin. But the roots continued their inexorable work, snaking around the girl's ankles and wrists, lashing her to the river bank. Last, the finishing touch—one for her throat. Tight enough to muffle sound, loose enough to keep her conscious.

He leaned closer, breathing hard.

Time to see.

First the legs, though her energy source hardly posed a question. Ignoring her panicked whimpers, he slid her long skirt up and examined the silver swirls marking her calves. Perfect. Now the eyes—to confirm what he'd seen from a distance. Chocolate pools, deepened by terror. Relief flickered through him. He stroked a claw delicately along the curve of her cheek, then over the root holding her left arm. The root loosened, allowing him to hook one claw beneath the cuff of the girl's long sleeves. She seemed to hide her wrists just to spite him.

Thunder and wind nearly drowned out the sound of ripping fabric. His eyes roved eagerly over the symbols twining around her wrist.

Blue.

Blue for water.

Disappointment flooded him, bitter, galling. It wasn't *her*, after all. His claws bit into the girl's arm. Her strangled cry of pain wasn't enough to ease his frustration. He dug his claws in further, savoring her sobs as her blood slicked his skin.

A fire soul... the *proper* fire soul... was it too much to ask? How did this disgusting boarding school teem with their fragile, foolish lives—insects exploding from every crevice—yet not hold the single girl he needed?

Hunger gnawed at him, exposing one threadbare consolation: this one was now expendable.

He pushed back his hood. The girl's eyes widened, her lips twisting in a near-silent scream. He pulled her wrist to his mouth, carefully piercing the blue energy tattoo with his long fangs. Her body arched and bucked.

The first taste of her life force brought Shadow's hunger roaring to life, full and terrible. He clamped down, fangs nearly breaking through to the other side of her wrist. He gulped eagerly as the girl convulsed. Sweet. Oh, so sweet.

Her body shuddered. Stilled. The flow of energy slowed.

Shadow continued teasing those last delectable remnants from her as the girl stiffened and began glowing with the faint luminosity of moonlight. Cracks raced over her skin, her eyes, nails and teeth and hair—a ruined star nearing annihilation. He drew in one last draught...

She shattered. An implosion of ash and light, hovering in a girl-like shape for mere seconds before collapsing into a pile on the ground.

Shadow smiled.

He stood, staring down at the faded essence—all that remained of the vibrant laughing girl—and swept one foot out to dispel the dust. It floated away, shining motes in the rainy night. "Ashes to ashes."

2

Pebbles on a Windowpane

◆

*T*ap. Tap. Tap.

The distinctive sound of pebbles hitting a windowpane echoed softly in the predawn hours of a nippy winter morning. Destry jiggled the last few rocks in her palm and scowled up at Cam's window—second story, third from the front, facing her house next door. Dew from the Waters' neatly trimmed grass soaked her shabby canvas sneakers and chilled her feet. Cam's lawn was more brown than green, like most Texas lawns in December, but it looked better than her weed-infested yard.

No movement from the bedroom. Destry pressed her lips into a tight line. Cam might sleep like the dead, but he had exceptional hearing, and a handful of pebbles usually woke him—without alerting Mr. and Mrs. Waters. Still, he'd been gone for an entire semester. Maybe he'd gotten used to sleeping without early morning interruptions.

Well, Mr. Camden-Fancy-Pants-Waters better get used to them again. She lobbed her remaining rocks towards the window, then grabbed more from a flower bed. Too bad she couldn't call him. But even if her cell phone had service at the moment (it didn't), the ringing might wake his folks. Finding out that their fifteen-year-old neighbor made early-hours visits to Cam's room—even for entirely innocent reasons—could rile the nicest of parents. No sense getting Cam grounded. She tossed more rocks.

As the seventh stone clacked against the window, it slid upwards, and Cam poked his rumpled head out. "Seriously, Des? It's four in the morning."

She glared, folding her arms and flipping her hair over one shoulder. A stray breeze blew some pale cornsilk strands back, catching on her eyelashes and tickling her nose. Destry shoved them away, but they tangled on her fingers instead. How was she supposed to strike an impressively annoyed pose with one hand caught in her hair? She yanked loose, ripping out a few wisps in the process. *Owwww.*

"You okay down there?" Cam's voice brimmed with suppressed laughter.

Destry chucked her last pebble directly at him.

He caught it, of course. Groaned. Then ducked inside, returning in seconds to unfurl the rope ladder that was (theoretically) to help him escape in case of a fire. The fire safety company probably hadn't included *this* in their sales pitch.

Destry sucked in a steadying breath and forced her legs to move, her hands to curve around the smooth metal rungs. This part never got easier, no matter how many times she did it. *Just don't look down.* She clambered up, eyes trained on Cam's face. Relief shuddered along her spine as he helped her over the sill. He shoved the window closed, gave Destry a rough side hug, tousled her hair half-heartedly, and collapsed on his bed.

"I can tell you're happy to see me." She tried not to sound *too* snippy.

"Give me a break, Des. My flight got in after midnight. I can't focus well enough to see you. If you'd waited until a normal time, I'd be leaping for joy."

She smacked him in the head with a stray pillow, then kicked off her sneakers. They rolled over some empty snack wrappers before coming to a stop next to his bed. Cam trained bleary eyes on her bare feet. "You know, at school, I learned about these cutting-edge inventions called socks. Keep your feet warm in the winter. You should try 'em sometime."

She'd been too excited to see him to scrounge up a clean pair in her dark house, but admitting that felt minorly pathetic. Instead, she smacked him with the pillow again. "Sorry to mess with your beauty sleep. Gotta be at work by five." She hurried to the adjoining bathroom, tripping over some clothes and a discarded backpack on the way. He'd been home less than four hours. How had he already gotten the bedroom this messy?

The warm tile floor felt good against her chilly feet. Destry dug through the cupboards and tossed a towel and washcloth on the shining countertop. Cam's voice carried past the half-closed door. "Still amazes me that any newspaper does delivery routes. Who reads an actual paper nowadays?"

Destry snorted. "Nothing changed while you were gone. My boss is as determined as ever to run 'an honest small-town paper like my daddy produced.' Good thing we have about a million retirees in this town."

"Good thing your boss doesn't need to make a profit."

Destry didn't bother answering. She didn't have time to rehash the eccentricities of their town's wealthiest citizen—not when he was such a stickler for employees being on time. And especially not if she wanted to beat the rain headed their way. The thunder and lightning hadn't started yet, but the sense of an oncoming storm tingled in her bones and pressed against her skin.

In decent weather, she'd be counting down the minutes until she could race outside to soak in every drop, revel in the peals of thunder shaking the sky. But pedaling her bike through a wintery downpour in barely-there morning light? That ranked lower on her happy list.

She scooted back into the bedroom to rifle through Cam's dresser. In her eagerness to see him, she'd also forgotten to grab a jacket. Her fingers brushed soft flannel—one of his ever-present button-ups. Not for the first time, she felt grateful for Cam's height and solid build. He'd always complained about being the biggest kid in class, year after year. But those broad shoulders and muscles meant his shirts fit a chubby girl like Destry.

Not like she would've made it a condition of their friendship. Still, being able to steal his clothes was a serious side benefit. She tucked the flannel shirt in the crook of her arm and shoved the drawer closed. "I'm glad you're back. I'm sick of cold showers."

"Your power got turned off again?"

She ducked into the bathroom, tossing the purloined shirt on the counter before making a beeline for the shower. "Yep. Bright side, though... cold showers and living by candlelight keep Pervert Number Twenty-Seven from staying overnight at our place."

The bedsprings creaked, like Cam had jerked to a sitting position. "Beverly changed boyfriends? I thought she liked Kenny."

"You know Mom." Destry turned on the hot water in the shower, giving it a chance to warm up. Her mother never liked the nice ones very long. Or they figured out that she wouldn't let them be some knight in shining armor and save her from herself. "Kenny's been history for weeks now."

"Is the new guy trying to mess with you?"

Nothing good could come from this conversation. She concentrated on the wisps of steam creeping out from the shower, carrying the scent of Cam's soap. Silence stretched between them.

Cam's voice dropped an octave, into a familiar tone of command. "Destry, I asked you a question."

"I can hear."

"Then answer me."

"You sure are getting bossy. Guess that's what happens when you gallivant across the country to attend some fancy-pants leadership academy. Are you supposed to use winter break to solve world hunger?"

"Quit evading."

She fiddled with the cold water and stuck a hand in to check the temperature. The droplets seemed to seep into her skin, sending energizing tingles up her arm. "It's nothing I can't handle. I lock my door, I stay out of his way. He hasn't touched me."

"But he's trying." The thump of feet hitting the floor meant Cam was fully awake now—and upset. "Maybe it's time to get my folks involved."

No. Her stomach dropped. She scrambled to the doorway, water temperature forgotten. "You promised not to tell! Your parents will call social services, and I'll end up in foster care!"

Cam was already at the bathroom door. A frown settled over his well-defined features. He ran one hand through his hair, making the chestnut waves stick out at odd angles. "I won't let that happen."

"How will you stop it? You're seventeen. No one's gonna consult you on what to do. As soon as you tell the adults, *their* opinion on what's best for me is all that matters. Why do you think I climb that stupid rope ladder whenever it's super late or super early, or I want to hide out here for a while? I can't risk your parents thinking something's wrong."

"Something *is* wrong, Destry. Your mom drinks away most of her paycheck. You don't have power half the time, the only food in the house is the food you buy, and you barely go home because of the freaks she dates. On top of all that, you're working your butt off."

She twisted around, looking over her shoulder. "Nope. My butt is definitely still there." He didn't even crack a smile, and she bit her lip. "Please, Cam. At least here I know what I'm dealing with. And I have you."

"Don't do that to me... the please and the sad brown eyes. I hate it."

"Look, it may not be an issue soon. I was gonna tell you later, when it was a sure thing, but I better spill it now. I've been offered a scholarship to a boarding school."

Cam's eyebrows slid upwards. "I didn't know you'd applied anywhere."

"I didn't. The guidance counselor at the high school gave them my name. The scholarship covers everything—tuition, room and board, even travel costs." She hesitated, biting at a hangnail on her index finger. "That is, if I get it. I meet with the scholarship committee tomorrow. Mrs. Meech says it's just a formality."

Cam tugged her hand away from her mouth. "You'll make your cuticles bleed," he said absently. He'd said it a thousand times before. "So what's the name of this school?"

She picked at the hangnail with her fingers instead. "Can we talk about it later? Even if that committee approves me, I need my job until I leave. Can't be late."

"Sure, Des. Enjoy your shower."

"I'd enjoy it more if you had my favorite body wash."

"Yeah? Well, you forgot to hide it under the sink last time—and Mom cleaned the bathroom that day. My folks gave me odd looks when I explained that I like the scent of 'Sparkling Sea Mist.'"

Destry snickered. Cam's soap preferences were depressingly plain. "Should have told them you were exploring your feminine side." She faltered at the bathroom door. "Cam? You won't say anything, right? It could really screw things up for me."

"You better not be lying about that scholarship."

"When have I ever lied to you?"

"Every single day."

"Good thing I'm telling the truth now."

Cam grumbled something under his breath, but he also made an irritable shooing motion before flopping on his bed. Destry heaved a sigh of relief. If Cam was willing to go back to bed, he felt better for the moment. She kicked the bathroom door closed and undressed, listening to the water hiss against the shower's granite floor. It was ironic. The one guy her mother had ever worried about—the older boy next door—was one of the few who'd never tried anything at all.

Cam wasn't actually sleeping. He wanted to. But his concern over Destry ruined all attempts to slip into blissful unconsciousness. He'd been worrying about her too long to break the habit now.

Admittedly, she wasn't the same kid he'd met four years ago: a chubby, awkward eleven-year-old in torn jeans and a messy ponytail, tripping over her own feet as she tumbled out of a banged-up sedan. She'd turned a slow circle, taking in the neighborhood at the edge of the historic district with its hodgepodge of houses—some stately like Cam's home, some just older. The place Beverly Adams had inherited was the smallest on the block, and the yard had become overgrown in the months since Destry's grandma died. Des still gawked like it was a castle. "We're really gonna live here?"

Cam's dad stepped forward, offering introductions and a set of keys to Destry's mom. "Your mother gave these to me after your dad passed, in case of an emergency. She knew—"

Beverly's face stiffened. "That she couldn't count on me?"

"That I was easily available," Dad supplied smoothly. He always knew the right way to handle people. Cam wished he could emulate that near-kingly confidence, but it seemed to be an inborn thing. "We live right next door."

Beverly's shoulders relaxed. "You're the ones who were always helping her, hauling groceries and doing repairs. Mom mentioned you in her last letter. I'm very grateful." She sniffled and pulled Destry closer. "I couldn't be here because... Well, the reasons are private."

Cam studied her surreptitiously. Although Beverly hadn't visited in the seven years since Cam's family moved into the neighborhood, old Mrs. Adams had kept photos on her mantel. They showed a bright-eyed young mom holding a giggling, well-kept toddler. But the woman standing before them looked like a plant starved for water—an undernourished replica of the mother in the photos.

Dad offered his pleasantly-reassuring-but-not-overly-friendly smile, the one Mom said made women feel safe. "We're here if you need anything. I'd have helped more on the house, but your mother was a very independent woman."

"Don't I know it. She couldn't understand anyone who struggled to manage life, in any capacity." She sighed, then pushed Destry towards Cam. "Look, baby. There's someone close to your age. Go make friends while I discuss what needs repaired with Mr. Adams."

Friends... A familiar regret pinched Cam, like it did every time he recalled that first meeting and the initial months after Bev and Des moved in. He wished he'd been as nice to Destry as he'd been to her grandmother.

You were a stupid thirteen-year-old who cared more about being popular than being a good friend. You know better now. Let it go.

Cam sighed and re-adjusted his position. The cotton sheets rustled gently. He closed his eyes, letting the comforting darkness pull him away...

Pull him away...

Pull him...

It wasn't working. Cam groaned.

He opened his eyes again and snagged his phone from the bedside table. 4:21 a.m. "Seriously, Des," he muttered. But he couldn't put true rancor behind the words. They'd gone from seeing each other every day to a few emails a month—all he could manage but not enough. Especially for Destry, who he'd basically deserted.

Cam heaved himself from the bed and shuffled to his dresser, digging out his smallest pair of socks: the Captain America ones. See how she liked that. With a faint grin, he tossed them next to her shoes. Then he rummaged through the drawer in his bedside table for the lotion Des always stashed there. He dropped it on the end of the bed, where she couldn't miss it, and collapsed on the mattress.

The shower water shut off, allowing him to hear Destry's tuneless humming. She came out moments later wearing one of his favorite flannel shirts over her Iron Man tee, weaving her hair into a messy braid. "I thought you'd be asleep by now."

He pushed up onto one elbow. "We haven't seen each other in months. I can sleep later."

A pleased smile brightened her round face. She bounced onto the end of his bed, still braiding. She managed to sit on the tube of lotion. "Exams are done, and tomorrow is the last day before vacation. I could skip school and come over after my paper route."

Cam sat up all the way, running a hand through his hair. "I told you in my last email. I won't be here the next two days. My grandparents' fiftieth anniversary party...San Antonio...they postponed so I could make it? Remember?" He nudged her knee aside, found the lotion, and tossed it in her lap.

Destry's fingers stilled a moment before winding an elastic band around her braid. "The last email I got said you'd be home today. That's it. But I...I haven't checked my email in a while." Her voice came out small. "My phone ran out of service a few weeks ago."

Cam cursed inwardly. When he'd left at the beginning of the school year, he'd known she would take it hard. Now he was letting her down again. "I'm sorry, Dessie. My folks and I leave for San Antonio at eight."

A shrug, a forced smile. "Don't worry about it. Not like I've been counting down the days until you came home or anything." She palmed the lotion, turning it over and over in her hands, gaze trained on the plastic tube.

He chucked her under the chin. "Well, that's disappointing. I marked off every single day on *my* calendar."

Her eyes flew to his, and Cam grinned. Destry's shoulders relaxed visibly. She tossed the little tube at him. "Sure you did." She leaned over the edge of the bed, snagging her tennis shoes and his sock offering. Her eyebrows quirked when she saw the red and blue shield emblazoned across the shin, but she pulled them on anyway. "I wish your leadership academy allowed cell phones. A few emails aren't the same as being able to text."

Cam repeated the explanation he'd given her several times already: "Cell phones distract from the goals I'm supposed to be focusing on." He adjusted her shirt collar (*his* shirt collar) which had gone askew. "But you're right. It wasn't enough."

Finally, a real smile, even if it was less bright than before. Cam uncapped the lotion and handed it back. Had she run out at home? Her skin looked chafed and irritated. Destry's lotion addiction was more necessity than vanity. She applied it with a sigh of relief, then wriggled her shoes on. "Fine. Hang out at your grandparents' fancy party. I've got papers to deliver." She stood, heading for the window.

"How about I drive you?" That would make her happy. Destry hated biking during the dark morning hours.

She hesitated, fiddling with her braid. "I think...I think I better do it myself." Cam opened his mouth to reply, and she took another step towards the window. "You won't be here again in a couple weeks. Got to stand on my own two feet, right?"

She opened the window and clambered over the sill, knuckles white from her grip. "See you Saturday," Destry whispered. And she was gone.

WRONG

---◆---

Destry regretted turning Cam's offer down exactly one hour and twenty-two minutes into her route: the moment it started raining.

No, "rain" was the wrong word. Maybe deluge? Gullywasher? Sheets of icy water sluiced down from the sky, soaking her clothes and making her teeth chatter. Why hadn't she listened to her thunderstorm-spidey-sense when Cam offered to drive her? What could have been more important than a relaxing car ride with the heater going full-blast?

A traitorous little voice whispered, *Showing Cam you can manage on your own, of course.*

She was officially an idiot.

Shivering, Destry distracted herself with pleasant thoughts of having phone service again. She'd gotten paid—a tiny check, but enough for a month of service with some left over—and it sat securely in her pocket wrapped in a newspaper baggie.

The downpour made it hard to see holes in the residential street. Destry hit one, and the bike shimmied. She extracted a paper from the bag hooked to her handlebars and flung it towards the correct house. It landed on the hood of a red Mini Cooper. *Close enough.* Two more houses and she could start home.

She pedaled harder, building speed to top the hill ahead. In the distance, a fork of lightning broke the sky in half. She'd barely reached the crest when a thunderclap cracked the air. Panting, she yanked her next-to-last paper from her bag—

And fiery pain shot up both calves. Destry yelped, losing her grip on the paper and her control on the bike at the same time. It swerved into the curb, bounced off, and the world dissolved into a swirl of granite sky and blurred trees and wet asphalt.

The tick-tick-tick of a free-spinning bike wheel slowly seeped into her ears. She gasped for breath as rain drummed against her upturned face. A deeper boom of thunder rolled across the neighborhood. It seemed to sink into her chest, sending a jolt of energy through her body and making every pain sharp and vivid. Destry groaned.

The world turned right-side-up again, and she forced herself to a sitting position, disentangling her legs from the bike. One hip ached and her left knee burned. She examined a tear in her jeans with a bloody scrape underneath.

Her calves throbbed—the pain that had caused this whole mess. She tried to peel up her sodden jeans, but the water-heavy denim clung to her legs. *Never mind.* Wincing, Destry stood and inspected her bike. It was mostly unharmed, and the new scratches blended in with the old ones gracing her secondhand, rust-tinged ten-speed.

She shoved sopping hair out of her eyes and scanned the gutters. The paper she'd been about to throw lay several feet away, water gushing over it and creating miniature rapids. She retrieved the plastic-bagged newspaper and flung it towards the house. It thumped against a window, startling a cat sleeping on the sill. The cat fell off its perch and out of sight.

Destry smirked, though her smile faded when she climbed onto her bike again. She pedaled painfully to the last stop, tossed the paper, and began the long ride home.

Destry slogged into the house thirty minutes later, kicking the kitchen door closed with unnecessary force. Her mom sat at the table, one hand propping up her forehead; the other clenched a piece of paper—their water bill, from the look of it. Envelopes littered the tabletop. Bev glanced up, red-rimmed eyes falling on her daughter, then darting away.

"Hey, Mom." The shivering ruined Destry's effort at a casual tone.

"You're wet." Bev smiled wanly. "Were you playing in the rain again, silly girl?"

Silly girl. Destry gritted her teeth even as the words dislodged a long-ago memory: *Mom on a chilly, drizzly day, holding out a tiny raincoat emblazoned with Spiderman. "Silly girl, of course you want to wear this! It'll give you superpowers if you leave it on."* The game had appealed to her imagination. For months afterward, she'd worn the coat even when it wasn't raining, certain it let her see shimmering red lights in the air.

She hasn't always been like this. Destry forced her jaw to unclench. No sense getting mad. Mom probably didn't even remember it was cold outside. "I got caught in a thunderstorm on my paper route."

"Good thing you enjoy them."

The tail-end of that memory pushed at her: *"Destry Gale, I know you love the rain, but your teeth are chattering. Come inside. You can wrap up in a blanket while I make cocoa."*

Not much chance of blankets and cocoa today. Bev didn't even notice her torn jeans and bloody knee. Destry swallowed past a suddenly tight throat. "I gotta get ready for school."

Bev's murmur grabbed her seconds before she reached the hallway. "Destry, we have a little problem."

The water bill. Heart sinking, she forced herself to turn back. "How much are we short?"

Bev's fingers trembled as she smoothed out the billing statement. "Just thirty-two dollars. I...I wouldn't ask, but it'll already cost extra to get the power restored. If they turn off our water, too..."

Two reconnect fees and a house without water? *Putting service on my phone will have to wait.* She dug in her pocket for the check.

Bev accepted it with a watery smile. "I don't know how this happened. It's so hard to keep track of everything. I was sure there was enough money in the bank." She rubbed her forehead.

Destry sighed. "Might be easier if you laid off the schnapps."

She regretted the words even before shame flashed across Bev's face, before her mom snapped, "I'm trying, Destry. Doing my best."

I wish that wasn't true. But as far as she could tell, it was. Mom had always been a little flaky, though it had gotten steadily worse over the past five years. Destry couldn't remember if the drinking had started before or had come afterwards.

Bev's anger faded as fast as it had come. She sniffled. "I really am trying, baby. Thanks for helping. I'll pay you back soon as I can."

By next week, you won't even remember you owe me money. Destry squeezed her mom's shoulder. "Don't worry about it."

Bev brightened. "When I get back in town, Brandon is taking us out for dinner. That'll be nice. You...you like him, don't you?"

Faint worry lines on her forehead clashed with the hope in her eyes. For a second, Destry considered telling her mom the truth about Pervert-Number-Twenty-Seven. *He hasn't done anything, but the way he looks at me is wrong. There's a reason I'm always at the library when he comes over.* Bev would believe her. If Destry said she didn't trust Brandon, he'd be history within the hour; she'd seen it twice now.

But she'd also seen depression consume Bev both times afterwards, self-recrimination and self-loathing fueling the fire. Increased drinking. Losing her job. Weeks before she regained her equilibrium. They couldn't afford that.

The silence stretched a beat too long. Bev's lips trembled, and the impulse died with barely a whimper. "He's great, Mom. But what do you mean, 'back in town?'"

Bev shuffled the bills into a single stack. "I told you. My boss is sending me and a few co-workers to a regional conference. We leave this morning, stay at the hotel overnight, home by tomorrow night. I'm sure I mentioned it."

No. But it's a good excuse to get away from me for two days. Bev loved her—she was certain—but she seemed to love her best from a distance, judging by her frequent weekends with the "guy of the month" at his place. It happened too often to sting anymore.

The chill of Destry's wet clothes seeped into her bones. "Guess I forgot." She squeezed Bev's shoulder again and turned towards the stairs, knee burning with the renewed movement. "Have a good time, Mom. Remember to pay the water bill before you leave."

Destry grabbed a towel and first aid supplies from the bathroom. She kicked off wet shoes, peeled off socks and jeans—wincing as they scraped her bloody knee—then carted everything to her room where the bigger windows let in more light. She plopped down on the desk chair and lifted her banged-up leg onto the bed. First, she would bandage the knee, then fix whatever was wrong with—

Her calves. As Destry's eyes fell on her elevated leg, she froze, and the supplies dropped from her nerveless fingers.

Up and down her calf—all along the area that burned—swirled a silvery design. The thing looked like a tattoo...more than seven inches long, twisting and twirling in shades of gray and black and silver.

Destry rubbed her eyes, but when she opened them again, the marks were still there. Bloody knee forgotten, she poured peroxide onto the towel and scrubbed the design. It didn't smear, didn't lighten. She scrubbed harder, until tears came to her eyes and the skin edging the marks grew red and irritated. No change. Her pulse sped up. How had this happened? *What* had happened?

Destry kicked her injured leg down and frantically examined the other calf. The same design swirled over it, beautiful and alien and wrong. She forced herself to breathe slowly—in and out, in and out.

Had she hit her head when she crashed? Maybe she was hallucinating. Destry felt her scalp for sore spots or lumps or blood. Nothing. Not a single indication of a head wound. But what other explanation was there? *People don't magically get tattoos from riding a bike in a thunderstorm!*

"I'm off to work!" The words echoed through the bedroom door, and for the first time in ages, Bev's voice brought Destry a sense of relief. Mom might be flaky, she might be drunk tonight, but right now, she was reality.

Destry ran for the door, yanking it open and thudding down the hall. "Mom, wait!"

Beverly stood in the entryway, one hand on the knob. She was too busy rifling through her purse to look up. "I can't chat now, baby. My boss has this thing for people being on time."

"But I need—" Destry stopped. What did she need? Somebody to say she wasn't crazy? Someone else who could see these marks on her legs? Or someone who couldn't, who would confirm Destry was seeing things?

Tears stung her eyes. *I need some help.*

But Beverly couldn't offer that. If she didn't see the marks, she'd get hysterical and freak out about concussions. If she did see them, that might be worse. Destry's father—whoever he was—had several tattoos. Bev had railed about them when Destry made the mistake of admiring the multicolored butterfly on some woman's arm. She might not act like a mom often, but that point was non-negotiable. No ink for her daughter, ever.

Destry backed into the shadows. "Never mind, Mom. You're gonna be late for work." Her voice came out small.

"You can always call me, okay?" With a vague smile, Bev hurried out the door.

Destry trudged to the bedroom and sank numbly onto the bed. She stuck her legs out, examining her calves. The marks were still there. So was the cut on her knee. Mechanically, she treated it and put the first aid supplies away. She stared out the window at Cam's house, at his bedroom window that faced hers, although at unequal heights. Cam was probably downstairs eating breakfast with his parents.

She could tell him about this...but his family was leaving in less than an hour. Did she want to pull him aside and explain the situation in hurried whispers?

Destry lowered the blinds. She would wait. Maybe the marks would disappear the same way they had come. Or maybe she really had hit her head, and once she was better, everything would go back to normal. She yanked on dry clothes and sneakers. Maybe if she couldn't see the marks, she would forget they were even there.

Hours later, Destry breathed a weary sigh as the final bell shrilled through the school. Forgetting about the marks on her legs had been like relaxing during an Algebra test. In other words, impossible. A couple of class-mates waltzed past her desk. One whispered in the other's ear, and they smiled—too sweetly—at her.

"Excited for Christmas break?" the first asked.

Destry shrugged, shoving books into her backpack.

The second girl giggled. "I hear Jared is coming home for the holi-days."

Destry's skin ran hot, then cold. She zipped her bag and swung it onto her back. "I don't care."

The girl smirked. "That's not what Moira said."

Destry's stomach clenched, like it always did when someone men-tioned Cam's old girlfriend. "Moira doesn't know what she's talking about."

The first girl rolled her eyes. "Sure. It's not like you and Moira hung out together for weeks after Cam left for that high-falutin' school. Oh, wait. You did."

Her friend added, "She also says Jared is dating some girl from his dorm, so you might be out of luck when he comes home this time. Hope it doesn't ruin your vacation."

Destry forced a smile. "I won't see your face for two whole weeks, so my vacation will be perfect." The girls tossed out a few not-so-complimentary names as she strode into the hall, but she ignored them. She had no homework with the holidays looming. She could spend the evening at the warm library lost in some piece-of-fluff book and forget this day ever happened.

"Oh, Destry!" A cheerful voice halted her mere feet from the front doors and freedom. Shoulders drooping, she turned around. Mrs. Meech stood in a nearby doorway, glasses askew and a pencil poked into her gray braid. "I need to speak with you, dear."

Destry trudged into the guidance counselor's office, decorated with motivational posters (Shoot for the stars!) and dozens of tiny cacti in pots. Her neck tightened. Guidance counselor was just another name for "nosy adult," and she didn't need anyone poking into her life.

Mrs. Meech waved her to a chair. Destry edged around the desk, trying to avoid the spiky decor, and her backpack swung into a pile of file folders. Papers cascaded to the ground, a waterfall of tan and white. Mumbling an apology, she bent to retrieve them, and her backpack tumbled forward, sliding up her back to whack her in the head. She stumbled, off balance.

"Destry, dear!" The counselor hurried over, grabbing her bag. She placed it by the door as Destry clambered upright, face heating supernova-style. "Just leave those folders. I'll get them later. We need to discuss your meeting with the scholarship committee. We spoke rather briefly last time."

Destry scooted into a chair and knotted her hands in her lap. "Um...yeah. Sorry." Mrs. Meech's pronouncement about submitting Destry's name had rattled her, and she'd escaped as quickly as possible.

The counselor lifted a cactus plant off a pile of papers and pulled one from the stack. "Not to worry, I'm sure you needed time to absorb the good news."

Destry took the paper—some form—as Mrs. Meech moved another cactus off a glossy pamphlet. She handed it over with a flourish. "There we go! Your mother needs to sign the form, and you must be here tomorrow at 3:30 for the interview. Dress nicely—" She eyed Destry's Iron Man t-shirt and faded jeans dubiously. "You don't have to wear a dress, of course, but perhaps a lovely sweater?"

A lovely sweater. Yeah, she had so many of those. But Destry nodded curtly. Mrs. Meech's lips tilted down for a moment, then turned determinedly upwards again. "No need to be nervous. I've given you a glowing recommendation. Your acceptance is almost assured, but the interview is a time to confirm the committee's good impressions and to ask questions."

Destry stared at the pamphlet, preferable to meeting the guidance counselor's eyes. Flowing script proclaimed:

– Mountainview Academy –

We nurture gifted youth!

Located in scenic Missoula, Montana,
our merit-based academy offers the perfect backdrop
to inspire youth with unusual talents and abilities.
Every teacher is a former graduate of this school,
with a unique perspective that allows them to connect
meaningfully with our handpicked group of students.

Destry stopped reading. "The school is in Montana?"

Mrs. Meech shuffled a stack of papers. "I'm afraid so. That distance may seem daunting, but it is one of the premiere private schools in the country. When they asked for recommendations for their scholarship program, you immediately sprang to mind. In fact, you're the only student I submitted."

Destry's fingers tightened on the brochure. "I just... I thought the school would be closer. I thought I could come home on the weekends." Who would check on Beverly? Who would remind her to pay the bills, to eat food instead of living on energy drinks and alcohol?

Mrs. Meech released a nervous laugh. "Weekend travel would be cost-prohibitive, obviously. But there are the longer holidays." She met Destry's eyes. "I hope you won't dismiss the offer out of hand, dear. This would be a chance for you—a chance to overcome some of your...challenges."

The way she said that, weighted with significance... Was Mrs. Meech more perceptive than she seemed? Destry had tried to make things look normal from the outside, but she'd slipped up a few times. Mrs. Meech's past remarks came back to her, comments on how Beverly never attended school functions or how tired Destry always seemed. Did she suspect?

The counselor held her gaze, intent. Destry's stomach dropped. If the school thought there were problems at home, refusing to attend that scholarship meeting might have unexpected consequences. She forced a shaky smile. "I'll try to impress the committee. Thank you for the opportunity."

Mrs. Meech beamed. "That's the spirit! Everything will work out for the best. You'll see."

The counselor's words echoed in Destry's head a half hour later as she biked towards her house: *Everything will work out for the best.* The library was closed because of some big fundraising party, and cold rain drizzled steadily from the cloud-soaked sky. Mrs. Meech might be perceptive, but she definitely wasn't psychic.

A gleaming black and chrome truck rumbled up alongside Destry and slowed. Frowning, she angled her bike closer to the grassy edge of the sidewalk. The passenger window lowered with a faint electric hum, and a college-aged boy leaned across the seat. "Need a ride?"

Destry's breath froze in her lungs, and her foot slipped on the pedal, jerking her to a shaky stop. She clutched the handlebars so hard the bumpy rubber grips dug into her palms.

Jared.

Smiling, he flipped his dark hair out of his eyes. "You look cold. Want to toss your bike in my truck bed? I'll drive you home."

Fury rolled through Destry, setting her cheeks flaming. "I'm cold, not stupid. Do you think I would ever get in a truck with you?"

"C'mon, Destry. It's been two years, and I apologized."

She pressed her lips together so Jared wouldn't see their sudden trembling. Pushing her bike into motion, she stood up on the pedals to get moving faster. "Stay away from me!"

Jared called after her, but the rumble of his motor and the rushing of blood in her ears drowned out his words. He spun the truck around in the middle of the street, tires squealing as he peeled away.

IMPOSSIBILITIES

D estry made the ride home in record time. She dragged her bike onto the front porch and stomped into the house, throwing the locks on every outside door. Then she scrambled to her bedroom. Shivering, Destry shimmied out of her jeans, barely reacting to the sight of the silvery marks on her legs. This entire day—Cam's return home, the tattoos, Jared's reappearance after his semester away at college—felt too far removed from normal life to merit normal reactions.

She took a moment to slather some dollar store moisturizer over her face and body, run lip balm over her lips. After an entire day at school, her skin felt tight and itchy. But she'd had to stop using them during the lunch hour, ever since Moira complained to a teacher that the smell of "cheap lotion" made her sick.

Destry pulled on sweats and a hoodie, then threw a blanket around her shoulders for good measure. Hurrying downstairs, she took some of the wood stacked next to the fireplace and started a fire. The scent of woodsmoke filled the living room as a small fire grew, crackling and popping. Aching for heat, she stretched her fingers towards the blaze.

The fire flared and roared, filling every inch of the fireplace. Destry jerked back so quickly that she stumbled over the blanket-cape and landed on her butt. *What was that?* No way could the moderate amount of wood in the fireplace create that massive fireball. She pushed to her feet, but the fire looked normal again. Cautiously, she held her hands closer.

Nothing. What had she expected, anyway?

Another shiver rolled through her, one that had nothing to do with the cold. She left her blanket on the couch and padded into the kitchen; there should at least be bread for toast. There was, along with a ten dollar bill stuck to the fridge underneath a happy rainbow magnet— probably what was left after Mom had paid the water bill.

She stuffed it in her pocket, then yanked open a drawer. The cutlery inside rattled and clinked. Grabbing a toasting fork, the bread, and some jelly, Destry scurried to the fireplace. Fingers trembling, she positioned bread on the toasting fork. The silence of the old house felt heavy, as if it knew she was alone and disapproved. *Stop acting so jittery*, she scolded herself. *You've spent dozens of nights alone, even after Cam left for school. Tonight is no different.*

Destry was on her second piece of toast before she realized: that wasn't true. Tonight *was* different, because Jared Morgan had come home. And the only other night like this—Cam and her mother gone, Jared here and acting so friendly—had gone very, very wrong.

Calm down. You're not a stupid kid any more. She breathed deep, trying to settle her nerves. But memories pushed at her.

A lonely night. Cam gone on a date with Moira.

Don't think about that.

The older boy from Cam's high school, the junior who kept flirting with her at Cam's football games. Her thirteen-year-old self had been flattered.

Don't think about that, either.

Schnapps filched from her mom and hot grasping hands...

Destry jerked to her feet. Staying in the house wasn't good for her mood. She could bike to Andy's Restaurant. Some cheesy bacon fries and a soda would make the chilly ride worth it. But Andy's had its own memories. Like a conversation with Cam, and his warning: "Jared is no different than the guys your mom brings home, the ones you're always avoiding. Promise you'll stay away from him."

A reluctant promise—one she'd broken.

Destry yanked the bread off the toasting fork and tossed it on the brick hearth. A bike ride to get food was definitely in order. Andy's wasn't the only place nearby. She hurried to the hall closet, digging out a jacket, getting the sleeves tangled up in her rush to put it on. Night would fall in less than two hours. Destry pushed open the front door, stepped onto the porch...

And stopped.

Climbing her front steps was Jared Morgan.

He stopped, too, a foot on the stairs and another on the porch, and gave her one of those easy smiles. "Hey, Destry. You going somewhere?"

She backed up, bumping into the still-open door. "What do you want?"

He glanced at Cam's house, then her. Jared wet his lips. "Just need to ask you something. I can give you a ride, if you want. We could talk on the way."

"I told you—leave me alone." Her voice shook. She took another step back, into the house, gripping the cool doorknob tightly.

"Destry, wait!" He closed the distance between them in a few bounding strides. Jared grabbed the outside knob, keeping her from pulling the door closed. "Just give me five minutes!"

"You got too much from me already!" She yanked harder, struggling to close the door.

Jared shoved his foot into the gap, talking fast. "Listen, would you? I have a new girlfriend!"

"Why should I care?"

"She's spending Christmas break with my family, she'll be around town meeting my friends. Maybe run into you. And Moira told me what everyone at school says about us. I want to make sure..."

He hesitated, and Destry glared. "What? That I don't tell her what you're actually like?"

"That you don't ruin my chances because of one stupid mistake! I'm not the same guy anymore!"

"Really?" She pushed at his foot with hers. He didn't budge. "You seem exactly the same to me!" She kicked him in the shin and the ankle, again and again.

Jared yelped and jerked his foot back. Eyes narrowing, he pressed his free hand against the door frame, trying to wedge the door open again. "It was one night, Destry! A couple kisses!"

A couple kisses. The words, the fury, the fear, built in her chest, and she wanted to scream the truth in Jared's face. She gripped the knob with both hands. Rage boiled through her. It stung her skin, sent fiery pain along her shoulder blades. Even her hands burned, powerful and painful. Destry looked down at them, straining on the knob.

The metal glowed like iron heated in a forge. Jared shrieked and let go. Destry caught a glimpse of angry burns across his palm before the door slammed shut. Shaking, she threw the deadbolt and stumbled back, staring at her hands, at the knob that looked completely normal again.

"DESTRY!" The door shook, the sound of boots against wood loud in the entryway.

She was thirteen, hiding in her bedroom. Jared pounded on her door. "C'mon, Destry, I know you're in there. Look, I just got carried away. I won't do it again." Bam, bam, bam. Jared's voice raised to a roar. "Destry! Let me in!"

The front door shivered as another round of kicks thudded into it. Destry whimpered. The burning behind her shoulder blades increased, and she gasped, reaching for her back.

The coat's heavy material ripped open. Something sharp nicked Destry's palm, and she jerked her hands away. A subtle weight grew along her shoulder blades. Breathing raggedly in time to Jared's pounding on the door, Destry turned her head. Something hovered in her peripheral vision, something on her back.

Something shimmering.

No, not thing. Things. She turned her head the other way, so far that her neck protested. Impossibly large, impossibly attached, waving furiously in the air and blowing her hair into her face...on her back beat a set of...

Wings?

Destry barely noticed that Jared had stopped banging on the door. She bolted to her room, tripping over her own feet, falling and slamming her knees against the wood floor, scrambling up again. Panting and off-balance, Destry shambled to a stop in front of the long mirror on the wall.

The wild-eyed girl in the reflection stared back. Numbness rushed her, river-swift. Destry watched her mirror-self sink to her knees. Arching behind her, as foreign and beautiful and terrible as the marks on her legs, was a pair of silvery wings. They beat more slowly than her racing heart, and as they moved, faint patterns of red flame appeared and disappeared.

Still numb, Destry lifted both hands to touch them. They wouldn't be real, they couldn't be real, it was fear or stress making her see things. She reached for the pointed upper curves, gleaming like a newly sharpened knife.

Pain sliced along her fingers and palms, and she yanked her hands away. The sense of detachment evaporated as she stared at the bleeding, razor-thin cuts.

Her breathing sped up.

Her breathing sped up.

Her breathing...

Her head spun. She swayed dizzily.

You need to breathe slower.

Can't.

You're hyperventilating.

Don't care.

You'll pass out.

Please.

Seconds later, she got her wish.

BROKEN

---◆---

Her eyes fluttered open—little splashes of reality trickling in with each blink.

No.

No.

No.

She let sleep pull her back under.

Destry was spinning.

Hot wind swirled past, twisting her in circles until she couldn't see straight. Images rushed over her, colors blurred by the inexorable gusts.

Cam inviting her to his first varsity football game, so proud and excited, the youngest guy chosen for the team.

Celebrating with the team at Andy's...no one cared she was only thirteen. Cam said she belonged, so she did.

She was getting dizzy...

Sitting in the stands alone, one of the few games Cam's parents missed.

A dark-haired seventeen-year-old—asking to sit with her, slipping a piece of paper into her jeans pocket, fingers lingering on her hip.

Red strands of light twined around her wrists, her chest, her waist—warm, comforting. The spinning slowed. Destry stumbled to a stop, trying to orient herself. Where was she?

She stood in the doorway to a cluttered bedroom. Potted plants hung from the ceiling, smelly football gear was piled on the floor, and a replica of Captain America's shield hung on one wall. Books were strewn across the unmade bed, and a raggedy kitten slept on the rust-colored comforter. Cam's room.

She remembered now. Friday afternoon. She'd rushed home from the junior high school, hoping Cam would be done with football practice and ready to hang out. Destry rapped on the doorframe and peeked inside. "Cam? You up here?"

He poked his head around the bathroom door, hair dripping and face aggrieved. "Just got out of the shower. Toss me those slacks...the ones on my bed."

Destry chucked the tan dress pants at him and plopped on his bed to wait. The kitten, looking offended, hissed and scooted to a clothing-draped chair. Moments later, Cam came out shirtless, wet hair dropping rivulets down his muscled back. He started rifling through a drawer. "Mom should've warned you that I was showering. What if I'd been wandering around my bedroom in a towel?"

His mom had been cooking when Destry dashed past the kitchen. If she'd said something, Destry had missed it in her eagerness to start their traditional Friday night hang-out. But suddenly, admitting her excitement over baking brownies and watching movies on the couch felt juvenile and silly. She shrugged, trying to act blase. "If you'd been wearing a towel, I'd have closed my eyes. I'm not some little kid anymore."

He abandoned the search through the drawer and moved to the clothing pile on his chair instead, displacing the kitten to the floor. "Sure about that? Because you're still ignoring your homework. You got four C's this last report card. I saw it on your kitchen table."

She scowled. Cam's family believed in academic excellence, so he thought Destry should care about her grades, too. But she couldn't concentrate on stupid math problems when there was so much to worry about at home, and she was sick of Cam's determination to "help." "In case you didn't notice, I'm a teenager now, same as you. I've matured."

Cam gently detached the kitten, who'd started climbing his pants leg. "Getting older and maturing aren't the same thing. Everyone gets older. You want to be more mature, stop making me hassle you into doing homework. Stop lying to me to avoid a lecture. And keep your promises."

Destry shifted restlessly. "Sometimes people don't mean to break promises. It just happens."

"It's a choice. You don't break promises on accident. You keep them on purpose." Cam finally located an undershirt and yanked it over his head, the jerky motions a study in impatience. "Please tell me this isn't about that idiot Jared Morgan."

"No. I'm just saying—"

"Because we went over this Thursday—when he thought I wasn't looking and slipped you his phone number."

That hadn't been all. After Cam's last football game, Jared had offered to drive her home. Cam intervened, saying they were riding with his teammates. Then he'd spent the first ten minutes at Andy's listing the dangers of a junior high girl getting involved with a high school guy. She'd only promised to avoid Jared to stop Cam's litany of warnings.

The kitten followed Cam to his dresser, pouncing on his toes. Cam snagged the cat, handed it to Destry (it squirmed away and dashed out of the bedroom), and grabbed a dark blue button-up from his drawer. "You said you wouldn't call him."

"I didn't!" she flared. "But even if I did, what's the big deal? We're not gonna run off to a chapel in Vegas. He just likes talking to me." And she liked talking to him—or at least, listening to him talk. Jared made her feel special, beautiful, grown-up.

"*Four years* older than you, Des. He's no different than the guys your mom brings home, the ones you're always avoiding."

Destry crossed her arms tightly. She could name one important difference between the middle-aged perverts and the handsome teenager. But explaining that might make things worse. She sent a sidelong glance at Cam. "They never try for long. I don't know why." The men always backed off after she told Cam about them. But how could any fifteen-year-old—even a tall-for-his-age, muscled-out one—discourage grown men?

"Stop trying to change the subject." This was Cam at his sternest...someone Destry rarely saw. Most of the time, having Cam in her life was like having a fun older brother, one who took her places and let her hang with his friends and helped with math problems. He hunkered down in front of her, shirt crumpled in his large hands. "You lie to me about piddling stuff all the time, but you've never broken an actual promise. Don't start now."

Why did he act like she was some little kid too stupid to decide for herself? "You're in a bad mood tonight. Did you have another discussion about the future with your dad?"

Cam stilled. Locked gazes with her. Without another word, he stood and strode to the mirror over the dresser, shoving his arms into the shirt, buttoning the front and adjusting the collar. He didn't look at Destry.

Her stomach squirmed. Gregory Waters was the nicest dad in the world, but he wanted Cam to attend his old school—The Academy for the Future Leaders of America—for junior and senior year. Cam wasn't certain he wanted to go to a leadership academy, let alone be a 'future leader.' Of all the troubles he shared with her, his worries about disappointing Gregory were the biggest.

And like a jerk, she'd brought it up.

"Cam," she whispered. "I'm sorry. Really."

"I know, Dessie." He pulled in a deep breath, letting his shoulders relax. "Look, I don't want to argue about Jared Morgan. He isn't worth your time or mine. Could you just trust me on this?"

Destry thought about the phone number put carefully away in her backpack. Her eyes fell on the dresser—and the concert ticket there. "Are you going out tonight?"

He scrubbed at his jaw, freshly shaven with a tiny nick near his left ear. "Um...yeah, it's kind of a last-minute thing. Moira Wilson invited me to go with her family. A guy at her dad's office gave him tickets to some symphony concert."

Moira, the girl he wanted to take to homecoming. Destry tried to be happy for him, but an angry voice inside asked why Cam could have a date on Friday night while she stayed home alone. She *knew* Mom would stay out all night. She always did.

Destry made a split-second decision. "That's okay. I've got lots of math homework."

He sat on the bed next to her. "Tell you what. Get it done by tomorrow, and we'll do something fun."

"It better be something good."

"Everything I do is good." He chucked her under the chin. "We *are* on the same page about Jared, right? You're going to ignore him?"

"Of course. Now, go get pretty for Moira. She won't want you if you look like a troll."

He snickered. "Trolls aren't real, Destry."

Hot wind whipped around her, jerking her into motion.

More memories blurred past.

Running to her house...her empty house.

Digging Jared's number out of her backpack.

"Stop," she whispered, grabbing the warm strands of light.

Opening the door to let Jared in, a bottle of Beverly's schnapps in her hand.

The spinning slowed, depositing her on the living room couch—with Jared. The TV flickered, an inane comedy playing across the screen as he took another swig of peach schnapps. Destry grinned. "This is the dumbest show ever." The movie was Jared's choice, and the schnapps made it hilarious.

"We could do other things." Jared rested one hand on her knee, his thumb sliding up her thigh.

Her breath hitched. "I told you, I want to take things slow." It wasn't very grown-up, but she didn't want her first kiss to taste like peach schnapps and feel so...confused.

He leaned closer. "You wouldn't say that if you had some experience. But you're such a little girl."

"I'm big enough to know what I want." She shifted her leg out of his grasp. "And that's for you to get going before my mom or Cam gets back." There. Maybe he would leave. Destry felt a little queasy, and Jared's suggestions were growing more pointed.

"Waters won't be back for another couple hours. And your mom stays out all night. You told me so."

Had she? Her brain was too fuzzy to be sure. Jared had asked where Cam was when she called him. She remembered that much. Destry tried again. "If the concert ends early—"

He turned off the movie, then tossed the remote aside. "Those symphony things last forever, and Waters is stuck at that concert until her parents drive him home. We've got time." His hands, sliding under her shirt to her waist, felt too warm.

Destry pushed against his chest. "I told you when I called, I just want to hang out."

He laughed, the alcohol on his breath nauseating. "Are you such a baby you don't know what that means?"

She pushed harder. "I know what I meant. Let go!"

"Silly baby girl. How will you get any experience?" He leaned closer, pinning her down on the couch. "Trust me, Destry. You'll like this." He twined one hand tightly through her hair, and his hot mouth covered hers.

She whimpered and shoved at him. His kiss was hard, wet, rough, nothing like she'd imagined. His body pressed her into the couch, unyielding. Destry's heart raced, blood pounding in her ears. He pushed her shirt up, and she writhed. She couldn't think, couldn't concentrate, couldn't get her body to respond.

Destry dug her nails into his chest, but all she got was shirt. She bit at him. Jared laughed and kissed her harder. Panic and disbelief crashed over her, a tidal wave stealing her breath.

Can't breathe...

Can't breathe...

Can't...

She pushed Jared with all her strength.

A sizzling sound split the air, and he flew away from her, thudding into the wall and crumpling to the floor. Destry scrambled off the couch. Two burn marks smoldered on the front of Jared's shirt. Her head spun. How...?

Jared stumbled to his feet, looking dazed, and Destry bolted to her room, slamming and locking the door, jamming a chair under the knob. She heard him stomping down the hall, opening doors. "Destry? Destry, come out. I'm sorry, okay?" Jared's feet thudded closer. "C'mon, Destry, I know you're in there. Look, I just got carried away. I won't do it again." Her door shook—*bam, bam, bam, bam, bam!*—and his voice raised to a roar. "Destry! Let me in!"

She scuttled to the far wall. "Leave me alone!" Tears clogging her throat made the scream hoarse.

He hammered on the door a few more times, until the rumble of a truck motor sounded outside. Destry rushed to the window. A shiny late-model Ford was pulling into the Waters' driveway. Jared must have gone to check out the sound, too, because the banging stopped. Footsteps thundered through the house, across the porch, and seconds later Jared's truck zipped down the street.

Cam got out of the Ford's passenger side and stood there, watching Jared's tail lights disappear. He glanced at her window. From the thunderous look on his face, he knew exactly who had just left. She heard him thank the driver for the ride home. Then he stalked towards her place.

Destry removed the chair and undid the lock with shaking fingers. She collapsed on the bed before her trembling legs gave out. Cam's footsteps, steadier than Jared's, heralded his appearance in her doorway. Eyes snapping, he held up the half-empty bottle of schnapps. "So much for being on the same page. Why was Jared Morgan here?"

"I thought you were at a concert with Moira."

"I was. But I kept thinking about you here, alone and lonely, so I ticked Moira off and asked her dad to take me home during the intermission. Only you didn't need me to keep you company, did you?"

She could lie. She should. Say Jared had stopped by, unasked, but she'd told him to leave. She opened her mouth to do it—and instead the entire story tumbled out. Cam listened, expression hard, until she got to the part about Jared kissing her, ignoring her protests. He knelt in front of her, checking her up and down. "Did he hurt you, Dessie?"

She gulped in a huge breath of air. "No. I... I shoved him off me and locked myself in here. It's just...just..." Tears pooled in Destry's eyes, spilled over to trickle down her cheeks. "That was my first kiss, Cam. And it was awful. I don't ever want a guy to touch me like that again." She rubbed her hand across her mouth, as if it could erase the feel of Jared, as if that could dam the sobs building in her chest.

Cam sat on the bed and pulled her into his arms as the sobs broke loose, rubbing her back and rocking her. When the tears finally slowed, Destry said, "The worst part is, it's all my fault. He thought that's what I wanted when I invited him over."

Cam pulled her up to look in her face. "No, Destry. No matter what, he had no right to take something you didn't want to give." His eyes searched hers. "Do you trust me?"

She didn't even have to think about her answer. "Of course."

"Then close your eyes." When she blinked, confused, Cam said again, softly, "Close your eyes, Dessie."

She did, and Cam's warm hands came to rest on her shoulders, steadying. The next thing she felt was the gentle pressure of his lips against hers—soft, tender, achingly sweet. It only lasted a moment. Destry's eyes flew open, and Cam released her. "That was your *real* first kiss. When you have to remember something about tonight, remember that one."

Beep. Beep. Beep. Beep. Beep.

Destry woke to the shrill alarm of her battery-operated clock. She flung out a hand to whack it, but her palm only hit wooden planks.

Wood?

Destry peeled open bleary eyes. She was lying on the floor in her bedroom...lying on the floor, smacking her stinging palm into a non-existent alarm clock. Why did her hand hurt? Memories hovered at the edge of her consciousness. Destry shied away from them. She closed her eyes, ready to fall back asleep.

Beep. Beep. Beep. Beep. Beep.

Stupid alarm. Destry heaved herself to her feet, stumbling across the room to silence her clock. Her hand stung, and she turned her palm upwards to stare at the dried blood there. Everything hurt.

Her knees, her shins, her hands, her—

Her back.

Memory rushed over her, a tsunami of image and emotion. Destry spun around, searching for the mirror. Too dark to see well... She fumbled with matches and her nighttime candle. Finally, light (after three shaky attempts). She examined her reflection.

The girl standing there looked exhausted, with dark circles under red-rimmed eyes and hair escaping her braid. Her jacket hung oddly. Long rips split the fabric from hemline to shoulder. But—no wings.

Relief loosened her chest, allowed air into her lungs. No wings. Maybe it had all been a dream, sparked by seeing Jared on the way home from school, like her memories of that horrible night.

She could never forget those moments of fear, but the vivid details had faded after two years. Destry didn't try to remember them. That weekend and the months following it still made her cringe. Though life fell back into a normal pattern, she'd lost Cam's trust, and it had taken months of determined effort to repair the damage.

There had only been one bright spot during that time. Ironically, it came from Jared, who had shown up at her place Sunday morning, face white, babbling apologies. He stayed at least six feet away the entire conversation. Then he left, tripping over his own feet and looking around wildly, like he was under surveillance. Vindicating, but odd. She'd never figured out what prompted his unexpected penitence.

She didn't have the time to consider it now, either. Sore, tired, weird dreams... She still had a paper route to run. Groaning, Destry smoothed her hair. Stinging pain zigzagged her palms. Where had those cuts come from, if last night was only a dream?

Okay. Maybe Jared had come by. She'd gotten scared, torn her coat and cut her hands struggling to close the door, hurt her legs falling in the hall. And her frightened brain had dreamed up the wings and the glowing doorknob to make her feel less weak. More powerful.

Her body remembered it: that sensation of strength, of fire burning through bones and sinew. Dream, perhaps, but remembering brought a smile to her lips.

The smile faded when Destry looked at her clock again. *6:30? No. No, no, no! I completely missed my route!* Her boss was unforgiving about no-shows. He'd give the route to someone else. She wouldn't have her own money, a way to take care of herself when Beverly did something stupid with her salary.

Destry pressed the heels of her palms against her eye sockets. *It'll be okay. I still have that meeting with the scholarship committee. If they like me, losing my job won't matter. Of course, the committee might not want a crazy person attending their school.*

"I'm not crazy," she said out loud.

Convincing, Destry. Real convincing.

LATE BLOOMER

◆

3:28 p.m. Destry stood outside Mrs. Meech's office, waiting. She fidgeted with a strand of hair, then dropped it, chewed on a hangnail, then remembered not to. Applied some lip balm and wished she had moisturizer. Blowing out a long, frustrated breath, Destry shoved her hands into her pockets. She still wore jeans and canvas sneakers, but she'd dug a "lovely sweater" out of Beverly's closet and combed her hair until it shone.

The guidance counselor opened the door. "Destry! How long have you been waiting, dear?" Before Destry could reply, Mrs. Meech waved her inside. "Never mind, the review board is here."

A man and a woman waited in Mrs. Meech's cluttered office. The woman sat ramrod straight behind the desk, a leather-bound book of handwritten notes open in front of her. One elegant black eyebrow arched as she surveyed Destry.

Her companion sat in a student chair, skinny legs stretched out and crossed at the ankles. One foot bobbed cheerfully, keeping time to some internal music. He seemed to have bought every piece of leather clothing available at the Harley Davidson store.

When Destry edged her way in, a smile lit the man's thin face, then disappeared as quickly. "Elena! Do you see—"

The woman's expression turned severe. "I see that the student we're evaluating has arrived. Destry, correct?"

She nodded, sinking into the third chair.

The man's foot had stopped swinging. "But you cannot miss it!"

Miss what? Destry looked from his agitated face to the woman's calm one.

"Our obligation remains, Riamon—no matter what." The scholarship lady glanced at Mrs. Meech. "Thank you for accommodating us. We'll inform you if we need anything further." She handed the counselor an envelope. "The details of the scholarship and Destry's signed permission form. You should evaluate them while we interview your student."

A frown wrinkled the counselor's brow. Destry started to say she hadn't given them the form with Beverly's (forged) signature, but Mrs. Meech opened the letter. "What a generous scholarship! I'll review it in the hall." She hurried out, closing the door behind her.

A barely-there smile settled on the scholarship woman's face. "Now to business. You may call me Ms. Elena for the time being. I'm headmistress at the Academy. This is Mr. Riamon, my second-in-command and deputy headmaster at the school."

The man adjusted his wire-rimmed glasses. "Riamon, to be precise. No mister."

Waving one hand dismissively, Ms. Elena turned to Destry again. "So, you truly are fifteen. I hoped we were mistaken."

Destry's concern over the permission form took a backseat to this new worry. "Is fifteen too young for your school?"

"Hardly. Most students start in their eleventh or twelfth years. Fifteen is quite a late bloomer."

"Late bloomer?" Destry had heard the term applied to teenage girls who hadn't hit puberty yet, but she didn't exactly have that problem.

The headmistress said, "This shall be a long conversation. However, we must establish two points of understanding before we begin. First, you are unlikely to believe anything I say. And second, everything I am about to say is true. Riamon, seal the door and windows."

Seal the door? This didn't sound like a scholarship meeting. Destry stood, and Ms. Elena sighed heavily. "If we intended you harm, would we have chosen an office in the midst of a crowded school to do the deed? Riamon is simply ensuring our privacy. Now, sit down—and pray, avoid any hysterical outbursts."

Riamon circled the room, skirting cacti and piled-up books. He made the same graceful gesture at every window and the door, lifting both hands as if grabbing something delicate from the air, then making a long smoothing motion. He picked his way to Destry's chair, holding it with old-fashioned courtesy. Destry hesitated, and he said gently, "Hear us out, Destry. What can it hurt?"

Mrs. Meech *was* right outside...

She sat. So did Riamon.

Ms. Elena tapped a pen on the leather book. "Our first order of business is to establish how far along you are. Let's begin with the markings on your legs. How long have you had them?"

It took a minute to find her voice. "I... How do you know about that?"

The woman stood and walked around the desk. She slid up her flowing slacks, revealing a set of blue and silver swirls, exactly like Destry's except for color. Riamon struggled to slide up his leather trousers; they stuck halfway up his calf. Ms. Elena's lips thinned. "Ridiculous human clothes." She pointed at his pants and jerked her hand as if cracking an invisible whip. They split six inches up the leg.

Riamon looked aggrieved. "I like human clothes. Leather ones, to be precise. I especially liked these pants."

"And she cannot see your markings when you wear them!" Ms. Elena sat behind the desk again. "Accommodate me, so that we may move along to more important things."

Riamon sighed and pulled his pants up, displaying greenish-blue swirls.

Slowly, Destry lifted her jeans. "I didn't... I didn't go and get them—not at a tattoo place or anything. They just appeared yesterday."

Ms. Elena glanced at her marks, then looked more intently. Riamon grimaced. "Of course she would be a storm faerie. Why should she be something easy?"

"A...a what?"

Ms. Elena met Destry's eyes, and her gaze softened. "A faerie, Destry. You're a faerie. The changes in your body indicate that you've come of age and can now utilize your magic abilities."

A long beat of silence passed. What should she say? If she bolted for the door, could the crazy people catch her before she escaped? The headmistress turned businesslike again. "Don't bother running. I already said you wouldn't believe us."

"Late bloomers are so difficult to convince." Riamon patted Destry's hand. "Not your fault, of course. Your mind became too humanized. Eleven and twelve-year-olds are still open to the possibility of magic in a way older teens aren't."

Destry jerked her hand back. "Faeries don't exist. Even if they did, I couldn't be one." Faeries were small, graceful, powerful—not clumsy girls with squishy stomachs and substantial thighs. More importantly, they belonged to the land of make-believe, and Destry had left that behind long ago.

"I assure you, they do." Ms. Elena sounded brisk. "And why should you not be one? Because you don't fit the parameters of an uninformed stereotype?"

Memories from last night resurfaced: power in her palms, wings on her back. But she couldn't—wouldn't—accept those memories as real. "No!" Destry's hands balled into fists. "I don't have wings, I don't have magic! If I did, I'd be able to change things, make them better."

"You're referring to your family?" Riamon asked. "Your mother, to be precise?"

Destry shrugged, pressing her lips together.

Ms. Elena said, "Magic can't remedy everything, child. Changing your mother would alter her nature. Do you have the right to change another person?" She considered Destry, hands steepled. "Late bloomer or not, you should've had some indications. Has nothing happened that you couldn't explain?"

Oh, she had explanations. Bad ones (that didn't make sense) or depressing ones (like losing her mind) but explanations just the same. But looking into Ms. Elena's clear-eyed gaze made her determined excuses ring false. "A few times," Destry whispered.

The headmistress's eyebrows climbed her forehead. "Hmm. And your leg markings are quite recent..." She jotted a note in the leather-bound book. "I assume the power markings on your wrists haven't appeared."

Destry's throat squeezed. "What?"

Ms. Elena slid her long sleeves up. A design like rushing ocean waves circled her wrists, bright against her warm brown skin. She glanced at Riamon, who hurriedly shoved his fringed leather sleeve up. He must've liked the jacket even more than his torn pants.

Riamon's markings resembled swirling gusts of wind. He pointed to Ms. Elena's and then to his. "Water and air. We'd have a complete set if yours were fire."

The headmistress shot him a repressive glance. "Perhaps we shouldn't borrow trouble."

"Oh. Perhaps not." Riamon smiled at Destry. "Don't worry, the chances are quite small."

"The chances of *what*?"

Riamon pulled his sleeve down. "Elena is correct. We shouldn't worry you for no reason. But be prepared: you'll get your second set of power markings soon. It might be a bit dramatic."

This was his attempt to not worry her?

"Enough, Riamon." Ms. Elena stood and walked around Destry's chair. "Let's discuss wings." Her fingers traced the inner line of Destry's shoulder blades. "Oh, dear."

The area stung. Destry jerked away. Sighing, Ms. Elena circled the chair, facing her. "They've already appeared, haven't they?"

"NO." Destry stood, trembling. "If I have wings, where are they?"

Ms. Elena turned her back on Destry. "The same place mine are: furled beneath the skin, waiting to be called upon."

Her blouse had a triangular cutout, baring Ms. Elena's shoulder blades. One second, everything looked normal; the next, silvery-blue wings blossomed out at Destry. She yelped and stumbled backwards into her chair, saved from falling by Riamon's bracing arm.

He patted her shoulder. "You see? You are not insane, nor are you alone in this."

Destry could only stare. The headmistress's wings waved softly. Water patterns caught the sunlight, appearing and disappearing with each movement. The upper edges and points gleamed like newly-sharpened knives, sparking another memory. Destry spread her fingers, displaying the cuts across her palms.

Riamon pressed her into the chair. He sat, too, pulling his seat closer to hers. "Poor girl. The first time is so distressing. How long before they went away?"

"Went away?" Her voice sounded as watery as Ms. Elena's wings. (Did she still call her "Ms. Elena?" It sounded wrong, with wings popping out of the woman's back. Unfortunately, Destry's English class had somehow omitted the all-important lesson on correct titles for storybook characters.)

"Yes," the headmistress said crisply. One deep breath, and her wings furled in on themselves, shrinking until they disappeared in a poof of blue mist. "You won't have this sort of control yet. Fear and danger often bring your wings out. Once you're calm, they recede."

Destry shook her head. This was a prank, a joke—anything but the truth.

Ms. Elena turned, gaze implacable. "Denying this will not make it untrue. I'm sorry you had to deal with it alone. We usually find new faeries before their wings appear."

Riamon smiled at her. "Mine took three days to go away, the first time. I had such long, glorious hair before that. Not after. I caught it too many times on the sharp edges." He rubbed his short-cropped hair ruefully.

Was Riamon's sympathetic reminiscing meant to reassure her? If so—it was working. A little. "Then...this isn't a joke? You're really saying I...I'm a faerie?"

"A half-faerie, to be precise," Riamon said.

"I don't know what that means."

"It means only one of your parents was faerie. Your father, in this case." Riamon shoved his glasses, which had been slowly slipping down his nose, back into place. "Not to worry, though, you may still attend school. The faerie academy, to—"

"Riamon, if you say 'to be precise' one more time, I shall obtain a scalpel and surgically remove the phrase from your tongue," Ms. Elena threatened calmly. "There's a limit to how often I may hear those words and remain a rational, reasonable faerie."

Destry didn't care if Riamon had his tongue carved on. "What do you mean, attending school?"

Ms. Elena looked impatient. "Being faerie does not predispose us to unnecessary deception. We're still here to speak with you about school, to which you still have a scholarship—though admittedly, Mountainview Academy is a pseudonym. The proper name is The Academy for the Education and Advancement of Faeriekind. Especially for half-faeries raised in the human world, attendance there is essential to managing your powers."

"But I don't *have* powers." Burning Jared's shirt and superheating a doorknob—two things in two years—hardly added up to grand displays of magic.

"Yet. Your powers have not developed yet." Riamon's eyebrows contracted. "Although, it *is* rare for magic to go undetected for so long. The last time I saw such late development, the lad in question lived at the edges of goblin land, and their power was suppressing his."

"Goblins?" Destry repeated weakly.

Ms. Elena favored Riamon with a black stare. "As goblins dwell only in the Fold, the girl hardly needs to worry about them congregating in her suburban neighborhood."

She turned to Destry. "Though the school is located in the Fold as well, goblins know better than to cross us. They rarely come to Si'fliegen—which is our kingdom's seat of power and the township encompassing our school—and never to the Academy. You'll be perfectly safe from those monsters while pursuing your education."

Goblins...are real. Monstrous. And I'm supposed to live around them? Just hope they keep some gobliny promise to stay away from the school?

Ms. Elena made another note in her book, apparently unaware that Destry's insides had just twisted into a massive knot. "About your father...has he ever contacted you? A visit, a letter?"

"No." Destry didn't even know his name. Beverly would only say that he'd walked out on her.

"Unsurprising," the headmistress said. "Faeries cannot maintain long-term relationships with humans. Society frowns upon such liaisons, which means few faeries will admit to their indiscretions."

Destry crossed her arms. "So my father left us because of some stupid 'don't- associate-with-humans' rule?"

"Not quite. In most scenarios, the fey partner leaves because their presence is damaging the human partner. Adult minds are unequipped to cope with the existence of magic. When constantly exposed, they sense it, and the resulting mental imbalance becomes evident in their behavior—such as your mother's drinking."

"But if my father left..."

Ms. Elena said, "Your mother has been exposed to *your* influence as well, Destry. I assume her drinking worsened over the years, as your power grew. That, and her frequent absences, are her instinctive way of shielding her mind from power she's ill-equipped to endure. Your father should have ensured your removal from the home years ago."

"My mom has been destroying herself with alcohol for years—because of me?"

"Because your father chose not to do the right thing, child. But leaving home will remedy the problem. Your mother's mind will adjust when not constantly exposed to magical influence."

"Can I..." Destry tried to still the tremble in her voice. "Can I ever see her again, after I leave?"

Riamon leaned forward, eyebrows drawn into peaks. "Of course! You simply must limit her exposure."

If it would help Beverly, how could she refuse? "Okay. Tell me more about the Academy."

A half hour later, Destry followed Ms. Elena and Riamon from the office, clutching an envelope with a letter for her mother and a plane ticket to Missoula, Montana—the city nearest the mysterious Fold. Sunlight poured through the entryway's glass panes, splashing over the gold and purple Townsend High design on the floor.

Mrs. Meech sat in a row of plastic chairs. "All settled?"

The headmistress nodded. "Destry, I'll see you the first day of term." A quick handshake, and she strode towards the main office, heels echoing down the corridor. Mrs. Meech gave Destry a cheery thumbs-up and followed.

Destry frowned. "Riamon—"

"Fey Riamon," he corrected gently. "It's the proper way to address your teachers, as well as the heads of the school."

"Fey Riamon, how did Mrs. Meech know to give you my name for that scholarship?"

He smoothed his jacket's fringe, a pleased smile wreathing his face. "She didn't. Our surge seekers discovered you, and Elena and I dealt with the matter from there."

"Surge seekers?"

He nodded. "When a faerie comes of age, the magic strands threaded throughout the world respond. They're attracted to the energy of new fey. The strands light up in the faerie's vicinity, like a beacon. A Surger's primary job is discovering people like you."

Destry held out her arms, as if she'd find some magic glitter dust there. "I don't see anything."

"Neither do I. To see them, I'd have to perform a specific spell or be in communion with my element." He tapped the wind tattoo on his wrist. "But they led the Surgers to you. Elena and I gave your counselor a letter enchanted with small magic. The spell is harmless. It encouraged Mrs. Meech to accept our explanations at face value."

"Like telling her she submitted my name for a scholarship." Destry fingered the letter in her hands. "Are you putting a spell on my mom?" Maybe it was learning that Bev's problems were the direct result of faerie magic—Destry's magic—but doing a spell on her felt wrong.

Riamon patted her shoulder. "Most parents are too addled by fey magic to challenge their children's claims about a scholarship. Like the pamphlet Mrs. Meech gave you, those papers aren't magic. They're window dressing to reassure your mother." He strolled towards the front doors. "The photos in the brochure bear little resemblance to our school. None, to be accurate."

She followed Riamon, her rubber soles squeaking on the linoleum. "Why?"

"Including photos of a magical location in material intended for the non-magical would be unwise." He stopped by a trophy case. "Once a person has seen something, they can never un-see it. Like that chip in the glass." He ran his finger along a miniscule broken spot in the left-hand corner. "You probably passed this cabinet every day and never noticed. But now, you'll never forget it's there."

Riamon started towards the doors again, Destry keeping pace beside him. "This world has been your home for fifteen years, but you don't belong here. You must treat it with caution now that your powers are developing. Unintended displays of magic or explaining to friends what you learned today... Well, teenagers cope with the existence of magic little better than adults."

"You're saying don't tell anyone."

He opened the door with a regretful smile. "To be entirely precise—yes. Enjoy your vacation. I look forward to seeing you at the Academy."

A DEFINITION OF FAMILY

✦

Cam was fuming.

He didn't let it show. An observer would see a young man sitting calmly in the backseat of an economy car, knees bent nearly to his chest, texting with his sometimes-girlfriend, Moira Wilson. The car swerved, and an enormous birdcage slid across the few unoccupied inches of backseat, digging into his ribs. The mangy parrot inhabiting the cage shrieked, making everyone in the car wince.

His mom twisted in the front seat. "Only a few more miles. Who knew Grandma Miller wanted to pass Rupert along to you?" Her face pinched in anxious apology.

Cam shoved the cage away. "I'm fine, Mom."

And he was, when it came to the birdcage and even the bad-tempered bird. Moira, however... The phone buzzed again as they turned onto the last few blocks leading home. Cam juggled it into a better position to read Moira's text. *Why are you upset? I called your mom to see when you'd get home and she invited me to dinner. Was I supposed to say no?*

Cam pressed his lips into a thin line. Moira knew her phone call would prompt a dinner invite. He texted back: *We already made plans to see each other Monday. I want some time alone with my family.*

Seconds ticked past. Finally, Cam's phone buzzed. *Your family? Or Destry?*

Cam blew a slow, measured breath through his nose. *Same thing.*

More silence on Moira's end. Why hadn't he anticipated this? In the months before Cam left Texas, Moira's possessiveness had gone from sweet to stifling. Though their breakup was mutual—neither wanted a long-distance relationship—Moira seemed determined to pick up where they'd left off.

The phone buzzed. *Fine. I'll leave after dinner, and you can spend the whole night with your "little sister."*

Cam sighed gustily.

"Everything okay?" his dad asked, pulling into the driveway.

Cam stifled an ironic laugh. After all, he'd learned a lot about leadership in the past three months.

He'd learned how to state his expectations tactfully but firmly.

He'd been tutored in curtailing excess demands on his time.

He'd received intensive training in the art of diplomacy.

Handling this situation should be easy.

It wasn't. How could he tell his mother she'd screwed up by inviting Moira to dinner? How could he tell Moira their relationship should stay in the past? And how could he show Destry that she mattered more than a pushy ex-girlfriend, when the ex was intruding on their first night together in months?

His dad was still waiting for an answer.

Cam kneaded his neck, angling his arm to avoid Rupert. "Everything's great."

Rupert screeched again.

Good thing Rupert wasn't a talking parrot. He might have learned some inappropriate words when Cam and his dad maneuvered his cage upstairs. They set it in Cam's room, ignoring the spilled birdseed marking their path like Hansel and Gretel's breadcrumbs.

Rupert bobbed unsteadily on his perch. Dad sighed. "You should have told Grandma Miller 'no' about taking this bird."

Cam opened the cage and stroked Rupert's scraggly head. "Grandma knows I'm good with sick animals." Mom said he attracted every homeless animal in Texas.

"He's still another project for you to deal with."

"When we have the ability to help, we have the obligation to help." Cam tossed the words at his dad, exasperated. How many times had his parents said that while their family worked in soup kitchens, animal shelters, community outreach programs, or some neighbor's house? Hadn't that been the rationale when Destry moved next door, and his parents incessantly pestered Cam to include her in his friend group?

He'd resented it, of course.

Cam had spent eighth grade trying to lose his old reputation—the kid who was way too big for his age, who couldn't play a single video game but knew every edible wild plant. The kid whose dad took him camping instead of visiting Six Flags. The kid who liked growing flowers instead of playing sports, who made the honor roll and did service projects with his parents. Cam wished the list stopped there, but he knew exactly how different he was from his peers.

Well, he'd taken advantage of his height and muscle and gotten on the football team—the fastest route to popularity in Texas. He earned money for a video game console and pretended he didn't like gardening anymore. Started wearing the right clothes, making friends, fitting in.

And his parents wanted him to commit social suicide by inviting some awkward eleven-year-old to join them? No thanks.

He *had* felt bad for Destry. Since she made crummy grades, Cam tutored her—which mostly got his parents off his back—and told his football buddies that his folks made him do it. If Cam noticed the longing in Destry's face when he left her to hang out with friends or ignored her waving to him at school, it was easy to dismiss.

The compromise worked until the night several months after they moved in, when he hosted a Super Mario tournament, and Destry showed up. His mom had been upstairs, luckily, or she'd have invited Destry to join the others, no matter what Cam wanted.

He'd ignored his friends' ribbing and stepped onto the porch instead of bringing her inside. "Hey, Destry. I'm too busy to help with homework now."

She held some sad, wilted seedling in a cardboard container, an equally wilted ribbon tied around it. "I just...I got this at that Earth Day assembly. And...um...you're always helping me. So I wanted to say thank you." She held it out. "I know you and your dad like gardening."

Cam's ears heated. Why didn't she announce it over the loudspeaker at school? He glanced at the window where his football buddies jostled for space, snickering. "I don't do that anymore. Thanks anyway."

Destry drew the pathetic plant to her chest like a shield. "Oh."

"But you can leave it on the porch. Dad would like it."

She nodded. Set the plant down. Chewed on a fingernail.

If he didn't get rid of her before Mom came downstairs, he'd be in worse shape than that stupid seedling. "Want me to walk you home?" Like a lot of kids, she was still scared of the dark. He ignored a wolf whistle from one of the guys.

She tossed a hungry look at his house but nodded again. They walked in silence until they reached her yard. "Why don't you tell your friends the truth?" Destry asked.

"What?"

"Your flowers. I wish my place was that beautiful. And you helped make it that way. Why don't you want your friends to know?"

He didn't bother lying; she saw him gardening every day. No matter what his friends thought, he couldn't stop doing it. He needed it in a way they'd never understand. "If I tell them I love planting flowers, I won't have friends, Destry." His voice came out rough.

She chewed on that stupid fingernail again. "Do you like video games?"

"They're okay." He had the sudden urge to confide in someone...someone who wouldn't remind him that a strong leader was true to himself no matter the consequences (Dad) or promise that good friends would accept him no matter what (Mom). "Actually, I think they're boring. But it's what everyone does, and I'd rather do boring stuff with everyone than do my own thing alone."

She pantomimed locking her lips and pocketing the key. "I won't tell anybody."

Cam rolled his eyes. His folks did that same goofy thing. "I'll give you some middle school wisdom: Don't do stuff your parents do, if you wanna make friends."

Destry shrugged. "Not like I'm bringing anyone from school to *my* house. What are we gonna do? Eat peanut butter sandwiches and watch the weeds grow? Besides, other parents want a mom or dad home."

Cam pushed down the part of him that remembered being different and ignored. He would invite Destry over tomorrow. A light glowed in the kitchen window, with Beverly silhouetted against it. "Looks like your mom's home now. You having a girls' night?"

Destry's eyes darted away from him. "Sure. Painting fingernails and stuff."

Cam sighed in relief. Maybe hanging with her mom wasn't super exciting, but it was fun, right? Girls liked painting nails. Destry waved half-heartedly and trudged to her house.

Cam headed home, but his chest felt tight and wrong. Especially when he went in the back door and saw the snacks overflowing the kitchen counter—including his mom's homemade cookies. Definitely better than plain peanut butter sandwiches.

Dang it.

No. He'd never hear the end of it if he brought Des over. *Oooh, Camden's got a girlfriend!* Instead, he tossed some cookies in a baggie and rushed out before anyone noticed him. He jumped the picket fence between his yard and hers, jogging towards the back door—and almost ran over Destry, sitting on the rear porch reading by flashlight.

He held out the cookies. "Brought some snacks for you and your mom. What happened to girls' night?" Muffled voices came from inside Destry's house, one of them masculine.

"Mom's new boyfriend is visiting." She slapped a fat mosquito on her arm.

"And they won't let you read inside? Where the mosquitos can't eat you?" Cam teased.

Destry's expression shuttered. "I want to read out here." When Cam opened his mouth to respond, she glared. "It's more fun reading out here, okay? Just leave me alone so I can keep having the best Friday night ever."

He almost walked off. Until she tossed a fearful look at her own back door. Until a tear slid down her cheek, and then another. She turned her face away, but he'd already noticed. Cam had never seen her cry in the entire three months they'd lived here. And—in a painful flash of enlightenment—it occurred to him that there were worse things than having parents who taught you to love nature and other people and animals, or even getting bumped back down the social ladder to "that weird big kid who likes plants."

Don't... his lonely-self whispered.

But how was he supposed to walk off when Destry was afraid to go into her own house? How many other nights had she sat here, staring at his place like this?

Cam sucked in a fortifying breath. "If you think it's more fun to read in the dark, whatever. But since you're not busy... I mean, it'd be nice having someone else at the party who isn't all about video games." He offered her a hand up.

Destry wiped her cheek on her shoulder. "You don't want me there."

"Of course I d—"

She shoved his hand away. "No, you don't! You talk to me if no one's around, but you don't want me there with your real friends."

Cam's chest squeezed. What was he supposed to say? *You're right, I don't want you over. I want people to like me, and my popularity probably can't outweigh some awkward eleven-year-old sidekick.*

Or *I want to have friends, but I also want to like myself. And liking myself is hard when I'm acting like the kids who ignored or teased me for years.*

He couldn't say either of those things, though they were both true. But he could say the truest one. "I only have one real friend, Destry. She likes me even though I'm a big weirdo who loves gardening. She likes me even though I act like a jerk."

Destry sniffled. Shrugged. Maybe that was a good sign? Cam dared to sit on the steps next to her. "If you're up for it, I really do want you to come."

Finally, Destry nodded. Gave him a wobbly smile. "Don't tell anyone I've never played before."

Cam lifted one hand to his lips, in a pantomime of locking them and pocketing the key. "Promise."

A sharp, hot pain jerked him into the present. His momentary inattention had given Rupert a perfect opportunity to try out a new snack: Cam's finger. He swore, dislodging Rupert. Dad closed the cage with a knowing expression.

Cam sighed. "I've gone down that road once, Dad—caring about dumb stuff and having an easy life more than caring about people—and it turned me into a selfish jerk. It hurt the person who turned out to be my best friend. I won't take that path again."

Dad rested a broad hand on his shoulder. "Saying 'no' once in a while won't change your core values. And you have more on your plate now, things of greater importance than a sick bird. People will take advantage if you don't set boundaries."

A shout from downstairs provided merciful distraction. "Cam! Moira's here!"

People who take advantage of my time: Exhibit A. Cam groaned. "She's early. I haven't even talked to Des."

Dad patted his back, green eyes twinkling. "I'll distract Moira. Slip out the kitchen door. Or there's always that fire ladder *no one* ever uses."

Cam laughed. "Thanks, Dad." He loped to the window and shoved it open, unfurling the ladder. In seconds, Cam was sprinting across the lawn to Destry's place.

"What are you doing?"

Destry's voice interrupted Cam's search among the dead potted plants scattered over the Adams' front porch. He twisted around. Destry stood at the base of the stairs, smiling quizzically.

"Looking for the spare key." Cam indicated her bike, parked around the corner of the wrap-around porch—the reason he'd assumed Destry was home. "You didn't answer the door."

Destry held up her keychain; the spare key hung there, along with Destry's house key. "You're the only person who uses it. When you left..." She shrugged and walked up the steps, more slowly than usual.

"Why didn't you ride your bike?"

Her smile faltered. "I...had an accident on my paper route."

"And it messed up your bike?" He gripped her shoulders, looking her over. "Are you okay?"

"Just scraped my knee."

Her movements seemed too stiff for a single bloody knee, and Cam could see several long cuts on her palms, scabbed over. He pushed up her sleeves. Bruises marred her arms. Destry yanked loose. "I'm fine."

Cam strode around the porch, examining her bike. The chain hung loose, ripped from the gears, and spokes were broken, sticking out at odd angles. Torn brake and gear shift wires dangled limply. He frowned. "Looks like someone deliberately damaged your bike. Sure you had a wreck?"

Color rode high on Destry's cheeks. "I did have an accident, the morning you left for San Antonio."

"But?"

She twisted a strand of hair around her index finger. Cam waited. The silence grew heavier. Destry rubbed one hand along the beaten bike. "Jared Morgan came by the other night." She shot a glance at Cam, and her words tumbled out, tripping over each other. "I didn't want him to come, I didn't ask him over! I don't like Jared, no matter what Moira says!"

Tears glimmered in her eyes, and Cam's heart stuttered. "Did he hurt you?" Unintended, his voice descended to a growl. Destry took a step back. Cam caught her elbows, forcing himself to move slowly, to speak calmly. He indicated the bruises and cuts. "Did Jared do this?"

"No." Her voice hitched. "I really did have an accident. And Jared scared me, but I got rid of him."

Cam waved one hand towards her bike. "Except he did this in retaliation."

She shrugged again. "Doesn't matter. I won't be here long anyway. I...I got the scholarship."

A spurt of relief—a small one—broke through Cam's anger. "That's perfect, Des. Congratulations." He fingered the broken wires. "But this still matters. I'm going to deal with Morgan."

Her brown eyes sparked. "No, you aren't."

"This isn't up for debate."

"Good, because I'm not debating it! I'm telling you I handled the problem, and you don't need to. Got to stand on my own two feet, right?"

She'd said that when he offered to drive her for the paper route, too—and this time, Cam recognized the phrase. He'd tossed out that nugget of wisdom right before leaving Texas: *You'll be fine without me, Des. Got to stand on your own two feet sometime.*

Destry lifted her chin, daring him to contradict his words. Cam scrubbed a hand over his face. "I didn't mean you should never get help."

How could he explain? Though Destry tried—so hard—to hide it, she'd been miserable about him leaving. Cam had intended to acknowledge her strength, to challenge her to use it. Instead, he'd made Des think he was withdrawing his support.

Lost for a response, he swept her into a bear hug, feet dangling. She squeaked in surprise. Cam hugged her harder. "Try standing on your own two feet when I won't put you down."

She broke into helpless laughter. "You're...squishing...me!"

"A little squishing builds character." Snickering, Cam set her on her feet and flicked her under the chin. "Your problems are my problems, Dessie. That's what family means."

She chewed the corner of her lip; he held his breath. Finally, she smirked. "What am I, your second cousin twice removed?"

"Of course not. You're my little sister. Emphasis on little."

"In case you missed it, I grew while you were gone. I'm five feet, five inches. Almost tall."

An invisible hand plucked Cam's heartstrings. "You're growing up." He ruffled her hair. "But you'll be short to me forever."

She batted his hand away. "That's what I get for being friends with an enormous freak of nature." Her eyes were bright now, and Cam's heart twanged again. She forgave him so easily. She always had. That acceptance was a comforting constant—one of the best parts of Cam's life—but it made their relationship seem unfairly balanced in his favor.

He propped hands on his hips. "Tell you what: we'll discuss Jared Morgan and the subject of justice later. For now, come to my house. I need to deal with something." He hadn't missed her earlier comment: *I don't like Jared, no matter what Moira says.* It brought to mind an email Des had sent months ago—an email that mentioned her becoming fodder for the school gossip mill. With this new information, things that hadn't made sense suddenly clicked into place.

Frowning, Destry followed him. The scent of pepperoni and baked crust wafted out when they opened the front door. Moira perched on a sofa, chatting with his folks. Cam felt Destry stiffen.

His mom's eyes brightened. "There's my girl. I've hardly seen you since Cam left for school."

Dad stretched until his shoulders popped. "Pizza's here. Ready to eat?"

Cam held up a hand, palm forward. His course of action, so muddy a half hour ago, had become clear. "I'm sorry to change plans at the last minute, but neither Destry or Moira or I can stay for dinner."

Moira smiled brittlely. "Oh? Are we doing something together, like the Three Musketeers?"

Cam leveled a steady gaze on her. "Des and I are spending time to-gether. You're going home, or wherever else you want, so long as it isn't here."

A flush crept up Moira's neck. "Excuse me?"

"Cam!" Mom looked from him to Moira, eyes wide. "What in the world—"

"If you trust me now, I'll explain later." Cam turned to his ex-girlfriend, whose lips were white and pinched. "I confided in you, hoping you'd help Destry at school, and you betrayed that confidence and twisted it into lies. You made her school life miserable. I don't care why. You aren't welcome here any longer."

Moira's gaze flitted to Destry, back to him. "I'm not sure what she told you, but—"

"Oh, Des was infuriatingly silent about what you did. But I'm not stupid." He *had* been. He'd believed Moira's claim to love Destry like a little sister. He knew better now, and there was no question who he'd choose.

His ex-girlfriend turned pleading eyes on his folks. "Mrs. Waters, Mr. Waters, you know me. I would never do anything to hurt Destry."

Dad cleared his throat, face slipping from pleasant to sternly regal—his "I'm disappointed in you" expression. "I know that Cam isn't the type to believe unsubstantiated rumors. I'm sorry, Moira, but I trust his judgment."

Warmth expanded Cam's chest. He strode to the front door and opened it, sweeping an ironic, old-fashioned bow. "Goodbye, Moira. It's been delightful knowing you. It'll be even more delightful to forget you."

She flounced out onto the porch. "You think Townsend High is miserable now?" she hissed at Destry. "Wait until next semester. You won't have the great Camden Waters to protect you."

Cam glanced at Destry, wiggling his eyebrows to show how little Moira's threat mattered in light of Destry's scholarship. She offered the older girl a jaunty salute. "Have a good year, Moira." Cam shoved the door; there was enough time to see Moira's face crumple into confusion before it slammed shut. And then, silence.

He faced his parents. "Des and I are going to Andy's, if that's okay. We need to catch up."

Mom crossed her arms. "As long as I get that explanation. Your actions seemed terribly unkind, Camden."

This might be one of the first times Dad understood better than Mom. "They *were* unkind. But they were also necessary." Cam added, more gently, "I promise to explain. Later."

Dad waved towards the door. "Better move it. Andy's fills up quick on Friday."

The silence in Cam's car was absolute. He didn't break it—another thing he'd learned over the past three months. Silence had its own power.

Des started nibbling that hangnail...again. Automatically, Cam pulled her wrist down. She clenched her hands in her lap. "How did you know?"

He stopped at a stop sign. The *click-click-click* of his blinker filled the car. "One of your emails mentioned someone spreading rumors about you. You claimed it wasn't a big deal, just irritating, but I emailed Moira. She said the entire school thought you'd slept with Jared when you were thirteen, that you two hooked up whenever he came home from college. She also said Jared started the rumors, which seemed odd, since he never said anything before."

A flush heated Destry's cheeks. "So when I mentioned Moira on my porch..."

"You thought she'd repeated those lies to me," Cam said flatly. "Why didn't you tell me how bad it was?"

Destry turned towards the window, blinking fast like she might cry. "You couldn't do anything. I figured it was time to quit expecting you to fix my problems."

If he ever made an idiotic statement like *Stand on your own two feet* again, Cam would cut his tongue out with a piece of jagged glass. What made him think Des was ready for that? "This is my fault. I wanted Moira to keep an eye on you when Jared came home for visits, so I said he'd tried to mess with you. I didn't give her details, but it must have been enough."

He'd only meant the request as a safety net. He hadn't expected a recurrence, badly as he'd scared Jared after the first incident. Yet another miscalculation. He turned the car left. "I'm sorry for making things worse."

"You didn't. Moira went out with Jared one of the times you guys fought and broke up. He told her I was a slut who teased but didn't follow through." She pulled a loose thread on her t-shirt. "After you left, me and Moira talked about you a lot. We both missed you. But the day I got your first email, I mentioned it—and she hadn't gotten one. She was so mad, Cam."

Regret chewed at him, leaving stinging puncture wounds. Yes, he'd emailed Destry first and more often. With his time so limited, she took priority. But he'd tried to be conscientious about emailing Moira, too. Apparently, it hadn't been enough.

"What happened?" he asked quietly.

"She told me what Jared said, she asked if I was the reason—" Destry broke off, eyes skittering away.

"The reason for what?"

Silence.

"Dessie. I know better than to believe anything Moira said about you."

"This...this wasn't just about me." She sucked in a breath and blurted, "She asked if *I* was the reason you two had never—um—done anything. She said you and me...we were probably..." She stopped, lips pressed together so tight a crowbar couldn't have pried them open. More questions were useless.

Unfortunately, Cam understood. No more questions needed.

From the beginning, he'd tried to tell Moira...to explain that physical attraction wasn't simple for him. He needed a strong emotional connection with someone before it was even a possibility. But she'd taken it like some challenge, and Cam never felt certain how much Moira liked him, or if she just wanted the satisfaction of achieving something no other girl had.

He'd always hoped it was the first.

Had Moira really thought he'd slept with Destry? Or simply wanted to humiliate Des in as many ways as possible? Shame burned his cheeks, his neck, but he forced himself to ask, "The rumors started after that?"

Destry nodded.

Cam didn't trust himself to speak. He'd grown accustomed to friends and teammates giving him the side-eye, expecting something more "normal" from the school's football hero. But this went past snide comments at his expense, and it was Des who'd suffered it. He fought the urge to whip the car around, hunt down Moira and confront her. Satisfying, yes—to eviscerate his ex with words like she'd done to him many, many times. Still, it wouldn't help Destry, looking miserable and embarrassed in the front seat.

Cam pulled into Andy's parking lot and killed the engine.

He reached for Destry's hand but remembered the cuts on her palm. Instead, he stroked one thumb along her wrist, one of the few places that remained un-bruised, uninjured, and blessedly unmarked. "Listen. Life is changing for us. We both know there won't be many more weeks like these. But you'll always be part of my life—no matter how little we see each other—and you can always turn to me. Remember that, okay?"

She rested her head on his shoulder, cornsilk hair spilling down his shirt. "I sort of forgot that, this semester. I won't forget again."

A BIT DRAMATIC

✦

For Destry, the next two weeks were the best in recent memory, despite her worries about the new school, her new powers, and leaving her mother.

Christmas came and went, made special by Beverly's effort to stay home (and sober). Destry and Cam spent their days together, though she watched closely for signs that her magic was unbalancing him. While the force driving Destry's powers seemed to slumber for the moment, it wouldn't stay away. Her wrist markings had yet to appear.

But Cam seemed fine, and Destry felt unusual gratitude for his months away at AFLA. Because Cam had put off private school until junior year, they'd required him to complete some preparatory class-es over the summer. He'd traveled back and forth before leaving on a longer-term basis in September. Much as Destry had missed him, she suspected that the forced separation was what allowed them this holiday together—without negative consequences.

Destry and Cam used his last day at home to have a Nothing Day: hanging at his place, watching movies, eating junk, and taking naps.

Cam's parents weren't due back for another hour. They had the house to themselves.

Darkness crept along the windows by the time Cam clicked off the TV. "I'm officially movied-out. Any more, and I'll have no brains left and flunk out of school." As the screen blackened, the living room grew dimmer, given shape only through indeterminate gray forms and crouching dark objects. Even Cam, sitting at the end of the loveseat with Destry's calves draped across his lap, was little more than a faceless figure cloaked in shadow.

Destry's chest tightened. In three hours, Cam and his dad would leave for an overnight drive to Georgia, where AFLA was located, and Destry's flight to Montana left the next afternoon. She'd been trying to forget that invisible finish line—the one marking the end of her life here, her time with Cam, her years (flawed though they were) with Beverly. It would never be the same again.

Her throat followed her chest, squeezing too tight for speech. The silence stretched out, broken only by the *tock-tock-tock* of the grandfather clock. Cam tickled her feet. "Too early to fall asleep, Dessie, even for you."

Her laughter came out strangled. Cam's shadow-self stilled. He leaned closer, looming in the darkness; Destry's heart gave an inexplicable jump, and she pressed back against the couch arm.

Cam snapped on the side table lamp. Buttery light transformed him into her friend again. "Sorry," he said, slate-green eyes crinkling. "Sometimes, I forget how bad your night-vision is." He strode around the room, turning on every single lamp and the ceiling light, morphing the room from night to day in bright-brighter-brightest succession.

Destry sat cross-legged, watching him. Cam didn't mind the dark. This gesture was entirely for her. Would anyone else ever know her so completely? Did she even want them to? The ache in her chest grew, and tears stung her eyes.

Cam clicked on the last lamp. "Better?"

Nodding, she tried to blink the tears away, but Cam saw. He knelt in front of her, face level with hers. "Hey. What's this all about?"

"Nothing."

"You hardly ever cry. It's something."

Destry could admit the truth, if not the reason behind it. "I'm gonna miss you. That's all."

His mouth pulled up on one side, into a smile more melancholy than happy. "Know what? I missed you, too. And I'll miss you again. That part just plain sucks." He rubbed her cheek with one warm, calloused thumb.

For a moment, Destry saw something in his face that she couldn't name. She knew only one thing: if she leaned forward the tiniest bit, and lifted her face to Cam's, he would probably kiss her, like he'd done when she was thirteen.

Wait...kiss her? This was Cam! Kissing him would be like kissing a brother. A squawk echoed through the house, breaking the mood. Cam groaned, pushing up to sit on the loveseat. "Rupert." He said the name like a curse word.

"He still won't let you feed him?"

"Oh, he'll let me feed him." Cam held up one hand, covered in small cuts. "But my fingers are his preferred food."

Destry giggled. Cam gave her a dark look, and she flopped over on the couch, still laughing. Her head landed on Cam's thigh. "Maybe your parents should take care of him. Maybe they're less tasty."

"Dad already has this *I told you so* face every time that bird screeches. He's not getting the truth unless I lose a finger and need driven to the hospital. And he better not hear it from you, either."

Still grinning, Destry lifted one hand to her lips and pantomimed locking them and pocketing the key. "Ravenous, man-eating trolls couldn't drag it out of me."

Cam chortled. "Trolls aren't real, Destry. I'd be more impressed if you withstood the temptation of Mom's cookies."

Her stomach twisted. Troll, goblin—pretty much the same thing. And according to Riamon, she'd live near the monsters soon. But Cam needed to stay blissfully ignorant of that fact. "Okay. Even your mom's fudge cake couldn't persuade me to tell."

Eyes dancing, Cam tapped the tip of her nose. "Now that's commitment."

Destry woke up in a tree.

That in itself was strange enough. After all, she'd gone to sleep in her bedroom after her Nothing Day with Cam. But here she was, twenty feet off the ground, with only moonlight to illuminate the white branches wrapped around her like cradling arms.

She pushed at them, and they slid away, leaving her sitting on a large branch near the trunk. A glimpse down set her stomach churning and the world spinning. Destry whimpered, clinging to the silky smooth trunk.

The branches only went down another five feet. There must be a better option than a fifteen-foot-drop to the ground, but what? She squeezed her eyes shut. "I got up here somehow. I can get down."

The branches rustled, despite the complete lack of wind, as if the tree was whispering to her. "It's a tree, Destry," she snapped, mostly for the sound of her own voice. "It can't think, and it can't help you."

The tree went still, the way a person might if she'd insulted them beyond belief. She squashed the ridiculous urge to apologize. Rustling filled her ears, and branches snaked around her arms, yanking her into the air. A shriek hung, suspended, in her throat. She tensed for impact.

But...

It never came. Destry jerked to a stop—stomach dipping, legs swinging free, branches still wrapped around her arms. She peeled her eyes open.

She dangled six feet above the ground. To the left was a large pile of grass and leaves. On the right stood a hard-packed dirt path. The tree limbs slid back and forth, swishing her with them, like the tree was debating. Then, with an impatient sigh that fluttered every leaf, they flung her to the left.

Destry landed with a gasp and a *whump*. Leaves flew up around her, crunched beneath her...but they cushioned her fall. She scrambled up, stumbling to more stable ground.

She was in a forest. The same white, smooth trees stretched endlessly on either side of her. Destry reached for one, curious—were all the trees as *alive* as hers had been?—but a rustle nearby stayed her hand. Why did that small sound seem ominous?

Another rustle, closer—and the trees weren't moving. Destry's heart sped up. Instinct pushed her away from the sound in hasty strides. She tripped on a tree root, fell, stumbled upright. Thunder rumbled nearby.

A streak of lightning sliced the night in two. The flickering light turned the forest into a maze of disorienting, many-limbed silhouettes. But there, up ahead—a break in the trees. Destry's jog turned into a sprint.

At the edge of the clearing, she stopped. Where the trees ended, an expanse of rocky ground began, and past that a river, parallel to the tree line. The water drew her, a deep, aching need. Movement flickered on the periphery of her vision. She spun, pulse jumping.

Just a branch, waving in the breeze from the oncoming storm. It seemed to beckon her into the forest. Destry hesitated, until another rustle pricked her ears. Something creeping along the softly carpeted ground. Something stalking its prey.

Prey. The thought sent tingles up her shoulder blades. The skin there began to burn, stretching and splitting. The rustling grew closer.

Destry bolted for the river.

She felt more than heard the pursuit, somewhere to her right—a shadow with quicksilver movements too fast to track. She swerved back towards the forest, her rasping breaths loud in her ears. The first drops of rain fell, soaking into her skin. Energy surged through her.

But even as her body channeled the new energy, the shadow flew into her line of sight. Claws caught her clothes, flung her to the ground near the pale trees. Breath whooshed from her lungs. Strong hands flipped her over, and vines broke through the ground in a shower of dirt, snaking up and binding her.

A hooded figure crouched over her, cloak hiding everything except its fingers. The flicker of lightning played over obsidian claws. The shadow creature sliced the vines, pinning her in place with its weight instead. A guttural voice asked, "Are you the one?"

It grabbed Destry's left arm; those iron-hard fingers burned. She cried out, but the creature ignored it, muttering fluid, incomprehensible words. "Show me," it hissed. "Show me!"

The pain in her wrists blazed, a branding iron under her skin. Destry screamed, struggled, strained. The creature squeezed tighter, claws biting into her forearm. "Tell me who you are!"

A flash of white at the edge of the forest—a tree twisting, branches whipping, but not from the wind. The longest branch slashed the creature across the face, knocking it off Destry. She scrambled up, rocks gouging her hands and knees, and lunged for the forest.

She slammed into a tree as her attacker flew at her again. The tree swung a heavier branch around, catching the shadow creature in the stomach, flinging it away. "NO!" the monster bellowed. The scream broke across her ears, shattering the night, the forest, and the dream.

Destry woke clutching her hands to her chest. Fiery pain twisted into her skin, and her heart stuttered. Twin circlets of flame surrounded her wrists. She yelped and tumbled off the bed.

The impact barely registered. Destry leapt to her feet, arms thrust away from her, but the fire was dying. It sank into her skin, leaving a delicate pattern of red and silver flames. Gasping, Destry crumpled to the floor.

She leaned against the bed and hissed in pain.

No.

Not again.

Her fingers flew to her shoulders, exploring the rips in her long-sleeved t-shirt, the soft membrane poking through, stretching and expanding in the cool bedroom air. She jerked to her feet, then stumbled as the weight change threw her off balance. Unbidden, the newly appeared wings stretched wide, compensating. Destry faced the mirror.

She'd left a candle burning, like always. Light flickered over her face, her tense stance, the curves of those...those wings. They arced from her shoulders, hovering gracefully in the background.

Not "those" wings. My wings. Destry made herself at least think the words. *They're part of me.* She stood there for a long time, breath making frosty puffs in the cool air, trying to adjust to this new image of herself. It wasn't working.

She whirled away from the mirror, reaching for those—her—wings again, avoiding the sharp edges and points. They felt cool, like water made into flesh. Too bad they couldn't soothe the burning on her wrists. That pain still lingered.

Fear trembled in her stomach. Hadn't Riamon mentioned fire markings at that meeting? Hadn't Fey Elena implied that fire markings were a problem? Maybe this was why. Maybe the burning never went away. Bad enough to be a freak with wings. Would she spend the rest of her life suffering this bone-deep ache?

Destry hurried to the window. It fogged as she pressed her wrists against the chilled panes of glass—first the tops of her wrists, then the undersides. Slowly, the pain diminished. She staggered to the bed, moving awkwardly to avoid catching her wings on any furniture. She collapsed on the edge, examining her new tattoos. Riamon's warning ghosted through her mind: *You'll get your second set of power markings soon. It might be a bit dramatic.*

Anger heated her cheeks. A bit dramatic? Her wrists had been *on fire*! What qualified as true drama? She'd been prepared to like Riamon, but now she would rather stuff the Master of Precision in a dumpster.

Yawning, Destry rubbed her grainy eyes. The shock of waking up to flaming body parts must be wearing off. It felt like she'd run for miles, probably because of that nightmare... Her stomach stirred uneasily, and so did her wings, making their own breeze. Strands of cornsilk hair blew into her face.

The bad dream must have made her wings appear again. Fey Elena said feelings of fear and danger brought them out, but how did she get rid of them?

Another memory played in her head, a crisper voice than Riamon's: *Once you are calm, they recede.*

Destry stifled a hysterical giggle. Calm. She had thirteen hours—at best—before she was supposed to ride with her mother to the airport, and fifteen hours before she boarded a plane for Montana. Who could relax under that sort of deadline?

Another yawn edged out of her. The last time they'd gone away was when she passed out, then slept. Maybe that would work again. If she could sleep...

If she didn't dream...

Destry locked her door, in case Bev felt unexpectedly maternal and checked on her. Then, gingerly, she lay on her stomach on the bed.

Chill air bit at her feet, but Destry probably couldn't pull up the blanket without cutting off an ear with her new razor-bladed body parts. She burrowed into her pillow and concentrated on the breath whispering in and out of her lungs. As her back muscles relaxed, so did her wings, lowering to cover her torso like a thick blanket.

The sensation was oddly soothing. She drifted into sleep, carried on waves of exhaustion.

FIREWINGS

"**W**ould you like another drink, Miss?" The airline stewardess leaned over Destry, face concerned. Maybe she'd noticed her crying.

"I'm fine." The lie wasn't up to her usual standard, but she couldn't manage anything better. Just hours ago, she'd said goodbye to her mom at the airport—a goodbye more final than Bev realized. The necessity of leaving didn't make doing it easier.

The captain's voice crackled over the speakers, announcing the plane's upcoming descent into Missoula, Montana. From there, a bus would take Destry (and the other half-faeries who'd come by plane, bus, or train) to the school in Si′fliegen.

Destry still had trouble understanding the location. Fey Elena had explained that the Academy—in fact, all the lands magic people called home—wasn't located in a normal human spot. Rather, one went through a "fold" in the world to reach them. When Destry asked, "But where is it?" Fey Elena had waved her hand impatiently.

"Nowhere. Everywhere. It is a real location, suited for magic dwellers, inaccessible to those who can't handle magic. A pocket sewn into the fabric of the earth. But it could not be put on any map."

The school had a post office box in Missoula—the town nearest the entrance to this magical Fold—where families sent letters to the half-fey students. But a mailing address couldn't soothe Destry's nerves over entering a place she couldn't find on Google Maps.

The dry air in the plane was making her skin itch. As she applied moisturizer, she also eyed the other passengers, looking for potential classmates. The girl with the short sleeves and unmarked wrists was out; same for the boy wearing shorts despite the chilly winter weather. But one girl—a redhead with bright purple glasses and a long-sleeved peasant blouse—was a possibility. She kept glancing at Destry, at the letter she'd been holding. It contained Fey Elena's instructions on traveling and what she was allowed to pack for school.

Not much, apparently. Destry stuffed the moisturizer in her backpack, then peeked at the flowing script, though she'd read the letter at least twelve times.

The school board wishes all half-faeries to make a smooth adjustment to our world. Therefore, certain items (judged to hinder the student's adjustment) are prohibited or may only be used in specific circumstances.

As access to clean air, water, and fire sources is essential to the well-being of faeriekind, the royal family established mandates to keep the fey kingdom untainted by human technology. In support of this endeavor, the school board prohibits laptops, electronic tablets, radios, and cell phones.

No big deal. Destry didn't own the first three, and her phone still had no service.

New students will be outfitted with garments appropriate to their status as children of the fey. Clothing from the human world may only be worn on trips away from school (barring field trips), in dorm and common room areas, and on weekends. Students caught in human clothing in public areas of the school during the academic week will be subject to discipline.

No sense getting in trouble right away. Destry had packed a few fa-
vorites: her Iron Man and Spiderman t-shirts and some flannels stolen
from Cam.

*Illicit food items from the human world (including chocolate, candy,
and the fizzy sugar drinks referred to as "soda") are strictly prohibited, as
is the buying, smuggling, and selling of said items. Illicit substances lead
to ill-considered and illicit behavior on the part of those consuming them.
Students found in possession of contraband face stiff disciplinary penalties.*

They made candy sound like an illegal drug. Were all faeries crazy
health nuts, or was it a school thing? Destry had ignored the temptation
to sneak in some treats, though, deterred by that unspecified punishment.

At least she'd been able to pack light.

The plane touched down with a series of grinding bumps. The "ding"
cleared everyone to disembark; Destry slung her backpack over one
shoulder, grateful she didn't have luggage. Wandering around looking
for the correct bags on the correct conveyer belt would intensify this lost,
uncertain feeling.

Spotting the driver in the pick-up area wasn't hard, with his uniform
and sign: Mountainview Academy. A handful of other kids, ranging
from pre-teen to almost-adult, headed that way too.

The red-haired girl from the plane bounced over to the man, waving
vigorously. "Arnie!"

His round face broke into a smile. "Good to see you, Sara. Last flight
of the day! We've been waiting here for hours." He jerked a thumb
towards the glass doors. A sleek bus stood outside, gleaming under the
streetlights. Night had fallen during their flight.

Sara shifted her bag. "Want me to man the clipboard? I think we have
some new ones." Her eyes fell on Destry.

Arnie pulled at his scratchy-looking outfit. "Anything to get home and
into my water-weave clothes. I'm dried out as a dwarf canyon."

"Okay, move it, everyone." Sara loped towards the bus. A few kids followed, bored expressions suggesting this was routine.

Most of the younger kids hung back. Arnie smiled reassuringly. "Sara's been with us four years. She'll take good care of you while I catch stragglers."

Destry hurried outside, trying to look more confident than she felt. Coming in late was bad enough; it probably meant taking remedial classes with kids three to four years younger. She couldn't afford to act like an uncertain preteen, too.

Sara, sitting cross-legged in the driver's seat with a clipboard, watched Destry top the stairs. "Name?"

"Destry Adams."

Sara made a check mark on the paper. "Fifteen, huh? You're old for a newcomer."

"They told me so."

Destry's stiff response made the girl's hazel eyes crinkle. "It wasn't an insult." She jerked her chin towards the back of the bus, where the seats were mostly full. "Find a seat alone, and I'll sit with you once the newbies are settled."

Destry stumbled on her way down the aisle, catching the sole of her sneaker on the rubber-covered floor. They ground together with a painful squeak. She grabbed an empty seat to keep from falling. She slunk into it, trying to make herself invisible.

In front of her, a hulking boy filled his entire bench unaided. His hoodie, stretched across broad shoulders, looked ready to rip at the seams. The boy twisted to face her. His grin flashed white against warm brown skin. "Newbie!"

Did he have to bellow it for everyone to hear? Destry slouched down in the seat. "Um...yeah."

He offered a hand to shake; it engulfed hers completely. "David Tuilagi. Unofficial welcoming committee of one. I have something for you."

"You...you do?" Her cheeks warmed.

He dug in a drawstring bag. "Yup. Call it a welcome gift or a free sample, whichever floats your boat." The boy pulled out a pile of t-shirts and rifled through them. "Most of these are sized for junior high kids. New halves are usually—"

"Eleven or twelve." Destry tried to keep the impatience out of her voice.

David nodded. Finally, he separated two tees—one pink with the words *My wings bring all the boys to the yard!* and one gray stating *#faeriesrule.* Squinting at Destry's sneakers, jeans, and navy hoodie, he announced, "You don't look like the pink type," and tossed the gray shirt in her lap.

She took the t-shirt with a mumbled thank you. David tapped his chest with a thick finger. "Just tell people where you got it!" He turned away in time to catch a few more kids coming down the aisle. They jumped at his shout of, "Newbies!"

Arnie climbed on, too, and the door swooshed closed. Sara bounded down the aisle, squirming past David as he thrust shirts in two more students' arms. She plopped into the seat, shoving Destry over with her hip. "Looks like you met my magic partner."

Magic partner?

The overhead lights dimmed as the bus lurched forward. David steadied himself, threw one last shirt at a startled kid (it landed on her head), and grinned. "'Course she has. Hey, check out my new creation!" He yanked off his hoodie. In the light from the streetlamps outside, Destry made out air tattoos on his wrists and a lavender-colored shirt proclaiming *Real men have wings.* "Color even matches your glasses. Kinda."

"Nice." Sara curled her feet up on the seat. "I'm gonna talk to Destry, but catch me later. I need help with that metalworking report."

"Nothing like leaving it to the last minute." David turned away, squeezing down the aisle towards some older students.

"You don't have to stay with me," Destry said. She didn't want to be a social charity case.

"I see David all the time. And I think you'll be interesting." Sara cocked her head. "I might as well ask: why'd you come in so late? I'm only a year older than you. How long ago did your powers show up?"

"I got my leg tattoos a few weeks ago."

Sara whistled. "Weird."

Destry considered a dozen ways to answer that, but not a single one was nice. Since Sara seemed friendly (if tactless) she kept them to herself. The redhead started chattering about things she might like at the school. She jumped topics quickly, and Destry—exhausted from her less-than-restful night—found her attention drifting. It snapped back when David dropped into his seat again, shaking the bus floor.

He grinned at Sara. "Almost forgot! I made you something over break." He handed her a paper cylinder. She unrolled it. The dim streetlamps illuminated a drawing of two faeries—obviously Sara and David. Rays of light shot from their palms, splitting a distant mountain in two. A title was inked across the bottom: *Sara and David- Team Unbreakable!*

Sara rolled it up and carefully stowed it in her bag. "That's your best one yet. Definitely going on my wall."

David beamed. Humming, he turned and propped his feet on the seat across from him, to the chagrin of the kid sitting there.

Destry considered the pair. Sara had called him her magic partner. Was that another name for boyfriend or girlfriend? "Are you guys...together?"

Discomfort flitted across Sara's face. "Not exactly. We're best friends, and we work as a team at school so our magic will function right."

What was wrong with their magic? Asking seemed rude, so Destry chose a less direct question. "Do all half-faeries get partnered up?"

"Yeah. Fey Elena will explain."

The girl fell silent, and Destry frowned. The chatty redhead had been eager to talk about school, even when Destry hadn't asked. Why the sudden reticence? "Will I get to choose my partner?"

Sara fiddled with her blouse hem, eyes trained on the embroidered flowers. "Sort of. Your magic already chose him."

"What does that mean?"

"I'm supposed to let Fey Elena explain this. She meets with every new person on their first day at the Academy."

Worry bloomed in Destry's stomach, a nauseating ache. What hadn't the headmistress told her? "I don't want to get you in trouble. But I can't wait for hours and hours, wondering what else will happen to me."

David's voice drifted over the seat. "Don't do it."

Destry leaned into Sara's line of sight. "Please, Sara? Weren't...weren't you scared, your first day here?"

The redhead groaned. "I never have this problem with younger newbies. *They* want to know how long before they can fly." She lowered her voice. "Fine. But when Fey Elena repeats this, play dumb."

David sighed. "She'll know. Fey Elena always knows."

Sara ignored him. "You understand that humans and faerie magic are a bad mix, right?"

"Yes..."

"Well, if a faerie and a human hook up, and the woman gets pregnant, that's what you have: a mix. The baby inherits magic from their faerie parent. Since babies are adaptable, it doesn't cause problems like it does for grown-ups. But they're not full magical beings, and they can't handle all that power, so their magic splits. That's why you're half-faerie and not full-faerie."

The light in the bus dimmed as they headed away from town towards rural roads.

Sara leaned closer. "Did Fey Elena say if you have a faerie parent?"

Destry furrowed her eyebrows. "Of course. How else could someone be half-faerie?"

"Because the other half of that split magic has to go somewhere. It searches out another baby—a regular human baby—and latches on, making that baby half-faerie too. Being faerie is about how much magic you hold, not whose DNA you have."

Destry rubbed her temples, trying to sort everything out. "So, if my father was fey, then I'm the baby whose magic broke. It found some other kid—"

"Some boy," Sara interrupted. "The magic does this ying-yang thing. It chooses the opposite sex, complementary personalities, different magic signs." She pushed up one sleeve, letting Destry see her tattoo. "Like I'm air, and David is water."

"Okay." The word cracked on the way out. "My magic chose some boy. And he's my magic partner?"

"You got it." Sara rushed on before Destry could ask another question. "You'll have to work with him for your magic to be at full capacity. And you'll like him—fey's honor. Magic partners always get along, because they're perfect complements to each other."

A permanent study buddy...a ready-made friend in a new place. That might be alright. She shushed the little voice whispering, *Who cares? He isn't Cam*, and smiled shakily. "I can live with that. It's not like I have to marry the guy."

"Yeah." Sara's voice shot up a couple octaves and came out a squeaky falsetto. "Nothing says you *have* to marry him. You don't even have to do the bonding ceremony until you're eighteen."

Her relief dissipated. "Bonding ceremony?"

"Destry, I really think Fey Elena should explain the—"

"What's a bonding ceremony?"

David said, "You told her the first part, Sara. No fair to stop now."

The redhead flopped her head back on the seat and pressed the heels of her hands against her forehead. Destry waited, clutching her *#faeriesrule* t-shirt, until Sara sat up and straightened her glasses. "This is how it works: while you're a kid, your magic is flexible. You can work with your magic partner at school, and that's enough. But the rules change when you become an adult. You have to be bonded with your partner—commit to them in a ceremony—or you both lose your magic."

Destry's hands turned clammy. "You said I don't have to marry this guy!"

"You don't. The bond indicates a strong emotional commitment, the willingness to be part of that person's life so your magics can feed off each other. It's a soulmate kind of thing, not a romantic one. But unless they're completely unattracted to their partner—and obviously, there's more than one situation where that can happen—" She gestured at the kids ranged around the bus, like that told Destry anything. "Well, you have a connection with this person you don't have with anyone else. Lots of bonded couples *do* end up together."

"Makes sense," David added. "How many romantic relationships are gonna work out when the person already has a magic partner waiting at home?"

Sara hurried on. "Look, I didn't like the idea at first, either. But your magic chooses really well. Even magic partners who aren't romantic are the most amazing best friends ever. You'll understand when the school finds him."

The clammy feeling crawled into Destry's chest. There had to be a loophole. Even as friends, she didn't want tied to some random guy. "You said if I don't do the ceremony, I'll lose my magic. Do people ever let their magic die and go back to their old lives?"

Sara's eyes grew wide, obvious even in the shadowed bus. "No. Not happily, anyway."

"Why not?"

"Because magic is part of you, even if you don't feel it. You don't particularly notice your arms or legs, but if you lost them, you'd feel the absence. When a person's magic dies, they struggle. Forever." She glanced at the boy in front of them. "Being half-faerie means caring about someone else as much as you care about yourself. If I walked away, David would also lose his powers. I could never do that to him."

Destry turned towards the window as the bus swerved onto a winding mountain road. She already had that sort of relationship—with Cam, with her mom. Now, she was supposed to care about some new person the same way, all because her magic said so?

The road turned narrower, dark trees crowding close on either side. It looked too small for the bus to squeeze through. Destry held her breath, but no branches scraped against metal, and the bus barely jostled them. Sara poked her in the ribs, grinning. "You're going to a school for *magic*. Don't worry, the bus has special properties." It must have, because the path shrank to little more than a hiking trail, and they trundled on.

The trail wound between a sheer pass of rock. Sara grimaced. "This part always makes me sick. Hold on."

Destry clutched the seat. Her stomach swooped, the sensation of an elevator going down too fast. Blinding light flashed through the bus. An impression of weightlessness swept over Destry, even though the seat felt solid beneath her thighs.

And that quickly, it was over. The light faded. Destry's stomach resumed its proper place. She peered out the window. They were driving along a wide, smoothly paved road. The sun shone brightly, gilding the trees dotting the landscape. The older students began talking again like nothing had happened. The newer ones sat open-mouthed.

Sara pried Destry's hands off the seat. "That was a figure of speech. Grabbing something doesn't help."

"What was that?"

"We entered the Fold. A non-magic person who tries to go through will feel so sick it drives them away. For us, it's just disorienting."

"Disorienting" felt like the wrong word. Acting blasé must be easier when you'd done it four times a year for several years. "Um, it's daytime now."

"Yep. Some things here are reversed from the outside world." Sara glanced at her watch. "7:46 p.m. there, 7:46 a.m. here. The weather is upside down, too. In the human world, in the United States, January usually means winter. Here—" she pulled down the bus window, and balmy air rolled over them, "it's full-on summer."

Upside down...a good description of her life. Destry didn't answer. Instead, she stared at her new home.

The road they were on swept around a valley. Down in the valley nestled a small town. Streets wound between stone houses and shops. The architecture soared: slender arches of pale marble, airy bridges that looked like they would never hold weight. Buildings tended to go up rather than out; small or large, everything had a second floor, and every house had at least one balcony.

As they drove closer, Destry spotted people on the balconies: sitting, talking, eating, playing. Some didn't have wings. Others did. People walked the streets—smoothly cobbled stone in various pale shades—or sat on the edges of fountains. There were fountains everywhere. Small or large, delicate or flowing, inlaid with multicolored stones or marble designs. Sara leaned closer to the window and breathed deeply. "Finally, a little moisture. Faeries aren't meant for the dry Montana climate."

The bus continued past the town, rounding a curve in the road. Destry's breath caught. In the distance, a lofty palace reached toward the sky. Sara said, "That's where the royals live: the Faerie Queen and her court. The Imperial family lives right next to the palace, in a separate building with their own grounds."

Destry managed to smile, though the new information jumbled in her head, unmoored by any relevance to her former life. Sara pointed out the window. "There's the school."

It didn't look like any school Destry had ever attended. The same delicate style of the local buildings graced the school, but on a larger scale, with a few improbably high towers thrown in. "Faerie mansion" might've been a better description. Gentle hills surrounded the three story structure, with bunches of tall, slender trees scattered across the grounds. The trees grew thicker and closer together behind the school.

On the left and right sat smaller buildings—three on each side—curving away from the school along another smooth-cobbled road. It ran in a horseshoe shape around the school and its grounds. On the right, the road stretched towards the palace Destry had seen, and on the left, into the forest created by the ethereal trees. The bus's road intersected it directly in front of the school.

Arnie pulled the bus to a stop, hauled on a lever, and the door opened with a hydraulic whoosh. "Everybody out. Take your luggage, or we'll give it to the goblins."

The veteran students offered dutiful laughs, the kind reserved for jokes repeated too often. But one girl about eleven squeaked, "Goblins?" Apparently, no one had mentioned the monsters to her.

Arnie nodded. "Very little fashion sense, goblins. Always on the look-out for clothes from the more civilized denizens of these realms." He winked. "Their forest is naught but a wing's width away."

Hadn't Fey Elena said those goblins knew better than to come to the academy? Destry grabbed her bag and scrambled after Sara. "The goblins live nearby? Like, in those trees or something?" She pointed toward the woods behind the school.

Sara hitched her backpack more securely on her shoulders. They began trudging up the lawn. "Goblins don't live in trees. They live in houses, like us. Their kingdom backs up to ours."

She lifted both hands, waggling the left one. "Look, this is Si'fliegen. Our palace is here—" she waggled her pinky finger— "and our school is here." She waggled the index finger. "My left thumb is the faerie forest—those trees you pointed to. It marks the boundary between the two kingdoms. My right hand—" she placed it next to the left, thumbs together— "is Rí Kobold, the seat of power for the goblin realm. Our forest leads into theirs." A wiggle of her right thumb. "And my right index finger is their castle, where the goblin king lives. Some people say they built it close to the line to spite us, but Fey Elena says the king has to be close to their willa trees, and that's where the grove is."

"Willa trees?"

Sara shivered. "Goblin trees. They're terrifying. But unless you have to see the goblin king, that forest is off-limits anyway. You'd get in trouble for trespassing."

They approached the school entrance. Destry swiped at her sweaty forehead. Her hoodie was wrong for the summer weather. "Guess I'll have to break my habit of dropping in on royalty."

Riamon's upbeat voice interrupted Sara's reply. "Ah, our last group!" He stood in an enormous arched doorway, thin face stretched in a smile. Through the open door, Destry saw kids milling around an entry hall.

Riamon spread his arms as they assembled on the short staircase leading to the entrance. "Hello, hello! Welcome to the Academy for the Education and Advancement of Faeriekind. Or, for our more experienced students, welcome back is more precise. And as veterans, you know what to do. New students, follow me."

The oldest students headed for the buildings on either side of the school. Other veteran students veered off as they came through the front door, heading up curved staircases situated directly to the left (the boys) and the right (the girls). Sara mouthed, "Good luck!" and bounced away.

Destry had been wrong; this wasn't an entry hall. It was an enormous rectangular room stretching the entire length of the school. The ceiling rose three stories, and floor-to-ceiling windows flooded the area with light. Three massive, marble fountains—each a different color—played in the middle of the room, water leaping in sparkling tiers.

The veteran students' laughter drifted back to them. The staircases led to open, atrium-style hallways on the second and third floors, and sound carried easily. Students leaned over marble banisters, waving to friends. Doors opening and closing punctuated their enthusiastic babble.

Riamon had the new students leave their luggage along a wall, then led them past several doors. Destry spied a dining hall through one, long corridors through others. Riamon gestured them into a circular room. Windows took up two-thirds of the wall space. A pedestal of white stone, carved like ocean waves, stood in the center of the room. The waves blossomed out at the top, twisting around a crystal basin of water. Fey Elena stood behind it, elegant in flowing robes.

She motioned towards crescent-shaped marble benches built into the walls, where other students (presumably from earlier groups) already sat. Destry ended up at the end of the row. Fey Elena cleared her throat. "All of you have gained one, if not both, sets of power markings...or, as half-fey youth are wont to call them, faerie tattoos. These markings indicate which natural sources strengthen you and your magic."

Fey Elena motioned to a dark-haired girl sitting in front. "Marisa, come up." The girl stepped hesitantly forward, and the headmistress said, "Your power is centered in your marks. Touching them is the easiest way for another person to draw your power. The water ceremony makes their magic inaccessible to all except yourself."

She motioned the dark-haired girl to roll up her sleeves. Her wrist tattoos were cerulean waves, like Fey Elena's. "Water," the headmistress said. She looked at the other students. "Wrist markings indicate what elemental source facilitates your magic: water, air, or fire. Partaking of these sources is as important as eating or breathing for any faerie."

Fey Elena positioned the girl's wrists over the basin. The headmistress scooped up water and trickled it over Marisa's wrists. The tattoos turned luminescent. Fey Elena dipped her hands into the water again, drizzling it over the girl's head. She peered into the basin. Destry stretched her neck, trying to see what Fey Elena saw.

Words rippled across the surface of the water. The headmistress read aloud, "Sea faerie, water faerie—heaving waves and moonlit calm. *Fálkom*, Marisa Waterwings, born of the fey."

Fálkom? What language was that?

Azure light glowed all over Marisa; the sound of rushing surf ghosted through the room before the light faded and her tattoos returned to normal.

Fey Elena repeated the process with every student. Faeries with an air element were christened Windwings. Destry kept listening for fire—that *had* to be her nature source—but no one else had flame tattoos.

Destry's legs were shaking by the time her turn came—last, since she'd been the last person seated. Nerves and excitement twisted her stomach into a confused mess. Fey Elena glanced at her sleeves expectantly. Destry took a deep breath and bared her wrists.

The crimson flames blazed against the water sparkling in the bowl. Fey Elena's eyes widened, and she glanced at Riamon. What had the headmistress said before, when Riamon mentioned fire elements? *Perhaps we shouldn't borrow trouble.*

Fey Elena continued the ceremony. Water flowed over Destry's wrists, cool silk against her skin. Then the water on her head. It seeped through her hair and trickled down her neck. Fey Elena peered into the basin. Before the headmistress could speak, the air around Destry crackled, bathing her in iridescent flames. Thunder rolled through the room, along with the scent of an oncoming storm.

Fey Elena's eyes widened again. But she said the words shimmering, ghostlike, in the basin: "Storm faerie, flame faerie—lightning and war. *Fálkom*, Destry Firewings, born of the fey."

ROOM THIRTEEN

✦

*L*ightning and war? Destry walked to her place along the wall, feeling dazed. Who was she supposed to be warring with?

However, Fey Elena gave no further sign that Destry's induction into the faerie world had been unusual. She gestured for the students' attention. "The other markings—the ones on your calves—indicate what type of water strengthens you physically: ocean water, spring water, or rain water."

"Storms, to be precise," Riamon said, face grumpy.

The headmistress sighed. "You'll share dorm space with others who have the same water type." Once students were called up and sorted into groups, Fey Elena said briskly, "Lunch is at one o'clock. Wear your school uniform. Your dorm leader will take you to the tailor and explain the rules and schedule. Be warned: although this is a faerie school, that does not indicate a laxity of standards. Students who ignore curfews and other guidelines will be punished."

She waited for their nods of acknowledgement before continuing, "Either Fey Riamon or I will meet you tomorrow to discuss accessing

your magic-giving element. For most of you, this will pose no problem."
Fey Elena's eyes flickered briefly to Destry. "As for your physical water
preference, the dorm showers are equipped with water suited to your
type, and the three fountains in the great hall contain salt water, spring
water, and rain water. Utilize them whenever you need to recharge."

Riamon clapped his hands. "On that pleasant note, let's head to your
quarters." Everyone retrieved their luggage from the great entry hall.
Riamon led the boys up the right-hand set of stairs, and Fey Elena led
the girls up the left-hand stairs to the third floor.

There were three doors along that hall, painted the color of the leg
tattoos—pale blue for spring water faeries, blue-green for ocean faeries,
and silvery-gray for storm faeries. A dorm leader greeted each group of
faeries at their corresponding door. Soon, only Destry and the few other
storm kids were left. There'd been two or three in the spring water and
ocean groups for every storm faerie.

As they headed for the silvery door at the end of the hall, Destry
asked, "Fey Elena, what language was that word in the water ceremony?
Fálkom?"

The headmistress waved one hand as if brushing away an annoying fly.
"The ancient language of the Fold. The word simply means *welcome*."

This place had its own language? An *un*welcome image flashed
through her head: sitting in a classroom, struggling to understand as the
teacher droned on in some foreign tongue, and the other kids snickered
at her cluelessness. Maybe Cam—

The automatic thought stung...lemon juice in a paper cut. Of course
Cam couldn't help her. "Does it take long to learn it?"

Fey Elena stopped at the storm faerie dorm. "Learning the ancient
language is unnecessary. It's used almost entirely by goblins for working
magic. Fey folk have progressed past written spells and utilize a more
elegant method."

"Then why—"

The headmistress scanned the hall—possibly looking for the absentee
dorm leader—and sighed. "Using the ancient language in our water
ceremony is a necessary anachronism. Some of our oldest spells only
work in spoken form, and the magic refuses to function properly if key

words are translated into more modern parlance." She said it like the magic was a misbehaving student.

At least I don't have to learn another language. And yet...a trickle of disappointment tainted her relief. The new word had felt right, as if her tongue was meant to shape the sound. She ignored the feeling. What would it say about her, if she loved a language only spoken by monsters?

Fey Elena pushed open the silvery door and led the group into an eclectic-looking common room. Comfortable couches warred with delicate tables; squashy leather bean bag chairs dotted the elegant rugs and cool marble floors.

Tables and chairs were spaced along the walls. No TV, of course, but floor-to-ceiling bookcases held everything from leather-bound tomes to battered paperbacks. One bookcase held games—some familiar (Monopoly), others less so. An arched door with glass panes led onto a balcony.

Other girls were ranged around the room, although few looked older than Destry. Two teens, one of them her companion from the bus, were having a vigorous discussion over a set of dominos with odd symbols. Sara tapped a domino with a gem carving. "I'm telling you, a dwarf-marked piece always defeats a—"

The headmistress cleared her throat, and the girl spun around. "H-e-e-e-y, Fey Elena. Sorry I didn't meet you at the door. We got into an—um—academic debate."

"Sara is one of your dorm leaders," Fey Elena said.

The redhead winked. "That means I'm mature and responsible."

"Or it means no one else would take the job," her domino opponent said.

Fey Elena gave them a severe look. "Sara will help you learn the rules and information necessary to integrate at school." She walked to the door, robes swirling. "I hope you'll each have an excellent experience here."

As the door swung shut, Sara grinned. "Alright, then. The grand tour." She waved one arm like a ringmaster. "Obviously, this is the common room. You can do whatever, use whatever, so long as you treat it right. People mark their personal stuff. You better leave those things alone, because sometimes they're enchanted. You could end up with three thumbs or a green nose.

"Meals are in the dining hall downstairs. If you bring food to the dorms, clean up after yourself. The rules say we have to deal with pest infestations, and trust me...dragon-mice are not cute, not cuddly, and really not fun."

One of the younger girls squeaked, "Dragon-mice?"

Sara gestured down a wide hall. "Communal bathrooms. Bedrooms too, and you don't even have to share. Empty room numbers—" she hefted a jar with folded papers inside— "are in here." She passed the jar around. When everyone had drawn a number, Sara made a shooing gesture. "Go find your rooms, people. We still have to see the tailor."

Destry glanced at her paper: Room Thirteen. She hurried down the L-shaped hall, past rooms one through twelve. There it was, where the hall bent to make the bottom half of the L. Destry shoved the door open and gawked. The circular room could have fit three beds, three chests of drawers, three desks and chairs, rather than the single set occupying the space. The pale furniture was inlaid with delicate marble designs, and sheer hangings draped the four-poster bed.

Footsteps thudded down the hall behind her. Sara bounced past, hauling Destry into the bedroom. The redhead grinned. "Fancy, right?" She pointed upwards, where a mural rolled across the high ceiling: storm-swirled sky, purple and blue and gray, flashes of lightning gilding the clouds.

Destry dropped her backpack on the floor. "Are all the rooms this big?"

"One perk of being a storm faerie right now. Every dorm—ocean, spring water, and storm—can accommodate seventy-five students. Same for the guys' dorms. But like in nature, things fluctuate. Our generation has lots of spring water and ocean faeries, not many storm types. Another twenty-five years, and the storm faeries might be three to a room, while the ocean or spring water faeries lounge around in all their extra space."

"What about the older kids? The ones who broke off from the group earlier?"

Sara dragged Destry across the room, past round cushion-lined windows deep enough to sit in, and through a door. It led to the balcony she'd glimpsed in the common room. Other rooms opened onto the same balcony, which ran the length of the dorms.

Destry slid her arm loose as Sara sauntered to the edge. The redhead boosted herself to sit on the marble railing. Destry's stomach flip-flopped. *Three stories up, and she isn't holding on to anything?*

Sara gestured to the buildings flanking the school. "Students sixteen and older get to live separate—practice for being independent. One side for guys, one side for girls. I could've, too, if I hadn't applied for dorm leader."

A breeze wafted across Destry's face, cooling the sweat dotting her forehead. Sara said, "Come to the edge. View's spectacular."

"I'm fine here." She pushed on before her new dorm leader could ask the inevitable question. "Do all the dorms have these balconies?"

"Nope. We're special, and we require special accommodations." Sara's smirk ruined her attempt at superiority. "Fey Riamon hates it."

"Why?"

Sara hopped down. "We gain energy best from stormwater charged with lightning, but once it's collected—like in the hall fountain—the charge lessens fast. We need to be in the storm. Whenever it's raining, they have to let us out, even during classes or the middle of the night. The balcony lets us take advantage of storms after curfew."

All the times she'd run outside to dance in the rain... Cam had rolled his eyes when she came in dripping and smiling. She shied away from more thoughts of him. "Sara, how bad is it that I came in late?"

"You'll have to work harder. That's about it, as long as you aren't some fire faerie. That one's basically a death sentence." She laughed, like the possibility was so remote as to be ridiculous. Destry slid her sleeve up. The older girl stared. "I— Destry, I didn't mean—"

"Yeah, you did. And Fey Elena wasn't thrilled, either. So tell me the truth: what's wrong with fire faeries?"

Sara grimaced. "Nothing. But those fire marks mean you have to do something no faerie wants to do."

"What?"

"You'll have to face the goblin king."

Twenty minutes later, Destry followed Sara and the other new students through the lofty halls of the Academy, headed to the school tailor. She glared at the redhead's back. After that one terrifying statement on the balcony, Sara had refused to explain further, past saying that the goblins controlled Destry's elemental energy source. "Talk to Fey Elena. I already botched one explanation. I'm not messing up another."

But it might be hours before she could speak with the headmistress. In the meantime, Destry could only wait—and worry—about facing an enemy so fearsome that he made the irrepressible Sara shiver.

The sound of burbling water drifted down the hall, along with a rhythmic wooden clatter. Sara shepherded them into a spacious room bustling with activity. Along one wall sat a row of wooden-framed machines. Hundreds of threads stretched over various bars, and a person sat in front of each on a bench, pressing foot levers while pulling a wooden bar back and forth.

Destry had seen machines like these on a school field trip: floor looms, used to weave cloth. A set of faeries stood on either side of each loom, passing a different wooden bar to each other. At the museum, they'd called this bar the shuttle; it had held yarn for weaving between the taut threads. Here, it seemed to hold water that slipped from the shuttle like fine thread, weaving itself into the material forming on the loom.

Sara gestured to the weavers. "Most fey clothing is made from water-woven cloth. Keeps us hydrated, even in dry climates. It's a big industry, and the school partially supports itself through our production line. Decide to go into the business, and you can apprentice here."

She waved them on, to the other side of the room past faeries winding cloth onto boards. They passed an open door, where men and women cut and stitched clothing. They gestured for items they wanted, sending sharp objects flying across the room. Everyone seemed used to it. They ducked as pins or scissors came too close, then returned to work.

Sara led them into a room filled with clothing. "Got new students who need outfitting," she announced to the man and woman tidying the shelves.

"Of course you do!" the woman snapped. "First day of term, why else would you be here?"

The man smiled apologetically. "Gabrielle had a difficult morning. We'll get you outfitted, never fear." The woman sent a rolled measuring tape flying at him. He caught it and bowed. "I can take care of this group and give you a break, Ga—"

"Do I look like a wilting flower? Take your half." The woman counted down the line, waving a group of kids to the left side of the room. Destry breathed a sigh of relief as the man waved her group to the right.

The tailor lined them up along one wall, then gestured Destry forward. Sara followed, chattering. "I don't get it, Cezanne. You're in charge of this entire outfit, and you let her boss you around like that."

Still smiling, Cezanne motioned Destry to come with him. "Gabrielle and I are both aware who makes the final decisions. As I had little expectation of being promoted over her, I can allow her some forbearance as compensation."

"Everyone knows you're the best. Just because you're a man—"

"Precisely." He whipped his measuring tape around Destry's waist. "I'm fortunate to work for Headmistress Elena, who promotes based on performance rather than gender or class. Under any other headmistress, I would still be an assistant."

He measured her shoulders and along her back. Destry asked, "Shouldn't the best person get the job?"

"Theoretically." Sara leaned against the wall, arms crossed. "But sometimes, it doesn't work that way. We're always ruled by a queen, and historically, women held most of the power. Also, faerie society is rigid about tradition. Guys can be at a disadvantage, especially if they aren't from a noble family or want a job usually held by women."

Cezanne twirled his finger. His tape measure rolled itself around his wrist. "Times have changed, affected by the outside world and half-faeries who carry new ideas here. But there's some advantage to being female. Headmistress Elena has created a more equitable environment in the school than exists outside of it. As I benefit from her wisdom, it seems fair to repay it by exercising my own."

Across the room, Gabrielle snapped at the youngest girl, and Sara sighed. "I better keep her from traumatizing the new recruits." She hurried off.

The tailor turned to Destry. "Pants or skirts, my dear?"

"You don't have jeans, do you?"

He chuckled. "The school board finds them repellant, though you're not the first student to ask." The man bustled to the shelves, pulling one item after another into his arms. He brought the pile to Destry. "These are as casual as I can offer. Let me see the fit of at least one set of clothing." He pointed at a dressing room before turning to the next student.

Minutes later, Destry edged into the main room, flushing. Compared to jeans and oversized t-shirts, this uniform made her feel underdressed. The pants—leggings, really—stopped just below her knee, and the tunic-style shirt reminded her of Fey Elena's, with a plunging cut-out to allow for wing movement. Short of a bathing suit, she'd never worn anything that left her back so exposed.

Cezanne clapped his hands. "Ah, I truly am good. Do they feel as wonderful as they look?"

Despite the "need-more-clothes" sensation, they were the most comfortable things Destry had ever owned. Every item was sewn from the same material, probably that water-woven cloth. It felt cool in the nicest of ways, like being in a just-right swimming pool on a blazing summer afternoon. The clothing quenched the constant thirst in her skin better than any lotion.

Destry nodded, but she fingered one elbow grazing sleeve. "Do you have anything longer?" None of the shirts he'd offered would cover her wrist tattoos.

The tailor made a *tsk*-ing sound. "You'd hardly want long sleeves. The weather will remain warm for another month or two. And there's no need to hide your power markings. Everyone has them."

Most of them aren't red. Destry didn't say it, but Cezanne cocked his head as if she had. He swept one arm out, indicating the students clustered at the mirrors. "Look around. Here, those marks on your legs show that you belong, that you've come home. And the flames on your wrists...well, my own wife is a fire faerie and quite amazing. Sometimes being different means being exceptional."

Sometimes, it just meant being weird, but Destry didn't want to argue with this smiling man. He pulled ankle-length leggings and a long-sleeved tunic from the shelves. "In case you truly feel the need. Wear them in good fortune, my dear."

A WARNING

---◆---

Destry didn't wear the long sleeves when it was lunchtime. Different or not, she'd spent enough of her life hiding things. She put on a black sleeveless tunic, short gray pants that tied at the knees, the soft sandals that had been one of her footwear options, and pocketed her ever-present lip balm. As she followed Sara downstairs, though, it occurred to her: she hadn't felt the slightest itch in her skin since their visit to the tailor.

Babbling voices broke over them when Sara pushed open the dining hall doors. Destry's heart skittered. Students were everywhere, crowded about the round tables, arm and leg tattoos shimmering in the sunlight from the arched windows. Teachers sat at the front of the room.

Sara dragged her to a table of older students—four guys, including Sara's magic partner David, and three other girls—introducing her casually as "the new fire faerie." Fey Elena welcomed the students before giving everyone permission to serve themselves. Food sat in the middle of every table. Destry peeked at the options. What did faeries eat?

Normal food, apparently: rolls, roast beef, mashed potatoes, broccoli, shining red apples. There were a few oddities: mottled pinkish-blue grapes, oranges with spiky tops like a pineapple, violently turquoise string beans. Destry stuck with familiar foods, not ready for another new experience.

One of the girls poured a glass of water from the pitcher, drank, and made a face. "School water. I must have my parents send a more palatable option."

Destry took a cautious sip of hers, but the water was…wonderful. A thousand times better than tap water, where Destry tasted chlorine and dirt and many other things Cam and Beverly swore weren't there. Her surprise must have shown; the girl flipped her glossy black hair over one shoulder with a condescending smile. "I suppose compared to the human world, anything is a step up."

Sara rolled her eyes. "Julya is better than us peons. She's never been subjected to tap water."

Their tablemates were friendly. Even Julya spent a few awkward minutes pointing out unattached half-fey boys who might be Destry's magic partner. Following Sara's revelations on the bus, that conversation made her stomach ache, so she asked, "Which one is your magic partner?"

Julya sniffed. "I'm full-faerie, from one of the oldest families in the land. I don't require a magic partner."

"But she wishes she had one." Sara sounded teasing. "It's why she sits with us lowly half-faeries."

Julya lifted her chin. "Why in the Fold would I want some predestined soulmate? I simply believe in being charitable to those less fortunate." But her eyes, when they fell on Sara and David, seemed wistful.

Conversation turned to school gossip. The names were meaningless to Destry. She tuned out, surreptitiously looking for potential magic partner candidates again. Julya's sharp voice drew her attention back. "Sara, do you truly think my information is wrong? Mine, of all people? My mother is assistant to Queen Liselle's most trusted advisor, Executor Faris himself. I heard this directly from her."

Sara glared. "Yeah, your mom's a big shot. She can still make mistakes. Becca's been missing two months now, and her commitment ceremony to Adam is coming up. He's worried."

Julya crossed her arms. "I told you, he doesn't have to be. Mother says the Queen put her own Surgers in charge of finding that girl. She's at her house in the human world, and they're trying to convince her to return to the Academy. She ran away, simple as that. It's not the first time some half-faerie couldn't handle the pressure."

"The pressure of what?" Destry asked.

"The commitment ceremony." Sara shot another angry look at Julya. "Becca has two human parents. Adam's magic pulled her in. When her powers manifested, it freaked out her parents, so she kept running away. But that changed when she came to the Academy. Becca loved being here. No way would she run off."

Julya shrugged. "Think what you want."

Sara started to reply, but David not-so-surreptitiously poked her in the ribs, tipping his head toward Destry. The redhead sat back, fuming.

Destry didn't know what to say. Did David think they were being rude, talking about people she didn't know? Or did he think the story of some girl running away from her magic partner would make Destry want to run away, too? To cover her awkwardness, she reached for another roll. She had to stretch to reach the bread basket, and, in the process, her elbow knocked over her water glass. David lunged to save it, missed, and knocked over the water pitcher. The contents of both containers swept across the table to cascade into Julya's lap.

She jerked in a startled breath, then glared at them. Ignoring their hurried apologies and the napkins they offered, she swept from the table.

Silence.

"Destry," Sara said, as she cleaned water droplets off her purple glasses, "You're officially my friend."

The table broke into laughter. "I didn't think anyone was as accident-prone as David," one of the guys chuckled. David grinned ruefully and reached across the table for a high five. Destry stretched to reach him, wobbled, and they both missed. Her cheeks burned, but their classmates' amusement seemed friendly, at least.

Every student received two small pieces of chocolate on the way out of the dining hall. They took it excitedly, as if this was a huge deal. Sara grinned. "Best part about the first day back!"

They moved into the entry hall. Dozens of students milled around the fountains. Sara was nudging her towards the storm-water fountain when the headmistress strode out of the dining area. Destry pulled loose. "I need to talk to Fey Elena." The redhead smiled sympathetically before getting swept up by a group of girls.

Destry wound through the students, catching up with the headmistress before she reached the opposite side of the hall. "Fey Elena. I…I need to talk to you."

The woman sighed. "I thought you might. Sara has no sense of discretion."

Destry followed the headmistress to an elegant office. As the door closed behind them, Destry held up her wrist. "What does this mean for me?"

Fey Elena's eyes were unflinching. "It means that you may have to walk a harder road at the Academy than most."

A harder road. Destry had come to the school hoping for a better life, not to exchange one set of challenges for another.

Fey Elena lifted her hands in a soothing gesture. "I said 'may,' child. We'll know little until you supplicate to the goblin king."

"Why do I have to see him at all?"

Fey Elena turned to the bookshelves covering one wall. She did a twirl-and-jerk motion, like some faerie cowboy spinning a lasso, and a book soared over, depositing itself on the desk. The scent of leather and paper wafted up as she flipped it open. "Our bodies are attuned to our elemental sources. Magic is contained in each source, and through them we gain an innate understanding of the power we control."

The headmistress beckoned Destry closer to the desk. She tapped a page with handwritten notes surrounding a depiction of flame. "Magic is a tangible thing, and when we speak of 'working magic' we mean it in a real sense, as a potter molds clay. But to make it do your will, you must understand it. You must be around its deepest source on a regular basis."

Destry fingered the waves carved into the edge of the wooden desk...satiny, as if they'd been worn smooth by hundreds of other fingers before hers. "Sara said the goblins control it."

Fey Elena nodded. "There are four elements—water, air, earth, and fire—from which magical creatures derive their abilities. The more intelligent beings, like faeries or goblins, utilize these sources purposefully. Water, air, and earth are easily accessible elements, so there's little competition for those resources—particularly since faeries either attune to air or water, whereas goblins attune to earth. However, within *both* races, a small portion of the population is attuned to fire. And that is a less convenient power source."

She flipped to a map of the world. "The areas where a permanent fire tap has been developed—like a well for drawing water—are few and far between." Her finger traveled over the page, touching five flame marks ranged across the continents. "Only one is easily accessible. Both goblins and faeries must visit it, which led to conflict in the past as the races crossed paths. The firewell became a hotly contested area."

The hooded creature from Destry's nightmare flashed through her mind. What if she had to cross paths with a monster like that? The skin edging her shoulder blades burned. She sucked in a calming breath and focused on the carved waves pressing into her palms, on the scent of polished wood and parchment. "Why didn't someone dig a new firewell? Or create a big bonfire?"

"Typical fire is one result of your magic, not the source of it. As for creating a new firewell, that is no easy task. Few knew the art years ago, and none possess the ability today. Which is why goblins and faeries eventually signed a treaty. We agreed that each race would take turns possessing the firewells. Whichever group controlled the majority would cede control of the central—and most desired—one. The ownership changes every hundred years. At present time, the goblins have custody of the only firewell that matters, and it will not revert to us for another eighty-seven years."

"Can't I use one of the other wells?"

"If you care to make a weekly journey to Siberia," Fey Elena said dryly. "Otherwise, we shall utilize the traditional method of gaining access.

You must go before the goblin king and request permission to use the firewell."

Siberia didn't sound too bad. Destry concentrated on the map, on the flames so far away from the North American continent. "Have any other students done it?"

"Yes. There are six fire faeries at the school, and others who aren't students. The goblin king has rarely refused access to a supplicant. Doing so would strain our already-tenuous peace."

"But he *can* refuse?"

Fey Elena closed the book, lips thinning. "I'll not let the whims of a monster ruin your chance for a decent life. We must add to your school schedule. You'll have lessons with me on deportment, the correct way to address the king, and what to say when making your request."

"For how long?"

Her dark eyes turned steely. "Until I'm satisfied that the king can find no fault in your manner or words. Gaining access to the firewell is imperative, Destry. I'll contact the necessary personages and arrange the meeting. Until then, do the best you can."

Over the next week, Destry tried to settle into her new life. Some parts were satisfying, like the decreased responsibility. Even with the heavier workload designed to catch up a new student, she had more time on her hands than at home. Those spare moments would've been better if they weren't peppered with bittersweet memories of Cam.

A few things were more than satisfying. They were sumptuous. Faeries didn't skimp on anything water-related. Even the dorm showers could put a fancy spa to shame. Daily rainwater showers, excellent drinking water, the storm fountain in the great hall, and water-woven clothing allowed Destry to shed the never-ending tightness in her skin. Which was good, since she needed all her focus for classes.

These had surprised her—not because of the unusual courses, but because of the normal ones. Most core academics—math, science, English—were required. Destry was also enrolled in magic classes: Basic Magic, Magic in Real Life, Growing Plants and Herbs, Magic with Metals, and Everyday Combat.

Her classmates varied. In the normal classes, Destry was with students her age. In the magic classes, she learned alongside other starter pupils or students who hadn't mastered a particular skill. The only magic class with a significant portion of older students was Magic with Metals; for most faeries, metalworking proved difficult.

Almost everything was a difficult subject for Destry...at least, everything magical. To her surprise, keeping up in the academic classes was easier with her old responsibilities removed. But her success in nearly every aspect of magic was based on locating "strands" of magic and catching them. It was an elusive ability, with few hard-and-fast explanations. Destry's inability to sense the magic around her made doing class exercises impossible.

Combat was the exception, because it didn't rely solely on her magic-sensing abilities. A married couple—half-fey magic partners—taught the class. Their first lesson, Fey Renalt made it clear he wouldn't tolerate fooling around. "Combat is a serious art. We teach it because, as magical beings, you have natural magical enemies. It's not intended as an aid to fighting your classmates in the corridors. I'll dismiss any student found abusing their abilities, and you won't return." His face was stern beneath his shock of red hair.

His wife, Fey Sassandra, added, "Some of you will never take more than the required year of combat—the basics of defending yourself. Others may find they're naturally gifted in this area and will make it the focus of their education." Had the woman's eyes flickered towards Destry's fire signs?

Their first lesson focused on faerie wings. Sassandra displayed hers. They waved gently above her short-cropped blonde hair. "Notice the razor edge on these babies. Your wings may look like a tool for flight, but that's not their main purpose. Has anyone tried flying?"

About half the class raised their hands, and some groaned. Renalt chuckled. "I assume it didn't go well. Your wings won't support you in the air until they've strengthened. We'll have lessons on that when you're ready."

Hovering midair, with only some unreliable wings for support? Destry's stomach lurched.

Sassandra continued, "Even once they're stronger, your wings aren't made for transport. Defense. That's the purpose behind these beauties. To get you out of the way quickly, to keep an enemy at a distance. Use them right, and it's hard for anyone—even an enormous goblin—to get their arms around you."

A boy laughed. "Sounds good."

Renalt looked at him soberly. "It can be. But caution and knowledge are essential when employing your wings. If you aren't careful..." His wings shot out—or rather, one wing shot out. The other was a shred of tissue along his shoulder blade. "This is what happens when you employ your abilities before you're ready."

"How did you lose it, sir?"

"I was young and arrogant and had a run-in with a goblin. We could've walked away peaceably, but neither of us was willing. Which brings me to today's second lesson: respect. For your enemy, for yourself. Unnecessary fights are a foolish way to prove your mettle."

They were given exercises (one for strengthening the wings, another for learning to move them with purpose) and ranged about the room at safe distances from each other. Before they could begin the exercises, they had to make their wings emerge.

Destry felt stupid, standing there trying to force her wings to appear. She concentrated on Sassandra's instruction: "Wing movement is involuntary when faced with an imminent threat, at least to the untrained faerie. This lesson comes first because the ability to control these puppies is as important as the ability to control your own hands and feet."

At least she wasn't the only one having trouble. Destry sighed, thinking of the times her wings had shot out without permission. That nightmare... An image of the cloaked creature flickered across her mind.

Fierce pain burned along the edges of her shoulder blades. Destry frowned. Was it really that simple? She pulled up the image from her nightmare again, remembering the hooded figure in minute detail, especially those shining claws.

Her wings flew out so fast they almost clipped Renalt, who was circling the room. He grinned. "First one. I thought you might be." Destry looked askance at him, and he said, "Fire faeries often excel in Combat. Part of our heritage, maybe."

His long-sleeved shirt hid his wrists. "You're a fire sign?"

He nodded. "I'm fortunate my firewell access wasn't revoked when it changed hands. But I'd already been before a tribunal, as had the goblin who fought me. We'd faced the justice of our people, and I'd lost my wing. The goblin king didn't pursue that matter further."

"What did you mean about our heritage?"

"Certain fey families were renowned for their combat ability. Many had fire as their element and acted as bodyguards to royalty. You'll find a disproportionate number of fire faeries in that profession."

A question hovered on the tip of her tongue. Destry debated whether to ask it, but Renalt seemed like her best chance for a straight answer. "At the water ceremony, Fey Elena said something about lightning and war. Is that why?"

Renalt shrugged. "The benediction varies, depending upon your combination of signs, and something more elusive. You're a storm faerie?" She nodded. "Two tempestuous signs in one girl... It's safe to say The Waters saw possibilities in you, possibilities you may not recognize yet."

"I can barely walk without tripping over my own feet. You think The Waters expect me to become some warrior woman?"

Renalt chuckled. "'Combat class' is a misnomer. Fey defense relies less on physical coordination and more on trusting your magic and using it in intelligent ways. And in cases of imminent danger, your hereditary instincts can take over for brief moments and guide your body, if you learn to heed them. Becoming a 'warrior woman' isn't necessary to defend yourself." He added solemnly, "Just don't allow those instincts to lure you into rash foolishness. The benediction sometimes doubles as a warning, even against ourselves."

FIREWELL

T he end of Destry's first week at the Academy came, along with one absolute certainty: she'd better like Combat. It was the only magic class she could pass.

Well, no. Occasionally, she excelled in Growing Plants and Herbs. The class, steeped in the scents of green things and fresh-turned earth, called up memories of gardening with Cam and his dad. Sometimes, remembering was a comfort—reassurance that she'd been accepted, even loved, despite all the shortcomings she needed to hide. In those moments, her plants bloomed so quickly that the teacher glowed with excitement. But if the memories turned sour—reminding Destry that she could never return to those moments, that life, with Cam—her plants withered, and the teacher scolded her like she'd done it on purpose.

When Fey Elena summoned her by note on Friday evening, Destry assumed it was about her dismal performance in classes. It couldn't be for those "how-to-be-proper" lessons; she'd had one Tuesday night and didn't have another until Sunday.

Which was good... Fey Elena had taught her how to curtsy to a king and ordered her to master it, but a proper curtsy in the Fold entailed more than quickly bending her knees. It involved sweeping one foot behind her, folding her legs until she was practically sitting on the floor, then dipping her upper body towards the ground, arms spread wide the entire time. Destry had practiced every night, but she always wobbled or slipped or outright fell.

Now, as she hurried to the headmistress's office, the note clutched in sweaty fingers, she tried consoling herself. *At least Fey Elena won't be checking my curtsy. I have two more days to get it right. Unless they've kicked me out by then for not being magic enough.*

Destry knocked on the headmistress's door.

"Enter!" The terse command wasn't reassuring, and neither was the headmistress's expression when Destry edged into the office. Eyebrows lowered, Fey Elena sat looking over some document. A folder lay near her elbow, one corner jutting off the desk.

Setting the paper aside, Fey Elena motioned her to a chair. "I've spoken to the goblin king's representatives."

Destry curled her fingers so tightly, the note rolled into a ball. "And?"

"The goblin king is currently on a diplomatic visit. His aunt, Lady Valda, manages affairs in his absence. Normally, no firewell access would be granted without the king's permission, but his absence will be lengthy—another three weeks, with a tentative return date in early February. Lady Valda granted us a concession: you may visit the well once a week until the goblin king returns to Rí Kobold, at which time you must appear before him. Once a week isn't enough for a new student, but perhaps it will allow progress in areas you find challenging."

So, she did know how poorly Destry was doing, and she didn't seem angry. "Thank you, Fey Elena."

The headmistress smiled dryly. "You won't thank me when it's time to meet him, nor for losing many of your evenings over the next few weeks. Now that we've a date to work towards, your lessons are even more urgent." She stood. "Speaking of which, let's see that curtsy. I assume you've mastered it enough to fine-tune it tonight."

The curtsy? Now? Destry shoved the mangled paper into her pocket. "Fey Elena, I...I really did practice."

"I assumed you would, given the gravity of the situation. Show me the results." The headmistress swept around the desk, but her skirt caught the edge of the folder, sending it flying to the floor in front of Destry.

Several papers cascaded out: sketches of two pale-haired fey girls, one on each page. Destry bent to pick them up. A name was written on the top page: Becca Tommin. That sounded familiar, but why?

"Destry! Leave them!" Fey Elena's sharp command made her jump. Destry yanked her hand back as the headmistress scooped up the papers. "Your desire to help does you credit, child. But these are not for your eyes."

What could seeing a couple of drawings hurt? Destry nodded anyway. Fey Elena deposited them in the folder, along with whatever she'd been reading earlier. "I'm still waiting to see that—"

Footsteps thudded down the hall, drowning out the last word. The doorknob twisted. A dark-haired boy shoved his head into the office, face flushed. "Fey Elena...I'm sorry, ma'am, but Fey Riamon needs your help! It's an emergency!"

The headmistress flung the folder onto her desk. "Fire and wings!" The boy's eyebrows shot up. Fey Elena snapped, "You did not hear me say that, either of you. And I shall personally scour your mouths with soap should you repeat it!" She hurried to the door. "Destry, practice that curtsy while I'm gone."

The boy sent her a conspiratorial grin before jogging after the headmistress. The office felt too quiet once they left. Destry squashed the urge to follow them, to see what counted as an emergency at a magic school. She didn't need to give Fey Elena another reason to be upset. Instead, she stood in the office, slipping and dipping and wobbling, for a good five minutes before slouching into her chair again.

It was useless. She needed help, not practice. Her eyes strayed to the folder on the desk. That name still nagged her. Maybe Becca was one of her classmates or one of the many, many people Sara had introduced her to over the past week.

Sara…at the welcome dinner. A full-fledged memory shoved the nagging aside. *Becca loved being here. No way would she run off.*

The missing girl? Destry eyed the folder with more interest, all thoughts of the curtsy disappeared. What *was* that drawing? Some sort of "Missing" poster, like the authorities hung in public places in the human world? But that didn't make sense, if Becca had already been found, and it didn't explain why Fey Elena had snatched those papers so fast.

I shouldn't do it.

But she was tired of being left in the dark, powerless to do anything but wait until some adult decided to share the next piece of information pertinent to her life. *Guess what? You're a faerie! Guess what? You have this predestined magic partner! Guess what? You've gotta beg a monster to use his super-ultra-special magic campfire!*

It wasn't a hard decision. One quick peek out the door, then—leaving it cracked open so she could hear Fey Elena's return—Destry hurried to the desk and snatched the folder. She examined the first drawing: Becca Tommin, pretty with her gold-blonde hair, knowing brown eyes, and reluctant smile. Notes ran along the bottom of the page: age, height, energy source, magic source, and last place seen (the river). But the words that caught her attention were written in all caps—STATUS: MISSING—along with the current date.

Frowning, Destry flicked to the next drawing: a whip-thin girl with a pale blonde bob, freckles, and brown eyes light enough to approach amber. She scanned the information at the base of the page, stopping at the girl's energy source: storm water. Prickles crept along her neck. That had been Becca's energy source, too.

And mine.

Distant footsteps echoed along the hall, and Destry jumped, jerking the folder. Papers went flying, escaping across the desk. One slithered over the edge and out of sight. Destry scrambled for them as faint voices joined the footsteps, indistinguishable but getting closer. Panic heated her face.

The voices became clearer: Fey Elena and the boy from before. They'd reach the office in seconds. Drawings in hand, Destry dropped to the floor, searching under the desk. Nothing. She swiveled on her knees, whacking her head on one corner. There, beside Fey Elena's chair! Eyes watering, she grabbed the paper—some letter that began *To Their Honored Majesties of the Goblin Court*—and stood...

The dark-haired boy opened the door. His blue eyes fell on Destry, standing there with papers in hand. Half a second after stepping in, he stepped back out and pulled the door closed. The headmistress's voice carried through it, crisp and irritated. "Entering my office is easier when you're not standing in the way, Tristan." Destry shoved the papers into the folder, ears straining for the boy's answer.

"Yes, ma'am. But I'm supposed to tutor some newbies tonight. Could I be excused? I wasn't involved in that...um...situation—fey's honor—and I already told you what I know about it."

Destry replaced the folder and rushed to the center of the room. Hopefully, Fey Elena would chalk her sweaty face up to curtsy practice.

"Situation? The correct word is disaster! Any idiot knows that dragon-mice and growth spells are a poor mixture." Fey Elena sighed. "Then again, you may be a rapscallion, but you never have been an idiot. Go do your tutoring."

Destry dropped into another mangled curtsy as the door opened and Fey Elena stalked in. The headmistress stopped, eyebrows climbing towards her hairline. Destry wobbled one direction, overcorrected, and tipped the other way. Tristan still stood in the hall. Grinning, he peeked over Fey Elena's shoulder, just in time to see Destry fall sideways in a heap.

The headmistress's eyes glinted—a dangerous look that might've been meant for either of them—and she said softly, "Tristan? Were you not in a flaming hurry just seconds ago?" She shut the door in his face.

Destry scrambled upright as Fey Elena turned back to her. "Kindly tell me that this graceless exhibition was due to surprise at our return and not evidence of your current level of ability with the curtsy."

She could lie and say that, except the next curtsy would reveal the truth. Blood rushed even hotter in her cheeks.

"I see." The headmistress sounded chilly. "Was I not clear enough, Destry? These are not sweet niceties. They are essential for going before the goblin court."

"I understand, Fey Elena. I really did—"

"Do you?" Fey Elena threw up her hands. "Do you understand that failing to impress the king means no access to the firewell? Do you understand that no access will leave you nearly incapable of succeeding at school? Do you understand how that will impact your future?"

New worry crept into Destry's stomach, adding to its ache. Of course she'd known the meeting was important. But in her fear over appearing before the goblin king, she hadn't thought about the long-term consequences of failure.

Fey Elena waved at the book she'd shown Destry before. It sailed from the bookcase —less gracefully this time—and flung itself open on her desk. She jabbed the firewell map. "The challenges involved in getting you to another firewell are immense, child! We may be faeries, but this is no fairy tale. I cannot magic you across miles or offer instantaneous transport. You *must* take this seriously."

"I am." Her voice rasped with the effort of keeping steady. This was life in the human world all over again. Teachers scolding her for "lack of effort," Destry protesting that she had done her best. She couldn't explain that Beverly was too drunk to help with math problems, that they couldn't afford materials to make some silly paper mache volcano.

I'm sick of this. Destry forced herself to meet the headmistress's eyes. "Fey Elena, I practiced over an hour every night. I know it doesn't look like it, but I did."

The woman snorted. "Unless you are uncommonly uncoordinated—" Destry felt her cheeks go hot yet again. She looked down, unable to hold Fey Elena's gaze, and the headmistress stopped short. Several seconds ticked past in absolute silence.

Fey Elena's footsteps echoed on the polished floor, and cool fingers pulled Destry's chin up. The headmistress's face had softened. "That was inexcusable of me. My apologies, Destry. I shouldn't have allowed my worries over other matters to affect my behavior with you, nor assumed your struggles were due to lack of effort rather than...personal challenges."

It was the nicest way anyone had ever called her clumsy. Destry managed a wobbly smile. Fey Elena released her. "I've changed my mind. We shall spend tomorrow night working out the intricacies of that curtsy. This evening would be better spent on a visit to your magic source."

Relief—and a spark of excitement—loosened her chest. "The firewell?"

"Yes. Most fey enjoy communion with their element, so it should offer a pleasant end to your day. Come along. We don't wish to be caught out after dark."

A light drizzle misted down as they stepped onto the front steps. Fey Elena swirled her hands as if grabbing a large quantity of magic strands. She spread her fingers, turned her palms upwards, and swept them above her head in an arc. She repeated the action going in different directions. When she lowered them, the steady mist ghosted around Fey Elena, but none fell on her—an invisible umbrella.

"Shielding magic," the headmistress said. "Would you like one?"

Destry shook her head. The gentle rainwater was no storm, but it felt energizing. Her hair dripped by the time they reached the curving road in front of the school. They followed it past the senior student houses, towards the goblin forest. Faerie trees arched over the smooth cobblestones. A river burbled on their right, some distance away.

Soon, the faerie trees thinned, opening onto a rocky clearing that led to the river. Across the clearing, a fringe of white trees began, growing into a thick forest. No foliage... Wait, they did have leaves. Transparent leaves, in gentle shades of blue, purple, green, yellow, orange, and red. The muted colors shimmered against the pale branches, like living stained glass. Destry stopped, assailed by a sense of déjà vu. This looked exactly like the forest from her dream. It *was* the forest from her dream.

Fey Elena stopped as well. "Is something wrong?"

She couldn't tell the no-nonsense headmistress she'd visited this place in sleep. "No. It's just—um—those trees are beautiful."

Fey Elena raised an eyebrow. "You'd be among the first to think so. Most faeries find the goblin forest intimidating."

Destry considered the trees again. Maybe they *could* look scary, with their smooth trunks and branches reaching like hands, especially when they rustled and moved despite the lack of wind. But she yearned to touch them.

If Cam were here, he'd understand...probably be as fascinated by the strange foliage as she was. But he could never know about the pale forest's haunting beauty. A sliver of loneliness slid beneath her skin, accompanied by an equally uncomfortable sliver of guilt. She hadn't written to Cam since arriving in Si'fliegen. She'd begun a letter, but the blank page already felt full—saturated with things she couldn't tell him.

Ironically, writing to Mom had been easy. Hiding things to protect Beverly felt like business as usual, and Destry had dropped the letter in the school's mail bag days ago. But she couldn't make herself copy those half-truths for Cam. It was like losing him all over again.

The headmistress spoke, pulling Destry from her guilty thoughts. "Kindly remember that the forest is off-limits. Those trees possess sentience and will tell the goblins about trespassers, both on their lands and at the firewell. Fey who trespass find themselves summoned before the goblin court, and you do *not* wish to be subject to goblin punishment. Our government won't intervene if a student knowingly breaks the rules."

Destry nodded. Should an intelligent tree seem creepy to her? It didn't. But breaking the rules would be stupid, with her firewell access already limited. Who knew what terrible punishments a goblin might conjure up?

They continued walking. The road curved away from the clearing and the river, to a path up a steep hill. She slipped several times on water-slicked grass as they climbed. Destry watched her feet for better stability. She was panting when they reached the top, unlike the headmistress, who'd somehow skipped the heavy dog-breaths. Destry finally looked up and understood. Fey Elena's wings had emerged, helping her along.

The headmistress saw her looking. "My wings inevitably appear, say I may or say I nay, this close to the goblin forest. It's prudent to take advantage of them." She evaluated Destry with a perplexed expression. Was she not reacting in the normal faerie way? Fey Elena motioned her toward a long flight of stone stairs leading to a covered pavilion. "I'll wait here. Don't be afraid of the fire. It won't hurt you."

Destry mounted the steps, heart hammering. With the greater height, she realized that the firewell was situated quite close to the goblin forest. The faerie forest sat on one side of the hill, the goblin forest on the other. The ground rose up between them like the firewell was a hat on a fringed bald head. The irreverent thought eased her nervousness.

In the center of the stone pavilion, under a shining metal roof, a huge hole took up most of the floor space. Warmth crept out the second Destry stepped over the pavilion's threshold. Ghostly flames flickered along the edges of the pit, rising higher in the center. She stepped closer. They drifted in her direction, transparent fire creeping across the floor.

Destry stumbled over her own feet backing away, but Fey Elena's reminder echoed in her ears: *The fire won't hurt you.* She righted herself, took a deep breath, and stood still as the russet flames wrapped around her ankles.

They sent faint patterns of heat everywhere they touched. The warm air was comfortable, especially after the drizzle outside. Destry waited, but the flames didn't move further. She took a few cautious steps closer—the firewell had no walls or even a lip—and peered into its depths.

Heat swept over her face, harsh enough to make her gasp. Glowing molten rock lined the sides, and flames crawled restlessly along them, more real than the ghost fire. The pit seemed endless, a miniature volcano waiting to erupt. Destry felt lightheaded. She backed away until her legs bumped one of the stone benches built into the pavilion. She flopped down and squeezed her eyes closed.

The phantom fire had followed, still tickling her legs. Its softer warmth was comforting. Destry pulled in deep, shaky breaths until the world stopped spinning.

She opened her eyes again...and nearly fell off the bench. Incandescent streaks of red glowed everywhere: in the air, in the distant trees, even twisting down the steps to the ground. She blinked and rubbed her eyes, but the shining strands remained.

Strands. That was how her teachers kept describing magic, as strands of power wreathed throughout the world. Tentatively, Destry reached for one of the shimmering threads floating nearby. She caught it, and it broke into sparkling motes. Destry tried a few more times, with the same result. Soon, the air looked like someone had upended a bottle of glitter into it.

She reached for another, but this time, rather than grabbing it, Destry turned her hand so the air movement made the crimson strand twist. It curled around her wrist, a friendly snake sliding towards her palm, coalescing into an insubstantial ball. Destry cradled it, spellbound. Her skin tingled with the promise of power.

What to do with it? The exercises she'd tried in class revolved around doing simple but specific things with magic. There were no marbles to roll across a table here.

Destry shifted, and her still-damp hair drifted over one shoulder. She considered the ball of radiant heat in her palm. Destry lifted it above her head, spreading her fingers. The magic sifted through them and over her. It caught her hair, blowing warm currents through it until it dropped, dry and soft, to her shoulders.

Destry caught more strands and did the same to her tunic and her leggings. Everything felt like it had been run through a clothes dryer. A happy warmth, better than the heat of the ghost flames, blossomed in her chest.

She stayed as long as she dared, with Fey Elena waiting on the hillside. Sighing, she made her way down the stairs. The clouds had broken while she was in the pavilion, and the setting sun peeked out. But despite the summer temperatures, Destry shivered as the heat of the firewell slipped away.

That wasn't the only thing that faded; as she and Fey Elena walked down the hill, the red strands shimmered away. Destry reached in the direction she'd seen one of the magic threads. Warmth slid across her wrist. She twisted her fingers and felt the strand slide through them and then break.

Fey Elena noticed. "The Sight—the ability to actually see energy strands—only lasts when you're in communion with your element. The ability to sense them lasts longer, though it will dissipate before the week is out. You should make your next visit on a Sunday afternoon, when you'll get more advantage from it. And under no circumstances should you come this late. Curfew must be observed."

This late? Destry smothered a snort of laughter. Fey society ran on a dawn-to-dusk time frame—a culture shock after the human world. The faerie tendency toward night blindness probably explained it. But the school's curfew seemed ridiculously early, even among the fey.

Fey Elena added, "You should also be aware: if a goblin arrives to use the well, you are legally required to give the goblin deference."

"What does that mean?"

"Essentially, you do what you're told. If the goblin is unwilling to share space with you, leave until the goblin is finished. If the goblin doesn't want you waiting at the base of the well, then you must return to our forest or the river until the goblin finishes. You should always allow extra time in case of that particular inconvenience."

Inconvenience? That felt like the wrong word. What Fey Elena described left Destry feeling vaguely ashamed, for reasons she couldn't identify.

The headmistress patted her shoulder. "Having rules avoids conflicts, child. Better to shelve your pride than to get into an altercation with a goblin."

When they reached the road, Fey Elena said, "The next step towards having fully functional magic is locating your magic partner. Normally, the signs on your wrists facilitate the process. Because the magic chooses someone complementary to you, the elemental signs are never the same. However, with so few fire signs, that hardly rules out a significant portion of students."

Destry wasn't sure she wanted to find her magic partner, anyway. Not yet. Fey Elena attempted a reassuring smile. "There is a positive. At your age, far fewer students are left unmatched. Even with your disadvantage, finding your partner shouldn't take long."

PARTNERS

The weeks following that discussion certainly felt long. Very, very long. Because Destry had to work with each guy for several days to determine whether their magics meshed, she could only get through two potential partners a week.

February breezed in, accompanied by more candidates. Destry cringed whenever Fey Elena appeared with some guy. So far, they'd all been dismal failures; neither their magics nor their personalities clicked. Worse, most of the candidates were particularly skilled at magic. Destry was probably ruining their GPA just by sitting with them.

The boy she started February with (Magic Partner Candidate Five) wouldn't have been bad: shy, nearly as accident-prone as Destry, and he also struggled to work magic. She might be comfortable with him. But by the end of their three-day trial, she had a new friend but still no magic partner.

The only upside to the whole grueling process (she'd dubbed it the MPC Marathon) was the distraction it offered. Her meeting with the goblin king had been set. For better or worse, she would appear before him February 9...and she only had hazy ideas on what to expect. Fey Elena had evaded Destry's efforts to get a description of the goblin king, like she thought details would scare Destry into abandoning her firewell quest. Not exactly reassuring.

So she'd gone to the next best source—her classmates—but their accounts varied widely. From giant, strangely-morphed animals to humanoid stone monsters, no one agreed on anything except the claws: wicked, black, and razor-sharp. They sounded unnervingly like the ones in her nightmare. With less than a week until the interview, she desperately needed other things to think about.

She was in Everyday Magic (Basic Level) when Fey Elena brought in MPC Six. This class should've been Destry's easiest, but the instructor made it her worst. Fey Gerald had once been the combat teacher. Rumor said the muscular faerie man was shuffled into this class because of excessive aggression. His resentment was clear. Gerald ridiculed any student incapable of mastering such a "remedial" subject. The subsequent nerves kept Destry from demonstrating even those skills she did master.

She was trying to bring a pot of water to a speedier boil by strengthening the flames beneath it...without success. Four days past her last firewell visit, Destry could barely sense the energy strands enough to maintain a simmer. Gerald had already mocked her in front of the class: "A fire fey? And you can't even boil water? Sure those power markings are real?"

Next time would be worse.

He turned in her direction. Panic flared through Destry. The flames roared into a small bonfire, so hot they melted the pot into a shapeless blob. A stray flame set Gerald's goatee smoldering. He patted it frantically and aimed a blast of water from his palm. It doused the pot and her. Destry stared at him through the rising steam.

Some of the steam looked like it was coming off his head. Gerald glared. "Thought you should show off, Firewings?" Which was both ironic and unfair. For the first time in weeks, Destry didn't feel like retreating. She glared right back.

The sound of laughter broke their staring contest. Destry and Gerald turned to the door. Fey Elena stood beside a faerie boy with air signs on his wrists—the guy who had covered for her that day in the headmistress's office. Destry's pot going up in flames had distracted from their arrival.

The boy doubled over, still laughing. Fey Elena crossed her arms. "Some decorum would be preferred, Tristan." Her lips twitched, though. "I have a new candidate for you, Destry."

Oh, no. Please not this guy. After that near-disaster in the headmistress's office, Destry had made a point of learning about her rescuer. His black hair, blue eyes, lean muscles, and troublemaker smile left more than one full-faerie bemoaning Tristan's "half-fey-I've-got-a -soulmate-somewhere" status. Any girl at the Academy would be thrilled to be his magic partner—any girl except Destry.

Tristan wouldn't *want* to be with her, same as the other guys. No matter how polite they were, the fact remained: her magic hadn't improved. Destry got a few days' use out of each firewell visit; then the warmth from her energy strands stopped registering. And Tristan was an advanced student; he shared few of her classes.

So Destry had to navigate her awkwardness with the male gender...while working with an intelligent, good-looking guy...in her worst class with a teacher who hated her?

Well. This was gonna be awesome.

Tristan stifled his laughter and joined Destry at her work station. Fey Elena gave Gerald a pointed look; he stalked away. The headmistress smiled. "Tell me how it goes."

A murmur broke across the class as the door closed. Gerald scowled. "Back to work, people. And clean up that mess, *Firewings*. Next pot you melt, I'm zapping you."

Gerald's favorite way to prod students was jolting them with magic. Like getting snapped with a rubber band, the first time was annoying, but repeated zaps became painful. He'd gotten her multiple times today.

Destry sighed and turned to Tristan. "Gotta clean up. I'll be ready in a minute."

But he was doing his own magic. The water on the floor, the table, and even her clothes evaporated in puffs of steam. It didn't feel warm, like when she dried things with fire magic, but it was effective. Tristan offered her the ruined pot. "Afraid I can't fix this. Metals are tough."

Destry took it, cursing herself for blushing. She grabbed another from the supply cupboard, but before she could fill it at the sink, Tristan swished his hand around the rim of the pot. It filled like someone was siphoning water into the bottom.

Destry couldn't even get water in a pot to respond, and Tristan could produce it out of nowhere? "Impressive," she said tightly. "Thanks."

He looked closer at her. "I wasn't trying to show off."

"I know." The gesture had been as offhand as drying her clothes. She put the pot on the metal supports and bent to light the fire. "I'm sorry you're stuck in here with me." At least the fire gave her an excuse not to look at him.

"Don't be. Everyone starts somewhere. And if you're my magic partner, we'll have to work that out anyway." They murmured quick introductions—Tristan with a mischievous grin and a knowing expression. Clearly, he remembered her, too.

Gerald prowled by their table several times, always with some biting comment. Flustered, frustrated, and humiliated, Destry tried to ignore him. When would this hour of misery end? She glared at the pot of simmering water, wishing she could vanish the stupid thing along with her stupid teacher.

Instead, the pot went up in flames again. The whoosh of heat made people across the room jump back. Boiling water leapt out like a geyser. As it splatted the ground, Destry jerked away, pulling Tristan with her.

He patted her hand. Then he slid his arm free, stepping towards the fire. With a swirling, pulling motion, he made a whirlwind circle the fire and funnel the air away—removing the oxygen feeding it. The flames flickered and died. *Smart, Tristan.*

But she didn't have time to thank him. Gerald was stomping across the room.

Destry set her jaw. She would *not* flinch. She might have to take Gerald's zaps, but she didn't have to show that they bothered her. Tristan looked at Gerald, then Destry. As the teacher flicked his fingers in their direction, Tristan stepped in front of her.

He acted like it was an accident, like he was going to the supply cupboard, but his shoulders tensed with anticipation. The jolt hit him squarely. Gerald barked, "Not another pot, Tristan. If Firewings is incapable of doing the exercise, we'll wait until she mends the pot herself. Zero marks if it's still in that shape by the end of class."

A few students tittered. Others looked sympathetic. Face burning, Destry ignored both reactions. She saw Tristan about to evaporate the water on the floor and snapped, "Don't. You already got zapped because of me."

Annoyance flashed over his face. The water began steaming away, though. Destry snatched the pot. Tears of frustration sprang to her eyes, and she blinked them back. Tristan's expression softened. "Hey, I had Fey Gerald too. Got zapped plenty of times."

"So you were feeling nostalgic?"

He grinned. "Not so much. But the first time doesn't hurt. The third or fourth...ouch."

Destry winced. "Or the sixth."

"He got you five times today? You should have sent more of that fire into his goatee."

She smiled—a real smile—but it faded fast. "Wish I could. I didn't make those flames on purpose."

The conversation had come full circle. Tristan must have been thinking the same thing. "Destry, do you know what it's like, spending years at this school, watching half-faeries find their partners, and never finding yours? Worrying you'll lose your magic because the person who completes it hasn't been found? Knowing you only have three years left to accomplish what you haven't accomplished the previous four?"

She shook her head. Tristan said, "Every one of the guys working with you...we do. We don't mind repeating some assignments or that you aren't good yet. We're just glad for a chance to find what everyone else has."

Nice. He had to be nice, on top of all the other perfections. But a tiny flame flickered in Destry. "Thank you for taking that jolt for me. I should have said it before."

"Eh, first time's no biggie. Don't make me into a hero. I'm just a really amazing, very awesome guy." She laughed, and he added, "You know, we *all* used to be bad at magic. Me and those other candidates managed for years at partial strength. We've adapted, learned the trade secrets. I can teach them to you, even if we don't end up being partners."

The little flame blossomed, warming Destry as thoroughly as any fire strands. She intended to thank him, but Tristan's expression stopped her—focused entirely on her hands.

Before she could ask what was wrong, heat blazed through her palms and fingers, burning every joint and rippling over her skin. Destry yelped and dropped the pot. As it clunked to the ground, she realized: it was a pot again. Not a deformed hunk of metal with a handle, but a real cooking utensil.

The burning in her hands died, and Destry picked up the pot. "Did you do this, Tristan?"

"I told you, I'm no good with metals. Most faeries aren't. That's why Fey Gerald gave you that assignment. He knew you couldn't do it." He grinned. "Except apparently, you could."

Apparently *they* could. By the end of the day, it was clear: Destry's magic worked better with Tristan around. And Tristan's weakest areas (plants and metals) were better with Destry along, too. Fey Elena seemed pleased when they reported to her.

"Excellent. Now we coordinate your schedules. The substantial learning gap presents a challenge. In the past, we've allowed the more advanced student to work with the less advanced one—eliminating all but your essential classes, leaving that time free for tutoring. Often, magic partners are excellent teachers for one another." She flipped through a file folder. "I believe Fey Gerald's class should go in the non-essential group."

Not have to see Gerald again? Destry tried not to smile too widely. Fey Elena made a note in the folder. "You have approximately one week until the goblin king returns. Once you receive permission to visit the firewell daily, you'll progress faster."

Tristan grinned as they shut the headmistress's door behind them. "The next couple weeks will be fun. New pairings always get extra freedom." She gave him a questioning look, and he added, "Close friendships lead to stronger magic bonds."

The glint of mischief in his eyes should have made her nervous. One day together, and she already suspected that Tristan used his quick wits to break the rules as often as he followed them. But a funny inner *pull* towards him made her smile back. He grinned wider. "It won't last forever, but we should enjoy it while we can."

LEARNING CURVE

Tristan was good at enjoying life, as Destry soon realized. He had an impressive ability to judge exactly what he could get away with—and do it. Fey Elena left their mornings free for tutoring. Destry learned more over the following three days than she had in the previous three weeks, both about legitimate subjects and less scholarly things.

She learned the shortcuts through the school, even those that students weren't supposed to take. She learned which teachers could be persuaded to let them out of class early, and which ones tolerated tardiness. While she was no good at weaseling out of trouble, Tristan was persuasive enough for both of them. They shared one magic class—metals—and the academic ones.

When Sunday rolled around, Destry looked for Tristan at breakfast. So far, they'd breakfasted together each morning, then practiced in a private study room. But with the serving hour nearly over, Tristan was nowhere in sight.

She joined Sara, David, and Julya. David and Sara were sharing an enormous plate of bacon (just bacon) and poring over new t-shirt sketches; Julya had an air of extreme boredom. Destry glanced once more around the room, and the dark haired girl gave a superior smile. "He's not here."

Destry jerked her gaze to the table. She grabbed a biscuit, sliding egg and bacon between its halves. "What?"

"Tris always skips Sunday breakfast. Likes to sleep in."

How did Julya know? Destry decided not to ask. Tristan had probably had some girlfriends in his time at the Academy. Sara looked up from the sketches. "Everyone knows Tristan skips Sunday breakfast. Always has."

Irritation brightened Julya's eyes. "You must be thrilled with your good fortune, Destry. Not every half could hope for a partner like Tristan. You may pass your basic year yet."

Destry wanted to make some scathing remark, but what could she say? The scales *were* unbalanced. Before she mustered a response, someone dragged a chair out next to her and plopped into it. She turned to see who it was.

Tristan grinned back at her. His hair was rumpled, as if he'd barely rolled out of bed. He was barefoot, and his loose tunic and pants looked like something he'd slept in. He grabbed a piece of bacon. "Actually, I'm the lucky one. How many guys get paired with a fire faerie? Believe me, there's heat in more than their magic."

Destry's jaw dropped, but Julya didn't notice. She wavered between a glare and a pout. The first won. She flounced from the table. Tristan pushed Destry's chin up with one finger. "It's more believable when you keep your mouth closed. A smug smile might've been good."

David laughed. Sara kicked him under the table, and he tried to dodge, making it shift and shudder. Silverware clinked against the dishes. Destry was still staring at Tristan. "I—you—why did you do that?"

Sara snorted. "Because Julya's a hypocrite. She acts like she's better than us half-faeries, but she wants a magic partner, especially if it's Tristan."

The fey boy sent Destry a measuring glance. "She never got anywhere with me. I won't say no one has...but not her. I don't have a girlfriend now, either."

She couldn't believe they were discussing this in front of Sara and David. "Good to know."

"Might as well be up front with each other," David said. "You've got a lot riding on creating a good relationship."

The reminder was even less welcome than the too-frank conversation. Destry bit into her breakfast sandwich to avoid answering.

Sara poked Tristan's shoulder. "How come you graced us with your presence today?"

He was half-watching Destry. "I figured someone might want my company. Though it looks like I figured wrong." His good-humored remark couldn't quite hide the uncertainty in his voice.

The ever-confident Tristan, insecure? Maybe Destry wasn't the only one who worried about things working out. She swallowed and forced a smile. "Then that someone is stupid. But *I'm* glad you're here. Want to come to the firewell later?"

Tristan's shoulders relaxed. "Love to. The firewell is one of the only things around here I haven't done."

The sun was lowering by the time Destry and Tristan started across the grounds, late that afternoon. Tristan was quieter than usual. As they reached the curving road, he said, "I've been thinking."

"That's dangerous."

Destry's teasing made him smile but didn't forestall his next comment. "I realized this morning—I know almost nothing about you. We've spent the last four days talking magic or school or other students. Exclusively."

"There's not much to know."

"And," Tristan continued, "every time I ask something personal, you shrug it off with comments like, 'There's not much to know.'"

Too bad he hadn't taken the hint. But Tristan *was* her magic partner. He'd need to know her better eventually. "Fine. Ask a question, and I'll answer."

"What's your home life like?"

Destry's pace faltered. "Seriously? That's what you're leading with?"

"What's wrong with it?"

"I thought you'd start small. *Did you get in much trouble in normal school?* Something like that."

Tristan snickered. "Why ask a question when I already know the answer? You aren't a big rebel. You can probably count the times some teacher hauled you to the office on one hand."

"You probably can too. But not for the same reasons."

He gave a self-satisfied smile. "You still haven't answered me."

Destry sighed. "My home life is...not great. Mom was drinking herself into oblivion because of my magic."

"Wasn't there anyone you could count on? Aunt, cousin, boyfriend?"

Destry had a feeling Tristan mostly wanted to know about the last. "I had a good friend who lived next door, but he left for boarding school. There was no one else."

Tristan shoved his hands into his pockets. "My folks are divorced. Going back and forth kept my power from affecting them much. And the Academy found me early, too."

"Were you sad to leave home?"

"Are you kidding? I was eleven, and some lady told me I had magic powers and could fly." He bumped his shoulder against hers. "Sure was nice of you to share your magic with me."

"Was it?" Destry worried over this. Did Tristan resent being pulled from a normal life by her powers, however unintentionally?

His eyes softened. "Yes, Destry. It really was. Look, I've had four years here to see how awesome working magic can be. Give it until the end of the school year. You'll feel the same."

As the road neared the rocky clearing, Tristan's wings shot out. They were as beautiful as the rest of him: darker silver than Destry's, pointed sharply at the tips, like some avenging angel. The indigo markings were more obvious than Destry's red ones, but less widespread, highlighting the curves and points of his wings.

He noticed her staring and blushed. "I don't know how you keep your wings in, this close to the goblin forest. Then again, you like combat classes. My magic partner is tougher than I am."

Surprisingly, Tristan didn't try to follow her to the actual firewell. He settled in the grass at the base of the stairs, smirking. "You're shocked, I know. Tristan, following the rules? What in the Fold is going on?" He pointed at the white forest. "I've heard enough about the leafy Gestapo to know better. Creepy trees."

Destry didn't feel ready to explain that the trees intrigued more than scared her, especially since Tristan didn't share her affinity. That was a concern for another day. She didn't linger at the firewell, either. Tristan watched her descend the stairs mere moments after going up. "That was fast."

"I have to get back early. Tomorrow—" She swallowed, then forced the words out. "Tomorrow is my meeting with the goblin king. Fey Elena wants to drill me again on what to say. She also wants to take another stab at that curtsy."

Tristan made the choking sound of a boy frantically suppressing his laughter. His voice came out strained. "I'm sure it's improved a lot since we first met."

Destry glared and walked faster, but her foot caught on a stone. She pitched forward, arms pinwheeling. Tristan caught her before she could eat dirt; he twined his arm through hers and started downhill.

They'd never been so close together. Destry shot a sideways glance at Tristan. He smiled like it was totally normal. "Are you nervous? About tomorrow?"

"Terrified."

"Want me to escort you there?" His eyes flitted to the white forest, and his wings (which had been waving idly) picked up speed.

Warmth expanded Destry's chest, even though she couldn't accept. "Fey Elena says no one can go with me. Goblin law. Proving I'm brave enough to come through the forest alone is the first trial. Meeting the king is the second."

"Well, I would have if I could. Remember that when I need your help in metalworking."

Destry laughed shakily.

Tristan squeezed her arm. "It'll be okay. The goblin king won't be able to refuse someone like you."

The next morning, Destry tried practicing faerie magic with Tristan, but stress rendered her worse than useless; it made her dangerous. The third time Tristan had to douse a fire on his shirt, he said, "No more practice until this is over. You're a walking flamethrower when you're nervous."

Destry scowled. She needed something to keep her mind off that meeting. "Then what should we do?"

He grinned like a kid about to raid the cookie jar. "Follow me."

They slipped down several halls and into a steamy kitchen. One of the faeries working there, a plump lady with lavender-colored hair, rolled her eyes. "Look who's here. I'm not giving you sweets."

Tristan's eyebrows drew together, sad-puppy style. "I just wanted you to meet my magic partner. Destry, this is Gertrude."

"You know I hate that name." The cook waved a batter-covered spoon. "It's Trudy, young miss. Can't believe they found a magic partner for this scapegrace."

"Not just any magic partner," Tristan said proudly. He pulled Destry's arm out. Her red and silver flames shone in the kitchen light.

Trudy's eyes widened. "You're the one headed for Rí Kobold today. Fire and wings, child, aren't you nervous?"

Tristan said, "Well, she set me on fire three times this morning."

"We can't have that. Wait here." The woman bustled off, apron strings swinging.

Destry turned to Tristan, eyes narrowing. "Did you bring me here to cadge food?"

"Of course not," he said loudly. Quieter, he added, "I brought you here to cadge *treats*. Don't mess it up."

Trudy hurried back and plunked a cardboard box into Destry's hands. "Something I baked for the teachers. You need it more than they do."

She poked Tristan's chest. "Don't share with this one. And don't eat too many. Best to have your wits sharp when you meet the goblin king."

Destry tucked the box under one arm. "I won't. Thank you."

Trudy shooed them out of the kitchen. Partway down the hall, Tristan reached for the box. Destry slid it behind her back. "I promised not to give you any."

He stretched both arms around her. "Yeah, but I'm the reason you have them."

Her breath caught. Tristan was so close. She backed away, bumping into a wall. Her magic partner laughed. "Trapped."

A stern voice made them jump. "What are you doing in these halls at this hour?"

The box slid from Destry's fingers; it disappeared as Tristan pulled his arms away. They turned towards Fey Renalt.

Tristan shrugged. "Destry's nervous about her meeting today. She lit me on fire too many times, so we went for a walk."

"Looked like more than a walk. But I know how it is." Renalt's face turned friendlier. "Maybe it's good that we haven't discussed palming power yet."

Destry tried to look politely interested...difficult, since she also wondered where Tristan had hidden the goodies. "Palming power, sir?"

He lifted his hand, palm forward. It glowed, giving new meaning to "hand-held light." "That's the process of gathering magic into our hands, to focus it. If young Tristan was overstepping his boundaries, for example—" he eyed her too-warm cheeks, "you could give him a nice jolt to the chest."

"Or she could ask *young Tristan* to step away," Tristan grumbled. "I'm not that kind of guy."

Renalt closed his fist, and the light faded. "The more experience you gain, the stronger your magic becomes, the stronger jolt of power you can summon." Destry nodded. The teacher said, "Alright, get to wherever you're supposed to be."

They hurried along the corridor, but when Destry turned toward their study room, Tristan said, "Wrong way. This meeting thing is gold. We're playing it for all it's worth." He steered her outside.

Tristan plunked to the ground under a tree, pulling Destry with him. He slid the box out of nowhere. "And you thought I would take them and run."

"How'd you do that?"

"Reflecting spell. Handy little thing." He set the box in her lap with a flourish. "You wanna open that?"

"This?" Destry cracked the lid and raised it to her nose. Her plan—to tease him by dragging it out—vanished with the first whiff of chocolate. "Brownies!"

Thick, fudgy brownies, garnished with glistening chocolate ribbons. She had no more objections to Tristan's methods. They each devoured one, then a second. Destry licked chocolate off her thumb. "Heaven."

She reached for a third, but Tristan slid the box out of reach. "Two is enough. Trudy's right. You don't want to be buzzed for that meeting."

"Nice try." Destry held out her hand. "Share."

Tristan shook his head. "Hasn't anyone explained this to you yet?"

"Explained what?"

"Aside from the start-of-semester chocolate, have you ever seen dessert served here?"

She didn't need to think about it; the school was depressingly health conscious.

Tristan said, "They hardly ever serve dessert because too much sugar makes faeries drunk. I can't believe no one explained."

Destry stared, but he was entirely serious. "Wait...you mean...really?"

"Yeah. Haven't you noticed?"

Memory rushed over her, of Cam taking her drink away during one of their junk food marathons. "No more soda. Good grief, sugar makes you crazy." And it had, always turning her giggly and relaxed. But it never made her drunk like when she'd gotten in Beverly's schnapps.

Destry must not have looked convinced. Tristan said, "It doesn't hit kids as hard. But once the magic comes on full force, the changes in our bodies make us metabolize the sugar differently. It'll affect you now, Des."

"Destry," she said firmly. She didn't want him using Cam's name for her.

"Okay. I'm your magic partner, *Destry*. I'm in charge of helping you get in trouble *and* keeping you from getting caught. You show up tipsy this afternoon, we'll both be in trouble."

She flopped her head back against the tree trunk. "This is the worst news ever. Worse than having to see the goblin king. I love chocolate."

Tristan patted her leg. "I'll save the other as a reward for making it through the meeting."

"You'll eat it."

"Nope. Fey's honor."

"What was the point of the brownies if I can't have them?"

"You can. Just not too many. And the point was to help you relax."

"It didn't work."

Her perversity seemed to amuse Tristan. "You're much more relaxed. I never realized what a brat you can be."

They stashed the box under a bush and roamed the school grounds. Destry felt like her old tense self by lunchtime. Tristan tried coaxing her to eat, but she refused. She didn't want to be known as the faerie who'd puked on the goblin king.

Riamon appeared at her table near the end of the meal. He smiled at Sara, David, and Tristan. "I must borrow your friend. For an extended period, to be precise."

Destry stood to a chorus of good luck wishes. Tristan squeezed her hand, his forehead puckered. "Now, now," Riamon chided. "Your magic partner will be fine."

They made their way out of the dining hall. Destry said, "I thought the meeting wasn't until five."

"You need time to prepare for the interview."

"Fey Elena drilled me so many times, I could do it in my sleep."

"I mean your appearance, to be more specific. You are going before the goblin king. Casual attire in a formal situation indicates either a lack of respect or that you take the situation lightly. Neither would be wise." He stopped at the stairs to the girls' dorms. "I sent some dresses to your room. Any will do. Elena is sending someone to arrange your hair."

What sort of dresses would be waiting for her, given Riamon's taste in clothing? But none of the three dresses on her bed had leather or fringe. She wavered between a blue gossamer silk and a red gown with black and silver accents. The blue might help her seem vulnerable and appealing. But she found herself fingering the jagged hem of the crimson dress, the fitted bodice, the floating wisps at the shoulders. It had a wide, corset-type belt of swirled black and silver. This dress said bold, confident. A little confidence could come in handy.

By four o'clock, Destry stood in the headmistress's office, waiting for inspection. Fey Elena had sent several people to bully her with their beauty tools. She'd been bathed, lotioned, dressed, adjusted, plucked, and poked. Hopefully, the effect wasn't wasted on a monster.

Fey Elena strode inside. One elegant eyebrow slid upwards. "Of all Riamon's offerings, you chose the one that most blatantly screams 'faerie.'"

"I liked this dress." Destry felt like she'd somehow failed a test.

"Exactly." The headmistress circled her, murmuring something about strong blood. "The effect is nice. And my stylist did excellent things with your hair." Loose braids were twined into a complicated arrangement, with silver ribbons woven throughout. Destry itched to undo the whole thing.

Fey Elena adjusted one of the wispy strands the stylist had left around her face. "You're going to be nervous, but try not to be afraid. You'll only give that monster the satisfaction of watching you grovel. Just remember: you will leave in one piece, no matter how the interview goes."

This was supposed to be reassuring? Destry nodded curtly, hoping to forestall more helpful hints. Fey Elena held out an ornate pocket watch. "Do not dally in the forest, either out of interest or fear. You must arrive at the goblin castle in a timely manner." She waited until Destry pocketed it, then hustled her through the door and onto the paved street.

Interview with a Goblin

Destry's walk to the forest passed in a haze of tense blankness. She paced across the rocky expanse near the river, through the trees onto a trail of hard-packed earth. Her direction was clear. The path led unerringly to the castle looming in the distance.

The silent wood served as little more than pale background to her fear. The very air felt heavy with magic. Indecipherable whispers drifted on the breeze. The susurration of rustling leaves and swaying branches sent shivers along her skin, pressing her to move faster. She checked the pocket watch repeatedly.

Destry rounded a curve in the path. Ten feet ahead, the forest ended abruptly, a stone castle visible through the gaps in the tree trunks. She pulled the watch out again, popping it open with a faint metal *snick*. The walk had taken less than twenty minutes. Destry clicked it closed, thumb lingering on its etched designs. Something solid...something familiar...something real.

Taking a deep breath, she shoved it into her pocket and plunged out of the forest.

The castle loomed over her, a strangely cohesive hodgepodge of architectural elements. Roman arches nestled among rough stone walls fit for a fortress; graceful spires perched near crenelated turrets. The sun glinted over the coppery roofs—some smooth, others made of overlapping metal tiles shaped like dragon scales. A huge balcony, one floor up, rested atop wooden pillars carved with Celtic knotwork. No grand entrances, though. Clearly, this wasn't the front.

A cobblestone path circled the castle. Destry followed it. Flowers and plants bloomed, overrunning their beds to spill onto the ground. Their cheerful disarray seemed wrong for a castle full of monsters. She reached a more impressive entryway; wide steps led to a massive pair of arched doors, their polished wood accented with coppery metal.

Destry looked for someone—anyone—but in vain. Wasn't that odd? Shouldn't there be workers or servants or monstrous minions? Had the goblin king cleared his castle so there'd be no witnesses to this event?

Breathe. Fey Elena would never have sent you if it was really dangerous. Just worry about impressing the king.

She climbed the steps and lifted a hand to knock, but that seemed ridiculous. Instead, she placed both hands on one of the knobless doors and shoved. It swung open more easily than she expected, thunking against the inner wall. The sound echoed inside a palatial foyer, with tall ceilings and gleaming wood floors, inlaid with leaves and vines of semi-precious stone. Tapestries hung on the walls, swirling designs accented with shimmering metallic threads.

A girl stood in the foyer, leaning against the wall reading a leather-bound book. She looked several years older than Destry. Her cream-colored silk blouse contrasted with her tawny skin, and a black vest with gold patterns emphasized a lithe figure. The girl's russet pants tucked into calf-hugging leather boots, laced to her knees. The sunlight spilling into the foyer gilded her short raven waves, caught on one side with a gold and copper feather barrette.

Destry stared. The last thing she'd expected was another human. The girl cocked an eyebrow, and Destry realized she was still hovering in the doorway. She forced herself over the threshold. The girl's gold eyes followed her across the floor. "You're the fire faerie?"

Destry nodded. What was this human doing in a castle full of monsters? "I have an audience with the...the goblin king."

The girl snapped her book shut. "Follow me."

Double doors loomed at the opposite end of the foyer. They were partially open, and the murmur of voices, like buzzing bees, drifted out. But the girl turned left, up a twisting staircase to the second floor. Destry opened her mouth; no sound came out. She cleared her throat, tried again. "Where are we going?"

"The king meets supplicants in his private audience chambers. Less disruption, less drama. Particularly if things go poorly." They came out into a wide hall, and the girl indicated another double door. "Good luck."

The way she said it sounded more like *Goodbye*. Destry wiped sweaty palms on her dress and hurried past the carved desk situated near the vast doors. She pushed tentatively against them.

They swung open easily, into a cavernous room cool with shadows. She forced herself to pace into the center. Of its own accord, the door swung shut behind her. The loud *clank* seemed very final.

Another arched doorway led onto a balcony. The lowering sun silhouetted the figure standing there, his back to her. Destry's attempt to stifle her gasp failed.

The goblin king was huge; he had to be seven feet tall. A silvery cloak draped over massive shoulders, blending with the darker silver fur dusting his muscled arms. His charcoal-gray skin looked harder than human skin. Sharp claws, dark as obsidian, stood in place of fingernails. He tapped one on the balustrade—*click, click, click*—like a predator stalking along a marble floor.

"So. An unfortunate faerie wishes to beg a favor." His voice was deep, gravelly, though something in the cadence gave her pause. It seemed strangely...familiar.

Destry summoned her courage, but while her heart felt brave, her voice must not have. It came out breathy, scared—nothing like herself. "Yes, Your Majesty. I do."

He swung around, cloak swirling after him like a lost thundercloud, and strode into the room. "Then ask it."

Destry's breath caught. The goblin king's face was like nothing she'd expected. She had always thought of goblins as small green troublemakers, evil imps, when she thought of them at all. She would never have imagined this shadow creature who watched her with a terrible sort of majesty.

The skin on his face and neck was the same as on his arms and hands—like he'd been carved from granite. Dark silver fur dusted his muscular chest and swept down his torso in a V. No shirt, but at least he wore pants—loose black ones tucked into tall leather boots.

Her gaze traveled to his face. Wavy raven hair brushed his shoulders and drifted around faintly pointed ears. His features, from the strong jaw to the noble nose, the high cheekbones and sculpted lips, were startlingly human. They looked wrong paired with the granite skin. She left the examination of his eyes until last: pools of midnight oil, no whites at all. Framed by dark, winged eyebrows, they held her, the eyes of a snake on its prey.

For a long second, the goblin king examined her as thoroughly as she examined him. Then his lips pulled into a smile, exposing sharp fangs in place of canines. Destry barely noticed the discomfort as her wings shot out with unprecedented swiftness. The goblin king's smile grew. "Destry?"

The growling voice broke her numb stare. She tried to breathe normally, to remember how to sweep the elegant curtsy Fey Elena had drilled into her. It didn't work. She wobbled and nearly fell head-first onto the floor.

As she righted herself, a deep rumbling sound thundered through the room. Destry staggered upright, nearly losing her balance again. Her wings swept back and forth so quickly they stirred her hair and the floating red dress. What happened in the goblin court if you offended royalty through absolute clumsiness?

But the rumbling wasn't a growl, or it didn't seem to be. The goblin king was bent over, clawed hand pressed to his stomach, in the universal posture of someone laughing his head off. "It's definitely you," he chortled.

Destry's cheeks glowed. For all his fearsome alienness, she still didn't want to make a fool of herself in front of the goblin king. He straightened, stifling another chuckle, face settling into solemnity. "I'm sorry. I honestly am. But this is the last thing I expected. I promise not to tell anyone."

As his formal speech fell away, she sensed that same familiar cadence. The king lifted one clawed hand to his lips and made the unmistakable gesture of locking them and pocketing the key. Destry gasped, assailed by an odd combination of confusion and homesickness.

The goblin king smiled again. "We both get a surprise today." And his shape began shifting, his stature shrinking. Silvery fur coalesced into a silvery-gray shirt. His skin morphed from deep charcoal into normal flesh tones. Claws receded, forming regular fingernails, and his hair rippled, shades of brown shooting through, turning his hair a soft chestnut.

And those eyes...the black seeped away from the corners, ink being unspilled, uncovering irises the color of green slate. Destry gasped again, shaking her head as if that could make sense of the image before her.

Cam smiled. "Hi, Destry. Welcome to my kingdom."

"Get away!" Destry, backed into a corner of the dim room, had lost all sense of propriety. Forget impressing the goblin king. He must be playing some trick on her, probably so he could *eat* her instead of letting her use the firewell. After magicking himself to look like Cam, he'd strode forward, hands out and smiling—like she would let him get those clawed mitts on her. Her retreat to a defensible corner had taken mere seconds.

Now he held his hands in an attitude of supplication. "Des...Dessie...it's just me. There's nothing to be scared of, I promise."

Yeah, right. A bookcase stood to her left, filled with heavy tomes. She snatched one. Her stressed-out-scorching hands set the cover ablaze within seconds. She flung the fiery target with all her strength. It went wide, but her next one hit him in the shin. He yelped—sounding so Cam-like that tears filled her eyes—and patted sparks from his pants.

Destry spoke through gritted teeth. "I *saw* what you are! Cam is my best friend. I'd know if he was some shadow-monster!"

He rubbed his leg. "The same way I'd know if you were some flame-throwing faerie? I've been visiting this world for six years, and I *still* missed it!" He turned, stomping out fires on the books.

The door flew open. Destry spun around as the girl from the foyer rushed in. Would the other human help?

Except the girl didn't look entirely human now. Inky raven feathers sprouted along her hairline and down her neck, and her gold eyes were bright, almost glowing. Destry stifled a sob.

The girl surveyed the room with an air of bewilderment. "Cam? What's going on?"

He stomped out the last flame. "Nothing, Tyla, it's fine. Go back outside." She hesitated, and he shot a look at Destry. "Seriously, your presence isn't helping."

She tossed up her hands, and the raven feathers melted away. "Shout if she sets *you* on fire." She swept out, shutting the door with a bang.

The goblin king eyed Destry. She readied another book. He sighed and strode towards the nearest window. He flung the curtains open, then headed for the next. Destry tensed. Did she have enough time to run? But he said, "Don't move, or I'm never letting you use my rope ladder again."

Her mind stuttered to a halt. Rope ladder? How would he know?

The goblin king moved from one window to another, flinging open the curtains until the entire room filled with sunlight. Finally, he paced back to her, more cautiously this time. "Better? I know you're scared of the dark."

She frowned. "That could apply to lots of faeries." But the girl *had* called him Cam...

"Here's one that doesn't: you're scared of heights. Climbing my rope ladder is a major act of courage, but you did it several times a week whenever I was home." He took another step forward, eyes holding hers. "You like frosting on cupcakes but not on brownies. Eleven is your lucky number. You always sleep curled on your side. You can't carry a tune or keep a beat, but you love to sing and dance as long as you think no one's watching."

He was almost close enough to touch her. "You think eating cauliflower is funny because it looks like brains, but zombie movies freak you out. You love Iron Man and think Captain America is too much of a boy scout, even though he's my favorite. You've never had a boyfriend, because Jared and your mom's pervert boyfriends made you think every guy is hiding *something*. And if you believe I'm really Cam, you probably think that opinion is justified."

One last step...

He took the book from her hands. Destry didn't resist. Cam smiled, a little sadly. "You're my best friend. And I'm yours. Even though we've had to lie to each other for way too long about something incredibly important."

Destry burst into tears and threw her arms around him.

They moved to sit on a chaise lounge when Destry shifted too fast and her wing cut Cam's left ear. He staunched the bleeding with a handkerchief from his pocket (why was everyone so fancy here?), but the smile never left his face. "I can't believe I didn't see it. Your ridiculous reaction to sugar, your water fetish, your night blindness. They're such typical faerie things."

"They're also human things." Destry curled her feet up beneath her. "*I* can't believe you kept this secret for six whole years. Why... When... I don't understand how you're a goblin. And a king. I don't even know which is crazier."

He set the handkerchief aside. "My dad is the reason for both things." Cam pointed at a series of portraits on the far wall. One showed a teenage Gregory Waters, dressed in a high-necked shirt with a velvety cloak draped over one shoulder. The plaque underneath read *Gregor Darkwater, Eldest Son of Leopold Darkwater*. "He's a goblin, born and raised in Rí Kobold, and he was supposed to inherit the throne. But

Dad never wanted to be king. He wanted to leave for the human world, where no one knew he was royalty. Since there was no other male heir, my grandfather suggested a compromise: two years living among humans. He figured Dad would miss the Fold and come home, which might have worked—if he hadn't met my mom."

Destry remembered how Gregory and Madison were always hugging and kissing, their pleasure in each other's company.

Cam looked out a nearby window, to the white forest beyond. "Dad gave up most of his magic to be with her. His only special gift now is the ability to grow things. But my grandfather was beside himself. To placate him, Dad promised that any future sons would learn about their goblin heritage and have the chance to accept the throne."

"Did he tell your mom?"

"No. We'd have to explain to her about this world, and people don't always react well. Although she's surprised us—Mom hasn't been affected by my magic as I grew older. Dad thinks there's some goblin or faerie blood in her, generations removed."

"So when did you...find out? Or did you always know?"

Cam rested on his hands. "Dad waited until I was old enough to keep quiet. And like faeries, goblin magic doesn't become strong until adolescence. But he made sure to tell me before I transformed the first time. Dad didn't want me scared out of my wits."

"Must have been nice, knowing what was going on," Destry grumbled.

His eyes strayed to her wings. "Were you scared the first time they came?"

"Terrified."

"What about now?"

She shrugged. "I'm not afraid. But they're a pain, literally. Always cutting things or people."

Cam nodded, but he continued examining her wings.

Destry grinned. "You want to touch them, don't you?"

"Wouldn't mind. I've never felt faerie wings."

She twisted around, giving him access. "Be careful. They have a sharp—"

"A sharp edge, I know." Cam trailed his fingers gently along the softer tissue, and tingling pleasure rippled through her wings and down her spine. He sounded awestruck when he spoke again. "They may be a pain, but they're beautiful. Prettiest goblin-slicers I've ever seen."

She snickered. "Goblin-slicers?"

"What do you think these razor edges on your wings are for? They're one of the few things that will cut my skin in goblin form. And my fangs, my claws, are among the few things that can pierce the protection around your tattoos and access your magic."

Destry turned to face him. "I still don't get how you know so much about this stuff. I understand that this is the 'school' you attended last semester. But how do you become king in a few months?"

"I've been coming here for years, Dessie, ever since I turned eleven. Remember my guys-only camping trips with dad?"

How could she forget? They'd leave for a few weeks or even a month, several times a year. Gregory sometimes even took Cam when school was in session, saying the trip was "educational." She'd always resented the time apart.

Cam leaned forward, resting his elbows on his knees. "Those were the alibi whenever Dad brought me here to see my aunt—she runs things when I'm gone—and to learn about my heritage."

"But why was your grandfather determined for a grandson to take over? Couldn't your aunt rule the kingdom?"

"No. Formal rule only resides in the male heir." He glanced at Destry and smiled. "Don't get huffy. It's biology, not chauvinism. The firstborn male of the royal family possesses the physical ability to hold the King's Strength—the fundamental magic of our race—along with a particular talent with willa trees. This inherited magic resides in him and feeds the willas, which in turn feed the rest of our race, until the ruler dies. Then it moves to the next male heir. Because Dad gave up his magic, the King's Strength moved to me when Grandfather passed."

"Still seems unfair to all the girl goblins," Destry said.

"Look who's talking. Faeries are only ruled by a queen, and for the same reason. But you don't see me pouting over the poor male faeries who never have a shot at the crown."

Destry jerked her lower lip in. "Apparently, you decided to take the job."

Cam nodded. "They wanted me to come when I was old enough to take the Oath of Sovereignty—at the beginning of my sophomore year—but I made an extra year with you a condition of accepting the throne."

He'd thought she was important enough to put off coming here? Pleasure washed over her, tainted by a stream of bitterness: long-term, he'd still chosen this over a life in the human world. And Cam hadn't known she was faerie when he accepted.

She was a crummy friend for even having the thought. Why should Cam give up being king to hang out with her at Andy's Restaurant and deal with the messes she made of her life? Destry forced a smile. "I see why you chose this."

He gave her a considering look. "Do you?"

"Sure. I mean, you get to be king. How many people can say that?"

Cam shook his head. "That sort of power is more responsibility than fun."

"Then why?"

"Because eventually, I would've lost the only thing that makes the human world home: the people I love. My magic may not affect Mom now, but the chances go up as my abilities grow. Any committed relationship would require giving up my powers, and the relationship would be built on half-truths. And every day, I expected to see indications that my magic was hurting you...knowing when it happened, I'd have to keep you at arm's length for your own good."

He took her hand. "Coming here meant protecting the people I love *and* making a difference for the goblin people. The best choice was obvious." Cam shot her a mischievous glance. "Plus, here I can transform any time I want."

Destry's heart lightened. Cam had included her in his list of people. "I knew transforming was the real reason. You have zero self-control and wanna Hulk-out whenever the mood strikes."

Cam cocked one eyebrow. "Zero self-control? You threw flaming books, and I didn't transform. I'd get revenge by going full-goblin again, but you'd bolt for it."

She lifted her chin defiantly. "Go ahead. I was only scared last time because I didn't know it was you."

He looked amused. "You think so?"

"I'm a faerie, not a wuss."

"If you're sure..." He released her, and the process began in reverse: getting bigger, skin darkening, teeth elongating. Before she knew it, an enormous goblin loomed in front of her, and Destry's wings were moving at a hum, entirely without her permission. Cam's amusement made sense now. Her knowledge of who occupied that body didn't erase instinct—an instinct that recognized a being not only dangerous, but dangerous to her specifically.

She breathed steadily, forcing her wings to stop fluttering, and tried to look casual. "See? And here you think you're such a big scary monster."

His eyebrows slid upwards. He smiled wider, deliberately baring his fangs. Destry's wings picked up pace again. She smacked his arm. "Cut it out!" Then she massaged her fingers. Hitting Hulked-Out-Cam was less comfortable than smacking plain old Cam. His skin was harder than human skin, though not as granite-like as it appeared.

His rumbling laugh sent chills down her spine. "Are you okay?" He reached for her.

Destry froze, fighting the urge to pull away. She tried to look relaxed, but Cam obviously noticed. He set his hand on the chaise lounge instead.

Shame engulfed her. "I'm fine." She took his hand and held it on her lap, brushing her fingers over the fur on his forearm. It was surprisingly soft. She slid her fingers between his, testing the fit of their hands now. Cam angled his claws to avoid scratching her. Hesitantly, Destry ran a finger down the length of one claw, barely touching the tip—as razor sharp as her wings.

Like the claws from her nightmare.

"Want me to change back?" Cam's voice was pitched to be gentle, as much as a gravelly growl could be. What had her face had given away?

"No. I want my instincts to learn to recognize you as a friend. Can't be scared out of my wings every time we get together."

He frowned. "Destry...it can't be the same here as it was at home."

"Because...because I'm a faerie? I know goblins don't like faeries, but I thought that wouldn't matter to you."

"Of course it doesn't. But I have enemies in the fey court. Tell people you're friends with anyone of my race, and you'll be ostracized—at best. At worst, they might use you as a political tool to get to me."

Cam's frown was more intimidating as a goblin. Destry squelched the urge towards instant agreement. "So...what? I go back and say you gave me permission to use the firewell, and we ignore each other?"

"No. But we need to be smart. You shouldn't tell people we know each other from before, let alone how close we are. As for seeing each other, possessing the main firewell grants a kingdom certain rights. For example, the race holding the power can demand that a supplicant take magic lessons from the ruler of that race."

"You want to teach me faerie magic?"

Cam chuckled, sending more chills along her spine. "I want to teach you goblin magic. The law was designed to encourage understanding between races—kind of important when you're crossing paths all the time. No one ever invokes that requirement, though."

Her shoulders slumped. "Guess it's a bad solution."

"Nah. My subjects expect some oddity from me, being raised in the human world. We could meet a couple times a week."

Destry nodded, although she wanted more time than that.

"Don't look so depressed. It'll be more fun than math homework." Cam grinned, fangs bright against his granite face.

Now that she'd recalled that stupid nightmare, Destry's body was on high alert. A shiver shook her, and Cam couldn't miss it, with their hands entwined. His lips tightened. Without another word, he changed into the Camden she knew.

Guilt heated her cheeks. "You didn't have to do that. I said I wanted to—"

"Drop it, Des." He stood. "We should get out of this room so the burnt smell can air out. C'mon, I'll show you my favorite place in the entire kingdom."

PERSPECTIVE

The raven-haired girl sat at the desk, making notes in a leather-bound book, when they exited the audience chamber. Destry wondered what excuse Cam would make for leaving with his supposed enemy. But he just said, "I'll be back in an hour, Tyla. Cover for me?"

She examined her book with an air of exasperation. "I'll have to move that meeting with the dwarfish council. Goblin gourds, Cam. Do you have any idea what a headache that will be?"

"Yes. But I have every confidence in your ability to do it." He smiled ingratiatingly.

Tyla pursed her lips. "Fine. If you bring me willa berries."

"Done." Cam offered Destry his arm in an old-fashioned, courtly gesture.

She took it, feeling silly. Was he playing around? Or did Cam have to act this way because he was king? As they started down the hall, he called over his shoulder—like an afterthought— "Would you feed Rupert, too?"

The girl shot to her feet, hands on hips. "Camden Darkwater, I don't have time to placate the dwarves *and* feed that earth-cursed bird."

"But he loves you. It's that whole aviary connection." Tyla opened her mouth, and Cam added, "I'll get you extra willa berries. Promise!"

He pulled Destry around a corner before the girl could answer. She heard Tyla mutter, "Goblin gourds!" again.

"So," Destry said knowingly. "You still have Rupert?"

"Yes." Cam sounded a little grumpy.

"And he's still biting you?"

"Yes." More surly this time.

"But he doesn't bite Tyla?" Cam shot her a dark look, and she sniggered. "Why don't you give him to someone he likes?"

"I've never had an animal dislike me. Rupert will come around." Cam seemed to be trying to convince himself.

As they rounded a second corner, they came face to face with an older woman gowned in clinging silk. The dress emphasized her long, lean muscles. The woman's gaze fell on Destry, but she looked contemptuous rather than surprised.

Destry froze, nerves back on high alert. Her fingers convulsed around Cam's arm. The woman stepped forward, too close for comfort even though she was still several feet away. Within seconds, her eyes morphed from human to feline. Her lips parted in a predatory smile, displaying rows of needle-like fangs. Destry's wings picked up speed (without permission...again) and her palms began to heat.

Cam cleared his throat. It sounded more like a growl, and the cat woman's eyes flickered to him. His expression—so severe he might as well have been in goblin form—sent yet another shiver through Destry. There was nothing casual or friendly in his posture now.

The woman swept a curtsy, somehow making clear that Destry wasn't included in the gesture of respect. "Your Majesty. I heard there was a new supplicant for the firewell. In fact, I smelled her all the way through the castle." Another glance at Cam's chilly expression. "Fire types always give off whiffs of brimstone."

Cam cocked an eyebrow. "Lady Sylka. Good of you to stay abreast of the doings in *my* castle. You'll be interested to know that this particular bit of brimstone will be coming here regularly."

Sylka's eyes narrowed. "Indeed?"

Destry breathed carefully, forcing her wings to slow. No need for this woman to know how easily she'd frightened her. She was about to answer, but Cam shot her a warning glance.

His posture shifted again, almost imperceptibly. If Destry hadn't been holding his arm, she might have missed the way his stance changed from haughty to intimidating. He said coolly, "Indeed. It's been years since a king forced the fey to send one of their precious students for goblin lessons. An amusing departure from the norm, I think, and educational for all concerned."

The woman's expression wavered, like she couldn't decide whether Cam was inviting her to laugh at his power over the fey...or indicating that she needed a lesson herself.

Cam continued smoothly, "Since you're the second to know—after Tyla, of course—" That comment definitely felt pointed. Did the woman have some rivalry with Cam's assistant? "I hope you'll spread the word. Our treaty with the faerie kingdom will be *strictly* observed. Wouldn't want to scare off our fey visitor." He bent a meaningful look on the cat woman.

Her lips tightened, but her goblin features melted away. "Let me extend the first welcome. What a pleasure to have fey walk our hallowed halls again."

Destry gave her a shaky nod. Sylka laughed. "Don't be afraid, my dear. Our king has spoken. No one shall use you for a snack with their afternoon tea."

Yeah, that sounded more like a threat. Destry's palms seemed to blaze hotter, but she stood tall. "Thank you for the warm welcome, Lady Sylka."

Her sarcasm sparked grudging amusement in the goblin's eyes. "So entertaining when one's pet is clever, don't you think, King Darkwater? But not quite clever enough. His Majesty has leave to use my given name. *Inferiors*, however, must address me as Lady Lynxwood."

Heat tightened Destry's chest, crawled up her face. She longed to throw the woman's first name back at her, minus her title this time. But what would happen if she did? Wouldn't it look suspicious if Cam tolerated disrespect from a faerie to her goblin "superior?" "My apologies, Lady Lynxwood."

Sylka offered a barely-there nod of acknowledgment, smoothing one languid hand along her already perfect hair. "Enjoy the firewell, little brimstone." She swept another curtsy to Cam, then strolled away.

"Shall we go, Destry Firewings?" Cam's voice was more commanding than inviting.

At the end of the hall, he lifted a tapestry, revealing a doorway; they slipped through it into a much dimmer hall. The second they were hidden from view, Cam jerked his arm loose. She stumbled. He gripped her shoulders, steadying her. "Sorry. Didn't mean to pull away so fast. But you've been roasting my arm ever since that earth-cursed woman showed her fangs."

Destry glanced at her palms, where a faint red glow was fading. "I...I didn't mean to."

"It's fine, Dessie. Controlling new powers is hard." He rubbed his arm surreptitiously, though. She groaned, hiding her face in her hands. Cam pulled them down. "It's Sylka's fault, not yours. She shouldn't even be here today. It's well-known protocol to clear the castle when a faerie supplicates for the firewell."

"So, the place isn't always this empty?" She forced a grin. "I was certain you'd gotten rid of everyone so you could eat me."

Cam looked...embarrassed? "I won't deny that the supplicant set-up—walking alone through the forest, to a mostly-abandoned castle, to meet the monster king in a darkened room—is intended to give fey students a healthy respect for goblinkind. That's especially important with the willa grove and school so close together. But we also clear the castle to avoid conflicts. A freaked-out fire fey running into an unfriendly goblin? It's a recipe for disaster."

"Like roasting your best friend's arm."

He sighed. "Enough apologizing. Unless you want *me* to start the litany of things I regret, too. I've never felt much conflict about following the established protocols for meeting the fey...until I scared my best friend out of her wings doing it." He tipped her chin up, eyes intent on hers. "For the record, Destry—you are no one's inferior."

In that moment, everything else disappeared: wings and kings and rank and pretense. It was just her and Cam, wrapped in quiet shadow, his fingers gentle beneath her chin. His words soothed the sting of Sylka's demands and eased the hot tightness in her chest. She wasn't willing to ruin that by discussing the new complications in their friendship. Time to change the subject.

She stepped back, gesturing at the stone walls surrounding them, closer and dimmer than the other halls. "Are we in some kind of secret passageway?"

Cam half-smiled, tipping his hand in a *sort-of* gesture. "It's impossible to have truly secret passages in a castle full of goblins. Our affinity with the earth grants us certain abilities. We excel at creating and sensing hidden spaces. This place is a warren of hidden hallways, though there's an etiquette to who's allowed to use them. It's a good way to get some privacy...or get away from my more close-minded subjects." He rubbed one hand along the back of his neck. "Sorry about the royal act. I can't afford to display any vulnerability around people like Sylka."

"You acted really different around her than Tyla."

"*Tyla* is trustworthy." A real grin this time, a slash of white against the shadowy rectangle of his face. "Plus, after that fire show in my chambers, I'm one hundred percent certain she eavesdropped long enough to know who you are."

"Tyla...Tyla heard everything? All the things *you* said about *me*?"

He chafed her arms. "Officially, Tyla's my assistant, but her unofficial job is staying informed about the happenings and secrets in this castle. Still, she has a sense of honor. She won't have listened longer than necessary—just enough to be certain you aren't a threat."

Which didn't reassure Destry about the stuff she preferred to remain private, but she dropped the subject. Cam was a king in a kingdom of goblins. Of course things would be different here. The thought left her uneasy.

He started down the hall, boots clicking. Destry didn't follow, and he turned back. "Coming?"

She looked pointedly at a lantern hanging from a hook on the wall.

Cam snickered. "Faerie blindness. I almost forgot." He lifted the lantern and opened its door, blowing away dust.

Glaring, Destry crossed her arms. "Can all goblins see in the dark as well as you? Or is it just an irritating—"

"*Solasten*," Cam murmured. An orb of golden light popped into being above his cupped hand. He wafted the light into the lantern and said the incantation twice more, adding the new orbs. They bumped gently against one another, competing for space. He shut the door with a *snick*. "Ready?"

The passageway rambled, branching and twisting and turning, though Cam seemed certain of their route. As they neared a fork, he said, "And yes, exceptional night vision is a goblin thing. Mine is worse than most, thanks to my human heritage."

Destry tore her gaze from the magic lantern. "Cam? Don't they care that you're half-human? It sure matters to the faeries."

"That's because faeries—the ones in power, anyway—are elitist snobs. They don't want to acknowledge their human roots." Destry frowned, and Cam added, "Even a full-faerie is part human, same as a full-goblin. Has anyone explained how our races came about?"

"Not yet."

Cam snorted. "Not ever, if they had their way. A long time ago, it was common knowledge that parts of the earth were magical: certain trees, gemstones, waters. They held leftover energy from creation. And some humans were drawn to them and had the capacity to channel that energy."

He turned left at the fork, unhesitating. "For generations, human magicians worked with these objects, until their bodies started changing—a result of absorbing magic. The changes scared some of them. They stopped working spells, lost their new forms, and became 'normal' as most people see it."

Destry's foot caught on her hem. She stumbled, heard the fabric rip. "What about the ones who didn't stop?"

"The changes became part of them. They no longer needed magical objects, except for particularly complex magic. Those who were attuned to earthier items took on goblin qualities. The ones who favored water took on faerie qualities. And they passed those on to us, their descendants."

"Doesn't the human blood affect your magic?"

Cam shook his head. "Goblins believe in honoring our heritage. We haven't tried to remove ourselves from it the way faeries do. Might be why our magic doesn't split like yours." His face grew pensive. "Have they...have they found your partner yet?"

Destry nodded. "His name is Tristan."

"What do you think of him?"

She understood Cam's unstated question: *How do you feel, knowing you have to commit to this guy or lose your magic?* "He's nice. But I don't know him well yet." Meaning she had no idea how she really felt.

They reached a heavy door. Cam pushed it open. Evening light washed over them, comforting after the dim corridor. The forest of white trees stood sentinel a short distance away. "I know how you feel," he said. "When I accepted the throne, I also accepted that my marriage would be based on things besides mutual affection."

"You mean an arranged marriage?" Destry's wings beat faster.

"Noble goblin marriages are arranged according to human blood to keep us from getting too purely goblin. We don't want to end up like you faeries—so far removed from our humanity that our magic becomes unstable. For the goblin king, it's even more important to marry someone with recent human blood in her ancestry. Because of Mom, I'll have more leeway, but it still matters."

It seemed wrong, Cam marrying some unknown girl because she had the right amount of human blood. "What would make you accept that?"

Cam caught her wings along the bottom, stilling them. He gestured to the pale trees. "This. Come on, I'll introduce you."

The trees arched across the hard-packed path, more welcoming than they'd seemed on the walk to the castle. Destry followed Cam into the forest, craning her neck to catch details she'd missed in her earlier terror. The foliage created a shimmering, sun-kissed canopy. Transparent leaves glimmered with iridescent color. Like faerie wings, their colors changed according to the angle of the light. Cam stuck his hands in his pockets, his eyes on Destry instead of the willas. "Your wings finally stopped fluttering."

"The willas are comforting." Surprise flickered across his face, but she ignored it, running her hand along the nearest tree's trunk.

Sensations rushed through her: pleasure, recognition, welcome, homecoming. As quickly as they'd begun, they ended. Destry's fingers played over the tree's smooth surface. Even without the mental display, she would have recognized its sentience. It pulsed with life, like a heartbeat. "Amazing," she whispered.

Cam smiled up at the crisscross of white branches and stained-glass leaves. "The trees *are* incredible. Each one is an individual, yet they share a collective memory. Their magic feeds the earth, which in turn feeds goblin magic."

"Is earth your element, or fire?"

"Earth, like most goblins. That's why the majority of us grow things. Our kingdom has the most beautiful gardens I've ever seen."

A neighboring tree stretched one branch towards Cam; he patted it absently. Destry watched the tree she'd been stroking do the same. "Jealous," Cam chided. He pointed to Destry's tree. "This guy wants nothing to do with me unless another willa gets some attention." He ducked under the branches and took Destry's hand. "Come meet my favorite."

He led her off the path, towards the center of the forest. Destry stumbled often enough to set Cam grinning. He poked the new rip in the waistband of her skirt. "It's a talent, you know—tripping over nothing."

She wondered whether she could smack him without making the trees mad.

The willas opened onto a small clearing, and Destry forgot her pique. In the center stood a willa, bigger than any of the others. Its branches parted in the center, waving up and out like nature's version of faerie wings.

Cam released her hand. "She's called Wings, for obvious reasons. There's no way to be sure, because of the collective consciousness, but we think she was the first willa ever planted." He rested his hands and forehead against the tree's trunk, closing his eyes. The tree seemed to lean towards him, branches gravitating in Cam's direction.

Destry smiled. "Looks like she missed you."

"She did. This is usually one of the first places I visit when I return." He opened his eyes and pulled away, though he kept one hand on the trunk. "She wants you to come up."

"Up?"

"Into her branches."

Destry swallowed. "You know my answer."

"You have wings, Des." She set her jaw, and Cam rolled his eyes. "Talk about—"

"Yes, talk about irony," she snapped. "A clumsy, chubby faerie who's afraid of heights."

A smile played across Cam's sculpted lips. "Nothing wrong with any of that. Would you feel safe enough to come up with *me*? It's incredible. And Wings hardly ever makes this offer—even to other goblins."

Nothing like the promise of exclusivity. "Fine." It couldn't be worse than their rope ladder.

The tree lowered some branches to shoulder height. Cam twined an arm through one and slid the other arm beneath her wings, pulling her close. "Try not to slice me. We have healers, but that necessitates explanations."

They flew through the air, with no more warning than that. Destry scrunched her eyes closed and clutched Cam. She felt the tree swing them up, stop, and lower them onto something solid. Cam squeezed her gently. "Open your eyes. You need to see where you're going."

She forced them open. Cam's face was inches away, slate green eyes smiling into hers. "I'll help you along this branch so you can sit next to the trunk. Move your feet and remember that I won't drop you."

Destry kept her gaze on Cam's face, despite the temptation to see how high up they were. She might freeze if she did. In less than a minute, she was nestled in the V-shaped space between branch and trunk. Cam settled next to her, legs swinging, shoulders relaxed. Branches slid up around them, cradling Destry and creating a net below.

She took a deep breath in, out, releasing some of her tension. The fear of falling bothered her more than the actual height. Secured like this, she only felt dizzy if she looked down. Instead, Destry looked out over the tops of the trees. Sunlight gilded the glistening leaves. "Okay, I see why you like this."

Cam patted the branches. "This net is new. She senses your fear and wants to make you feel better. Wings likes you."

"She said so?"

"Not in words. Willas don't 'talk' the way we do. They communicate, mainly through emotions."

Destry remembered her dream, the sensation that the tree was trying to tell her something. "How do you understand them?"

"It's a goblin gift...specifically, a royal goblin gift. Few others have the ability."

Destry stroked the willa's smooth bark. "Tell her I like her, too."

Cam chuckled. "I don't think that needs translation." He plucked a cluster of pearlescent berries from beneath a grouping of leaves. "Willa berries. They're hard to get, because most of the trees aren't willing to share. I bribe Tyla with them."

"You mentioned a Tyla when you told me about 'school.' Guess that was her."

He offered her a berry. "We do apprenticeships instead of school here. More advanced goblins teach younger ones who share their interests. There are tests to move up: Apprentice, Journeyman, Master. Tyla has apprenticed at the castle since she was twelve. Once she achieved Journeyman, I requested her as my personal assistant."

They sat in the tree awhile longer, eating the sweet fruit and watching the sun set. "You realize I'll barely be able to find my way back?" Destry said.

"I'll walk you as far as I can. But don't tell anyone. Let the other faeries think I kept you late to make you stumble through a dark forest alone."

Destry chewed her lip, remembering Sylka, remembering Fey Elena castigating them as monsters. "Cam? Are most goblins like you?"

He hesitated. "There's no simple answer to that. I'm trying to nudge my kingdom towards better relations with the fey. Most goblins are willing, but some aren't, and there are centuries of bad blood. Ultimately, all goblins are dangerous. Don't ever forget that."

"But once they know me, I won't have to worry, right? They'll realize I'm harmless."

Cam snorted. "Says the untrained girl who burned my books, sliced my ear, and roasted my arm. Faeries are the farthest thing from harmless I've ever seen. By the time your education is finished, you'll have power blasting from your palms, razor-sharp wings, and an arsenal of knowledge. We're two races with an uneasy peace between us. Neither side will ever relax their guard."

"But why do faeries and goblins hate each other? Aren't they—we—all magic creatures?"

Cam popped another berry into his mouth. "Competition, mostly. The Fold is the only magical sanctuary of its kind, and centuries ago, there were a lot more faeries and goblins. Stick a bunch of people together competing for limited resources, add physical traits and magical talents that make each side the worst possible threat to the other, and you'll have conflict. At this point, the attitudes are so ingrained, and the history of conflict is so long, that few people ask 'Why?'"

"But there's an entire world outside of the Fold!" Destry gestured towards the horizon.

"There are also a lot of humans, and people fear what they don't understand...or they exploit it. We've always needed a sanctuary."

"Since we all need it, seems like everyone could agree to get along."

He laughed. "That's sweet, Des. Entirely naïve—but sweet. Our treaty is the closest thing we'll get. Goblins and faeries have disliked each other since before the days of the Grimm brothers."

"The guys who wrote the fairy tales?"

"'Wrote' may be a stretch. Those stories obviously came from the fey. They're ridiculously one-sided, with faeries as the good guys, goblins as the bad guys—even when we aren't named. Sometimes we're trolls, sometimes ogres, sometimes a big bad werewolf waiting to eat the little girl in the red hood. Which is, quite frankly, disgusting."

"How could they mistake you for all those different creatures?" Destry asked.

"Goblins are shape-shifters. You saw Sylka. Not everyone transforms the way I do. Some look like animals or have qualities associated with the earth." His face pulled into disgruntled lines. "Besides, the faeries didn't mistake us for those other creatures. They just didn't want to sound as prejudiced as they are."

"At least they're only stories." Destry tried not to laugh at Cam's expression.

"Most of those 'stories' really happened—though not the way faeries tell 'em." He wrapped an arm around her. "Time to go. Stay away any longer, and they'll think I drained your magic and buried the leftovers in the forest."

Destry held on tight as the branches lowered them to the ground. "I'll tell everyone what you said: the mean, scary goblin king wanted to make me pay for using the firewell."

He cocked one eyebrow. "You're more frightening than anything I've seen in these woods."

The walk back wasn't bad. Cam held her arm, stabilizing her uncertain footing, until they reached the forest's edge. "Can you make it from here?" he asked. "The fey can't see me escorting you."

Destry pointed at the faerie lights—balls of color similar to the ones in Cam's lamp—hovering above the cobbled pathway. "I'll be fine. You...you won't forget...about asking for lessons? I promise to act upset."

He chafed her shoulders. "I won't forget. This is the best thing that's happened to me in months. Besides, you might like goblin magic."

"Not likely. I'm not even good at faerie magic. Better when I do it with Tristan, but mostly because he's carrying me."

Cam lifted a finger, mock-scolding. "Study and make good grades, or I'm going full-goblin every time we meet. Your wings will never stop fluttering."

Grinning, Destry flicked the sharp edges. They slid together threateningly. "Better keep your distance, then."

Cam pulled her close. He kissed her cheek, ruffled her hair, then spun her towards the fey school. "Behave, Dessie. I'll see you soon."

Fey Elena—eyebrows drawn tight—was pacing the front steps when Destry stumbled up the path. She accepted Destry's explanation about a long interview and finding her way in the dark with an irritated, "Typical goblin behavior." Then the headmistress patted her shoulder. "But you received access to the firewell, which is all that matters."

After returning Fey Elena's pocket watch, Destry hurried to the girls' dorms; she found Tristan and Sara waiting on the stairs. Tristan pointed at her wings, still waving conspicuously in the air. "So, there are a few things that scare you."

Destry laughed nervously. "I think the goblin king would scare anybody."

Tristan took her hand. It felt strange after holding Cam's wider one. "You missed dinner. Trudy has something for you."

In the kitchen, between bites of fey-spiced chicken and sweet potatoes, Destry gave them an edited version of her visit to the goblin realm. Her friends might not be the kind of threat Cam worried about, but were they discreet enough to know the truth? She couldn't be sure. So Destry described Cam only in goblin form, told them about the castle and the forest and the girl called Tyla, and explained how she'd walked back in the dark—though she pretended to have made the trip alone.

Eventually, Trudy shooed them off to the dorms. Most of the storm faeries were eager to hear what had happened. By the time she repeated the tale, Destry was weaving with exhaustion. In her room, she let the fancy dress fall into a puddle on the floor and collapsed into bed.

HALF-TRUTH

✦

"**D**estry Adams. I need to speak with you."

Destry was absorbed in her current magic lesson: using energy strands to reflect light at Tristan. Fey Elena's comment took a minute to register. She released the strands and looked at the headmistress, standing in the doorway to their private study room.

Why did the woman look so stern?

Admittedly, Destry and Tristan had been unproductive most of the morning. They'd snuck outside to retrieve their last two brownies; then, relaxed and happy, Destry asked Tristan to teach her the reflecting spell. She'd been considering sharing the truth about Cam when the headmistress showed up.

But surely Fey Elena didn't know about their wasted hours. Destry followed the headmistress to her office, twisting her braid between her fingers. Fey Elena waved her inside with a flick of the hand, then closed and locked the door. "I need to know exactly what transpired between you and the goblin king yesterday."

Destry knit her brows. "Why?"

"Because he's done what no goblin royalty has done in decades and commanded you to attend him at the castle for personal lessons. I received the missive a half hour ago." The headmistress gestured towards the desk, indicating a letter with a broken wax seal. "Because while he has that right, the goblins—and, indeed, the faeries—rarely exercise that prerogative. Because he might have the same suspicion about your descent that many do and seek a faerie bride! Take your pick, child, any of them are a concern."

My descent? Does Fey Elena know who my father is?

She opened her mouth to ask, but the headmistress began pacing, cutting her off. "If he intends such a maneuver, then we must consider ways of circumventing it."

Destry frowned. "I could refuse, right?"

"Royalty is royalty, goblin or not."

That sounded like a "no." She debated before settling on a half-truth. "The goblin king...used to live next door to me. We've known each other for four years, only neither of us realized what the other was. I think the situation is funny to him."

Fey Elena halted mid-pace and stared. Then her face crumpled—into laughter. The woman laughed until tears came to her eyes. "This explains quite a bit. Quite a bit. Child, you do have the most atrocious luck."

She sat at her desk, gesturing for Destry to take the student chair. "This is a relief. I've been extremely worried over you. I never thought I'd be glad to see a student subjected to early goblin influence."

Destry didn't respond. The prejudice irritated her, now that she understood more.

Sobering, the older faerie continued, "Understand this: multiple things can affect the element your magic chooses. Lineage, temperament, ability...but two main conditions lead to the adoption of fire. One is to be exposed to goblin influence, to form sympathy for someone of their race. Goblins possess a greater affinity for fire than faeries. I assume you liked the boy."

Destry nodded. It was better than admitting she and Cam were practically family. Fey Elena nodded too. "What would normally be frowned upon is good in this case. Because the other likelihood is to be the illegitimate offspring of the Imperial family."

"Who?"

"A family of particular political importance. They frequently possess an affinity with fire."

"I couldn't have become a fire sign any other way?"

"Possibly," Fey Elena said. "But given your appearance, I doubt other explanations would ever be considered."

"My appearance?"

The headmistress said reluctantly, "You have physical attributes the family is noted for. Your hair, your eyes, your facial structure. Riamon noticed the resemblance during our meeting at your old school."

Destry leaned forward eagerly. "You're saying you know which family I'm from?" She'd come to the faerie realm with an almost unacknowledged, half-ashamed hope: to learn her father's identity. In her bitterness, Beverly had burned every picture of him long before giving birth. Destry didn't even know his name.

Fey Elena slashed her hand through the air. "No! I'm saying it's good we can rule out that possibility. Befriending a goblin is better than finding out you're a by-blow of the Imperial family."

Her words fell heavily between them. "The Imperials were the original ruling class of our society, until the reigning sovereign decided that the people should be ruled by a wider swath of the population. She handed the Queen's Line down, intending it to move through all families —not only the nobility. Whenever a sovereign relinquishes the title, the entire population gathers for a ceremony. Our communal magic chooses the next ruler."

"That sounds like a good thing," Destry said tentatively. "Why wouldn't I want to be part of that family?"

"To understand that, you must understand how Liselle—our current queen—came to power. Her mother was our last queen. When she relinquished the crown, she declared that the guiding magic had already chosen her daughter. The magic was handed over without being exposed to the populace.

"Many accepted the decision. Liselle and her mother were well-liked and politically savvy, and Liselle can trace her lineage to the Imperial family on her father's side—a distant relation, but enough to make the populace like her by association.

"The dissident families were of little political importance: people who'd grown tired of watching the Queen's Line pass from one branch of the current royal family to another, who were tired of our society's belief that noble families—generally full-faeries—are better suited to rule. They revere the Imperial family's willingness to share power and believe the throne should be restored to its original governors. They wish to depose our current ruler in favor of a true Imperial...especially a half-blood, to prove that full-faerie magic is not necessary to rule."

She gave Destry a pointed look. "As you can imagine, this makes the establishment nervous. Were you a member of the Imperial family, you would gain formidable enemies because of your lineage. That's far worse than some teenage disdain because you choose friends in...unusual places."

Destry understood the warning: if she ever had to name a reason for her fire preference, it would be better to claim Cam as her friend than to consider the Imperials as her family.

Fey Elena chuckled again, quietly. "The goblin king, of all people. No wonder you went undiscovered for so long. Goblin presence, goblin magic, suppresses and masks undeveloped faerie magic. And the goblin king is the ruler of his race. Had he not taken up long-term residence here, we never would have found you."

"Lucky me," Destry said.

The headmistress narrowed her eyes, like she suspected sarcasm. "Now, regarding these lessons, we can hardly refuse. However, we should keep your prior friendship with the goblin king between ourselves unless circumstances dictate its disclosure. Friendships with those in high places—they can win you enemies as well. Do you understand?"

Destry nodded. "What do I say when people ask me about the lessons?"

"What you already explained to me: that it amuses the king to use you as a plaything to ruffle our feathers here at the school. There are worse things to have hurt than your pride, and you might find a surprising amount of admiration. The goblin king frightens the wings off most faeries."

Cam would have been flattered by Headmistress Elena's assessment, had he heard it. He couldn't afford to seem weak to the faerie realm. It was hard to be a young king, even harder to be a young king raised outside the realms of magic.

Politically, that was an advantage. Most of Cam's constituents approved of his time in the human world and the fresh perspective it lent him. But among the nobility, where traditions were set, it created difficulties...especially among the older generations, who preferred a more mature ruler.

Aunt Val was an excellent advisor; she had a near-equal hand in ruling the goblin kingdom. While some kings might hide this, Cam didn't. People would realize, sooner or later, so in his coronation speech, he acknowledged his inexperience and intent to rely on those with greater expertise until he could shoulder the burden alone.

Brumal, an old friend of his father's—who was also Cam's chancellor—had discouraged that bit of candor. So had several other advisors, who probably hoped to control him without the kingdom realizing. He'd done it anyway, and his humility won many supporters.

Still, Cam needed to wean himself from his aunt's aid eventually. She had no complaints —Aunt Val had been indispensable for too long to be shuffled aside—but timing was important. While he was young, the kingdom admired Cam's willingness to learn; a few years down the road, leaning too heavily on someone else would brand him as incompetent.

At the moment, he especially couldn't afford that. Cam had a problem to resolve—one that brought him to the desk in his private audience chambers, the morning after Destry's surprise visit.

Of course, he quickly gave up the desk and began pacing. Tyla nearly hit him with the door when she came in with the day's correspondence. She tossed her bag on a chair and slipped back into the hall. Cam heard her telling someone goodbye, a masculine voice answering. Then a brief silence, which probably meant Tyla was getting a more satisfactory farewell. She looked pleased when she came inside.

Cam eyed her. "Let me guess. Erik?"

"How'd you know?"

"I thought he had the advantage when I saw you together last week. How about the guy in the blacksmith's wing? You still leading him on?"

She tossed her head. "I never 'led him on.' He knew from the beginning we wouldn't be tangling roots."

Well, he'd give her that. It was common knowledge around the castle that achieving her Master's rank took priority, even over her romantic life. Tyla made sure of it.

"What about you?" She poked his shoulder. "Have you deigned to notice any of the girls swooning at your feet?"

Cam snorted. "If anyone is swooning, it's over my title. Or because I grew up eating hamburgers and using a cell phone—so *exotic*."

"Don't forget that game. Football?" She assumed a breathy voice, batting her lashes in painfully accurate parody of one specific courtier. "You can teach me how to play, Your Majesty. I don't mind a little...contact."

Cam shook his head. "She seemed shocked when that didn't work."

Laughing, Tyla retrieved her bag. "She's an unobservant twit. Anyone who pays close attention knows you aren't a 'body-first' type of person."

He flushed. Tyla's observation might be accurate, but it didn't feel quite comfortable for her to say it out loud.

She glanced up from digging the day's correspondence out of her bag. Her gold eyes softened. "Nothing shameful about that, Cam."

He knew that. He didn't actually want to be a different person. But old habits died hard. He forced a smile. "Either way, I'm not looking. Every time I spend more than ten minutes with a girl, Brumal evaluates her for an alliance. Better to avoid the drama."

To Tyla, that probably seemed like business as usual. She'd been raised in the world of goblin nobility, where arranged marriages were the norm. She slid her hair behind one ear, gold eyes curious. "There's no one you like?"

Cam shrugged. "Not well enough to promise my roots to them."

He'd grown up hearing Dad murmur, "My roots begin and end with you," in Mom's ear. He'd always assumed it was some private joke—a silly way for a certified Master Gardener to say *I love you*. Not until coming to the goblin world had he understood the true significance of those words.

Goblin culture revolved around the willas, whose vast interlocking root system allowed the trees to communicate over long distances and offer each other physical support. If a willa was injured, the other trees would weaken themselves to support it back to health. Few willas could thrive away from the mycelium-like underground network. *My roots begin and end with you* meant more than a declaration of love. It encompassed the deepest dedication, need, and interconnectedness one person could share with another, and it was never said casually.

Tyla offered him a rueful smile. "Tough being at the top, isn't it?" She tossed a handful of missives on the desk. "What's got you pacing this time?"

He reached past the new correspondence to a small scroll with a broken seal. "This was waiting when I returned from my visit to the dwarf cities."

She scanned it, frowning. "From the headmistress at the faerie school?"

Cam nodded. "There's another like it, received before I left to visit my parents. She said the same thing: a faerie girl has gone missing, last seen headed for the river. Because of the close proximity to our forest, she asked me if the willas remembered anything. With the second letter, she included sketches so I could give the willas a visual reference."

He offered her two squares of parchment. Tyla's eyes widened. "These girls look—"

"Pretty similar, yeah. Blonde hair, brown eyes. Both storm faeries, although their elements were different. Both older students out after curfew—probably to take advantage of stormy weather."

Tyla's expression was entirely too perceptive. "In other words, like that fire faerie...the one you intend to have over for lessons."

Cam sighed. "I'll tell you the whole story later, okay? But yes, she fits the profile. The first letter, I went to see the trees. They didn't have anything. This second one, Aunt Val answered, explaining that she doesn't have the ability to communicate with the willas. So I spoke with them this morning. They're uneasy. I caught images of the last girl and another one, a different girl from either two."

He retrieved the parchment. "Those girls are going off the grid too close to our borders. We could be blamed. I'm sending a message to the headmistress, and I could post sentries in the forest, but I can't post sentries on faerie land—which the river is. Our people step over that line, and something still happens to another girl...you can see where it might end up."

"Then what do you intend to do?"

He made a face. "The last time I got a letter from Headmistress Elena, I sent out two responses: one to the headmistress, the other to the faerie queen, informing both of our efforts to help and the lack of information from the willas. I wanted to keep things transparent. But though Headmistress Elena sent a letter thanking me, Queen Liselle never answered, so I sent another. That time, I received a form response, saying someone in the palace received my missive and would pass it to the queen—which is odd, because I marked it as Liselle's personal correspondence. I plan to send another, sharing the new information we've uncovered and suggesting they station sentries near the river. That's all I can do, officially."

"And what do you intend to do unofficially?"

"I could use an extra pair of ears...someone to listen in on conversations, see if there's any talk about two lost girls from the school, or a third one. And there are ravens all over the place, Ty. Even in Si'fliegen."

She wrinkled her nose. "Little ones."

Cam raised an eyebrow. "You can't do it?"

"I just don't want to. But I will."

He grinned. "You're such a good goblin subject."

"You're such a crummy goblin friend."

"Hey, I brought you berries last night."

"I'd have had more if you weren't sharing with your pretty faerie girl."

Cam laughed. "I'll get you a whole bucket for this, okay?"

"You better." She picked up her bag. "Lady Val is waiting for me."

"I'm disappointed. I thought I'd get to see you transform."

He meant it—few goblins could shift both shape and size. His assistant's ability to go from normal-sized raven to a bird larger than most adults placed her in a special category of magical talent. But Tyla clearly thought he was teasing; her lips quirked into a sardonic smile. "Not this time. Sorry, Your Majesty."

"Being king isn't all it's cracked up to be." He sobered as he walked her to the door. "Ty...be careful. Your talons don't look like normal raven claws. They're too sharp, too shiny. Be sure the faeries don't notice."

She tossed her head, light catching the obsidian waves. The cinnamon scent of her perfume wafted over him. "I've been spying since before I was officially allowed to spy. Save the overprotective act for that sweet faerie thing."

He grimaced. "About that..."

Tyla rolled her eyes. "By the first goblin, Cam. I already know to keep my mouth shut. If you did the same, I could go."

He closed his mouth with exaggerated care and opened the door for her. Tyla swept a mock curtsy. "Your Majesty. Thank you for your time." She hurried down the corridor and out of sight.

Magic Lesson

✦

It was three days before Tyla brought Cam any information, right before his first lesson with Destry. Cam was pulling out some basic spell books when the goblin girl flew in the window to the private audience chamber. She alighted on the floor. Her bird form turned human, glossy feathers melding into shining hair and a black dress. Tyla smiled archly. "Lucky we have enchantments on our clothing. I'd hate to explain to an unexpected visitor, like your faerie girl, why I'm in here with the goblin king naked."

He didn't rise to her bait. "Or you could go to your room and dress first—if that were the case."

Tyla poked the books. "You're no fun. Want to hear what I found out?"

"Tell me while I get ready."

She cocked her head to one side. "Why are you getting these things out? Aren't the lessons just an excuse to see Destry?"

"They're the cover, yes. But her school will expect her to learn something."

"Defeats the purpose, if you do spellwork the entire time."

Cam smiled. "This is business as usual. I've spent more time than I care to count helping Des with assignments."

Tyla's eyes narrowed, as if measuring his response. Though he'd explained his relationship with Destry, the goblin girl probably wanted more details. He lifted an eyebrow. "Weren't you about to tell me what you learned?"

With a huff, Tyla slid onto a stool at the work table. "There wasn't much to hear. But what I did hear was interesting."

Cam placed the books on the table, the scent of leather wafting from their covers. He fetched the jars of water he'd enchanted earlier and a cloth measuring tape. He gestured for Tyla to continue.

"None of the Academy students seem to realize those girls disappeared," she said. "Both the girls from school were half-faeries—one from full-human parents, one with an unknown faerie father—and the second girl's magic partner isn't even worried."

In the center of the room, Cam measured out an exact square, ten feet on every side. "That's odd. Magic partners depend on one another entirely." Destry's partner hovered on the fringe of his thoughts, irritating.

Tyla nodded. "The girl who disappeared most recently is a student rep at court. Her partner is under the impression that she left with some other kids—nobles schooled at the palace—to observe a diplomatic mission. But when I scouted the palace, I didn't hear a thing about a group of kids gone, to learn diplomacy or anything else."

Cam placed the jars of water precisely at each corner of his square. The lazy afternoon sunlight made their contents sparkle. He double checked his measurements, then grabbed his last item—a large metal tray filled with sand and pieces of dry wood—and placed it in the center of the square. "What about the guy whose partner has been missing a couple of months?"

"He's more concerned." Tyla grabbed a handful of dragontree nuts from a bowl on the table, jiggling them in her palm. "The girl had a history as a runaway before they found her, and their commitment pledge was coming up. Everyone figured she'd caved under the pressure and would be back once she'd blown off steam."

Cam settled on the stool next to her, stealing several nuts from her and tossing them in his mouth. "Except she hasn't returned?" he asked around the mouthful.

"No. And here's the strangest part: word around the palace is that the surge seekers found the girl at her parents' house in the human world. But I eavesdropped on the Surgers. They're still trying to locate her magic signature...in secret. Why are they searching if they know where she is? And why is that headmistress sending you letters asking for help, if both girls are accounted for? It's like she doesn't believe her own government."

Cam wouldn't trust the fey government, either. "Is anyone—anyone at all—saying the girl might be dead?"

Tyla shook her head. "If a magic partner dies, their magic automatically goes to the other half of the partnership. The boy ought to be at full power if she's gone. He isn't, so they're assuming she's alive."

The faeries were missing a pretty obvious possibility. Cam rested one elbow on the table, staring out through the balcony door to the willa forest. Movement caught his eye: a flash of white-blonde hair. Destry skipped out of the willa forest and headed for the castle.

Cam's gut tightened. He forced his attention back to Tyla. "What about the last one? The girl the willas remember, the one who wasn't from the school?"

She made a grumpy face. "I deserve two buckets of willa berries for ferreting out that information. Nobody is talking, but not as if they're unaware she's missing. Hushed conversations, people shushing their kids or giving them half-baked excuses when they ask questions."

"Who is she?"

"Full-faerie, from one of the minor noble families. Distant relative to the queen, in fact. Schooled at the palace. Seems she liked this boy who attends the Academy, got caught a couple times sneaking out to see him. Anyway, the story everyone's telling is that she found some human she liked better and ran off to the non-magic world to be with him. That's a disgrace to faerie nobility, which means keeping it quiet."

Cam drummed his fingers on the table, a staccato beat to match the restlessness of his thoughts. "Do you think that's the real story?"

"It does sound like the faeries. Snobs all the way. But you'd expect the parents to search for their kid. She wasn't that old...about Destry's age. No one's looking, far as I can tell."

Cam grimaced. "So we have three nearly identical faerie girls missing, and three suspicious explanations. We have a headmistress who's worried enough to contact me, yet hasn't told the students to stay away from the river, plus a faerie queen who either isn't concerned or has her own reasons for not responding to my letters."

"What reasons are you thinking?" Tyla asked.

"I'm not experienced enough to be sure. I need Aunt Val's opinion."

Tyla kicked his stool leg. "That's a politician's answer. I want the real one."

"I'm honestly not positive. Things seem pretty stable with the faeries—more than they've been in years. But if someone wanted to start trouble, what better excuse than a goblin murdering faerie girls?"

Tyla's eyes widened. "There's no proof that anyone's been killed."

"Worst case scenario. These girls disappeared, and not one has returned. If they never do...only a few creatures are capable of feeding on a faerie's magic. We top the list."

A knock on the door interrupted them. Cam gestured to the lock; it clicked loose. "Come on in, Des."

She shoved the door open and stepped inside. "How'd you know it was me?"

"I'm the goblin king." Cam managed to keep a straight face. "I know all."

"Or he saw you out the balcony." Tyla easily dodged as Cam threw his last few dragontree nuts at her. She gave him a look of lofty superiority. "Be sure you pick those up." She swung out of the room, shutting the door behind her.

Destry watched her go, a frown pulling at her lips. Cam sighed and tracked down the dragontree nuts, dropping them on the table. He noticed that several large chunks of Destry's braid had come loose, wisping around her face and sticking out at odd angles. He tugged one, grinning. "The willas get too friendly?" Cam was aware of the trees' habit of reaching for people who intrigued them, though he did wonder why they had such intense interest in Destry.

Her hands flew to her hair, and a flush crept up her cheeks. "I guess so."

Why was she embarrassed? They'd seen each other more disheveled than this. Then Cam saw her eyes flit to the door—the one Tyla had exited—and he understood. Gripping her shoulders, he guided Destry onto the stool. He pulled the tie from her hair and began combing it with his fingers.

She leaned forward, making his pinky snag in a tangle. "I can—"

"So can I. Who taught you to braid in the first place?" At eleven, her cornsilk hair had been a constant mess. Cam had watched online tutorials so he could teach Destry how to contain it.

She sighed, but she stayed put as he carefully worked the snarls out. A second sigh —pleased this time—whispered from her lips. Her shoulders relaxed. Did all girls like having their hair played with? Cam didn't know. He did this for Destry, and only Destry.

"How are your firewell visits going?"

Destry hesitated a beat before answering. "Good. Definitely one of my favorite things about the Fold."

Cam frowned. She sounded sincere, but why the pause? He worked out the last snarl and started weaving her hair into a braid. "Do you get to go often?"

"Whenever there's free time in my school schedule...and nothing comes up when I get there."

Cam's frown deepened. He fastened the tie on and circled around to the other stool. "What would come up once you're at the firewell?"

Destry shrugged. "Nothing, today. I visited on the way here." She glanced at the leather books, tension seeping back into her face. "Hope it helps. I'm pretty bad at magic."

"Des, I won't think worse of you for having trouble learning. You know that."

"Yeah." The word had too much question for Cam's taste. "I'm just pretty crummy at being a faerie." She acted like it was a joke, but Cam could see the truth in her hunched shoulders and fidgeting hands.

He reigned in his temper with difficulty. He'd spent years trying to improve Destry's self-worth—an uphill battle with her mother's lack of concern and her struggles in school. A month and a half with those fluttering fools and she was back to square one.

He forced his voice to stay calm. "So you don't share the same talents as most of your race. Doesn't mean something's wrong with you."

"But it takes me twice as long to do things as it does the other students! I can't get a feel for manipulating the strands."

"Maybe you need to learn another way. We use the same magic energy, Dessie. The difference between faerie magic and goblin magic is mainly in execution. We rely less on instinct, more on structure." Cam pulled the top book closer and flipped it open. "I thought we'd start here."

Destry read the heading. "Spells for Manipulating Fire?" She tossed him an incredulous look.

"It's what you call up most easily. That makes it simpler to experiment with."

"Do you *want* me to burn down the castle?"

"I took some precautions." He led her to the practice area he'd set up. "See these jars of water? They're imbued with a four-corners spell. They act as a magic shield for anything inside the square. The square has to be exact for them to work, so we can't knock them out of place. But otherwise, anything that happens will be contained."

Destry started chewing a cuticle. "I could still set *you* on fire. It happens when I'm stressed. The day of my 'interview' with you, I set Tristan's shirt on fire three times in one morning."

Cam suppressed an unworthy grin. *Guess it's not all fun and games being Destry's magic partner, is it, Tristan?*

He pulled her finger out of her teeth. "It'll be fine. The whole point of a spoken spell is to frame the magic with words, to tell it what to do. Are you planning to make a spell to set my shirt ablaze?"

"Of course not, but—"

He pointed to the center of the square. "Sit down while I get the book."

She hesitated. Cam gave her his sternest look—the type she generally ignored. "Are you refusing to obey the king? Maybe I should go full-goblin for our lesson. You might cooperate then."

He expected her to snicker or roll her eyes, not swallow and step into the square without another word. Cam retrieved the book, guilt dripping like acid into his gut. He sat cross-legged on the floor across from her, the sand-filled tray between them. "Dessie?"

She looked up from her lap, face carefully blank.

"I was just teasing," Cam said softly. "I didn't consider... I'm not used to being someone who would frighten you." Shame flashed through him.

Destry's shoulders loosened, and so did her expression. "It's not you. Some of the other goblins are pretty scary. I shouldn't have reacted like that."

Cam frowned. Aside of Sylka, what other goblins would have been scaring her? But she hurried on. "So, does this containment spell only work with water?"

Would it do any good to press for details? She was definitely hiding something. But Destry's face had taken on that stubborn cast, and he refused to chance frightening her again. Better to see if Tyla could ferret out anything.

Cam shook his head. "I chose water because it's a natural deterrent to fire. The spell is most effective if you use an object that corresponds with your needs. If you wanted to soundproof a small area, for example, it would make sense to cast the spell on cloth and tent stakes, since cloth muffles sound. It's all about starting with a base and adapting it."

He opened the book to the correct page. "See how there are blank spaces in the spell? Official spells can be changed using different nouns, verbs, and adjectives."

Destry pulled the book closer, fingers tracing the words. "You can't work magic without knowing the official spell?"

Cam tipped his hand in a so-so gesture. "Learning the language of magic is a lifelong process. Those who have a firm grasp of the ancient language can work magic whether they know the 'official' spell or not."

"Is that hard for you? I mean, are you behind because you weren't raised here?"

Cam nodded. "There are definitely better magicians, even though I have more hereditary power. I spend a lot of time studying. And I make up for it with my instincts. For a goblin, I'm unusually good at manipulating magic without words."

"In other words, you're better at my own kind of magic than I am," Destry grumbled. "Fine, teach me these spells."

They spent the next thirty minutes working on pronunciation and meaning. Cam gestured towards the tray of sand and wood. "We'll start by lighting that, using the words for wood and heat in the spell. Remember them?"

"*Wiold* and *taesfier*?"

Cam nodded. "That'll start the flame going more gently than using the word for fire." Destry watched intently as he said the entire spell, altering it to the correct phrasing. The wood began to give off wisps of smoke before a small flame erupted.

Cam slid the book closer to her. "Now it's your turn. Think of something you could make the fire do."

Destry frowned, then repeated the spell, substituting the words *ciorreis* and *ainfier*. Nothing happened. She shot him a look of mixed embarrassment and annoyance. "I might be better at goblin magic, huh?"

"It takes time to learn new skills, Dessie." Cam traced a circle in the air with his finger. "You wanted to make a ring of fire?"

She nodded, flushing.

"Then you chose the right words. Let's work on pronunciation. And focus matters, too. With the four-corners spell, you can't inadvertently set wood on fire that's outside of the square. In a situation without a containment spell, you need to know precisely what you want and use it to give your words the proper direction. Try again."

Destry stumbled over the phrasing a second time. Cam corrected her pronunciation, ignoring her pained face. She tried again. The fire just flickered on its bed of wood. "Maybe I should stick with learning the theory," she mumbled.

Cam tweaked her braid gently. "Try again. And this time, concentrate on the meaning behind the words. You have to feel them. Like a song that hasn't been put to music yet."

"Which would make it poetry," she said dryly. But she bent over the book again.

Cam watched her lips silently form the words of the old language. Did she appreciate its innate, almost haunting beauty? It gave him an odd pleasure to hear it on her tongue.

Destry looked up from the book. Her chocolate eyes fastened on him briefly before she closed them and said the spell out loud again.

The tiny flame exploded into a three-foot-tall one. It leapt out of the tray, racing in a circle around them both. Destry's eyes flew open. "*Wasisse!*" she cried, shrill with panic.

Water swirled up from the jars, turning into mist from the heat. Cam grabbed her hand before she could draw more water out and obliterate the containment spell. "Let me." He grabbed earth magic strands, focusing on its ability to smother fire, and tossed them in a loop over the fiery circle. It softened and died.

Destry turned big eyes on him. "I didn't mean to—"

Cam grinned, wiping sweat from his face. "What? Make the magic strands obey you with a vengeance? Look, maybe you meant the words a little too sincerely, or maybe you need to be more specific about where you want your circle, but the fire did exactly what you asked. *That* is impressive, Des."

She swiped a bead of sweat from her temple, eyebrows knit together. "You...you really think so?"

"It took twenty-three repetitions of *my* first spell to get any results. So yes, I'm honestly impressed." He held up a cautioning finger. "But we need to discuss what happened with the water. There was no chance, with fire that hot, for the small amount of water to do anything but evaporate. You have to understand what you're doing, the mechanics of how things work, which is why studying magic—my way or the faerie way—is more than learning words and manipulating the strands." Cam took the slightly damp, slightly singed book and pointed to the lengthy explanation under the spell. "Studying this can help."

They worked on refining the spell, until Destry could keep it contained in the tray. Finally, Cam doused the fire and closed the book. "No more today. You have to leave in forty-five minutes, and we've done nothing but study."

"My work ethic should impress you, then." Destry ran a finger along the book's tooled leather spine.

He stood and stretched. "Take the spellbook with you and study between lessons. Just be careful about experimenting."

Destry accepted his hand up from the floor. "Cam? You know that students sometimes get free days away from campus?"

He'd been afraid this would come up. He kept his voice casual. "So I've heard. We post guards by the willa forest those days, to discourage students coming in on dares. The willas have some pretty hefty magic protecting them, but the forest is essential to my people's well-being. Too important to have teenagers fooling around in it, doing stupid things to prove their bravery. Injuring a willa is serious."

"You're a teenager, too...in case you forgot."

"Yep. But I'm also the goblin king. More importantly, I spent years dealing with you. Makes me far more mature."

She refused to be distracted. "Well, the first one is this Saturday. I thought maybe we could sneak a day together."

Cam hesitated, searching for a diplomatic answer. But his silence lasted too long. Destry's face fell. "Or maybe not. Never mind, it was just an idea." She turned away, grabbing two of the jars from the four-corners spell.

Cam picked up the last two. "Des, there's no one else I'd rather be with. You know that, right?"

She nodded, although something in her eyes made the affirmation into a question. Cam saw them flicker to the door. *Ah.* He set his jars on the desk, then took hers and did the same. "I'm not blowing you off because I'd prefer to hang with other goblins—even Tyla. I have official duties that day. And it's not good for you to disappear. Your friends would wonder what you were doing."

She shrugged. "I'd tell them I had something going on."

"What about your magic partner? You plan to lie to him also?"

"That's my business."

Cam felt his jaw clench. Irritation bubbled in his stomach and crawled up his throat. There was no point in lecturing Des about her selective honesty. She never listened, and it bothered Cam in a way that Tyla's occasional evasions didn't.

Hypocritical, he knew. Why give the goblin girl a free pass for something he deeply disliked in Destry? Maybe because Tyla usually lied for convenience's sake—like swearing Cam needed formal wear for some social function. She avoided Cam's complaints about uncomfortable dress clothes (when they weren't *strictly* required), and Cam's outfit made the right impression. Annoying, but Tyla's finely honed understanding of goblin society worked to Cam's advantage.

Destry's lies were inevitably attempts to hide something: a mistake that embarrassed her or a choice Cam would disapprove of. They complicated his life...and worse, left him feeling unworthy. Bad enough that his own father questioned his ability to govern a kingdom. (Dad might claim that wasn't true, but Cam sensed some reservations.) Bad enough to worry whether he *could* live up to the faith placed in him by his aunt and his subjects. After all their years together, hadn't he at least proved his worth to Destry? Proved she could trust him?

Whatever the reason, her dishonesty hit different than Tyla's—a slap to the face rather than a friendly punch in the arm.

Well, he might be a hypocrite, but he shouldn't take it out on Destry, whose expression had turned wary. "You still need to be careful. And I still have things to do. Go have a nice time with your faerie friends."

She nodded, but her disappointment was obvious. Cam groaned. "I hate those sad eyes. Why do you do that to me?"

"I'm not doing anything."

"Yeah, you are. But not on purpose, which only makes it worse. Look, cheer up, and I'll bring something special to our next lesson."

"What?" she asked suspiciously.

"A surprise."

Destry wavered, but she was a sucker for surprises; Cam smelled victory. Finally, she smiled. "Deal. Can we visit the willas now? Classes ran late today. I couldn't stop on the way here."

She bounced with excitement all the way to the forest. She ran to the first willa she'd met, the annoying male, patting his trunk tenderly. *At least it's a tree upstaging me, and not her idiot magic partner.*

Cam pulled himself up short. Where had that come from? Destry needed to form a bond with her magic partner, and they weren't exactly in competition. This Tristan would play a different role than brother in Destry's life.

It still felt strange.

Cam walked her through the forest until they were almost in sight of the river. She turned to him, smile brighter than before. "Gotta hurry. Fey Elena expects me by six." She started down the path, pale braid swinging.

He made a quick decision. "Des, wait." She turned back, and he said, "I have a request. Well, more of an order."

She smirked. "In case you haven't noticed, ordering me around isn't effective."

Gratitude spiked through Cam—this was an improvement over her instant obedience during their lesson. But fear overrode it. Better she be slightly scared than dead. He let the mantle of goblin king slip over him. "This isn't negotiable, Destry."

Dismay transformed her lighthearted expression, but at least she was paying attention.

"You need an escort when you come here from now on. Normal lesson times, I'll meet you at the edge of the woods. If you want to visit another time, alert me through your school's messenger service. I'll send someone if I can't get free. But *don't* come alone. There have been incidents of faerie girls disappearing—not in the woods, but close by."

She hesitated. "I saw something I wasn't supposed to, in Fey Elena's office. Pictures of a couple of missing faerie girls. But the kids at school say they're not missing, just gone for other reasons."

"School rumor isn't fact. Besides, missing girls or not, there are dangers in these woods —including the other goblins. Promise, and don't dare break my trust."

Destry frowned. They generally avoided reference to the incident with Jared, however oblique. "I don't like it. But I promise."

He breathed a sigh of relief. Destry never reneged on an actual promise. "Stay away from the river after dark, too. In fact, don't go out alone at night."

Her expression turned annoyed. "I have a curfew, remember? Why would I wander the grounds late? Why would I wander the grounds at all? I'm supposed to spend my free time with my 'faerie friends.'"

So he wasn't forgiven for refusing to meet her. Cam's earlier irritation flared, and he couldn't tamp it down. "I'm trying to help you have a good life! If it were up to me, I'd pull you out of faerie school, bring you to my castle, and you'd stay there forever as the goblin princess. But your magic partner might object. More importantly, *you* might object. And if the faeries find you different now, try publicizing that you're best friends with a goblin." Destry didn't answer, eyes wide. Cam waved one hand in frustrated dismissal. "Do what you want."

Destry caught his arm as he turned away. "Cam, wait. I'm sorry. I...I'm just a little lonely over there."

The tremble in her voice cooled his anger. These magic realms, a refuge for him, weren't home to her yet. Of course she was lonely. But in the eyes of certain goblins, she was also a threat to their way of life. He couldn't allow Destry to get lax about safety or to forget that the fey realm was her true home.

His heart gave a painful, rebellious jerk. Cam ignored it. They were already walking a dangerous line with these lessons. "But that's how you get less lonely: by making friends with the people who share your life."

She nodded. And she smiled brightly before heading down the path. But Cam couldn't shake the feeling that he'd done something wrong.

TEMPTATION

✦

Cam didn't do anything wrong. The thought pushed at Destry, making her feel guilty for her attitude—and her earlier anger. He was right, both what he'd said, and the one thing he'd left unsaid: *I don't share your life, Destry. Not really.*

She'd realized that from the moment Fey Elena explained how damaging her magic could be. This was much better than nothing. She still felt an inexplicable sense of loss.

Tristan was waiting on the front steps when she got back. "Where's Fey Elena?" Destry asked. The headmistress had made clear—both to Destry and the 'goblin king'—that she would watch for her charge's prompt return after lessons.

He held up two pieces of native fruit known as nectar-greens—peach-like with jade-colored skin and purple flesh, nearly as sweet as candy. "She said I could wait for you, as long as I made sure you got in on time. She thinks I'm a good student."

Destry sank down next to him. "She doesn't know you very well."

"I am a good student. Just not always a well-behaved one." Tristan pressed one of the nectargreens into her hand.

Destry ran her fingers along the fruit's fuzzy skin. "Good behavior is overrated."

Tristan cocked his head to one side. "You look bummed. Was the lesson bad?"

"Actually, that part was interesting."

"Did the king scare you?"

Destry shook her head. "He was...pleasant. And a good teacher."

"Then what's wrong?"

She passed the nectargreen back and forth in her hands. "Maybe it's too much new stuff at once. I think switching between different realms, different magics, will be confusing."

Tristan took her hand—a stark contrast to Cam's wider grip. "The lessons only take four hours a week. You don't even have to think about them when you're here."

Destry couldn't explain that the feeling of being torn went deeper than her lessons. She just nodded. Tristan spun his nectargreen on the tips of his fingers. "This isn't good comfort food. But at least it's sweet." He took a big bite. "Mmm-m-m."

She smiled at his exaggerated pleasure. "There's juice on your chin."

He swiped his sleeve over it.

Destry rolled her eyes. "You missed. Be still." She rubbed her thumb across the wet patch. Tristan stayed steady, blue eyes intent on her face. She swallowed and leaned back. "Better."

"Thanks, Des."

She didn't correct the nickname this time. Tristan opened his mouth to say something else, but a snide voice interrupted. "Fey Elena sent me to ask if Destry returned yet. Clearly, she has." They turned. Julya stood at the top of the stairs, expression sour. "Dinner started five minutes ago."

"Thanks for telling us." Tristan offered Destry a hand up.

Julya flounced into the school with a swish of black hair. Before Destry could follow, Tristan whispered, "Okay, the nectargreen wasn't good enough. I have something better. Meet me on your balcony after curfew."

He moved away too quickly for her to respond. She sighed and followed him into the dining hall, wondering what he had up his sleeve this time.

Tristan was waiting when she finally made it outside. "Took you long enough." He grinned, eyes bright with suppressed excitement.

"I couldn't get away. The other girls wanted to hear about my lesson."

"You're such a novice. We have to work on this." Tristan threw a leg over the balcony railing. "Come on."

Clammy sweat popped up on Destry's forehead. "What're you doing?"

"I didn't plan to stay here all night. This is the best way to leave without getting caught."

"I'm *not* climbing down a balcony."

"You don't have to. Use your wings to glide down."

"I can't."

Tristan thumped one fist against his forehead. "I forgot. Yours are too new. Guess we can use the vines."

She didn't correct his assumption. "The vines might break. Then where would we be?"

"On the ground." He laughed at his own joke. "I used 'em to climb up. They'll hold." She crossed her arms and planted her feet. Tristan sighed. "Alright, meet me on the stairs. Unless you want me to glide us both down."

She didn't. Tristan took one look at her face and vaulted off the edge of the balcony with another resigned sigh. Wings outstretched, he glided to the ground. They folded seamlessly into his shoulders with a faint poof of blue as Tristan darted off.

He beat her to the hall outside the girls' dorms. They slipped downstairs and into a side corridor, stopping in a patch of shadow to avoid some teachers. A few more dashes, and they were outside, the warm evening breeze lifting their hair.

Tristan grinned. "I haven't gone out that way in forever." He cupped his hands, like he was scooping something out of the air. Seconds later, a ball of blue light glowed there. Tristan deposited it in Destry's palm. "For milady." He conjured a second, tossing it into the air to hover near his shoulder.

The faerie light pulsed against Destry's skin. "Where are we going?" she asked.

"A little place in Si'fliegen. You'll love it."

Destry wavered. "What if we get caught?"

"Do you think I'd let that happen? And do you think I'd let you take the blame, if it did? Just trust me."

His eyes were appealing, but the deciding factor was something Tristan didn't intend her to see, half-hidden behind his confident smile: vulnerability. He seemed worried that she wouldn't like whatever he'd planned. Her opinion mattered to Tristan. That was enough to set Destry's feet in motion.

As they walked, she told Tristan about combat, where they'd started palming power, and her success in hitting the targets Renalt set up. Watching the beam of light—*her* beam of light—break through solid objects felt deeply satisfying. She also told Tristan about goblin magic and how much easier it seemed compared to theirs.

He made a face. "That's a lot of memorizing."

"Yeah, but it works. Would it...would it bother you if I used that kind of magic?"

Tristan looked surprised. "*I* don't care. But you may get a bad grade if our teachers suspect. Clue me in, so I can cover for you."

They crossed the marble bridge into town. Tristan took her faerie light. "We won't need these now." He snagged his out of the air, then cupped his hands around both energy balls. When he opened them again, ephemeral blue glitter filled his palms. Tristan blew it over Destry. The bits of magic glowed for a moment on her hair and clothes before dissipating.

Tristan's eyes were just as bright. "Pretty, Des." He led her down the main street. The business end of town was closest to the school. Gauzy faerie lights hovered around signs and doorways. People were still out on the streets, but they had an air of late-night festivity.

Tristan ducked down a side street to a café. A tinkling fountain played near the entrance; when the breeze gusted, it sent fine mist over her and Tristan. An olive-skinned woman with a long nose and orange-edged wings was sliding drinks onto one of the outdoor tables.

She smiled and led them inside, past other patrons to a quieter corner. "Out breaking the rules again, Tristan?"

"All for a good cause. Mellie, this is my magic partner. She hasn't talked to her mom since term started. Could we use your connection?"

"As long as you vouch for her." She motioned them toward a set of stairs at the back of the café. "Want me to bring up your usual?"

"Better double it. Can we have the room for a while?"

"It's all yours, my dear. Have fun."

Doing what? Destry's shoulders tightened, but she followed Tristan up the narrow stairs, into another hallway and through a door. The room was cozy, with a squashy couch, several small tables, and...a couple of laptops? Destry ran her fingers along one with a gleaming silver cover. "I haven't seen a computer since we crossed through the Fold."

He closed the door. "They're pointless in the magic realm. So is anything that relies on signals sent through the air. Magic disrupts those signals. But a few faeries—like Mellie—have a talent for keeping a line open. A lot of halfs come here to borrow her internet, e-mail their families. Makes you less homesick."

Destry loosed a pent-up breath of tension. He really was just being nice. "This is awesome. I know we can send paper letters, but it takes forever, and it's—"

"Not the same," Tristan finished. "Just don't tell anyone, because the fossils on the school board might shut her down."

Destry was curled up on the couch, computer on her lap, when Mellie poked her head in. "Something to make your evening more enjoyable." She slid a plate overflowing with treats onto the table. The scent of cinnamon and fresh-baked cookies filled the room.

Tristan snagged a lemon tart. "You outdid yourself."

"Finding your magic partner merits celebration. I don't have anyone else scheduled for this room tonight. Take as long as you wish." Her smile to Tristan seemed particularly warm.

Destry shook her head as the proprietress closed the door. "Do you charm every woman you meet?"

"The ones who can help me out," he joked lightly. "Mellie just likes the money I spend here."

Destry nibbled on a chocolate chip cookie and checked her e-mail for the first time in a month and a half. Right after she'd left for school, there was almost nothing from her mom. But as the weeks went on, emails appeared with greater frequency. They also grew more lucid, going from one line ("Hope you're having fun!") to a three-paragraph letter.

Destry spent a long time reading the last one. Bev mentioned that she'd been drinking less—and coming to a lot of realizations. She ended with, "I understand why you wanted to go to that school, even though it's so far away. You needed something better than I gave you. Maybe by the time you come home for the summer, I'll have a life worth *staying* home for."

Tristan noticed her rubbing at a tear. "Everything okay?"

"It's fine." Destry couldn't decide how to feel about that letter. Beverly was improving, just like Riamon had said—which was awesome—but returning to school each year would be much harder.

She answered the last email, gushing over the non-existent mountains, the school, her new friends. But what could she say about Beverly's drinking? Destry settled for a few lines about how her mom was making some great changes.

She clicked *send* and closed the computer with a sense of finality. Tristan looked up from his laptop. "Finished?"

She nodded. "Do you need help paying for the internet time or the food?" She wondered how she would pay if he said yes.

Tris waved a dismissive hand. "My mom doesn't make much, but Dad's loaded. He sends guilt money all the time." He grabbed a pair of brownies and handed one to her. "You gotta try Mellie's specialty: dark chocolate with salted caramel and pecans."

They spent the next ten minutes eating and fooling around on Tristan's laptop. When Destry polished off the last crumb, she said, "We better get back to school. Sneaking in may take a while, since we can't use the balcony."

Tristan slid the laptop onto the table. "I have vast experience sneaking around. That part's fine. But we need at least one more dessert, maybe two. Gotta enjoy this contraband." Grinning, he snagged a cheesecake square.

Destry snickered. "This from the guy who wouldn't let me eat three brownies the day of my interview. Are you *trying* to get me drunk?"

Tristan's smile slipped. His cheeks reddened. "I..."

"You *are*?" Memories rushed over her, of Jared, of grasping hands and the taste of liquor on her tongue. Destry shot to her feet and scrambled across the room, knocking into the table along the way. The plate of treats spun across the tabletop, flinging cookies and lemon tarts everywhere.

"Please, Destry, wait! Let me explain." Tristan's voice halted her at the door. He had stood, too, but he hadn't followed her, and it was the only reason she turned back.

"Fine. Explain."

"I wasn't trying to get you drunk. I wanted to get *both* of us tipsy," he blurted.

Power built in her palms. What would happen if she blasted him? "Wow. That was an explanation worth sticking around for."

He shoved one hand through his hair, sending glossy strands into disarray. "That didn't come out right. I just... I thought if we both relaxed, we could at least talk...without it feeling like an interrogation."

"What's that supposed to mean?"

"It means I can do the math. You and me—we complete each other's magic." His clear blue eyes met hers. "I don't want to give up my magic. Unless you do, we know where our friendship is headed."

"And that makes it okay to trick me into getting tipsy? Into getting too drunk to stop you, when you want to 'talk?'" Destry crossed her arms, the better to hide her trembling. "Losing my magic would suck. But sharing it with a guy who would force me into something is worse."

"Hold up." He ran a hand through his hair again. "'Talk' wasn't code for sex or even making out."

Jared's mocking voice echoed in her head. *Are you such a baby you don't know what that means?* She glared. "Sure. A heart-to-heart conversation is *so* much better than getting your hands under my shirt."

His gaze didn't waver. "I've been waiting for my magic partner for four years. I'm not gonna screw it up by trying 'friends with benefits.' And I would never *force* anything—or anyone—no matter what. The idea makes me sick."

Destry hesitated. Was it possible he actually meant that? Her stomach was twisting, her body still shaking, but the inexplicable *pull* she sometimes felt towards Tristan whispered that he did.

Tristan's eyes grew heavier. "I...I didn't know, Destry."

Didn't know what? He was watching her as if he suddenly understood something—something she hadn't intended to share. Did he also get strange whispers about her through their connection as magic partners?

Tristan folded to the couch, expression miserable. "Fey's honor, Des. I just figured you might open up a little if we relaxed and had fun together." He dropped his head into his hands. "Fire and wings. I really screwed up tonight."

That inner pull again, the feeling of knowledge outside herself...affirming that his idea to get sugared-up together was an error in judgment, like inviting Jared over to share Beverly's schnapps—not an effort to take away her free will. The sensation that she understood his motives unnerved her.

Avoiding the tart and cookie shrapnel, she edged to the couch and sank onto it, as far away from him as possible. "Yeah. You definitely screwed up." To her horror, tears gathered in her eyes. "I don't need some guy taking away my choices."

Tristan looked ill. "I'm so sorry—for not being up front, for making you think I'd hurt you. Can't believe you didn't blast me."

Destry swiped at the tears spilling over. "It was coming." She rubbed her palms, itching as the unused power drained away. "Tristan, why is this such a big deal to you? I get that most magic partners end up together, but they don't always."

Worry tightened his features. "I know."

"And they still do their commitment, right?"

He loosed a long, frustrated sigh. "Yes. But..." He stopped, like he was fighting for words.

"But?"

"I don't want to be like my parents!" His voice cracked. "All I've done, all my life, is go back and forth between them like some toy they're fighting over. Then I came here. Having a magic partner—knowing who my soulmate is—sounded awesome. Someone I could count on, someone who could always count on me." It was Tristan's turn to swipe away renegade tears. "Except I guess you can't, now."

Another of those inexplicable, annoying, enlightening *tugs*. It hadn't occurred to Destry that in some ways, Tristan might be as broken as she was. After a long pause, she said, "That depends. Are you gonna do this again?"

He gave a short, sharp laugh. "Des, if I could rewind the clock and change everything I did tonight, I would. I'm sure not doing it another time."

She shrugged. "Maybe you shouldn't change *everything*, then. I really did need the sweets. I miss brownies so much."

He managed a shaky grin. "They're your only weakness?"

Smiling back felt...natural. "I also miss sugar cookies. Dark chocolate. Cake. Pie and ice cream."

Tristan ticked off on his fingers. "M&M's. Ice cream, alone. Any kind of fruity candy. And soda." He closed his eyes dramatically. "I still feel Dr. Pepper calling my name. The first month here almost killed me."

"I'm dying," Destry admitted.

Tristan stood. "Considering how much we've already had, maybe it's time to leave this den of temptation." He reached to help her up, hesitated, then pulled back, eyes uncertain.

Destry's fingers trembled, but she grabbed his hand. "Everyone messes up, Tris."

His voice came low and subdued. "I just don't know how to make this up to you."

"How about letting things happen naturally, with no pressure—and no sweets—to move it along? If we're supposed to be together, it'll work out, right?"

"That's a promise I can make." Some of Tristan's usual self-assurance peeked through. "Besides, if you don't snatch me up eventually, Julya will come after me again. And I don't see you being okay with that."

She couldn't suppress her laughter. Both of them were smiling—if more tentatively than before—as they headed out through the café and down the street to school. Neither noticed the eyes that followed them, long after they'd left town.

20

HER

I t was her.

Excitement quickened Shadow's breathing as he stood in the alley of the small café, watching the young couple. That girl—he'd seen her leaving the tall pavilion on the hill earlier that day. Faeries only visited the firewell for one reason.

Her hair, her face, her eyes... Everything looked right. Still, Shadow couldn't afford a fourth mistake. Not after his sloppiness with the others.

He should have known better. He *had* known better. But desperation made fools of the wise and brought even the stalwart to their knees. Of the three girls he'd taken, only one had true potential to be the soul he required. Shadow's need had pushed him into reckless gambit with the other two, taking them too soon. Thorough research and firm self-control would have prevented those missteps.

So when the girl had hurried from the firewell into the willa forest, Shadow had tried to follow. But the white trees recognized him, even without his shroud, and drove him away. *Patience*, he'd counseled himself, and had come into town to slake his burning hunger.

Now, here she was.

She and her partner headed for the school. Shadow diverged from their route, circling to the bridge leading to the Academy. He slid beneath it a full minute before the children traipsed across the marble structure. He peered through the gaps in the railing at the girl's calves—at her stormy silver tattoos. Shadow breathed a shuddering sigh of relief.

She was the one.

He'd begun to lose hope. Perhaps what he'd overheard was wrong. Perhaps the fey man was mistaken, even about something so personal. But Shadow's efforts had finally borne fruit.

Need tightened his stomach. They had some distance yet to traverse in the dark, mere children with untried defensive abilities. He could grab them now...

No. He would assuage his hunger but lose an opportunity desperately waited for. Time to feed before he lost control.

He pulled his hood closer, gliding down the road towards town. Businesses were dousing their lights; the streets had emptied of pedestrians. Still, he kept to the shadows and alleys. Long experience had taught him how to find prey and not be found himself.

Finally, he heard it. A couple arguing on their balcony, too angry to be discreet. The man's voice: "Fire and wings! If you love him that much, go live with him!"

Next a woman's, shrill: "Maybe I should! I'm tired of fighting, Evan."

The man stormed from the house, hurtling into the alley. Excellent. The woman would have been fine, but the man's power, fueled by his anger, would satisfy Shadow longer. He crept after the faerie.

The man stopped, probably wondering where to go. Shadow examined him. Heavy-set, not particularly fit. A raven cawed, and the man turned toward the sound. Slowly, though. Poor reflexes.

No need for subtlety with this one.

The faerie didn't sense danger until it was too late. Shadow sank his teeth into the neck, careful to avoid the arteries; he craved magic, not blood. Paralyzing the man and piercing his tattoo took the last of Shadow's waning energy, but the man's power gushed into him.

Sweet. Oh, so sweet.

He lost himself in the pleasure of the feed, until...

That implosion of light, the shining ash.

Shadow wiped his mouth and stood.

He should be pleased. Individuals with some reason to disappear made the best prey. By the time the man's unfaithful wife stopped being relieved by his absence and started worrying, Shadow's business would be long finished.

He kicked the faerie's essence. It swirled apart, then coalesced again, sweeping away to wherever faerie souls traveled after death. Shadow's hands clenched, claws biting into his own skin. Such travels were forbidden him. But not forever, now that he had found her.

PERSONAL

◆

The day of Destry's next lesson with Cam, she found him waiting at the edge of the woods as promised. She held up the bag she'd brought along. "Got your note." The message— requesting that she bring the red dress from her "interview"—had been sitting on her desk when she returned from Si'fliegen the previous evening. "How'd you get it to my room that late at night?"

Cam smiled, though a bit tightly. "Tyla flew it over for me."

Destry had planned to ask why Cam wanted her to bring a dress, but his phrasing drove it out of her mind. "*Flew* it?"

He strode into the willa forest, Destry keeping pace beside him. "You noticed her feathers at our 'interview?' Tyla transforms into a raven. Being able to fly lets her see a lot of things other people miss." His voice was as tight as his smile.

Destry frowned. "Is something wrong?"

He waved a dismissive hand. "There's no time to get into a discussion."

"A discussion?" Destry forced the question to sound light despite her sinking stomach. "It's worse than I thought."

Cam's lips compressed into a hard line. "I just noticed that the curfews at your school aren't as effective as you claimed."

"What are you talking about?"

He shot her a black look. "You, walking around after dark and well after curfew, in Si'fliegen."

Destry stopped in the middle of the trail. "How would you even... Did you send your raven girl to *follow* me?"

"How about you give me an explanation first?"

It was more an order than a request. Destry's hands balled into fists. "No. Because even if I did what you said, I wasn't breaking my word. I wasn't breaking your trust. But spying on me? That's completely different, Camden Waters."

He turned, resting against a tree trunk and crossing his arms. "I didn't send Tyla to follow you...just to deliver that note. She already had some actual spying to do in the fey town. And she noticed you and some guy, strolling along without a care in the world. I thought you weren't going out after dark."

"I promised not to go out *alone* after dark. Tristan took me somewhere. We were just having fun."

Cam sighed gustily. "And didn't you think whatever's haunting my forest might roam other places too?"

"I did what *you* asked!" Destry said. "You don't have any right to lecture me. You don't have any right to tell me to create a new life and then tell me I'm wrong for doing it."

Cam pushed away from the tree, his jaw working. They began walking again in silence. Destry didn't break it. She was in no mood for lectures. Her day had begun with a tough quiz in metalworking and ended with getting in trouble in Combat. She'd only wanted to see how many bolts of power she could summon. Renalt said to stop at five, but—while most students seemed exhausted from that number—she'd felt exhilarated. When Renalt went to help another faerie, she'd tried three more shots in quick succession...

And nearly passed out.

When he saw her crumple to the floor, Renalt knew exactly what she'd done. He took her to his office for a glass of storm-charged water and a stinging scolding. As punishment, she had to write a three-page essay explaining the importance of safety guidelines.

Cam finally spoke. "You're right. I did tell you to make some friends. But I wish I'd known your magic partner is fond of rule-breaking before I said that."

"You should be happy. I'm trying to 'get less lonely.'"

He grimaced. "Throwing that in my face, huh? Alright, I'm sorry. I had no right to bring this up in any way, and the fact that I care about you and am worried about you is absolutely no excuse."

"You don't have to be sarcastic."

"I am sorry—mostly. Your other promises are still in effect, though. Three girls have disappeared, and they all resemble *you*. That's too much coincidence for comfort."

She didn't want to accept his apology after he'd made a bad day worse. But Cam's green eyes *were* worried. Destry sighed. "I'll keep my end of the bargain."

As they neared the edge of the forest, Cam said, "Things will be different today."

"Different how?"

"I need to introduce you at court. It's tradition whenever a foreigner spends much time here."

Her hands flew to her messy braid. "Cam!"

"Don't get your wings in a flutter. It's just a short formality."

This was why he'd asked her to bring that stupid dress. "You could've warned me!"

"You'd have gotten stressed for days beforehand, and there's no reason." He eyed her and shrugged. "Tyla can help you get ready. All you need to do is change clothes and brush your hair."

She scowled. Cam was as much a guy as ever, goblin king or not. Did it even occur to him that looking nice enough to stand up before an entire court of people took planning—not just throwing on a dress? Destry was still frowning when they came out in the hall leading to his private audience chambers. Tyla, sitting at the desk leafing through a book, looked up. "I told you."

"Seems I should have listened," Cam said.

Smirking, Tyla turned her golden gaze on Destry. "I told him to warn you about the presentation. He said, and I quote: 'Des doesn't need fancied up to look good.' Males." She closed the book with a muffled *whumph*. "Come on, I prepared a few things in case Cam stayed stupid."

Destry hesitated. Did she really want this elegant goblin girl to help her get ready? Tyla rolled her eyes. "I don't bite, even when I transform. Move it, we only have fifteen minutes."

Destry followed her into the audience chambers. A brush, some cosmetics, and an assortment of hair clips sat on one table. Tyla pulled the door closed and snagged Destry's bag, pulling out the red dress. "Get those clothes off."

She wanted Destry to undress in front of her? Destry hesitated, and Tyla raised one perfectly shaped eyebrow. "Clock's ticking, faerie girl."

Destry shimmied out of her leggings and tunic, trying not to look as self-conscious as she felt. She searched for a topic of conversation—anything to make this less awkward. "You and Cam are good friends?"

Tyla tossed the red dress over Destry's head. "For five years now. Started the year we both turned twelve. I'd just arrived at the castle to begin my apprenticeship, and the unsanctioned tradition is for older apprentices to set a task for the newcomers. Well, the other girls thought it would be funny to make me kiss Cam."

Destry jerked the dress down. "Kiss him?"

"Cam and I had barely met. It was guaranteed to be uncomfortable. But the others would have teased me mercilessly if I refused. Kissing Cam was the lesser of two evils." She fastened the back buttons on Destry's dress and undid her braid as Destry tied on the wide belt. "Brumal—Cam's chancellor—likes long hair. This'll win you points."

"So what happened?"

"I went to the stables one day when he'd been riding. Offered to help rub his horse down. While we were doing that, I tried flirting. Wasn't too bad at it, either. But when I leaned in for a kiss, Cam leaned away. I scooted closer, and he scooted even farther. He asked if I really liked him that much. Since I wasn't getting anywhere, I explained about the challenge and asked if I could kiss him to get the girls off my back." She handed Destry the brush, then turned to rifle through the hair clips.

Destry dragged the brush through her hair, wincing as it caught on tangles. "Did Cam say yes?"

"Why so interested?"

Destry schooled her features to bland unconcern (at least, she hoped that was the result). "Just curious. This happened before I met him."

Tyla grinned knowingly and held up a silver hair clip shaped like willa branches. "He offered something better. He let me kiss him, plus we walked around holding hands in front of the other girls for the next few weeks. Since they liked him, it was a most excellent revenge." She shoved Destry into a chair and started fiddling with her hair. "Cam's sense of honor was the one drawback. He felt compelled to remind me, repeatedly, that it was only a game. As if I'm the sort to go head over heels for some guy."

The muscles along Destry's neck relaxed. Why had she been worried, anyway?

"Cam and I have been friends ever since. I helped him learn important things he didn't know, and when the time came to appoint a personal assistant, he chose me." Tyla attached the hair clip with a quiet *snick*. "We can skip the makeup. You don't have to be fancy, just presentable."

Cam poked his head in the door. "You two almost done?"

Destry stood, holding her arms out to the sides. "Any better?"

"You'd probably think so. I thought you were fine before."

Tyla glared. "They should have given you fewer lessons in language and a few more in charm, O Goblin King."

She flounced out. Cam chuckled. "I like that dress, Dessie. Glad you didn't set it on fire when you were lobbing flaming books at me."

She took a deep breath. "Let's hope it impresses the other goblins."

Stepping into the vast throne room was like stepping into a kaleidoscope. A stained glass window—the biggest Destry had ever seen—graced the wall behind two carved stone thrones. The matching windows on either side were smaller but still massive. Sunlight shone through their free-form swirls, sending a riot of color across the polished floor. Unlike most of the castle, this floor was stone—a uniform shade of cream, the perfect canvas for the glowing jewel tones.

Destry swept her eyes over the waiting crowd, apprehension tightening her chest. How many would be in goblin form? But of the people waiting, only some looked inhuman. Cam's assertion that goblins could easily be mistaken for other creatures made sense now; no two were alike. Some reminded her of Cam: a humanoid version of natural stone. Others looked like they were carved from jewels. Still others had animal qualities or looked entirely like animals...huge ones. As they paced towards the front of the throne room, a leopard stepped into the wide aisle, glittering ruby eyes level with hers. Destry's heart sped up.

Cam raised an eyebrow. The creature backed away, claws tapping loudly against the stone. They resumed their walk. Destry understood why the goblins eschewed a wooden floor for their throne room. All the transformed goblins shared one similarity: those wickedly sharp obsidian claws.

Destry's shoulder blades burned. The sharp edges pressed against her skin, demanding release. But allowing her wings to shoot out would make it clear how much this crowd of goblins intimidated her. A quiet lick of internal fire bolstered her courage. *No.* She could control this, if nothing else. She concentrated on the normal goblins, the reassuring humanity of their faces. The stinging eased.

The self-control won her mixed reviews. A few people made disgruntled faces. Had they been looking forward to a show? Others nodded approvingly, and some random person made a loud comment about her being "a brave one."

A woman stood near the thrones; her long green dress outlined a statuesque figure. She bore an obvious resemblance to Cam—the same chestnut hair and slate green eyes—though the planes of her face were gentler.

On the other side of the thrones, an enormous wolf paced. Its dark fur seemed to swallow light. Destry's breathing sped up. That graceful predator's stalk reminded her of the hooded creature from her dream. The wolf headed for her and Cam.

As it grew nearer, the wolf's shape shifted, flowing upward until a tall man was striding toward them instead. His stiff clothes were the same deep black as his fur.

He stopped in front of Destry and bowed...not low, barely a bend of the waist. To Cam, he offered a deeper one. His pleasant smile didn't match his wolfish goblin form. "So, this is the faerie supplicant fortunate enough to receive such a broadening of knowledge. We're pleased to allow you the opportunity to know goblin-kind better. I am Brumal, high chancellor to King Darkwater and to High Lady Valda Darkwater."

The chancellor merited a curtsy—Fey Elena's lessons had taught her that—but she didn't want to fall on her face in front of the goblin court. She tried a deep bow with a slight bend of the knee instead. Brumal's expression turned strained. Destry straightened. How apologetic should her smile be? "I'm grateful for the opportunity, Lord Brumal."

The man's face softened into pleased lines. "Hardly a lord, my dear. My status as high chancellor was earned through service to the kingdom. I may thank King Darkwater's father for my exalted position."

The older woman moved closer to their trio. "High Chancellor Brumal has been our loyal advisor for many years."

Destry gave her the same mangled curtsy she'd given the chancellor. Lady Valda smiled kindly. "Welcome and good fortune, Destry of the Fey." Her green eyes crinkled at the corners. She added in an undertone, "Curtsies are an earth-cursed piece of business. I'd have told you to forgo them, but that would have offended our audience. And our chancellor. He prefers the structure of formalities."

Brumal murmured, "Someone must observe them and balance Your Majesties' tendency towards the casual." He pressed a hand to the small of Destry's back, turning her to face the crowd. "Our kingdom's friendship is extended to Destry Firewings of Si'fliegen. Her welcome is assured."

Apparently, it was a rote greeting. The court echoed, "Our friendship is granted." Destry gazed over the crowd. Some of the faces didn't look welcoming. She forced a smile.

A low babble of talking broke out as people began mingling with their neighbors. Destry turned to Cam. "Yeah, you should have warned me."

"I'd have ruined your week. Destry, this is my Aunt Val—Dad's sister."

"I've been hearing about you for years," Lady Valda said. "Interesting, the twists of fate."

Brumal cleared his throat. "As the nature of Camden's connection to Destry is to remain undisclosed, I suggest we not linger on the dais."

He wasn't telling people in the goblin realm? Destry turned surprised eyes on Cam. He said, "I'm a king, Destry. Kings have enemies—even among friends."

Lady Valda indicated a door off to one side. "You three leave. I'll mingle with the crowd. Another chance to visit with Destry will arise."

Cam kissed his aunt's cheek before heading for the door. Destry followed, watching his regal walk. He seemed so different sometimes...and while part of it was for show, part wasn't. Cam had an assurance here, a certainty of his place in the scheme of things. It left her feeling strangely bereft.

The door led into a small chamber furnished with chairs—a waiting room, maybe. As soon as the door swung shut behind them, Cam's face lost that intimidating formal expression. "Now we can relax. Sorry for the royal act, Des."

"You might have extended such formality a bit further," Brumal chided. "We've spoken about your casual affection in such situations."

"You've spoken," Cam said. "And I told you I didn't agree. I'm not bowing to my aunt like we're strangers every time someone's around."

"Certain members of your constituency don't approve," Brumal said.

"I don't care. Someday, I'll have a wife. Do you expect me to only show affection behind closed doors? The objections are all from the oldest courtiers."

"The very ones you should be trying to appease."

Cam grew stern. "I'm not planning to *appease* anyone. Appeasement would indicate an apology for who I am, and I make no apologies for that, Brumal. I'll do my best to reassure those who are nervous about my governing abilities. That's the end of it."

Brumal's smile was obviously forced. "I understand, Camden. You must realize, I only want what's best for you."

"And I appreciate your expertise. You know exactly how things have been done for centuries. Hopefully, you'll forgive me for instituting my own preferences—such as a less formal court."

The older man turned to Destry. "I ought to beg pardon of our visitor. I'd hate for you to return to your people and tell them this is how life goes on in the goblin court."

Cam chuckled. "Destry won't tell tales. Our secrets are safe with her."

The chancellor's eyes lingered appreciatively on her unbound hair. She owed Tyla thanks for the suggestion. "I'm sure she's all that is discreet. Tell me, Destry, what do you think of Rí Kobold?"

"It's beautiful…what I've seen, anyway. The willa forest is amazing."

His gaze sharpened. "Many faeries find the trees intimidating. Too much goblin magic for comfort."

"I guess it comes from hanging out with a goblin for four years."

Cam slid one hand along her back. "Speaking of which, this goblin has things to teach you. See you at dinner, Brumal." He whisked her down the hall.

"In a hurry to escape?" she whispered.

A wry expression flitted across Cam's face. "I'm grateful to Brumal. He guides me in a lot of areas where I'm untried. But one more word about 'court manners,' and I'll deliver him to your combat class for target practice."

"I'm surprised you told him about us, since you aren't telling your subjects."

"Didn't have much choice. When he heard about the lessons, Brumal nearly choked. He thought I'd fallen in love or lust or some such thing. I heard every possible consequence of getting involved with a faerie. He was on the second litany when I gave in and explained the real reason for asking you here."

Destry snorted with laughter. "Fey Elena thought you were gonna abduct me as a faerie bride."

"Yeah, we could install your magic partner in the room next door. Talk about cozy." He opened the door to the audience chamber and held it for her, grinning.

A raucous squawk cut the silence. Cam's grin slipped. Destry peered around him to the cage set in a corner of the room. Though it was fancier than the one at Cam's house, the occupant was the same. "Rupert?" Destry slipped under Cam's arm and through the door. "Since when is he in here?"

Cam let the door bang shut. "Since Tyla got tired of his shrieking. Twice now, she's tried to smuggle him out on dwarfish trading caravans."

"You made her keep your mangy bird? In her room?"

"Of course not. He was in *my* bedroom." Cam's neck reddened. "But Rupert still doesn't like me much. Everyone in that wing could hear whenever he got annoyed."

Destry shook her head. "You should let someone else take him...someone who likes ugly, ornery, screeching birds. At least Rupert could taste some new fingers."

"Oh, he doesn't bite any *other* goblins. He doesn't screech at any other goblins. Just me." Cam sounded grim. "But he can't hold out forever. That bird will accept me eventually."

Destry rolled her eyes. Cam added, "I better feed him before we start the lesson, or we'll have to do the entire thing in sign language." He strode to the cage with the air of a man steeling himself for battle.

Destry hurried over, snagging the birdseed from the shelf beneath the cage. "Blood makes the spellbooks hard to read. How about I feed him and save your fingers?"

"How about you don't? Rupert likes goblins—other goblins, anyway—because of the nature connection. He may not like faeries." Cam reached for the bag.

Destry pulled it out of reach and flicked the latch on the cage; the door swung open with a metallic moan. She stuck her hand inside, eyeballing Rupert in case he decided to expand his palette with some fey fingers. But the bird sat calmly on his perch, watching bird seed spill into his dish with a rapid *tap-tap-tap-tap*.

He chirruped. Destry lifted a finger to stroke his neck. Rupert stretched taller, allowing her access to his chest feathers. Behind her, Cam made a disbelieving sound—something between a cough and a choke. "This is getting personal."

"Guess he prefers things with wings," Destry said. "Too bad you're the almighty goblin king. Rupert might like you better as a faerie."

He grumbled under his breath; Destry didn't ask for clarification. She pulled her hand out of the cage, and Cam closed the door. The second he touched the bars, the parrot loosed a cringe-inducing squawk. Rupert continued shrieking until Cam retreated across the room.

Destry followed, scooting up onto her customary stool. "Do dwarves come through your kingdom often?"

"About every month or so, depending on the season. Why?"

"Because you're right: that bird hates you, and it's definitely personal."

A MONSTER MOST BEGUILING

✦

By the time Cam walked Destry through the forest to the edge of fey land, it was almost twilight. As promised the previous week, Cam had brought a surprise to their lesson—a creature with long rabbit ears and a rat-like but furry tail, small enough to fit in Destry's hands. She'd christened it Ratbit.

But between the surprise and her after-lesson visit with Wings, she'd left way too late. She waved goodbye to Cam and took off at a jog for the firewell. With tests in several classes tomorrow, communion with her magic source was essential to a good grade. *Please let the well be deserted.*

Destry had, on occasion, run into other faeries leaving the well. She'd passed goblins more often. Usually, they ignored her or offered a terse nod of recognition. A few even smiled or waved. But she'd had to give deference three times now, to two different goblins. The first—an older woman—had stated in cool tones that she preferred to commune alone. Destry had waited at the base of the stairs, and it had only made her run about twenty minutes late.

But the other goblin—a man in his mid-twenties—had gone full-goblin the second he saw her: a man-beast with leathery skin, bat-wings, and glowing red eyes. He'd watched *her* wings shoot out with obvious pleasure, then ordered her to wait by the river. It was over an hour before he left the firewell. The second time they crossed paths, he'd been leaving the well but turned around as soon as he saw Destry. He'd transformed with a vindictive smile and, when her wings didn't shoot out, prowled over to stand inches from her. She stood frozen as he whispered in her ear. "The river, fey trash." After two hours, Destry couldn't stay any longer without missing curfew. She'd flunked a quiz the next day as a result.

She didn't want to tell Cam about those experiences. They left her feeling lesser, somehow. So she skirted his questions about the well—careful to be honest, but careful what she shared. And she tried not to overreact again, like she'd done the day of their first lesson.

She didn't have time for delays today. Destry took the hill at a run. The daily visits were paying off; she was barely winded when she rounded the top...

And nearly ran into four fairies. Four intimidating faeries—two men and two women—wearing black uniforms with gold and silver flames embroidered along the arms from wrist to shoulder. They stood at the base of the stairs, backs straight and chins high. One man held out a hand. "You'll have to wait, miss."

"But I don't have long. I'll get in trouble if I'm not in by curfew."

"I'm sorry." He sounded courteous but unyielding. "You'll have to wait until Queen Liselle is finished."

The faerie queen? Destry hadn't even heard she was a fire fey. She tried to peek around him, but the guard sidestepped to block her, face stern. There was nothing for it. She'd have to come tomorrow night instead. Hopefully, the abysmal test grades wouldn't affect her average much.

A quiet voice echoed from the top of the stairs, "Let her come up, Clarent."

The guard turned, giving Destry an unimpeded view. An ethereal woman stood looking down at them, raven hair shining. She beckoned to Destry. "Come, my dear. Two of us can share the firewell's bounty. You should not get in trouble on my account."

A female guard protested as Destry slipped past her. The queen lifted one hand, palm forward. "I can defend myself against one young student, should it come to that. I have not become entirely useless."

Destry scurried up the stairs. Recalling Brumal's strained expression earlier, she took a chance and swept her best curtsy. It still wasn't good. She straightened, and Queen Liselle smiled, her deep brown eyes faintly amused.

The queen turned and walked into the pavilion. Destry followed but stopped a couple feet in. Queen Liselle had seated herself on a bench; where was Destry supposed to sit? Or should she not sit at all, maintaining a respectful distance between her and royalty?

Liselle wafted a hand towards the bench. "We shall not stand on ceremony, my dear. It's a rare novelty to have a companion."

Destry seated herself gingerly. "I'm grateful for your understanding, Your Majesty."

The queen's face had a timeless quality, though she must have been about the same age as Cam's dad. "Perhaps in return, you may answer a question for me. I hear that one of the fire faeries at the school is taking lessons from the goblin king. Might you know this unfortunate girl?"

Another bigoted faerie. Destry sounded stiff, despite her best efforts. "That's me."

"This is most opportune. I considered sending a message to your school."

"A message?"

"Indeed. Those lessons were instituted in an effort at mutual understanding, and they cannot be circumvented. However, I would caution you: do not be lulled into false security by the seeming normalcy of many goblins. Do not let your guard down in the goblins' presence."

Destry frowned. "I've been safe at the goblin castle." Unbidden, a traitorous voice whispered through her mind: *But what about out of it? Do you feel safe when the wrong goblin is at the firewell?*

"I'm pleased to hear it. Nonetheless, the circumstances merit caution." She smoothed her gold-hued dress with a slender hand. "Have you been presented at court yet?"

"Today."

"Then you should understand. Some of the goblins were in full-form, were they not? An opportunity to show their power, to frighten and humiliate you."

"Maybe they're just scared of us." But Destry knew it wasn't true—not for all goblins.

Liselle met her gaze. "You think me prejudiced. Would it surprise you to know that at one time, I ran tame in the goblin castle?" She smoothed her gown again, absently. "I considered my elders close-minded and ridiculous. I wanted to prove that the goblins are no different than us. So I visited, in an official capacity, and made friends in an unofficial one. I quite liked it there, and thought how ridiculous everyone was. Then I got to know them better."

Destry watched a strand of ghost fire twist in a figure eight around her ankles, trying to keep her face expressionless. Liselle said, "Goblins are closely attuned with the animal side of their natures. Their loyalty to each other drives them and supersedes all. Believe me, my dear—no matter how close you are to a goblin, he will turn on you in a second, should you threaten his world."

Her bitter tone left a sour metallic tang in the air. Destry said carefully, "Thank you for the advice. I know you have more experience than me."

"That rarely matters to young people. But perhaps you will prove the exception." The queen stood. "I've had enough heat. I visit the firewell out of pleasure more than need these days."

Destry stood, too, and curtsied. Queen Liselle sighed. "You're so very young. Have a pleasant evening, my dear, and remember my advice." She swept down the stairs, skirts whispering, leaving Destry with only the deepening twilight for company.

As February blended into March and then April, the summery weather turned cooler. The leaves on the fey trees at the school changed color, from light green to a pale shimmering gold. Destry's life fell into a pattern of mornings with Tristan and classes at school and twice-weekly visits to Cam. She became familiar with the firewell schedule of the unfriendly goblins, which made avoiding them easier. She spent more time with Sara and David, made some casual friends, and took quite a few unauthorized walks with Tristan to Mellie's café.

Cam still insisted on escorting her through the woods. The three girls hadn't reappeared, and the lack of further disappearances made no difference to him. Destry got to know Tyla better, and Cam's aunt dropped in on their lessons each week for a visit.

Learning goblin magic improved Destry's grades significantly. She spent hours studying the language and creating spells. Despite some improvement in using faerie magic, Cam's technique was more reliable. Destry mastered the art of using hand motions while speaking quietly, so the teachers wouldn't realize what form of magic led to her newfound success.

Around the end of April, Fey Renalt caught her on the way into Combat and said she'd be moving to the advanced class soon.

Destry paused on the threshold. "I thought students didn't change classes until the end of each semester."

"Generally. But with the sort of progress you've made, it's unnecessary to keep you with the beginners—most of whom will never take more than the required first year." He laughed. "Perhaps you can coax your magic partner to take another class. Tristan never lived up to his potential in this area."

Destry doubted she could persuade Tristan. He described combat class as the worst way he'd ever spent an hour. She sensed some deeper reason than simple disinterest, but Tristan turned aside her probes on the subject.

"It's not too early to consider making this the focus of your education," the Combat teacher added, as they started into the classroom. "Have you considered what you'd like to do after graduating?"

Destry hesitated. For years now, she'd only been able to worry about survival: finding ways to stay with her mom, to keep herself safe, to keep herself fed. She hadn't had energy to think past that.

But here in The Fold, she had space to think further than surviving. And while she loved learning to defend herself in Combat, she didn't want to spend the rest of her life using those skills to protect snooty nobles. No, if she was going to help anyone, it would be kids like her: half-faeries whose lives would never get better without someone to seek them out. Hadn't Riamon mentioned faeries who did exactly that?

Still, she didn't know how to say that to Renalt, who was easily her favorite teacher. She shrugged. "I don't really know my options yet."

He patted her shoulder. "Of course. And I'm not trying to pressure you. But with your natural bent, you might consider the option. Some of us find it very fulfilling."

"Rewarding, to be more precise." Riamon had entered the room behind them.

Renalt clapped the deputy headmaster on the back. "Here's our expert for the day." They'd spent the last few classes learning about less-friendly creatures and techniques to counter them. Each guest speaker had specific knowledge on the subject.

Riamon adjusted his glasses, knocked askew by Renalt. "I'm experienced more than an expert. But I may be of service, regardless."

The class sat on the mat-covered floor. Riamon handed around sheets of parchment covered with drawings of faeries and goblins. "What creature do you see?"

One girl said, "A handsome boy."

Another student wiggled his paper. "Little girl."

"An old lady."

Riamon said, "And, if you believe your eyes, that's all you will ever see. The creature we speak of today is among the most dangerous you will ever encounter. To faeries, to be more precise."

He held up a sketch of...nothing. "Today we discuss hobgoblins."

A couple students shifted uneasily or exchanged glances with their neighbors. One girl whimpered. Others, like Destry, looked confused. Riamon pointed to the blank parchment. "Hobgoblins have two forms:

the one they use to walk among other beings, undetected, and their natural form. Few know what a hobgoblin truly looks like. They only revert to their natural shape when hunting. In their true form, they cannot abide sunlight—giving rise to the human legends about vampires. But a hobgoblin isn't after your blood. He wants something greater: your life force. In the case of magical beings, this means your magic."

A boy raised his hand. "But we have protection around our tattoos."

Riamon nodded. "All hobgoblins have sharp fangs that can pierce either goblin skin or faerie tattoos. They may also hunt goblins. Most choose a single race as their preferred food source."

The girl who'd whimpered began crying. "A hobgoblin killed my gram when I was seven. At least, they think so."

Riamon nodded again. "Determining what happened to hobgoblin victims can be difficult. If the creature attacks animals or humans, it leaves a corpse with bite marks in the neck—thus the legends of vampiric slayings. A goblin, with more human blood than most fey possess, will be a withered husk. And a faerie, should the hobgoblin feed to the very end, will be reduced to nothing but their essence—the soul of a faerie. Upon that, the creature cannot feed, much as they would like to."

"Why?" The timid question came from somewhere in the back.

"Because a hobgoblin is an abomination. A creature created by the union of a goblin and a faerie."

Destry raised her hand. "But Fey Elena said goblin kings sometimes take faerie brides. Does that mean all their children...?"

A couple people tittered. Her lessons with Cam were well known. They probably assumed she was asking for personal reasons. Destry's cheeks burned, but Riamon ignored both reactions. "A hobgoblin is the result of the rape of a female, not a willing union—a violently unwanted pregnancy, to be more precise. The faerie magic fights the goblin magic. As in the act, the male's magic dominates, the two combine, and you have a creature with all magic, all intelligence, and no soul. There is no conscience in them. Just an insatiable hunger and two magics forever at war. The women thus violated usually abandon the infants at birth."

An older boy with blonde hair asked, "Then how do they survive?"

"Hobgoblins are cunning, even as infants. They can appear as a normal goblin or faerie—whichever was the dominant, or male, magic—and often find a family to take them in. For several years, they can subsist on regular food. Then they transition to their natural diet."

Sassandra, perched on a stool, added, "There are a couple defenses against these monsters. Your ability to palm power is good if you can hit the hobgoblin—they're wicked fast—and your wings will cut their skin."

Riamon grabbed a stick of charcoal and sketched fangs on the blank parchment. "These are meant to pierce deeply, but they have a flaw: the length makes them break more easily than regular goblin fangs. We've found them broken off in victims before. And they seem to be a hobgoblin's only way of draining life force."

"What happens once you remove the fangs? Do the people survive?" a young girl asked.

Riamon shook his head. "The fangs act as a poison. Those who stripped the hobgoblins of their ability to kill did so at the cost of their own lives."

The blonde-haired boy raised his hand. "Fey Riamon, how do you know so much about hobgoblins? Have you helped hunt them?"

"I was engaged to one."

No one spoke. The only sounds were the distant noises of a few students horsing around in the hall. Riamon sighed heavily. "She called herself Elisabeth. Her father had been a faerie, and when she wasn't hunting, she blended into our world almost perfectly. Quite beautiful, quite enchanting."

He half-smiled, but there was too much pain in it to succeed. "I suppose she'd decided to try life among us—the closest thing to her kind. Since she preferred to hunt goblins, her double-life might have gone on for years without discovery. The night after our engagement celebration, a two-day affair with many festivities, I finished my teaching duties and walked to Si'fliegen to see her.

"I reached her house in time to see a hooded figure leaving. I followed it down an alley, curious, and called her name. The figure turned. Elisabeth's voice came from the hood, though it sounded different than I was used to. She said only one thing: that I shouldn't have followed her. She'd been hungry too long, you see. Our engagement festivities made it difficult for her to leave to hunt. She'd settled for faerie nourishment that night, and I interrupted."

He slid the high collar of his shirt down. On his neck were two dark round scars. "She used the venom on her fangs to paralyze me—something hobgoblins seem to reserve for places where a quiet kill is necessary."

"How did you escape?" The girl in the back row almost whispered the question.

"Renalt may take credit for that. He, too, had come to the village—for an evening of enjoyment, to be specific. He saw me going into the alley and followed, thinking to catch me and Elisabeth kissing and to tease us. Instead, he saw me laid out on the ground, a clawed figure bent over me."

"I blasted her away from Riamon," Renalt said. "The creature fled. I didn't give chase, with my friend injured. For months afterwards, faeries combed the surrounding areas. The goblins did too. We never found her."

"I'm one of the few survivors of such an attack," Riamon said. "From my experience, you may learn the best way to protect yourself from a hobgoblin: observation. I might have noted that Elisabeth never used magic in front of me—one of the biggest hallmarks of a hobgoblin. Their magic relies on spoken spells only. Similarly, she rarely took food around others. She told me she'd lost her wings in an accident, and tragedy as that is for our kind, I didn't press the matter. Hobgoblins, fey-fathered or otherwise, do not possess them and cannot create the illusion. Her lack of family or friends, her secrecy regarding the rest of her life...these things should have warned me."

He stood. "Let us split up—into small groups, to be precise. I've written ten scenarios for you to consider, along with the hobgoblin's hunting habits."

The blonde boy raised his hand one more time. "Sir? Do hobgoblins have emotions?"

Riamon frowned. "They have sentience. One assumes they have emotion—whether or not they have a conscience."

"But do they love? I mean, why did she want to get engaged? Seems like a sure way to be discovered."

Riamon turned away, handing some papers around. "That will always be unclear—or more accurately, a mystery. Perhaps my proximity to the school, and thus the goblin realm, made her hunting trips less obvious. Whatever Elisabeth gained from our association, we can be sure it was not motivated by love. The attempt to kill me would indicate otherwise."

A MATTER OF TRUST

Destry was quiet that evening at dinner. Halfway through, Sara lobbed a roll at her. "What's got you so serious? Already stressed about finals?"

She forced a smile. "I was thinking about our combat lesson."

"They did hobgoblins today," Tristan said. His smile was teasing, but he squeezed Destry's hand under the table. She squeezed back, then slid her fingers loose and grabbed a nectargreen from the fruit bowl.

David glanced up from his current sketch: a close-up of fey hands manipulating glowing magic strands. "That's a freaky lesson. Creeped me out."

"Yeah." Sara bumped her shoulder against David's. "He kept dreaming that everyone we knew was really a hobgoblin in disguise."

"Traitor." He mock-glared. "My secret's supposed to be safe with you."

They were so easy together...like they'd been made for each other. Most of the joined couples were that way. Even those who would never be romantic, because of a lack of attraction or other barriers, were perfect complements—the sort of best friend that comes along once in a lifetime.

It was nice to watch, but uncomfortable to realize that was her future.

She shrugged the thought away. "In David's defense, it is creepy. A hobgoblin could take on your shape, or yours, or yours—" she pointed to each of them—"and I'd never know the difference."

"Not so," Sara said. "Hobgoblins can only shift between two shapes: their true form and their faerie or goblin form."

Tristan grinned at Destry. "You're the one we should worry about." He ticked off points on his fingers. "One: you came here late, with no friends and no easily verifiable past. Two: you're very private, even with your magic partner. And three: you prefer *goblin magic*." This last was said in a stage whisper that only carried around the table.

"So if we're massacred in our beds tonight, everyone knows the culprit," Sara said.

Destry took a big bite from her nectargreen. "But I eat. See?" she mumbled around her mouthful. A piece dribbled out and fell to the table.

David chuckled. "We can't miss it."

When dinner ended, Sara and David sheared off to finish homework; Destry and Tristan strolled into the great hall. They often spent a few minutes there after dinner, sitting at the edges of their respective fountains, getting doused with mist and talking. But Tristan took one look at the crowded edges and said, "Want to walk the grounds tonight?"

They didn't have long before curfew, but Destry agreed anyway. She'd learned to stop questioning Tristan's ability to slip in undetected. They'd gotten caught exactly once, leading to a Saturday afternoon detention spent catching the dragon-mice that had infested a classroom. Despite a few burns on her fingers, that wasn't enough to make Destry refuse Tristan's out-of-bounds excursions.

They walked to their favorite hill, one that gave a perfect view of the willa forest, its white branches and stained-glass leaves gilded by the setting sun. The foliage was thinning in response to the cooler weather. How long before she got used to fall temperatures in April? A chilly gust pulled at their clothes. She shivered.

"Cold?" Tristan wrapped an arm around her. Destry froze, torn between the impulse to pull away and the desire to lean into him.

Tristan's lips pulled into a wry smile. "Why do you do that?"

"Do what?"

"Every time I do anything besides hold your hand—not because I'm pushing, just because it feels normal—you move, or get all tense, or joke it off."

"I don't."

Tristan released her, taking her hand instead. He drew his thumb along her knuckles, lingering in the bumps and valleys. "Yeah, you do. At Mellie's, you said, 'How about letting things happen naturally?' You don't seem to mind me touching you. But every time we start to get closer, it's like you're fighting what comes naturally."

Destry chewed her lip, searching for an answer. "It's kind of...big. Once we go that far, we're done for life. You and me and no other possibilities, ever."

"Is that so awful? If you're happy with me—if we feel so right together you have to pull away to fight it—what's wrong with having that for the rest of your life?"

How could she explain that the end result wasn't what bothered her, but the sense that her free will was being eroded? Something that came too easily felt unreal. It seemed like the road to love ought to have more bumps and less certainty. How could she explain that to Tristan, though, with his enviable gift for accepting life—crummy or not—and creating happiness from it?

She couldn't. And she didn't honestly want to. Had she hand-picked a boyfriend, Tristan would have made the top of the list. Destry squeezed his fingers. "Nothing's wrong with that. Just let me take things at my own pace, okay? You've had four years to get used to the idea. I've had less than six months."

He gave her the same wry look as before. "Sure you want to get used to it?"

She'd hurt him. Despite Tristan's effort to pretend otherwise, Destry sensed that much. "I really do. And because we're magic partners, I'm gonna tell you a secret—one nobody at school knows."

"A secret, huh?" He raised an eyebrow, but he was obviously pleased. Warmth shot through her.

"Yes. I haven't told anyone because...it's embarrassing."

"An *embarrassing* secret? Tell away. Goblins with long, threatening claws will never wrench the truth from me. Neither will hordes of rampaging dragon-mice. Even Julya couldn't scare me enough to betray your trust."

Destry rolled her eyes. "I'm afraid of heights."

Total silence from Tristan.

She pressed her lips together, unwilling to look at him. "Go ahead and laugh. I know you're dying to."

He did chuckle—quietly. "Sorry, Des. It's not funny. But it sure is ironic."

"Yeah, so I've ...thought." She stumbled on the last word, because she'd been about to say, *So I've heard*. And that would have involved explaining about Cam.

Which she hadn't done yet.

Which was a problem for another night.

"How do you plan to take Advanced Combat with that issue?" Tristan asked. "They do some wingwork in there."

"*What?*" Her voice came out a squeak.

He smiled at her, a very nice smile with no laughter at all. "You trusted me, Des. If you'll trust me again, I'll help you out."

Relief rushed through her. If anyone would know a way around the flying lessons, it would be Tristan.

"Meet me on your balcony once everyone's asleep," he said. "I'll tell you all about it."

Destry glared at Tristan. "This is your idea of help? Throwing me off a balcony?" She pressed against the outer wall of the school like the sticky-footed geckos that climbed the porch posts of her Texas home. "Forget it. I'll skip the combat class."

Tristan slid one hand behind her lower back, trying to pry her away from the wall. "You know you want to take Advanced Combat. And you've gotta be able to glide to do it. Which means being able to look over the edge of a balcony and not hurl or pass out." He finally got one arm around her waist, pulling her loose with a grunt of effort.

"I'm gonna do both of those things *on you* if you don't let go!" Destry's voice rose so high, only dogs could have heard it.

Tristan dragged her towards the edge of the railing. "Shhh. If you wake everybody up, we'll get detention again."

"I don't care." She leaned into him, away from the death-drop mere feet away. "A month chasing dragon-mice would be better than this."

"Really? Getting your fingers burned and crawling under desks is better than standing here in the arms of your very wonderful, very understanding magic partner?" He winced when she kicked him in the ankle. "Who's now injured in the line of duty."

"Serves you right. I thought you were gonna get me out of that flying requirement."

His blue eyes crinkled. "I'm a magic worker, not a miracle worker." Tristan slid behind her and rotated them to look out over the railing. He pulled Destry tight against his chest. "Now, is this as bad as you thought it'd be?"

It was like being in the willa tree with Cam—not entirely terrifying when she had a sense of security against the height-induced dizziness. But they wouldn't just stand on the edge of the balcony. "Yes," Destry gritted. "Because you want me to leap over the edge and hope I don't plummet to the ground and die."

"All I want right now is to hold you and glide you to the ground. And maybe you could keep your eyes open." His wings ripped loose, unfurling to their full length.

Her stomach twisted. It was tempting to tell Tristan where he could stick those wings of his. But he'd been so understanding earlier. She couldn't say she didn't trust him now. "Can your wings support both of us?"

He flexed them to their full width, hovering at the edges of her vision. She turned her head to see better. Moonlight glinted off their points, the sharp silvery edges and indigo patterns. Destry felt a swift flash of kinship with Cam; no wonder he'd wanted to touch hers.

Tristan grinned. "Done looking yet?"

Destry jerked back around. The horrible view was better than his knowing smile. "I was just checking to see how strong they are."

He whispered in her ear, "I like yours, too, Destry. Wish I got to see them more."

Heat scalded her cheeks. "That doesn't answer my question."

"I've been doing this since I was eleven. My wings can handle it."

Destry didn't ask exactly what part he'd been doing since he was eleven. She just sucked in a deep breath and nodded. Tristan's face lit with excitement. He released her, jumping the railing of the balcony to stand on the ledge that ran in front of it, and offered a hand to help her over.

That ledge seemed much narrower than before. Destry took a half-step back, but Tristan grabbed her wrist. "No changing your mind. C'mon, I'll get you brownies if you make it." He tugged so she had to either move or fall. She kept her eyes trained on his wings as he helped her slide first one leg, then the other, over the rail. Her breath came faster.

Tristan twined his arms around her ribcage. "Be careful your wings stay put. You'll shred me if they pop out now."

Her wings were as unwilling to fly as the rest of her; they furled so tight, her back muscles ached. With a whimper, Destry flung both arms around his neck. Tristan sighed. "You could see better if you faced forward. And I could glide better if I could breathe. It's a quick drop down...just a few seconds."

"So is a fall to the death," she snapped. "Take what you can get."

He sighed again, but she felt his legs bending, gathering for a push-off. Destry reminded herself how badly she wanted to take Advanced Combat. She reminded herself how tired she was of this fear of heights. She reminded herself how much she loved brownies.

It didn't work. "Stop! Stop, stop, stop, I changed my mind!"

"Too late," Tristan said cheerfully as he vaulted off the edge.

She'd intended to close her eyes, no matter what Tristan requested. But they were frozen wide in terror. The wind rushed over them, the scenery sped past them. The ground got closer and closer. And then they landed with a thump and a stagger. It was over.

Destry gasped in a huge, hungry breath and buried her face in Tristan's shoulder. "We survived."

"Guess this means I owe you brownies."

She shuddered. "Give them to me first next time." It registered, faintly, that she was actually willing to do it again.

Tristan stroked her hair. "You're the bravest faerie girl I know."

This seemed ironic, since she was still shaking. "You must know some really wussy girls."

Tristan slid his hands along her jaw, under her hair, tracing gentle patterns with his fingertips. Her eyes met his. She felt breathless again, but not for the same reason. Tristan half-smiled. "Can I kiss you, Destry? One kiss?"

She almost said no. It was too fast, too much. But the night wind was cool, and his arms were warm, and he was her magic partner. So Destry nodded and allowed Tristan to pull her closer, with only the stars as witness.

RIPE

❖

He was ready. Everything was in place. The wait had burned, stretching him thinner and thinner until he felt like the Shadow whose name he'd taken—but the girl needed to ripen, fruit only to be devoured at the peak of freshness.

Her life had formed better than he could have hoped. That idiot goblin king, with his disdain for tradition and determination for change, might have ruined all. Shadow had observed the fool when Destry left him in the woods each week. Camden Darkwater loved a faerie, whether or not he knew it.

But his quixotic honor and determination to give the girl her own life had proved fortuitous. Her world was now full, moderately happy, growing sweeter by the day. How much worse, then, when everything fell. When Shadow came to her, she wouldn't resist.

She would give him exactly what he wanted.

Her.

25

PRESSURE

◆

"How long before you rejoin the faerie world?"

Tristan's voice startled Destry, curled up at the base of a fey tree in the grove they frequented. She'd been too absorbed in her goblin magic book to register his approach.

A gust of chilly air swept through the secluded area. Leaves rustled, whispering secrets to one another. Destry tugged her cloak tighter. "I'm learning a new spell. Hard to say how long it'll take."

Tristan sat next to her, grinning. He rubbed a thumb between her eyebrows. "You get this look on your face when someone disturbs your reading—a grouchy line between your eyes. It's cute."

"You interrupted my studying to say I'm cute when I'm annoyed?"

"Mean, too," he teased. "But that's not why I came looking for you."

Sighing, Destry set the book aside. She had less time for studying goblin magic lately. Tristan's efforts to teach her to glide (late at night, so she didn't have to explain her fear to everyone else)...the heavier workload from their teachers as the end of the school year drew close...time spent developing her social life (this at Tristan's insistence); they'd all cut into her study hours. And she and Tristan spent their private tutoring hours on faerie magic.

Destry had a lesson with Cam in three days and didn't want a repeat of the previous week. Cam had prepared an experiment—something he'd done as a new student—and been eager to share it. Unfortunately, the execution depended on knowing spells she'd failed to study. She explained about the party she and Tristan had attended at Mellie's, her lessons in Advanced Combat, her upcoming finals, and Cam insisted he understood. Destry still felt like she'd severed a tie—one she might not be ready to cut.

Tristan caught some magic, twirling it absently between his fingers. She could tell because he liked to make it glow. It was like watching someone play with an evanescent glowstick. "I missed you at breakfast."

Destry had skipped the dining hall because today was one of the free Saturdays. And Tristan would have plans, whether or not he'd thought to mention them. With most of her fellow students in town, this was the perfect time to do some serious catch-up...alone. "I wasn't hungry."

Tristan made the magic turn rainbow colors. "I thought maybe you were avoiding more gliding lessons."

Destry grimaced. Non-gliding lessons would be more accurate. Over the past couple weeks, she'd mastered her fear enough to stand on the balcony lip without shaking. She could allow Tristan to glide her down without absolute terror. She could even climb the vines up the balcony; it wasn't much different than climbing the ladder to Cam's room. But every time she considered jumping off the ledge, her wings furled inside so tightly that the muscles behind her shoulder blades cramped.

"No," she said. "If I can't move past this, I'll have to explain to Fey Renalt. We start gliding next week."

Tristan released the magic. It twisted mid-air, forming a tiny, perfect rainbow before the colors dissolved. "We'll tackle it again tonight. Today, though..." His eyes brightened. "A bunch of the others are going to Si'fliegen. There are lots of places you've never seen. I thought we could go, too."

"Who's going?" Destry hoped the question sounded casual.

Tristan ticked them off on his fingers. "Sara and David, Lenny and Cass, Avery and Aiden. Not Julya. She's ticked at David for spilling oatmeal on her this morning."

She'd been afraid it would be that group. Joined half-faeries gravitated toward other joined halfs—people who understood the hard parts and the better parts to being a working duo. Some of the couples had made things official. Others, like Sara and David, were in the "best friends" camp and saw other people. A few were even in the same netherland she and Tristan currently walked: not always just friends but not committed, either.

Tristan was unfailingly careful to get Destry's permission before kissing her, whether the permission was tacit or spoken. And he never asked for more than a kiss or two; he accepted her hesitancy, even if he didn't understand it. But his efforts couldn't erase the pressure to make a decision...a pressure that came from outside sources and Destry's own conscience more than from Tristan. Hanging out all day with three other sets of joined couples wouldn't help.

She smiled at Tristan, but regretfully. His smile faded. "Guess that doesn't sound so great?"

"It sounds fun. But I have a lesson in three days at the goblin castle, and I've hardly studied."

He shrugged. "Don't. Maybe the goblin king will stop insisting on these pointless lessons if you don't progress."

"Pointless?" Destry heard the coolness in her voice and tried to modulate it. "These lessons are helpful to me."

"I didn't mean it like that. But ultimately, you want to learn faerie magic, don't you? The kind we work together?"

"Of course. But I also want to hold my own when we aren't together. You should want that for me too."

Tristan ran one hand through his hair. "I do! Look, I just figured you'd be sick of those lessons, no matter how much you love that forest."

Destry didn't correct his assumption that the willas were the largest motivating factor in her visits to Rí Kobold. The longer she went without explaining about Cam, the harder it seemed to do. Tristan would be hurt that she hadn't trusted him from the beginning.

Destry pulled her knees up, twining her arms around them. "I like learning goblin magic. I'm sorry if that bothers you. I'm sorry it makes me weird, and I'm sorry you're the one stuck with me. But I don't want to give it up." She rested her forehead on her knees, wishing she'd hidden better so they could've avoided the entire conversation.

His heavy sigh was easy to hear. "I don't care about any of that. Forget I said anything."

She lifted her head to look at him. "You're mad."

"No. Just frustrated and confused." He stood. "I'll let you get back to studying."

What would he say if she asked him to stay? What would he say if she offered to share this part of her life with him? But his comment—"pointless"—choked the words off in her throat. "Have fun with the others."

His attempt at lightheartedness was better than hers. "Yeah. I'll bring you some brownies." He strode across the grounds.

A half hour later, Destry closed her book with a thump. Concentrating on the ancient language was impossible while guilt twisted her stomach. Maybe she should join Tristan, after all. She started for the school.

Partway up the stairs to her dorm, someone called her name. She turned. Riamon stood at the bottom. He jogged up to her, a package tucked under one leather-clad arm. "This came by way of messenger for you. From the goblin castle. Normally, I would be required to watch you open it, for your safety."

"My safety?"

"It comes from a foreign entity. A potential enemy, to be precise. However, I doubt the goblin king is sending you poisoned letters." Riamon's smile seemed secretive, amused.

Destry frowned. "What do you think it is?"

He dropped a pointed look on her magic book. "I am slightly more perceptive and less silly than people believe. You go willingly to your lessons at the goblin castle...eagerly, to be more accurate. Despite having a personable, attractive magic partner, I hear through the rumor mill that you have not yet—how do you young people say it—hooked up? And you like goblin magic."

Her insides congealed, turning to cold stone. If Riamon had noticed, how many other people realized Destry's preferences? He made a placating motion. "We all have secrets. I learned to watch closely some years ago, experience being an excellent teacher. Rest assured, I shall not tell about your admirer...or whom you admire in return."

He slipped her the package and hurried downstairs. Numbly, Destry turned towards her dorm. Two girls came out of the ocean faerie dorm, giggling. Without conscious thought, Destry slid her book to cover the parchment-wrapped parcel. She didn't uncover it until safely in her room.

There was no label; presumably, the carrier had told Riamon it was intended for her. Destry stroked the lightly textured parchment. Mottled with hints of gold, this type was particular to the goblin castle. She'd seen Cam use it for writing important letters. It seemed too pretty to destroy. Destry undid the paper carefully.

She lifted the lid from the dark wood box and gasped. A dagger nestled in a bed of burgundy satin. The silver hilt twisted gracefully upward, twined with opalescent black stone. The shining blade was perhaps an inch wide and six inches long, etched with black designs reminiscent of willa branches.

Destry picked up the weapon carefully. Underneath sat a sleek black sheath and a note written with an old-fashioned calligraphy nib—the type Cam used for official correspondence. *Keep this close—for me.*

Destry shook her head. Cam still worried about the forest. But if it made him feel better, she'd bring the dagger when visiting the castle. Maybe it would be handy for keeping him in line.

The last thought made her smile. She imagined Cam's reaction if she threatened him with this thing: green eyes crinkled at the corners, sculpted lips pulled into a mocking grin. He'd slide his unruly hair out of his eyes and say, "You're more likely to impale yourself than me, Des. Sit down and let's do our lesson."

And here she was, back to what had brought her upstairs in the first place. Destry's smile faded.

Until Riamon mentioned admirers, it never occurred to her that someone—past a few idiotic students—might assume Cam had any romantic interest in her, or the other way around. But Tristan never asked for details about her lessons, past what she willingly shared. She'd assumed he was respecting her privacy. Could there be another reason? Did he wonder why the goblin king wanted her at the castle, and why she went so eagerly?

Destry groaned. Why hadn't she told Tristan the truth from the beginning?

She sheathed the dagger and sat there, turning it over in her hands. Her chest felt tight, compressed from too many conflicting pressures and expectations. Loneliness added its own weight until she could barely breathe.

Destry jerked to her feet. There was one place she could feel peaceful. She slid the sheathed dagger into the waistband of her leggings, covering it with her loose tunic. Driving need sent her out the door, down the stairs, on the path to the willa trees. The guards posted on every free Saturday would be there; she could visit the forest without breaking her promise to Cam.

The burbling river sang out as she reached the rocky expanse of ground. Destry stopped short. No goblins stood sentinel at the edge of the trees, waiting to discourage troublemakers from the academy. Where were they?

The willas swayed like they were beckoning her. A gut-deep ache for Wings rose in Destry. The willa seemed to understand her in a way that transcended the need for words. More, Destry swore she could feel the tree's emotions. She felt too silly to mention it to Cam, though. Sensing the willas was a royal goblin gift, not a common faerie one.

The dagger pressed against her waist, reassuring. Surely, going to the *edge* of the forest would be okay. Not inside, she reminded her prickly conscience. She was still doing exactly what she'd promised. The willas weren't likely to tattle, either, since she was an approved visitor. The trees reached towards Destry as she drew closer. Smiling at their welcome, she touched the branches.

Unease shot through her mind. One branch twisted around her wrist. A sense of protectiveness—towards her—and a feeling of hostility followed the pressing uneasiness.

The hostility wasn't for Destry. She slid her hand loose and turned a full circle, ignoring the tree's attempts to snag her hair and clothes. Nothing out of the ordinary... Water babbled. Cool air kissed her cheeks. Sunlight streamed through colorful leaves, dappling the forest floor.

The tree grabbed her wrist again. When she didn't move, another branch pushed her from behind. She stumbled and fell, grazing her knee. Maybe it was the tree's touch, maybe the agitated rustling of the other willas, but the silence of the forest seemed threatening. A chill slithered down her back.

Destry clambered to her feet. The tree pushed her again, urging her into the forest. She shook her head; if something was wrong, heading for the school made more sense. Another willa, closer in, rustled angrily.

A sound like footsteps clattering over stones echoed from behind her. Destry froze. She turned slowly towards the clearing, but the rocky expanse was still deserted.

Another clatter—closer. The trees began waving, more agitated than ever. The closest willa shoved her. An image filled her mind: Cam. The willa's emotion flooded her: urgency, a need for shelter. The sound of stealthy movement on the rocks filled her ears, an invisible threat stalking nearer.

Destry ran—for the goblin castle and Cam and safety.

SEEING RED

---◆---

"Camden? Did you hear what I said?" Wulfrik Brumal, High Chancellor of Rí Kobold, looked decidedly irritated. He stood in the doorway to Cam's bedroom, watching his sovereign refuse the help of the valet who was daily dispatched to dress the young king.

Cam was rather annoyed himself. Every single day since returning, he'd made his feelings on the matter of a valet clear. Wardrobe suggestions? Fine. Press the clothes and shine the boots? Also fine. Suggest appropriate attire for public appearances? Fine three times. But he knew how to comb his own hair, tie his own shirt laces, and put on his own earth-cursed pants.

Cam had explained this—quite politely—to the valet. And yet, the man knocked on his door every morning. Cam started getting up a half hour earlier to preempt him. So the valet began showing up a half hour sooner, which meant Cam had to get up an hour earlier to render the man's assistance unnecessary. Unlike Destry, Cam wasn't a morning person; this didn't help his mood or his patience.

The valet snatched his (perfectly fine) boots and buffed at a spot. Cam turned to his chancellor. "Yes, I heard. I know you'd like to limit the hours we receive supplicants on Saturdays. And I won't do it just to give the courtiers more of my time. The people coming to the castle Saturday need help. The nobles don't need a weekly dinner party hosted by me. If they got more involved with the less-fortunate, I wouldn't be occupied all Saturday."

"That is not the only concern I mentioned, Camden." Brumal sounded stiff. "I also asked about setting a date to practice the King's Strength spell. It is an essential part of your duties."

Cam was as tired of this conversation as he was the previous topic. "I've been working on that spell since I took my oath. I've memorized it word-perfect."

Every king had to learn that particular bit of magic: insurance for times of war or the injury of a king. It allowed Cam to draw magic from the willas and use it to sustain himself or others. The lengthy spell was the hardest he'd ever tackled.

Brumal sighed. "Yet you've avoided the practical application. That spell requires a very delicate balance to do properly. Give too much magic to anyone besides a goblin—an ally from the dwarfish kingdom, for example—and the surplus of foreign magic will kill the person you wish to save! Worse, giving too much magic could cause your own death. You must have some hands-on practice, and Tyla already volunteered to be your test subject."

Cam's stomach dipped. Of course Tyla would volunteer. Always determined to prove that she'd achieved her position on her own merits, not through their friendship or her father's influence. Never considering the danger posed as the test subject, who had to voluntarily share enough magic with another goblin to cause a true deficit of life force. And if her self-preservation instincts kicked in, and Tyla was unable to voluntarily release that much magic, another goblin had to draw her magic instead. Painful and dangerous—what a wonderful combination.

After that, she'd be counting on Cam's ability to draw life force from the willa and restore her to health. If he couldn't, for some reason, or gave her the wrong amount, Tyla faced a lengthy convalescence. Other goblins would need to share small amounts of their magic each day to support her healing.

Even with Dante—the top healer in the castle—supervising the process, Cam couldn't feel easy about practicing that spell. He also couldn't say that to Brumal, who would point out (again) how this was a traditional rite of passage for all kings, that it conferred honor on the test subject.

Cam would have to do it at some point...some point farther in the future. "I'm not avoiding the hands-on practice, Brumal. My schedule has been packed, and I can't afford to have Tyla out of commission if something goes wrong."

"Your schedule would be less packed if we removed unnecessary obligations—lessons with the fey girl, for example, since you're unwilling to change the Saturday audiences."

"I've heard enough from you on that particular subject as well." Cam didn't try to curb the sharpness in his voice.

Out of the corner of his eye, he noticed the valet listening intently. Picking up gossip to share with anyone who would listen, most likely. Cam held out a hand for his boots. The valet clutched them to his chest, as if Cam intended to bludgeon him with the footwear. "These are not finished, Your Majesty."

"They're finished enough. I have things to do." Cam extricated his shoes and pointed at the door. "You're not hanging around to fiddle with the ties on my shirt or the crease of my pants, either."

Aunt Val walked in on this exchange. She watched the valet stalk out with an injured look on his face. "Why, Camden. It's unlike you to be rude to your servants." Despite the reproving words, her expression was amused.

Cam sat down and tugged on a boot. "It's unlike me to have to repeat myself every day, and yet no one listens. I've been getting dressed on my own for years. I didn't lose the ability because I took the oath of sovereignty. Brumal, I don't want to see that guy tomorrow."

The chancellor sighed. "It is simply a mark of your rank. But if it bothers you overmuch, I shall attend the matter." He cleared his throat.

"Your presence is fortunate, Lady Valda. I need to speak with both of you."

Wonderful. The man had a third topic to discuss. Cam glanced at the clock on the fireplace mantel. "I'm supposed to be in the throne room in fifteen minutes. Is that long enough?"

"Indeed. The subject is simple, but rather delicate. I refer to Your Majesty's marriage."

Cam yanked on the other boot. "I don't recall proposing to anyone."

"That would be the problem. Or rather, it soon will be. Particularly with the faerie girl coming here for lessons."

"How does one relate to the other?"

Aunt Val said, "Goblin engagements are drawn-out affairs, particularly among the nobility. The more important the engagement, the longer it may be. Royalty often propose a good three or four years before they intend to marry."

Brumal added, "With Destry's attendance here, some speculate that you intend to train her to be your bride, which would be unwise. As a young and untried king—one who wants to make significant changes in how the government operates—you need the political support that comes from allying yourself with another noble family. More, your subjects need reassurance that you'll uphold certain established traditions...such as marrying a goblin girl with the right amount of human blood, rather than some fey girl of uncertain parentage."

Cam met his chancellor's gaze. "I'm not trying to change that tradition. I understood it was necessary from the beginning." *One reason I took so long to accept the throne.*

"That's not how it appears. You show little interest in the ladies at court, even though most young men your age are courting. The more established nobility believe you should have already selected a wife."

"You mean the older ones," Cam said. "The same ones who want me to wear a starched cravat and bow to my aunt like we're strangers."

Brumal looked impatient. "Even kings must compromise. Aren't these changes you want more important than fighting something that's inevitable?"

Cam sighed. "Is there something specific you want me to do?"

Brumal slid a sheet of parchment onto his dresser. "Only consider the names on this list: young goblin women, all excellent candidates. You might get to know a few better." He pulled out his pocket watch, checking the time before snapping it shut. "It's a political choice more than an emotional one, Camden. Noble girls understand this. They won't expect you to promise your roots to them immediately—possibly ever. Perhaps that eases your mind?"

The chancellor thought that would comfort him? *Your wife won't expect true devotion from you, and she might not offer it, either. You might never say, "My roots begin and end with you," and mean it.* But Cam's wife would expect a physical relationship, at least. The kingdom would expect heirs. How could he manage that without mutual affection and trust?

This was what he'd agreed to, though. He'd find a way to make it work. Somehow. Cam stood, lacing the strings on his shirt. "Have you heard back from the fey palace yet?"

Brumal's expression turned long-suffering. "No more than before. They assure me there is adequate explanation for the disappearance of each girl."

"Explanations full of holes," Cam snapped. "Have you spoken to the queen herself, or arranged a meeting for me with her?"

"No, I have not. It would be foolish, politically, to insist upon meeting to discuss denizens not of our realm but theirs, based on a few letters from that headmistress and the vague memories of the willas. The queen's executor assures me that we shall be held blameless, having done all that was reasonable on our part. Let me be frank, Your Majesty—if they choose to ignore those missing girls, there is little you can do."

Cam ground his teeth. Aunt Val said, "My nephew might be concerned for reasons beyond the political consequences. We'll discuss it this evening and come to some agreement."

The chancellor bowed. "As you wish. Those matters being resolved, I'll make sure all is in order for today's audiences." He strode from the room, closing the door behind him.

Cam frowned. When had Brumal ever helped with the supplicant audiences? He always left that chore to Tyla.

Aunt Val squeezed his shoulder. "Ah, the joys of ruling."

He smiled faintly. "I don't regret the decision. But I didn't realize how much the pressure would increase once I took my oath." His eyes strayed to the parchment on his dresser.

Aunt Val followed his gaze. "Camden...I understand the challenges of weighing your own desires with the good of our people. At your age, I was off defending the kingdom, fighting monsters and having a grand time doing it. However, I left my warrior ways behind when Father died. I was needed here, as you are. You carry on the line. Without you, the goblins with the inborn ability to commune with willas die out."

"I know, Aunt Val. When I took the throne, I accepted the need to get married, to have kids, and that it would be a political choice as much as a personal one."

"We discussed this last year. You seemed less reluctant then. What changed?"

Cam smiled grimly. "Three hundred sixty-five days."

"The passage of time does tend to make a far-away sacrifice into a more immediate one. But are you sure that's all it is?"

Cam shrugged. "What else?"

"Your life has changed since last year. Examine your heart and mind, Camden. There are ways around almost any obstacle. It would be unfortunate to realize, too late, what you truly want." His aunt stood. "I'll see you in the throne room. Please be prompt. I believe the supplicant list was quite long."

"Your Majesty, my neighbor's garden is planted entirely in shades of red. Mine is a green garden of ferns and delicate beauties. The glare from his yard is an assault on my eyes, every single day. Surely you can see that."

The goblin in front of the throne had a nasal voice that grated on Cam's nerves. He kept his expression neutral as the man droned on. It was easier to do in goblin form—the way he always saw supplicants. The goblin form disguised his youth and carried more weight than his human one.

Cam glanced at the sunlight slanting through the stained glass windows of the throne room and adjusted his cloak. Despite the feel of a too-long morning, he was certain only a couple hours had passed. It couldn't be later than eleven o'clock.

The man wanted to force his neighbor to build a stone fence to hide his "clashing garden" from view. Cam didn't mind an honest grievance, but he'd been tired of this fool's idiocy since he opened his mouth.

The door to the side room opened. Relieved for an excuse to look away from the man's florid face, Cam turned and saw Tyla; she beckoned to him. The supplicant pulled out a stack of drawings (he'd actually brought visual aids?), sealing the deal. Cam stood hastily. "Something has arisen which requires my attention. I'll return momentarily."

He hurried across the dais, boots echoing on stone, and slipped through the door. "What trouble did you bring me?"

"Not trouble, exactly. I just thought you should know your faerie girl is here."

"This isn't the normal time." Cam frowned. "I'd better see what's wrong."

Tyla stopped him with a hand on his arm. "Finish with this family first. She's ruffled, but she says it's not an emergency."

"Then why'd you interrupt me in the middle of court?"

"Because if I didn't, you'd accept case after case, and she'll be cooling her heels for the next four hours."

"Good point." Cam dug a gold coin out of his pocket. "Please give this to whichever guard escorted her."

Tyla accepted the tip, but an expression of unease, quickly hidden, flitted across her face. Disquiet crept over him like strangling vines. "Tyla?"

She sighed. "Destry found me in the foyer. Nobody was with her, so I assumed the escort dropped her at the door. When I asked who to tip, she said the forest guards weren't at their posts. She...she came alone."

Cam froze. Alone. Near the river, in the woods, with the willas nervous and trembling over some unknown threat. His conversation with

Brumal rushed over him. *If they choose to ignore those missing girls, there is little you can do.*

He whipped around, striding away from the throne room. Tyla stretched out a restraining hand. Cam ignored her. The strangling vines tightened around his chest and throat until he couldn't breathe. He hardly noticed her following as he stormed down the hall. For once in his life, Cam was seeing red.

What is wrong with those stupid white trees?

Through a window in Cam's private audience chamber, Destry glowered at the willa forest. She'd run almost halfway through the woods with the willas screaming in her head: feelings of danger, urges to hurry, warnings and fear. Her wings had responded, pressing against her skin in response to the perceived danger. She barely managed to keep them in. And every time she slowed to anything less than a jog, the willas whipped their branches, hustling her along.

Then, inexplicably—they stopped. Calmed down. Like today was the same as any other day. Destry had shambled to a halt, gasping, and leaned against the nearest tree trunk.

Nothing. Nothing but pleasure that she was visiting.

Destry tried to call up the urgency that had pushed her into the forest, but the trees seemed to live in the moment. She didn't know the trick for directing their thoughts like Cam did. She hurried to the next willa, but it acted the same as the first. No more fear, no more urgency.

Destry wavered. She hated to show up at the castle and admit she'd come through the woods alone, but whatever had scared her into the trees might be waiting when she came back out of them. That could be much worse than hearing a lecture. Cam would understand once she explained.

When Destry slipped into the castle foyer, she had to navigate around a long line of people. Tyla stood nearby, taking names onto a sheet of parchment and informing a woman that her son needed to change out of goblin form (a wildly yapping dog with black fangs). The goblin girl accepted her explanation about the missing guards and waved Destry upstairs. "King Darkwater is seeing supplicants. He'll be with you as soon as possible."

But the longer she waited, the more stressed Destry became. Her wings finally got the message she wasn't in danger and subsided. However, that was her only comfort. The line of people had been massive. What if Cam needed to see all of them before he could see her? She might miss curfew and get in trouble at school.

She heard Cam's boots clicking rapidly along the corridor and breathed a sigh of relief. Tyla must have given him a heads-up. Destry turned. She'd barely taken two steps before the door flung open.

Cam wore his goblin form; that was the first thing she noticed.

Well, no—first she noticed that he was angry. A huge, angry goblin. Her wings shot out so fast that fire blazed along her shoulder blades.

He slammed the door. "What are you doing here without an escort?"

"Cam." Destry's voice came out a squeak.

He glared. "Yes, I'm full-goblin. No, I don't care if you're scared. I *hope* you are! Maybe I can scare some sense into you! You promised, Destry. I told you how important this was."

"I'm...I'm sorry." She wanted to tell him about her loneliness, about Tristan and feeling trapped, about the strange rustlings and feelings of being watched through the woods. But she couldn't, not with him so livid. Not like this. "The guards were gone."

"And you couldn't send an earth-cursed *message*? Or wait until they returned to their posts?" The growl in his voice made shivers prickle her spine.

"I didn't mean to come! I decided to visit the willas at the edge of the forest instead, and..." She trailed off, because that wasn't much better.

His jaw clenched. "The letter of the law but not the spirit?" He pointed to a chair, fury rolling off him in waves. "Stay here, Destry. I don't have time to escort you back right now."

At that moment, Destry understood exactly why Cam's subjects obeyed him. His face was hard enough to be the granite it resembled, and his bottomless black eyes held no room for understanding. He was foreign, beautiful, powerful...and so frightening that Destry couldn't even answer. She just nodded. He strode from the room, cloak billowing behind him. Through the open door, she heard him ask Tyla, lingering in the hall, "Watch her, will you?"

Trembling head to toe, Destry sat. Cam might as well have said it out loud: *Watch her, because I can't trust her.* How could she ever explain?

Tyla peered around the door as Cam's steps faded away. "He's good and mad, isn't he?"

Destry's *yes* choked off into a sob. She closed her eyes, trying to control the tears pushing against her eyelids. A warm hand gripped her shoulder. She looked up into Tyla's face. "Hey," the older girl said softly. "Cam will calm down. He gets mad, he gets over it."

Destry shook her head. "I broke a promise. I didn't mean to, but I did."

The goblin girl looked skeptical. "Walking through the forest is pretty purposeful."

Destry stared at her lap, exhausted. If she couldn't convince Tyla—who was considerably calmer than Cam—how would she get him to listen?

"Goblin gourds." Tyla heaved a gusty sigh and pulled another chair close. "Alright. Tell me what happened."

Destry didn't leave anything out. She even explained the comfort she felt with the willas, her inexplicable need to see them. When she finished, Tyla said, "You're the strangest faerie I've ever met."

"People keep saying that." Her voice sounded small.

Tyla stood. "You should tell all this to Cam. If I go to the throne room to speed things up, will you stay put?"

She nodded. "Thanks for listening, Tyla."

"Eh, you aren't that bad...for a faerie."

Destry roamed the audience chamber while she waited for Tyla to return. Her wings refused to furl, and even the airy space seemed confining. Destry shoved open the balcony doors, looking out over the white forest. Why couldn't she feel at home anywhere except in a grove of trees?

A flash of red drew her gaze. Squinting, Destry peered at the tree line closest to the castle, where something large wove in and out of sight.

So vivid, so wrong against the trees, its presence screamed "intruder."
Destry leaned over the railing to see better. Whatever it was, it looked
armored. Sun glinted off the creature's vermillion hide. It scuttled into
the willa grove before she could get a closer look.

A shiver shook the forest, like the trees sensed something foreign in
their midst. More than just foreign. A threat. Maybe whatever had sent
her running here was in the woods again. Were the guards at their posts
yet? She turned into the room; waiting for Tyla wasn't an option. She
had to find Cam. Angry or not, he'd want to know about a threat to the
willas.

She didn't even get to the doors before a scream knifed through her.
Not a sound...a feeling, a thought, a sensation of panic. Destry jerked
around. The trees were waving frantically.

Another scream. Destry gasped—this one felt familiar. Wings.

How she knew it was that particular tree, Destry couldn't be sure.
But it was as distinct in her mind as the taste difference between oranges
and chocolate. Without conscious decision, she leapt the balcony railing,
wings spread to slow her descent. That was all the thought she gave it.
Because with Wings' touch in her mind, she could no more stand by than
if a friend was being threatened.

Besides, surely Cam would feel this too. Surely he would come.

Destry ran for the forest.

DAMAGED

◆

Destry had found it difficult, on most visits to the woods, to locate the ageless willa. The forest was too vast, the trees too similar. Today, she unerringly chose the right path. She stumbled over roots and her own feet several times, falling, scraping her palms. But she kept running.

Though Wings hadn't screamed again, all the willas pulsed with fury and fear. Destry's heart hammered in her chest, her breathing rasped loud in her ears. She faltered. Which direction should she take?

The willa's second scream reverberated through her skull. Wincing, she clutched her head and stumbled in the correct direction. She yanked the dagger from its sheath, cutting her stomach. Blood from the shallow wound trickled onto her waistband. But when Destry burst into Wings' clearing, every minimal concern faded, replaced by leg-weakening, in-stinctive, absolute horror.

A crimson nightmare loomed near Wings. The creature was a cross between a scorpion and a spider—red scorpion body, but with eight long, agile legs that tapered to black at their tips. The front two had pointed pincers. Its armored body was easily five feet long without its tail, standing almost as tall as she did. Its stinger hovered a yard above her head. Silver liquid dripped from the barbed tip.

The scorpion rotated towards her, issuing a high, piercing chitter—a warning as instinctively frightening as the rattle of a rattlesnake. Obsidian fangs lined its obscene maw.

Destry looked past the creature to Wings. Her breath caught. The willa had been slashed. Silver liquid—the same as on the scorpion's tail—oozed from several shallow cuts and one deep gash. The willa's shudders of pain reverberated through Destry.

The creature watched her narrowly. She watched it back. It shrilled one more warning and turned towards the tree, raising its stinger.

Pulse leaping, Destry dropped the dagger and obeyed her natural instinct. She raised her palms and shot two bolts of power at the creature, hitting it in the side. It swung around, the eerie chitter rising. Too late, she remembered one of Renalt's warnings: *Certain creatures—especially armored ones—may take repeated blasts to breach their coverings. Anything less will just annoy them.*

Cursing her idiocy, she scrambled for the dagger. Her hand barely closed on the hilt before the scorpion charged. She flung herself to the side, towards the willa. Fast as it was, the creature didn't turn quickly—one small advantage. It spun a circle as Destry shifted her dagger, holding the point aloft.The scorpion hissed. Destry tried to shake off the *pain-panic-fear* sensations from Wings; they were weakening, disorienting. There must be something besides her bolts...

She knelt, whispering the word for what she knew best, the only word that would come to her fear-fogged brain: *ainfier.* Fire shot up in the grass and raced towards the scorpion, curving to create a wall between it and Destry. The beast hissed again and started around the flames. Desperate, she cried, *"Ciorreis!"* focusing hard on what size circle she wanted. The flames raced in a loop, closing her and Wings off from the scorpion and the rest of the forest.

Destry rushed to the willa tree. What could she do? She didn't know any healing words. Silver blood gushed from the largest cut. Sticking the dagger in the ground, she pressed each side of the gash and tried pushing the injury closed. Blood slicked her hands. The smooth bark was impossible to hold.

The circle was heating up. Acrid smoke stung her eyes, making them water. Releasing the trunk, Destry pushed hair off her sweaty forehead and looked at the scorpion. So far, it had just circled the ring of fire. How intelligent was it?

Smart enough. The creature swept its tail in an arc along the ground, grinding up dirt, flinging it onto the flames until a large section was doused. Destry grabbed the dagger again. Willa blood from her hands dripped down the handle onto the blade. She tightened her grip, breathing fast, as the scorpion scuttled through the cleared section.

How could she fight this thing? She lacked speed and coordination. Her wings wouldn't retract, and with no flight experience, they were worse than useless—they were a liability. Their sharp edge would barely scratch the thick insect shell. She furled them closer to her body.

So her defenses were a limited number of bolts and a dagger, which felt about as useful as a toothpick right now. Maybe it could stab the monster's eyes, except the eyes were near those fangs. Bad idea, getting that close. Could she intimidate it for a few seconds? If Cam would just hurry... Why hadn't he come?

She screamed, slashing out with the dagger. The scorpion whipped its tail sideways, slapping her wrist. Pain ricocheted up her arm. The knife flew from her hand, all the way to Wings, bouncing off her now-silvery trunk and landing on the ground.

One defense left. The creature swung around as Destry raised her hands. Her first two bolts hit the ground in front of it, sending up showers of dirt and ash and grass. Two more frantic bolts. One glanced harmlessly off an armored leg, but the other hit the creature in the face. Its chitter turned high. It stopped, rubbing one eye with a pincer.

A tremble raced along her arms, leaving an alarming weakness in its wake. The bolts of power were draining her. Could she summon more? Or would she pass out, like that day in Combat?

Destry had a last, unlikely idea. The armor might be thinner on the underbelly, or have chinks where the sections joined together. Heart hammering, she crouched in front of Wings. It took every ounce of fortitude to hold her ground as the scorpion lowered its pincer and charged. When the monster got within a few feet of her, she dropped to one knee, until she was almost beneath it. Aiming her hands upward, she sent two simultaneous blasts towards its sickening, insectoid underbelly.

Her bolts hit the upper left side, near the join of the legs. The scorpion reared, tail thrashing, armored legs stabbing the ground. One caught her thigh, gashing her legging and her skin. *Move, move, move!* Destry scrambled away, but there was no safe space to escape. Another leg slapped her back, her shoulder. She pinwheeled away.

Wumph. The tail slammed into her ribs, flinging her against the willa. Destry rebounded, thudding facedown on the ground. There was a mad scrabbling sound, an incomprehensible shriek, and the clearing went still.

Gasping, Destry rolled to her back. Fire crackled around her. Her wings stung, sizzling streaks of pain where rocks dug into them. Tears from the smoke blurred her vision. Above her, willa branches spun. *Too quiet... It's too quiet. Where's the monster?* Destry pushed herself up, panting, ribs burning...

The scorpion was gone.

It couldn't have disappeared that quickly. Was it behind her, approaching Wings from the other side? She jerked to her feet. Something shiny caught her eye, glinting in the firelight. The dagger. Snatching it up, Destry scrambled around the tree. Her pulse roared in her ears, an angry tide ready to swallow her.

No scorpion.

She stumbled in a circle, scanning the clearing. Nothing.

Then, above the thrum of blood in her ears, distant shouts. Finally, someone was coming. She staggered toward the voices, tripped over her own feet. Fell. Pushed to her feet again.

Wait...the voices were coming from behind her. She spun, staggered the other direction. Where had the scorpion gone?

The voices seemed to be everywhere. Not just voices—growls, yowls, bird calls, hisses. A huge raven swept overhead. Tyla's voice rang out, shrill. "Wings' clearing! Wings' clearing! Hurry!"

Seconds later, goblins began pouring in from all directions. The ruby-eyed leopard—the one who'd stepped in front of her in the throne room—bounded into the clearing, nearly running Destry over. She dropped to the ground, throwing her arms over her head.

Several more bodies buffeted her, but no one stopped. Growls and bird calls morphed to voices. Destry lifted her head as spells rang out, goblins summoning water or clouds of earth to smother the fire. But where was Cam? At least a dozen goblins in the clearing, and she couldn't see him from her spot on the ground.

Her legs felt too weak to stand. She watched numbly as most of the goblins circled Wings, including Tyla and Brumal. The goblins gripped each other's shoulders. A few of the nearest goblins shifted. She finally located Cam—kneeling in front of Wings in goblin form, pressing her wound closed. He completed the circle, the goblins closest to him resting their hands on his shoulders. He must have come in on the opposite side of the clearing, closer to Wings.

Cam began singing: fluid words in the ancient language. Her mind felt too muddled to decipher anything. The other goblins joined in, a wordless counterpart to Cam's melody that vibrated through the air. Cam's voice rose, twining with theirs. The tune was haunting and heartwrenching and beautiful, and Destry forgot for a moment...

Forgot her pounding head, aching body, and stinging wings...

Forgot her magic-induced weakness, her knee-trembling fear...

Forgot the all-encompassing smell of smoke and blood...

Forgot everything but the call of goblin song.

A rough hand yanked her to her feet, claws digging into her arm. Destry stumbled, wheeling around to face Sylka. She was in the same half-transformed state as the first time they'd met, teeth bared, eyes blazing. "Trying to sneak away, little hor d'oeuvre?"

Destry struggled to find her footing. "Sneak away?" Her voice came out a rough, weak thing.

The cat woman grabbed Destry's other hand—the one holding the dagger—and brandished it. "I'd sneak away too. We have no mercy for earth-cursed murderers." Her claws dug deeper.

Destry yelped. "I didn't—"

Sylka hissed. "We have even less mercy for wing-bearing liars!" She released Destry, backhanding her across the face. Pain exploded behind her eyes, along her cheekbone. She fell, only to be yanked upright by Sylka's clawed hands in her hair. She stumbled to her feet to keep it from being ripped out.

A roar sounded from across the clearing. "Release her!"

The cat woman whirled, dropping Destry and simultaneously dropping to one knee, head bowed. Cam crossed the clearing in a few swift bounds, Brumal close on his heels. The cat woman held Destry's dagger—when had she taken it?—above her head. "She had this, King Darkwater." Her voice was an odd mixture of plea and challenge.

Cam stared at the dagger, face as blank as Destry had ever seen. He swallowed. "What?"

Sylka glanced up. "She had this in her hands, Your Majesty, and was trying to sneak away."

Brumal snarled. "You brought this into our sacred forest?"

But Cam had told her to carry it... Mindful of Sylka's sharp gaze, she croaked out, "Yes, my lord."

Sylka loosed a triumphant hiss. A pit opened in Destry's stomach. Nothing that made Sylka triumphant could be good.

From across the clearing, Tyla shouted, "Cam! We're losing her!" She and the other goblins had continued their wordless song, but silvery blood still streamed down Wings' trunk.

He hesitated, gaze swiveling between Destry and the dagger and the goblin woman.

"Cam! We need you!" Tyla's voice cracked into a sob at the end.

"I will handle this," Brumal said, yanking his eyes away from the dagger. "Go."

Cam's eyes rested on Destry for a brief moment. "You will protect the faerie from further harm. Report Lady Sylka's actions to the fey officials. And get the faerie's account, so I can pronounce judgment." His voice was impossibly unreadable. Worse than neutral, it sounded empty. Hollow. He bounded back to Wings.

Sylka rose, movements coiled tight. "Report me?"

Brumal held up a hand. "First things first." He turned to Destry. "Do you have a sheath for this abomination?"

She still sat on the ground where Sylka had dropped her. Her head ached, her face and body were on fire, and nothing they said made sense. She stared at Brumal dumbly.

"The dagger," he snapped. "Surely you carry a sheath for it?"

What's wrong with the dagger Cam sent me? The pit in her stomach yawned wider, but it was too late to deny ownership. She pulled the sheath from her waistband, handing it over.

As he collected the blade from Sylka and gingerly slid it into the sheath, Brumal said, "Yes, Lady Lynxwood, we have no choice but to report you to the fey authorities. We do not mistreat prisoners, faerie or otherwise. Your unconsidered actions could bring faerie wrath upon us."

Prisoner. Did they mean *her*?

The goblin woman's hands curled into fists. "This faerie trash had the knife in her hand, covered in willa blood. She set fire to our grove. She's fortunate I restrained myself." Sylka stalked away towards the castle.

A dagger in her hand, willa blood all over her... Destry looked down at her torn clothes and bruised body. "Lord Brumal," she said slowly, "I didn't do that to Wings."

She waited for him to say, *Of course not.* But his face just hardened. Destry glanced at the other goblins in the clearing. The ones not gathered around Wings—one guard and two journeyman students—watched her with varying degrees of hostility. Hadn't any of them seen the monster? How could they miss something that large?

Destry gulped. "I heard the willas screaming from the audience chamber, so I ran here. There was a giant scorpion. It did this to Wings, I tried to stop it—" Her voice broke, tears snaking down her cheeks.

One of the journeymen—a young woman with long hair and cold eyes—snorted. "Heard the willas, she says. And just happened to have a willa slayer in her hand too."

Destry mopped at her tears with one sleeve. "I don't know what you're talking about."

"The enchanted knife you brought here," Brumal said coldly.

"It's just a dagger. King Darkwater sent it to me."

The other journeyman student—one who'd met Destry around the castle—frowned. "When?"

Destry pressed a hand to her aching head. "Today. This morning."

The student crossed his arms. "I acted as messenger today. The king didn't send anything to the faerie school."

"Maybe someone else—"

He cut her off. "There's a master list where messengers record every errand, whether it's a note or a delivery. The only deliveries this morning were made within the castle."

Brumal's lips tightened. "If you have anything to add to your story, tell me now. I must report to King Darkwater."

Destry stumbled through a more complete explanation, tripping over her own words. When she finished, the journeywoman scoffed. "If you'd fought a scorione, we'd be sending a corpse back to the faeries. Besides, High Lady Valda wiped them out of these parts years ago."

Brumal said, "Nevertheless, this is the report I shall offer King Darkwater. Wait here." He eyed the students and the guard. "You will uphold standards of treatment better than Lady Lynxwood, or the consequences will be—regrettable."

Destry watched him walk across the clearing. Throughout Brumal's explanation, Cam rarely stopped singing, though his eyes stayed intent on the chancellor. When the man finished, Cam quit singing long enough to say a few words, then turned his attention to the willa. Brumal paced over.

"Well?" demanded the journeywoman.

"The evidence isn't clear."

"Not clear?" Outrage limned her voice.

"Yes. Regardless of probability, a scorione could have done this damage. We cannot condemn without a trial." He looked down his nose at the student. "Unless you understand our laws better than myself and the king, of course. Should we defer to your expertise?"

The journeywoman flushed and looked away. Brumal gripped Destry's upper arm and lifted her to her feet. "I'll escort you to the holding cell. Let's go."

He'd pulled her several shaky steps before the words made sense to Destry. She dug her heels in, twisting against his hold. "Wait, I have to explain. Cam! Cam!"

He never turned. Cam didn't give any sign that he heard her. Brumal forced Destry into a walk again. "You'll have adequate time to explain at the trial. Come, Destry Firewings, before you make things worse."

The holding cell was chilly. Destry wrapped her arms around herself, wishing she had a jacket, a blanket, anything. But it probably wouldn't have helped. The cold came more from the deep fear crouching in her bones than her surroundings.

Situated in a lower level of the castle, the room wasn't exactly a dungeon—just a windowless utilitarian space bare of everything except a few hard chairs. The sturdy door bolted from the outside. Destry alternately paced and sat the endless time away.

How long had she been here? An hour? Two? She couldn't guess.

The door swung open. A goblin stood silhouetted in the doorway; Destry recognized him as one of the men who'd been helping with Wings. His white hair stood out like dandelion fluff, contrasting vividly with his brown skin. He waved off the guard's attempt to follow him inside. "I can manage on my own."

"High Chancellor Brumal's orders—"

The goblin sighed. "Wait outside the door, if you must. My work requires privacy."

The guard sent one black glare Destry's way. "I'll be listening for any trouble."

After the door closed, the goblin man stepped further into the room. He wasn't tall, but he was wide, with heavy-looking hands. Destry took an involuntary step back, heart hammering. What "work" would he need to do, alone in a room with her?

The man stopped. "There's nothing to fear. I'm one of the castle healers, come to check your injuries."

Why would the goblins offer healing to someone they considered a vicious criminal? Destry backed up another step. The man held out a leather satchel, opening it to show her the contents: bandages, labeled jars, scissors. Her shoulders relaxed fractionally.

The healer smiled. "All foreign prisoners must be given adequate treatment while in custody. So states our treaty with your realm. Will you sit?"

She perched on the hard chair while he examined her. Those clumsy-seeming hands were actually quite gentle. He cleaned several cuts, bandaged the wound on her thigh, and asked if her wings, finally retracted again, were alright. Destry fiddled with the hem of her stained tunic. "They hurt while they were out. Now, I can't feel anything. I don't know... I'm not sure if that's good or bad."

He sat in his own chair. "As long as there were no substantial rips or wounds, it's helpful. Minor abrasions, minor heat damage—those will heal best while your wings are furled. I recommend keeping them that way for several hours."

Uncertainty tempered her relief. How much would a goblin know about fey healing?

He must have noticed. "I prefer to be helpful to all creatures, not only those of my kind." He sighed. "There is some severe bruising I cannot easily treat. Healing songs aren't effective on faeries, and I'd be hard-pressed to gather rainwater today." He indicated the tattoos on her legs.

Destry frowned. "Rainwater?"

"Yes. Your water source is one of the best methods for supernatural healing. Fortunately, your own people should fetch you soon. Their remedies will be more restorative." He stood, packing up his bag. "My apologies for the delay in treating you. Few of our healers are educated on interspecies care. And I was rather occupied with Wings."

She was desperate for news, and this man had been kind so far. Could she risk asking? Before she could chicken out, Destry blurted, "Will Wings be alright?"

The man's bushy eyebrows slid upwards. "You ask about the goblin tree?"

"I just want to know if she's okay...if she will be." Destry's voice rasped. "Please."

He considered her for a long moment. "She's out of immediate danger. Her recovery will be full but slow. Wings lost a great deal of blood, and the delays caused when Lady Lynxwood assaulted you exacerbated the problem."

Her chest seemed to expand fully for the first time in hours. "Thank you."

The healer closed his satchel. "It seems an odd concern—to worry about the willa when you're alone and scared."

Destry was afraid to say again that she hadn't done it, after the barely-checked rage of the goblins in the forest. "I love the willas. I wish no harm on them." She looked down at her lap, tensing for his reaction.

The goblin's wide fingers, pulling her jaw back up, were considerate. He searched her eyes. "I would believe it, Destry Firewings. Send word through your guard if you need anything."

28

SCAPEGOAT

✦

That was the last time anyone visited her. Destry paced more often than sat, wishing she could outrun her thoughts. She waited for Cam to show up, to explain why he'd sent her here, why he'd turned away from her in the forest. When someone knocked on the door, Destry jerked to her feet, hoping. The heavy wood door swung open again.

Fey Elena stood there, the guard a shadow behind her. She surveyed Destry. "You look rather worse for the wear, child. Are you able to walk to the school?"

Destry nodded.

"Then come along."

She followed the headmistress out the door and into the hall, the guard trailing them. "Fey Elena, I don't understand what's happening." How often had she said that today?

The headmistress shot a look at the guard, whose jaw and shoulders were rigid. "What is happening is that you've managed to embroil yourself in a great deal of trouble. But for the moment, I'm allowed to take you to the school. That's all we need discuss right now."

Her tone was repressive. Silently, Destry followed her through a shadowy narrow hall, up an equally shadowed set of stairs, into a room too dim for any faerie to see more than a few feet ahead. "This is ridiculous," Fey Elena snapped, summoning a ball of light.

The guard whirled on them. "No filthy fey magic in *this* castle! Put it out!" The light illuminated rows of spikes popping up along his arms, covering him from wrist to shoulders in seconds.

Destry scrambled back, slamming into the doorframe and whacking her head. Fey Elena's wings shot out. She stepped between the guard and Destry, chin high. "You have escorted us along the dimmest path possible—to disorient and intimidate us, I imagine—rather than the well-lit main halls. As you've failed to provide a light, what else am I to do? I refuse to stumble about in the dark...and I shall report this bit of petty revenge to your superiors."

The guard sneered. "It's on the king's orders we took this route. Were it up to me, we'd have gone through the main halls so every single goblin could see this *felindeamhan* for themselves. They all have ideas on dealing with a would-be murderer."

Destry's heart pounded in time to the renewed throbbing in her head. Her fear must have shown on her face, because the goblin's lips stretched in a satisfied smile. He strode across the room to open a door. As light poured in, the guard offered a mocking bow. "They're waiting for you."

Gently, Fey Elena took Destry's arm. "Come, child."

The door led into the main hall. Brumal waited for them by the entrance, face as stiff as his bearing. Goblins congregated in small groups around the hall. Some wore their human forms, others were in various stages of transformation, but all fell silent as Destry and Fey Elena crossed the room to Brumal. The chancellor spoke to Fey Elena. "You realize that your ward's presence is required by mutual law at a hearing this evening."

"I'm aware. The situation is no different than others involving a troublemaker from the school."

An angry hiss came from one of the watching goblins. Brumal's eyebrows slid almost to his hairline. "I disagree, Headmistress. A charge of trespassing is far different than the attempted slaughter of a willa tree."

"I didn't, Fey Elena." Tears stung Destry's eyes. She concentrated on pushing them back.

The headmistress raised one hand for silence. "She'll be here this evening. But we need time to contact Executor Faris and the fey representatives. I won't allow a student to be tried with no defense."

"They've been informed of the situation. Six hours should give adequate time to prepare."

"Yes, exceedingly generous." Fey Elena's voice bordered on satirical.

The chancellor frowned. "Allowing you to remove a suspected felon from our custody *is* a generous decision. Especially one who received such condescension from King Darkwater. The hearing shall be held in the throne room." He glanced at the goblins scattered through the entry hall, then met the guard's eyes. "Your king is counting on you to bring them *safely* through the forest."

The guard nodded, face stony. "I would never betray King Darkwater's trust."

"See to it, then." Brumal strode away, swallowed up by the castle.

The guard gestured curtly to the front door, but the combined weight of the goblins' stares pressed into Destry, pinning her in place. The guard's words from moments ago echoed in her head: *Were it up to me, we'd have gone through the main halls so every single goblin could see this* felindeamhan *for themselves. They all have ideas on dealing with a would-be murderer.* Only when Fey Elena tugged Destry forward did her feet unfreeze. A low babble of conversation broke out again as they exited the room, punctuated by terse interjections and several growls.

The guard pointed toward the willa grove. "We're taking the path through the forest."

The scent of smoke still hung in the air. The second Destry stepped into the woods, a sense of wrongness assailed her. They'd walked several yards before she realized what it was. The willas weren't moving. No fluttering leaves or twisting branches waving at her, no trees leaning closer when she passed. What was wrong with them? Were they traumatized by what happened to Wings? She wanted to touch one, reassure herself that life still pulsed through the too-quiet tree, but didn't dare. Not with that guard here, his flat stare poor concealment for barely-restrained anger.

He did look away once—to trail *his* fingers along a willa as if in greeting. The willa didn't move, didn't shake its leaves or wave a branch in welcome. A bleak look washed over the goblin's face. Then he glanced at Destry, and his fury blazed to life again, hotter than before.

For once, Destry was happy to leave the forest.

The guard stopped precisely one yard outside the treeline—the demarcation between fey and goblin land. As Destry and Fey Elena continued alone into the river clearing, he spat on the ground where they'd been. The headmistress's lips thinned, but her pace remained steady. "Do not allow the barbarian to overset you, Destry. He'd enjoy it too much."

Destry limped after her. "Fey Elena, I didn't do what they said."

"I'm aware of that. Had I believed your guilt, I would have left you in the holding cell for the lesson to sink in more deeply. However, your innocence may not matter with such damning evidence."

"I tried to protect the willa! That's how I got hurt, how I got willa blood all over me!"

"Unfortunately, there's nothing to either prove or disprove your story, except your presence at the scene of the crime with an enchanted knife."

"They called it a willa slayer. I don't know what they meant. The goblin king sent me that knife."

Fey Elena frowned. "The king says otherwise. And despite the sneaking nature of goblins, I can't imagine why he would. That knife has a single purpose: to harm a willa tree. No sane goblin would create such a thing, let alone put it in the hands of a faerie."

"But it came by messenger from the castle! You can ask Fey Riamon, he brought it to me."

"And did he watch you open it?"

Destry bit her lip. "No. I opened it in my room, alone."

The headmistress sighed heavily. "Then his testimony may be little help. Understand that willas aren't as vulnerable as they seem. A veneer of magic protects them. A regular knife couldn't have done the amount of damage inflicted on that tree, and only dark faeriesmiths have ever created willa slayers. How believable is it that a goblin bought the dagger and sent it to a faerie girl with unusual access to the goblin forest?"

Fey Elena didn't break stride as they exited the river clearing and started down the path lined with fey trees. "Though your description of the scorione was accurate, those monsters are exceedingly rare, and no one else saw it. I've been informed that the willas cannot communicate with the goblin king. They've drawn in on themselves in an effort to support the injured tree and won't communicate with him until the tree is out of danger."

"Can't we put the trial off until then?"

"Willas heal slowly. It may be weeks. And even if the goblins were willing to wait that long, our kingdom's officials insist the matter be resolved with greater speed."

"Why? Wouldn't waiting give me a better chance for a fair trial?"

Fey Elena sighed again. "Our rulers do not like this bruited about, but we were liable to lose the last faerie-goblin war. Faeries have a shorter period of reproductive years than goblins, so our population has not increased at the rate theirs has. While we're well-matched in battle, it was only a matter of time before they overcame us through sheer numbers. The peace talks saved us from becoming a conquered race. And the government will do whatever they deem necessary to prevent that from happening again. Do you understand what that means for you?"

Destry shook her head. Too much had happened to marshal her thoughts.

"They don't want to give the goblins time to grow angrier. They want to leave no doubt that we're committed to our side of that treaty. The trial *will* be convened, and someone *will* be held accountable, no matter what."

Clammy sweat popped up on Destry's face and neck. "But if the fey government won't be fair to me, why did we even tell them about the trial?"

"*We* didn't. The goblins ran screaming to our officials the second that tree was injured. But our representatives need to be there in any case. Otherwise, you face double-jeopardy: the possibility of being punished twice for the same misdeed. As long as the necessary officials are present, mutual law states that one side or the other shall deal with a law-break-er—not both. So if the goblins find you guilty, then you cannot also be punished by the faerie court."

"But I didn't do anything!"

The headmistress jerked to a stop, face wreathed with impatience. "I know you're frightened, child. But repeating that statement to me, who already believes it, will help nothing. You were in the wrong place at the wrong time. You went through the goblin forest alone—after their king specifically requested you have an escort. The staff confirmed it. They consider it proof he didn't entirely trust you."

"That was for my own safety!"

"But the reasons matter not, unless he intends to admit them to the entire court, which might put you in an even worse position. I'll defend you as best I can. But what is wisest, long-term, may be unpleasant in the short-term."

The uneasiness in Destry's stomach congealed to true fear. Somehow, she'd thought Fey Elena could stop this whole trial mess, if she understood the truth. But there would be no stopping it...no escape from the angry goblins eager to vent their rage. Destry had made one stupid decision and was going to pay for it ten-fold. Cam didn't even believe her, or he wouldn't have left her in that holding cell. Her only hope was convincing him at the trial.

Tristan waited on the steps. He took them three at a time, skidding to a stop in front of her and Fey Elena. He reached for Destry's hands, then halted when he saw the cuts and bruises. "Are you okay?" The tears pressing against Destry's eyes finally spilled over. Tristan's eyebrows drew together. "I guess not."

Fey Elena said, "How 'okay' she will be depends on this evening. And this evening will go best with adequate time to prepare. You can help by staying out of the way, Tristan."

The headmistress led Destry into the school, to the rainwater fountain. "Immerse yourself. We need to start the healing process as soon as possible. I'll return momentarily." The hall was empty at the moment—one small mercy. Destry kicked off her shoes and slid into the water.

It lapped over her battered body, neither too warm nor too cool. Relief. Destry closed her eyes as the rainwater soothed aches and bruises, lessened the pounding in her head. The scent of thunderstorms drifted around her.

Tristan's voice sounded close by. "Better?"

Destry's eyes flew open again. He sat on the edge, blue eyes intent. She summoned a tiny smile. "Didn't Fey Elena tell you to go away?"

"You know how well I listen. Want to talk about it?"

"Not now. I...I can't."

"Then can I say something to you?" Tristan trailed his fingers in her water. "I just... I know I upset you this morning. And that's probably why you went to the goblin forest. I'm sorry for that. I'm sorry for making you feel bad about who you are. And I want you to know that I like all of you, even the strange part that loves scary white trees and thinks long, confusing, foreign spells are easy. Especially that part."

Too bad she hadn't known that before. But maybe it wouldn't have mattered. Destry tried to laugh and cry at the same time and made a choking sound. Tristan leaned closer. The fountain misted over him, water drops hanging on his hair like crystals. "I don't care what Fey Elena said. Do you want me to stay with you?"

"Yes. No. I'm not even sure what's happening."

He laughed quietly. "Decisive. You know where to find me if you change your mind."

She nodded. Tristan rubbed a thumb between her eyebrows, expression a mixture of regret and teasing. "The scowly line is worse than this morning."

Destry snorted and batted his hand aside. "You'd scowl, too, if a giant scorpion beat you up."

Fey Elena bustled in. "Do I need to give you detention, Tristan? Believe me, I'm in no mood to be restrained."

Tristan didn't stay to see if she meant it. Fey Elena confirmed that Destry's injuries were healing, then hurried her out of the fountain and to her room.

While Destry soaked in another rainwater bath and guzzled glasses of storm-charged water, the headmistress instructed her on what to say—and what not to say—to both sets of officials. By the time she got out of the water, her fingers were wrinkled, and her head was swimming with information. At least moving hurt less.

Someone tapped on the door. A fellow storm faerie poked her head into the room. "Um...Fey Elena? There are people downstairs asking for you."

The woman stood. "That will be Executor Faris. Be in my office by four, Destry. Wear the dress I send up. Do your hair the way I said. And take a nap, or you'll be a wreck for the trial."

She was already a wreck. "I can't sleep."

The headmistress pressed her fingers to Destry's forehead. Dizziness rushed over her, then faded. Fey Elena said, "A sleep spell. Get into bed or you'll pass out on the floor. Sara will wake you on time."

Destry collapsed on the mattress seconds before sleep claimed her.

When Destry left her dorm at four o'clock, she found Tristan waiting on the stairway. He held up a brownie. "Stress relief."

She took the brownie and broke it, handing half back to Tristan. He watched her take a bite. "I asked to come with you to the trial. But it's only open to your guardian at the school and the officials."

Destry forced herself to swallow. "That's okay. What's the worst that could happen?" She added quickly, to forestall any too-helpful answers, "I meant that more rhetorical."

He held her hand—careful of the cuts and bruises—all the way down the stairs. At the bottom, he faced her, eyes earnest. "I'd help if I could. More than this."

Destry leaned into the gentle strength of his hug. "This is enough."

29

INNOCENT

The trip to the goblin castle might have been interesting under different circumstances. Destry, Fey Elena, Riamon, and the officials weren't allowed to walk through the willa forest. Since the other route was longer—around the woods and through the official entrance to Rí Kobold—they rode in two old-fashioned carriages.

Executor Faris, a fat little man with thinning hair pulled into a ponytail, leaned against the velvet seat with a sigh. "So much more comfortable and attractive than that hideous bus you prefer for your school. Why our world is enticed by human 'innovations,' I will never understand." His yellow-tinged wings spread across the entire seat, making it impossible for anyone to sit near him.

Fey Elena furled her wings and took the seat opposite, gesturing for Destry to sit beside her. Riamon squeezed onto the edge of the executor's bench the best he could.

The other six officials stepped into a larger carriage, and the horses started off with a jerk. Destry craned her neck; she hadn't noticed anyone driving. A condescending smile settled on the executor's face. "Our livestock is well-trained and guided by magic. One benefit of living in the palace. In point of fact, there are many benefits to remembering tried-and-true methods. Such liberal thinking as graces the school leads to foolish mistakes." His eyes rested on Riamon, who was cleaning his glasses.

The fey man replaced them, gaze unflinching. "It was indeed a mistake to assume that package came from a friendly entity. However, it was my mistake and shouldn't reflect poorly upon the school." Riamon turned to Destry. "I haven't yet apologized. Begged your forgiveness, to be precise. Had I examined the parcel, I'd have seen the willa slayer and could have stopped this entire fiasco. Whoever sent it is no friend of yours."

Executor Faris smiled again. "That is one explanation."

Nobody questioned the meaning behind the statement. The executor had been oblique ever since Destry arrived at Fey Elena's office. He'd asked questions and listened to her answers, but when the headmistress insisted on knowing what direction they would take for the trial, Executor Faris said, "That depends on the goblins' choices, does it not?"

The carriage wound through faerie country, with its thin graceful trees and foliage turning gold for the fall-like weather. Gradually, the landscape changed. The trees grew thicker, their bark rougher. Leaves were changing colors here too—some to traditional autumn shades, others to black or iron-gray—but deep green still clung to the hills and fields, vibrant despite the cooling weather.

They rumbled up to a stone bridge with a ponderous bronze gate. A river swept beneath it. Two hulking goblins stood sentry, both in goblin form. One looked as if he'd been created from steel. His shape was human, but tattoo-like etchings covered every inch of his body. His obsidian claws rested on the edge of their carriage as it pulled to a stop.

The goblin gestured for his companion—a russet wolf man—to check out the second carriage, then turned to them. "Faeries, hmm? Why does a group of earth-cursed wing-bearers want to enter goblin lands?"

Executor Faris straightened and adjusted his fine robes, although his wings quivered. "We have business with your king."

The metal goblin's brown eyes skimmed over them. They were startlingly human and looked wrong with his statue-like appearance. He raised one etched-on eyebrow at Destry. "Did the willas rip your wings off, young law-breaker, for what you did?"

Her shoulder blades burned, but something stubborn in Destry refused to allow her wings free reign. "They'd have no reason to. I tried to help the willas, not hurt them." She was tired of repeating the statement, but she was also tired of getting blamed for something she hadn't done.

His eyes narrowed. "Either brave...or stupid. Good luck at the trial."

As the carriage passed over the bridge, the executor looked at Destry with open curiosity. Fey Elena said, "Destry is used to the goblins, after her many lessons at the castle."

"So I see."

The carriage bumped along a familiar cobblestone road; Destry recognized it as the one that ran past the goblin castle. Sure enough, the massive structure soon loomed into view. The carriages pulled to a smooth stop before the front steps. Riamon scrambled out, offering a hand down first to Fey Elena, then to Destry, and then (because he took it) to the executor. The little man stared at the forbidding rock exterior and sniffed. "How very medieval." He took the stairs at a fast clip.

Fey Elena grabbed Destry's arm before she could follow. "Release your wings," she hissed. "You're accused of trying to slaughter a willa tree. It looks good to neither side to flaunt your fearlessness in this world."

Destry wanted to rebel, to refuse to show the goblins her fear. The headmistress gave her arm a shake. "Release them, or I will punish you myself for sheer stupidity."

Fey Elena wasn't a woman to be crossed. Destry allowed her wings to rip loose. At the top of the stairs, the executor laughed smugly. "The castle *is* imposing. But you should be more worried about what's inside."

The other carriage pulled up. The officials piled out, wings waving freely. *That* must have been fun, with the closed carriage. A few looked irritated. The three women and three men hustled up the steps, stopping next to Executor Faris like a row of ducklings after a mother duck. The little man adjusted his robes again. "Shall we proceed?"

One official looked impatient with his posturing—a woman with a long brown braid and features that seemed oddly familiar, though Destry was certain they'd never met before.

Tyla waited in the hall; she bowed to the faeries. "On behalf of the goblin court, we extend temporary peace to you, in the interests of pursuing justice and executing it in righteousness. Follow me."

She led them into the throne room. Destry's breath caught. The room was packed. Every goblin in Rí Kobold must be there, sitting in rows upon rows of chairs, or standing where the chairs left off. They watched her progress to the front of the room. Some looked stony, some angry, some merely curious. Destry's wings picked up speed.

A section up front had been left clear. Cam and his aunt, in goblin form, sat on thrones on the raised dais. At least, Destry assumed it was Lady Val. She glittered, like miniscule emeralds were embedded in every inch of her skin. Her eyes were the same solid black as Cam's, her hair the same raven shade. Her obsidian claws tapped restlessly on the arm of the throne as Destry followed the executor.

Brumal, standing to the right of the thrones, announced, "The accused is present. Has she representatives?"

Executor Faris puffed out his chest. "I and my officials. Advisor Alissa Windwings will act as defender."

"Then we shall proceed." He waved Destry towards a heavy black chair at the base of the dais, several yards to the left of the thrones.

Her legs trembled; hopefully, her dress hid it. She glanced at Cam as she passed, but his face—immobile and severe—offered little reassurance. Destry seated herself while Fey Elena, Fey Riamon, and the officials filed into chairs on the opposite side of the thrones. A narrow table stood several feet from the faerie officials with a cloth-wrapped bundle atop it.

Brumal said, "Destry Firewings of Si'fliegen is herewith accused of damaging one of our sacred willa trees, with intent to slaughter. Initial evidence was declared unclear by King Darkwater, bringing us to trial to determine the guilt of the accused in goblin eyes. As high chancellor to His Majesty, I will conduct this examination. And as the injured party, we have the right to proceed first. After each point of accusation, the opposition will be allowed to question or call witnesses. Is there any objection?"

No one raised their hand.

Brumal smiled. For the first time, it looked as wolfish as his goblin form. "Then we begin." He lifted the bundle from the table. The wrapping fell away, revealing Destry's dagger. "Is this familiar to you, Destry Firewings?"

Her voice rasped on the way out. "Yes."

"Speak loudly, please."

"Yes," she said again. "I received it as a gift. I didn't realize what it was."

"But you do now."

Destry nodded.

Brumal asked, "From whom did you receive this...gift?"

Fey Elena had ordered her not to bring Cam's name up. It might spark outrage in the audience and disbelief of anything else Destry said. "A messenger told Fey Riamon that it came from the goblin castle. I've made friends here. I had no reason to doubt the message."

Brumal lay the dagger down with exacting care. Dried willa blood glistened on it. "This knife was found at the scene of the crime—in the hand of the accused." He looked at Destry. "It seems an odd gift: a dagger. Why would you accept such an item and carry it into our realm?"

Destry said carefully, "I was warned that some creatures in the woods are dangerous. I took it as a friend's attempt to offer me extra protection."

Brumal reached into a pouch, withdrawing a handful of glittering dust. "All will recognize this: the dust we compound to determine the origins of magic. To assure all of its impeachability, we'll test it on an object from our faerie officials. Who is willing?"

The woman who'd looked impatient slid her long brown braid back. "I am Alissa Windwings, advisor in the faerie court and defender of the fey child, Destry. I offer this ring, which was handled only by me and its maker, another wind faerie." She placed the ring on the table.

Brumal sprinkled dust over it. The ring glowed with a pale blue mist. Part of the mist wreathed around Alissa; the other swept through the room and out the door. Brumal lifted the ring between two fingers for all to see, then placed it on the table again. He sprinkled another measure of dust. This time, besides the blue mist, part of the vapor glowed green and flew to Brumal. He looked to the faerie woman. She nodded curtly. "It is acceptable."

He spread a handful over the dagger. The dust dissolved into red mist, wafting over to encircle Destry. From there, it separated into two other streams of mist: another green one that wreathed Brumal, and a stream that rushed into the audience, where Sylka sat a few rows back. Brumal said, "This proves that—besides myself and the goblin who relieved you of the dagger—none but yourself handled this object. Had a 'friend' from the castle done so, the mist would have claimed him or her. Do you wish to recant your story?"

Destry waved the red mist away. "No. I don't know why there aren't other magic colors, but I'm telling the truth."

He raised one eyebrow. "Then I shall allow Advisor Alissa her turn."

Unlike the executor, Alissa seemed to be firmly on Destry's side. She called Riamon up to explain how he'd received the package and why he'd assumed the source was trustworthy. He left out his romantic suppositions.

As Riamon resumed his seat, Alissa strode to the table where the dagger lay. "Destry, do you know how to make a willa slayer?"

"They don't teach that in my metalworking class."

A few—only a few—chuckles came from the audience.

"And how long have you been at the Academy?" Alissa asked.

"Since January."

The woman turned to Brumal. "A rare dark magic, one that takes years to perfect...that's common knowledge. And this child supposedly learned the art in mere months?"

Brumal said coldly, "Of course we don't think the girl manufactured the blade. That would be ridiculous, given her history."

"Then why aren't any other fey signatures present?" Alissa said. "It should hold the signature of its maker. Surely, you and Lady Lynxwood haven't perfected the art of slayer-forging."

Brumal scowled. "Of course not."

The fey woman turned to the audience. "If we accept that Destry could not have created this blade, then we must also assume that someone else did...someone with the nearly unheard-of skill to hide their magic signature."

She continued her questioning, asking Destry why she'd considered the package safe and letting her explain about the wrapping from the castle and the note inside. When she'd finished, Brumal stood again.

He immediately led into another point of accusation: her assertion that she'd run to the forest because she heard the willas. How would a faerie—any faerie—possess the ability to hear what most goblins did not? Surely she knew that gift was claimed only by goblin royalty.

Destry didn't back down from that statement, either; she had no idea why she felt the willas' emotions, but she did. Brumal said dryly, "A convenient claim, as the willas are currently incapable of verifying it."

Goaded, Destry snapped, "It would be more convenient if they *could*. They'd have shown everyone the truth, and I wouldn't be here." That won her some considering looks and grudging smiles from the goblin audience.

The trial dragged on. Brumal declared the scorione—a rare creature that did prey on willas—to be another great convenience. He suggested that Destry had made the creature up, choosing the one monster that could have done similar damage to Wings.

"And yet," Alissa countered, "the scorione roams goblin land almost exclusively and isn't covered in most faerie books or education. Few new students would have access to such knowledge."

Brumal said delicately, "Few new students frequent the goblin castle, either."

They called a man named Dante Bramblebaer next—the healer who had examined Destry in the holding cell. She was surprised to learn that he was Cam's personal physician, the top healer in the goblin kingdom. Under Brumal's questioning, he admitted that Destry's injuries might have been inflicted by a willa defending itself.

"But," he added, "a scorione could have caused the same injuries. And there was substantial damage. I consider it unlikely that the child would have stayed within striking range of Wings, allowing herself to be hit again and again."

Brumal released a stiff breath through his nose. "Thank you. You may—"

The healer spoke over him. "The same child asked—with what I judge to be sincere concern—about Wings, concerned for the willa despite her circumstances at the time: bloody, bruised, frightened, alone and friendless in a holding cell."

"Thank you." Brumal's voice came out thin. "Though I would not call the girl friendless, Healer Bramblebaer. It is clear she gained an ally in you."

The healer glanced at Destry. "Yes. I would say she has."

A murmur went through the audience. Some still looked angry; others seemed to be debating. The healer's opinion clearly carried much weight. But the face Destry was most concerned with never changed. Cam stayed as stony as ever, no matter the question or the response.

Finally, Brumal and Alissa declared themselves finished. They turned to Cam and his aunt. "The evidence has been presented and challenged," Brumal said. "The faerie Destry Firewings is charged with the attempted slaughter of a willa—with malicious cutting with an enchanted knife in an attempt to undermine the goblin kingdom. What say Your Majesties?"

Cam stood. Destry couldn't take one more second of his hard, emotionless expression. She jerked to her feet, too. "Cam," she cried desperately. "Cam, please, you know I wouldn't do that."

He turned to her, granite face severe and cold. "Do not address me in such a casual manner, Destry Firewings. Our lessons have not granted you that liberty."

Her chest contracted, crushing itself from the inside. She sank numbly into her chair. She barely heard the murmurs around the court, or registered that some were slightly concerned, or noticed Cam and his aunt turn away to confer with each other. Fey Elena came to stand with her, gripping Destry's shoulder. Executor Faris looked displeased with the gesture of support.

Cam and Lady Val turned to face the court. "We have passed judgment," Lady Val announced. Her voice in goblin form was clear, almost ringing, like glass speaking. "While the evidence presented is most damaging, the alternatives presented are equally motivating. The dagger's origin is in question, as are the faerie's motives for carrying it into the woods. The scorione's presence can be neither confirmed nor dismissed, nor can the faerie's injuries shed decisive light upon this subject.

"And we must raise the question: Why would a student with human background and little faerie experience be so motivated to damage the goblin kingdom—risking life and limb in a feat many seasoned insurgents are loathe to try? The evidence is too unclear for a conviction of guilt. In the goblin realm, Destry Firewings shall remain blameless. So say we. Is there agreement?"

Brumal raised his hand and called for "ayes" from the goblin audience. The answering response sounded loud to Destry, but it wasn't everyone; she was sure. Brumal raised the other hand. "We will have the nays."

She held her breath.

The nays shouted loudly, but the goblins in disagreement—while substantial—were less than the ayes. Brumal bowed. "The majority is in agreement, Your Majesties. The verdict stands."

A babble of conversation broke out. Across the room, the faerie officials talked rapidly amongst themselves. Destry sat there for a moment, stunned.

It was over. She'd been found innocent.

Her chest expanded, uncrumpled. Had this been Cam's intent all along? She looked at him, still on the dais, and chanced a small smile.

Camden Darkwater, King of the Goblins, looked right at her.

He didn't smile back.

30

CONDEMNED

◆

Destry couldn't breathe. Her lungs were blazing, consumed by phantom fire as surely as her wings.

Cam hadn't forgiven her.

The certainty pressed against her shoulders, wrapped around her throat.

He hadn't forgiven her.

Whatever the court had decided—whatever Cam might have done to keep her from experiencing goblin justice—he either still thought she was lying or that she'd purposely breached his trust. Destry's insides crumpled again, and this time, they stayed that way.

Fey Elena patted her shoulder, but when Destry stood, the executor waved her back. "A moment, my dear. We're not quite finished."

Not finished? She'd been found innocent. Destry turned to Fey Elena, whose face pinched up tightly. "What does he mean? You said I couldn't be tried twice if everyone was here."

The pity in the headmistress's eyes frightened her. "I said you couldn't be *punished* twice, child. The goblins found you not guilty."

Executor Faris bowed in front of Cam's throne. "Your Majesty, we must be grateful for the forbearance shown this fire faerie. But we would be remiss in accepting Your Majesties' verdict. Seeing the evidence gives us pause as to this girl's innocence. As representatives of the fey kingdom, we do not wish you to feel that justice went unserved."

Cam stood, rising to his full height. Especially with the dais, he towered over the little man. "If you have concerns, take it up in faerie court. The goblins have prosecuted this according to the exactness of our laws. We'll pursue it no further."

The executor smiled, but it wasn't a friendly expression. "How very forgiving the goblins have grown."

"Not at all." Cam's face hardened. "The law restrains us. Unlike fey law, we require more than unsubstantiated allegations. Proof must be stronger than doubt. We cannot pursue justice against the perpetrator—no matter our wishes."

The executor nodded. "Faerie law is more exacting. We prefer there to be no doubts, particularly in cases such as this. And your presence would be required at the sentencing, since the law broken involves a treaty of such import to both races. But we have all the officials necessary to convene...unless you have an objection?"

Cam's eyes roved over the faerie officials, stopping on Alissa's mutinous expression. They also rested, for a brief second, on Destry. "Fine." He flipped his cloak back and settled into the throne. "Brumal, you will quiet this room."

"Perhaps we could clear the room, Your Majesty," Executor Faris said.

Cam raised a pointed eyebrow. "Why is that, Sir Executor? Are you afraid for the goblins to see how faerie justice is done?" He smiled like it was a joke, fangs gleaming.

The executor swallowed, and his wings picked up pace. "I think of the girl, of course. Our purpose is to place this student on a path of proper, lawful behavior. We hold her no personal malice. Indeed, our deep concern for her well-being forces us to this unpleasant course. A goblin audience can only add to the strain of accepting the consequences of her actions."

"As you wish." Cam leisurely scratched an obsidian nail along the stone armrest of his throne; the sound made the executor wince. "But clearing the room may take hours. Goblins are gregarious creatures, I fear. It would be most unfortunate for your entourage to have to travel through Rí Kobold in the darkness."

Executor Faris looked dubious. "Hours? Surely Your Majesty has but to issue a command."

"Surely *you* don't presume to understand the intricacies of the goblin court? I said hours. Hours is precisely what I meant." Cam's face was carefully blank—and even in goblin form, Destry recognized the expression. It was his bluffing face, the one she'd seen dozens of times when they played poker. Why was he lying? Was he so angry that he'd purposely make this trial even more miserable for her?

The executor scowled, but he gestured curtly to Alissa. "We will proceed." He swaggered to Destry's chair. "I'll act as questioner. Advisor Alissa prefers to retain her role as defender. Our vote shall be taken at the end of the inquisition and approved by both the fire faerie's guardian and the wronged party—the goblin king."

The little man might not look as impressive as Brumal, but Destry quickly realized he was as dangerous. His first questions honed in on her receipt of the dagger. How again had she determined that the package came from the castle? Was she certain of how the wrapping had looked? Why hadn't she brought it as evidence?

Destry had been afraid this question would come up in Brumal's examination. She clenched her hands together. "I couldn't find it."

The executor's eyebrows rose in poorly-simulated surprise. "What? Something notably important, and you threw it away?"

"No. I set it aside, but when I got back to my room, the wrapping and note were gone."

"What do you think happened to them?"

Destry set her jaw. "I don't know."

"And are you aware that the goblin castle keeps record of every delivery made to the fey kingdom? I've been required to sign receipts of delivery myself. I requested their records. No messengers visited our kingdom today." The executor leaned closer, like he was inviting her confidence.

"Shall we be honest, fire fey? It seems more likely that you know who sent that package, and it was not a goblin. Perhaps someone who asked a favor...someone you could not refuse?"

"Why are we repeating this line of query?" Alissa demanded. "This question was asked and answered in the trial, Executor Faris."

"The dagger's origin was never verified," he said. "And some in our realm want to discredit the current administration and our queen. I wish to ascertain if this fire faerie is merely a pawn in their game or a willing participant."

Why did he keep harping on her element? Destry said, "I'm not part of any game! I thought the knife was from a friend!"

The executor turned away. "That part I believe, my dear. But what friend?"

His next question focused on the scorione. As Brumal had pointed out, the monster's appearance seemed terribly convenient. If she'd truly been attacked, why had the creature stopped? Why had it left her alive?

"I don't know," Destry said. "Maybe it heard the goblins coming."

"Had the goblins scared such a large creature away, they should have seen or heard its retreat. Yet none did."

"You're still rehashing information covered in the trial," Alissa said. "Unless there's something new to explore, I suggest we make our arguments and vote upon the desired punitive measures, if any."

Executor Faris waved one hand in Destry's direction. "I'm offering this girl an opportunity to recant what are clearly lies. And I wish to cover one last point before we end. Why were you in the forest today, Destry?"

She frowned. "For the reasons I said earlier."

"Yes, we heard your charmingly heroic tale of wanting to save the willas. But isn't it unusual for a faerie to conceive a fondness for these trees?" He walked a circle, stopped by Destry's chair. "Do you know what I think? Your supposed fondness for the forest was a ruse...a ruse to allow you access, to allow you the perfect opportunity to create damage."

"Why would I do that?"

He shrugged. "Personal reasons, perhaps? The goblins control your power source. That must be frustrating. Or an inherited vendetta, recently discovered as you learned about your heritage in the magic realms?"

"The goblins give me full access to the firewell. And inheriting some vendetta would be hard, since I don't know who my father is. He never claimed me."

"There are many ways to learn about your heritage, my dear. There are few—very few—faeries known for their appreciation of these white trees. Perhaps you're not pretending. Perhaps it's a matter of biology, which would give ample clue to your parentage. How can we trust anything you say? If you will lie about knowing your father, you will lie about other things."

"I'm not lying! I don't know my father!" Destry's voice caught, emotions bubbling over after the long trial. Some members of the audience frowned, though not at her...at the executor.

Alissa strode over, eyes flashing. "You've crossed into harassment, Executor Faris. The child was abandoned by her father and has stated repeatedly that she doesn't know her family. By all legal and ethical codes, you should end this line of questioning."

"So defensive." Smiling, the executor turned away, fingering the dagger's wrappings. "If I accept her claim, we have no explanation for her reprehensible actions. I suppose there's the oldest reason of all: resentment at being spurned. Perhaps a 'friend' who was not as loyal as you hoped? A friend who won't publicly recognize you, who won't protect you? Destroying something of value to that person would be immensely satisfying."

Alissa stepped between Destry and the executor. "These suppositions are mere fabrications, with no fact to support them." She turned on the other officials, braid swinging. "Why don't you raise an objection?"

The officials shot each other nervous glances, but they were clearly unwilling to halt the executor. The little man stood taller. "I merely wish to determine her motivations, Advisor Alissa. But if you believe the girl's best interests are served by allowing the mystery to go unresolved, then by all means—let's make our final arguments."

There was absolute silence in the throne room as the faeries made their points. The goblins that had remained (three-fourths of them, at least) were as centered on the outcome as if it had been their trial. It was either the best reality show ever, Destry thought hysterically, or the goblins were hoping her punishment would be horrible—nearly as good as punishing her themselves. She'd long since stopped looking at Cam and his aunt. Every time she saw him sitting there, stone-like, her chest crushed a little more.

Alissa pointed out that no fresh evidence had been offered—just unsubstantiated suppositions. She reminded the officials that Destry had arrived at the goblin castle before the willa attack began. Why wait until witnesses could place her in the vicinity, when she'd had unrestricted access earlier in the day? She pointed out that Destry was half-human, with little support in the human world, and had a magic partner who was in no way implicated in the day's misdeeds. Any significant punishment, such as expulsion from the school, would not only expose a young girl to the negligence she'd suffered for fifteen years, but also damn her partner to lose his magic at the age of eighteen.

When Alissa finished, the executor rose. "My fellow officials. Our law is different than goblin law specifically because it's exacting. The girl hasn't provided one shred of proof to uphold her claims, nor does she exhibit sorrow for her lies. And despite the statement that my claims are unsubstantiated, one fact remains: this girl trespassed on goblin territory. The king commanded she have an escort through the woods and generously provided one any time she wished! It's common knowledge that guards are stationed at the edge of the forest when students have free Saturdays, yet she took advantage of their temporary absence and chose to venture there unaccompanied."

Destry had worried someone would challenge her about the guards. She'd been relieved when Brumal never brought it up, confused when Executor Faris didn't. Now, she understood. He'd been saving it as a final nail in her coffin, something to use once Alissa could no longer call witnesses or ask Destry for explanations.

The executor raised one indignant finger. "This alone is a serious breach of behavior, a serious lack of respect for authority. If we do not correct her course, she heads down a dangerous road. As my colleague points out, it would be unfair to condemn the law-breaker to a life of neglect, or to deprive her magic partner of the opportunity to help her along a more fitting path. Therefore, I propose ten strikes with the golden rods."

Murmurs rippled through the audience. Apparently, they understood what that was, even if Destry didn't. Alissa looked outraged. "Ten strikes? For simple trespassing?"

The executor swept his gaze across the officials. "We all know simple trespassing is not the only issue. Queen Liselle wishes to assure that such an act is never perpetrated upon goblin-kind again." He sketched a bow to Cam. "We must choose a punishment strong enough to deter a recurrence, or else we must remove the girl from this realm and temptation. Would you not agree?"

Alissa stared at the other officials, either nodding agreement or avoiding her eyes. "Fine," she snapped. "But it will not go on her record. A youthful misdeed, to be dealt with and forgotten."

"Well, let us hope she will not forget it," Executor Faris said. "But in the eyes of our courts, it will be instantly erased. We shall vote."

There was no hesitancy from the other officials. The executor turned to Fey Elena, who nodded grim assent, and then Cam. "We have chosen a course of action in pursuit of continued peace with your kingdom. Where your law restrains you, ours does not. Thus may all parties feel that justice has been done. Does this meet your approval, King of the Goblins?"

A tiny vine of hope, unwanted and unencouraged, pushed its way into Destry's heart. Whatever those golden rods were, ten strikes with them was obviously bad. Cam could refuse to accept the punishment...but then what?

It didn't matter; Cam looked at the executor a long moment, then nodded. "So be it. Faerie justice shall be done."

The court broke into a low babble of conversation for the second time that evening. Fey Elena slid one hand under Destry's arm. "Come, child. The sentence has been pronounced. Now it's over."

Destry glanced across the room. The officials and executor stood together, deep in discussion, but nobody seemed intent on grabbing her.

She turned to the headmistress, stomach clenching. "Will they...will they do it tonight?"

Fey Elena patted her shoulder. "No. The rods have special properties. They'll drain your magic—your ability to sense and manipulate energy strands—for a brief period. But they take time to prepare and are only used in our justice building, located near the palace. Your sentence cannot be carried out until tomorrow evening, at least."

Relief shivered down her spine. "I'm more used to living without magic than living with it. That doesn't sound so bad."

"I will not lie to you, Destry. The aftermath is not what most dread. While the rods cause no physical harm, the Striking—the process of removing your magic—is extremely painful. But once it's over, you need never think on it again."

That wasn't especially comforting, coming from this side of the equation. "Do I get to come back to the school tonight?" Please say she didn't have to spend the night in another holding cell, this time a faerie one.

The headmistress nodded. "We must detour by the justice building. They'll place a band on you to prevent escape attempts. I'll make the practical arrangements, and you'll have a reprieve until tomorrow night."

Alissa came over, mouth pulled tight. "We're prepared to leave. Destry, I'm afraid you must come with us. But don't be scared, at least for now."

Destry met the woman's eyes. Alissa had done all she could. "It's okay. Fey Elena explained."

They followed the other officials across the room. Cam stood in front of his throne, watching Riamon and Lady Val converse in low tones. Destry paused in front of him. He turned to her, and she searched his face, hoping for some sign—some indication that he might forgive her. There was nothing.

Destry sank into the impressive curtsy she had, until now, failed to master. "I humbly beg your pardon for the damage that was done, Goblin King, and assure you that it was both unintentional...and regretted."

She didn't wait for his reaction. Destry swept from the room on the tail of the executor and his entourage, with the faerie queen's words from some time ago playing in her ears: *Believe me, my dear, no matter how close you are to a goblin, he will turn on you in a second, should you threaten his world.*

A HEAVY PRICE

✦

In the grand foyer, Alissa grabbed Riamon's arm. "Move it, Ri. I'm not riding with those overstuffed toads another minute." She hustled Destry's supporters past the more sedately moving executor and officials. The carriages stood on the cobbled road, gleaming dully in the early evening light. Destry, Fey Elena, Riamon, and Alissa piled into the four-person carriage. When the executor came to the door, the fey advisor smiled sweetly. "It seems we're full up, Executor Faris. Perhaps the other carriage would be more to your liking."

He bent a poisonous look on her before puffing over to the larger vehicle. Riamon frowned. "You seem adept at making enemies, Liss. To enjoy it, more specifically."

She laughed. "Making enemies at court is unavoidable if you have a scrap of integrity. Don't play the overprotective brother tonight."

Brother? No wonder Alissa looked familiar. Now that they were together, it was easier to see the facial similarities. But Destry felt too sick inside to comment on their surprise relationship. She huddled against the seat, staring out the window as the horses picked up speed.

Fey Elena leaned into her line of vision. "You look done in, child. Why don't you rest? It's a bit of a drive to the justice building."

She shook her head, despite the weariness dragging at her bones. Sleep was impossible.

The headmistress pressed a hand to Destry's forehead. "That wasn't a suggestion." Magic wrapped around her, weighting her eyes, dampening her awareness. She tried pushing it away, but Fey Elena's fingers pulsed with increased energy. "Rest." Within seconds, Destry succumbed to the darkness.

"Destry. Destry, wake up, child."

Someone was shaking her. Destry tried to ignore it, but the shaker was persistent. A masculine voice said, "You made the sleep spell strong. Too strong, to be precise."

Fey Elena spoke again. "She was fighting me, and she needed rest. I couldn't bear to watch her fear one more moment."

Another voice—Alissa's—said, "I wish I could have done more for her. But the executor handpicked officials he could lead around by the nose. He only included me because no one else was available on such short notice." She sighed. "Ten strikes is a steep price to pay for youthful foolishness."

Fey Elena sounded severe. "Let's be honest among ourselves. Her supposed crime is not what Destry is paying for. She's paying for her suspected parentage."

Alissa said, "You know which one is her father?"

"Of course not. Had I anything more than suspicions, I would have approached the family—convinced them to use their influence to make this a fair trial. But even without proof, I can see and think. The executor made every effort to discredit her tonight. That was more than simply covering his bases with the goblins."

Destry wanted to force her eyes open, to ask about her family...but Fey Elena had declared that subject off-limits. Besides, she was too tired.

Someone rapped on the carriage. Another masculine voice—not Riamon's—said, "What's taking so long? If the bracelet is applied soon, we may still make dinner."

Alissa said coldly, "By all means, Gordan, run along to the banquet hall. It's a fitting action for a cowardly pig."

The man's voice dropped to a hiss. "What did you expect me to do? Faris affects our positions, and he answers to no one but the queen. Be as high and mighty as you want. You'll fall if you don't march to his tune."

"If everyone stood up to him, he couldn't run roughshod over this kingdom in the name of protecting Queen Liselle's interests."

The man called Gordan made a dismissive noise. "Or there would simply be new advisors in Her Majesty's court. Are you taking care of the bracelet, then?"

Alissa sounded tired. "Yes. I'll get her banded."

Rocks crunched underfoot as someone—probably Gordan—strode off. Alissa said, "If you can't wake her, cast a rousing spell. I want to get my thirty pieces of silver and have done with it."

Riamon said, equally subdued, "You did the best you could."

"Well, dear brother, that wasn't enough tonight."

They stopped speaking, and Fey Elena didn't shake Destry again. Good. Maybe now she could delve into true sleep.

No such luck. Cool fingers pressed against her forehead, and a jolt zipped through Destry. Not an unpleasant one, like Gerald's. It was more the sensation that she'd been drinking strong coffee for the last hour and was instantly and irrevocably awake. Her eyes flew open.

Riamon offered her a wobbly smile. "Did you have a pleasant rest?"

"It was better than my day."

"That counts for little," Fey Elena said dryly. "We've reached the justice building."

They piled out. To Destry's surprise, the place where the fey dispensed justice wasn't a scary, imposing edifice. Less polished than most faerie buildings, but with an air of old grace, the circular building was ringed with columns carved to resemble fey trees. Delicate branches held up the roof, turning the walkway into a stone forest.

Alissa said, "This building was designed by Shiblo, an artist favored by the early Imperial family. It wasn't meant to be a place of fear, but of reckoning and restoring balance. Despite our occasional departure from that idea, I think it's one of the loveliest in all of faerie architecture."

They walked through the columns and then an arched door. Inside, the place was broken into several levels of balconies, each ringing the entire building. The floor recessed in the center, creating a circular room at basement level. Destry looked over their ground-level balcony railing. Marble mosaic covered the floor of the recessed room, depicting each of the elements: water, wind, fire, earth. Destry was surprised to see the last and said so.

Alissa shrugged. "Shiblo was a revolutionary thinker. He argued that our separation from the goblins and humankind was unnatural, removing us from the very things that create balance in our world. His thoughts were encouraged while the Imperial family held the throne. But as the administration changed, Shiblo's ideas became less acceptable, and he fell out of favor. This is one of his last major pieces."

Destry slid her hand along the banister. The floor level balcony seemed larger and more impressive than the others. Riamon said, "This is the level afforded to dignitaries who come to see justice meted out. The goblin king will watch from this balcony tomorrow night."

Cam would be here? Destry turned surprised eyes on Riamon.

He smiled bitterly. "I'm certain they will request his presence. Require it, to be more precise. That way, he may attest to his people that justice was served."

Alissa said, "Shall we do the banding? I still need to make arrangements with your headmistress."

Destry's heart thumped, but banding was just a name for the flexible gold bracelet Alissa slid over Destry's right wrist. She tapped it, made a circular motion, and magic rippled over the metal. It thinned, melding to Destry's arm above her wrist tattoo. When the magic stopped shimmering, the bracelet looked and felt like little more than a strip of gold paint.

"The metal is joined with you now," Alissa said. "Don't try to remove it, unless you wish to remove your skin." She slid a strip of gold around the balcony railing and repeated the tapping-circular motion. The strip melted into the marble. "Once you return tomorrow, both strips may be removed. If you go past certain geographical boundaries, the metal will burn, warning you to turn back. Obey the warning."

Destry didn't ask what would happen if she disobeyed. She didn't want to know.

Fey Elena waved towards the arched entryway. "Riamon and I must complete tomorrow's arrangements. Why don't you explore the grounds? The rousing spell will require some exercise to work off. Just stay within sight of the justice building."

Destry hesitated. Shouldn't she be part of this discussion? But the headmistress's face indicated this wasn't a "suggestion," either. She hurried out into the early dusk.

The grounds were as well-designed as the building. No sidewalks, though paths were worn in the neatly trimmed grass. Destry followed one, winding through groups of slender trees and past benches. A small pavilion, similar in design to the justice building, was surrounded by greenery. Destry turned in that direction.

As she drew closer, a gentle tenor voice broke the quiet—song gliding towards her on the breeze. Destry rounded the pavilion. A man knelt on the ground, tending the flower beds. He broke off as she came into view. "Ah. Another supplicant, come to beg me to cease my assault on her ears."

He looked about the same age as Cam's father, with long blonde hair streaked with gray. The faerie man's eyes were gray, too, and crinkled at the corners in amusement. Destry smiled hesitantly. "The song was beautiful. But I didn't recognize the words."

He sat back on his heels, brushing earth from his hands and wrists. His silver and blue tattoos gleamed in the light. "Well, it's an old song, an old language. Fairly unpopular with most here, which is perhaps why I sing it. Besides, it helps the plants grow."

"You're the gardener?"

"Among other things. It isn't exactly in my job description, but few have the talent or taste for this. I do what I can."

Destry fingered one of the vines wreathing the pavilion. "Will I disturb your work if I stay? It won't be for long."

The man returned to gardening. "You are welcome here, young faerie. Stay as long as you wish." He began singing again.

The words reminded Destry of the ancient language Cam was teaching her, of the music he'd sung to Wings. It gave her a sense of both homecoming and homesickness. She paced outside the pavilion and then inside, examining the craftsmanship. Restless, she rubbed the shining band on her arm.

"Did you receive that tonight?"

She turned. The faerie man stood at the steps of the pavilion, watching her. She hadn't even noticed that he'd stopped singing. Heat rushed along her cheeks. "Yes."

He came into the pavilion and sat on one of the benches. "Don't let it bother you overmuch. We all rebel from time to time. You'll receive a couple strikes, be suitably punished, and move on—older and wiser, with a new experience under your belt."

Destry laughed humorlessly. "My number is a little bigger than that. Ten."

"Ten?" The man's eyebrows drew together. "That seems a large number for someone so young. What did you do to merit such hefty punishment?"

There was no censure in his soft tones. Destry sat on the bench a few feet from him, and she found herself explaining about her lessons at the castle, the enormous scorpion no one else had seen, the bleeding willa tree, and the trial. The only thing she didn't mention was her friendship with Cam.

"Interesting," the man said, "that the goblin king didn't pursue retribution more stringently. The willas are essential to their race." He examined her, as if he suspected the single thing she'd left unsaid.

"I think he believed me, at least some of it. The executor didn't, though. That's why my punishment is so bad: because of how important the trees are, because of what I might have started between the faeries and the goblins."

The man laughed, low and ironic. "Faerie politics are rarely that simple. The executor has personal reasons for pursuing such harsh justice. You're merely a tool for advancing his agenda."

"How do you know?"

"Because that is what they do." His tone was final. "The question is whether you'll allow yourself to be used."

"I don't even know what he's using me for. How can I change it?"

Those cool gray eyes seemed to see right through her. "You must have some idea what purpose you'd serve."

Destry started to say he was wrong, but the assertion died, stillborn. She remembered Fey Elena's relief at learning about her friendship with Cam, her hints that Destry could be taken for an illegitimate member of the Imperial family, the overheard conversation in the carriage. The headmistress's warning: "Were you a member of the Imperial family, you would gain formidable enemies simply because of your lineage."

And then there was Cam. The executor insinuated that he must have private reasons to be "forgiving" of Destry. Faris was dedicated to bringing down the Queen's enemies; Cam qualified. Admitting his connection to Destry after the mess in the willa forest would be like condoning her supposed crime. It could cause instability in his kingdom...a convenient benefit for the faeries.

The executor wanted her to admit her connection to Cam; he wanted her to name a member of the Imperial family as her father. Since Destry wouldn't and couldn't do those things, he wanted someone—her father or Cam—to step forward and stop what was, by everyone's opinion, a severe punishment for something Destry hadn't even done.

If that was the plan, it had backfired. Her nameless, faceless father didn't care enough to acknowledge her existence; why would he care if his daughter suffered? And she'd ruined any chance of Cam stepping forward the moment she strolled into the forest. It must seem like the final breach of trust. No wonder he'd turned his back on her.

The man was still waiting. "Yes," Destry said. "I think I know what he wants."

"Then if you wish to thwart his desires, you must also thwart his plan—no matter how challenging that is. Physical pain is temporary.

There are worse consequences, ones that last longer and are far more difficult to endure."

The fey man stood and bowed to her. "I wish you good fortune, young faerie. And I would offer one piece of advice. The rods draw an essential part of you—your magic—which removes your defenses and leaves you vulnerable. The natural reaction is to fight, thus the pain. But if you can bring yourself to accept the loss of your magic, the pain from the strikes will lessen."

"But it's part of me. That's like telling me not to worry while someone cuts my fingers off."

The man chuckled. "The loss of your magic is temporary, unlike the loss of your fingers. Do you understand how magic works?"

Destry shrugged. "We pull it from the air—the magic strands, I mean—and make it do what we want."

"Correct in essentials, though not in understanding." He said it too nicely for Destry to feel embarrassed. "We refer to the energy wreathing the world as 'magic strands,' but the true magic lies within us, in our ability to sense and manipulate them—or in the case of spoken spells, to command them with words. And just as climbing a hill expends the caloric energy gained from food, exercising your ability to 'do magic' expends some of your magic energy with each spell. They're small expenditures. Magic regenerates quickly, so we rarely notice unless the spell is quite enormous."

After the stressful day, this technical explanation made Destry's head ache. "You're saying my magic will grow back?"

He nodded. "Each strike inhibits your ability to use magic for approximately five hours. Ten strikes would remove your magic for two days. Logically, that's a short time. And if remembering that fails, try this: they will draw your magic, whether you fight it or not. But *you* can choose how badly they make you suffer."

He bowed again, then strode out of the pavilion and down the hill, away from the justice building. Destry watched him for a moment before starting back to where Riamon and Fey Elena waited patiently beneath the stone trees.

MY KIND OF MONSTER

✦

Cam wasn't making Tyla's day easier. He knew that. He regretted it. But he also couldn't change it. *One of the perks of being my assistant,* he thought grimly. *Lucky Tyla.*

She'd spent the past twelve hours with him, offering friendship and help as he patched up Wings, sang health into her veins. She'd mediated his heated argument with Brumal, took Cam's part when he insisted that Destry hadn't caused the willa's injuries. Tyla had reminded him why he shouldn't visit Destry in the holding cell. She'd made sure Cam arrived at the hearing with the proper documents to make the verdict of innocence official. And she'd stayed to watch that travesty of faerie justice, even though she liked Destry and didn't want to see.

The trial had gone exactly as he feared. He'd been sure, the second he heard Destry's explanation, that he and Brumal could "pursue justice" without coming up with a guilty verdict. Enough goblins liked Destry to accept that, as long as they didn't suspect favoritism from him. Which was the only thing that lent Cam the strength to turn away from her earlier...to let them take her, scared and uncomforted, to a holding cell.

But he'd feared the faerie reaction. Nobles, in particular, were known to abandon friends and even family who disrupted their ordered existence. The executor was no exception. Cam knew the man planned on a fey trial when he brought all those officials. He would have no compunction about punishing Destry—whether she was the true culprit or not—in the name of keeping peace between kingdoms.

Cam barely remembered the walk to his bedroom after the fey left. Tyla was already there, waiting. She didn't comment as he slid into human form, as he paced the room from balcony to door and back again. Finally, she said, "Cam, you did the best you could."

He smashed one fist against the stone balustrade and watched in satisfaction as several knuckles split open and began bleeding. "Did you see her face, Tyla? I'm the only person she's counted on in the last four years, and I just fed her to the wolves."

"You did what you had to. You couldn't have trusted her to goblin punishment—not with an injured willa. And learning that you two are actually friends would have made the faerie sentencing worse. Those earth-cursed officials would've increased the punishment just to set an example. You won her more sympathy by snubbing her."

"A lot of good it did! Ten strikes, Ty. When's the last time you heard a youth sentence so high?"

"At least they didn't expel her. And it's not going on her record."

"I'm sure that's great comfort to her now." He clenched the stone railing, imagining Destry in her room, waiting fearfully for the next evening and the unknown pain it would bring.

Tyla laid a tentative hand on his shoulder. "I saw how she watched you, Cam. The fact that you're angry at her—or at least, she thinks you are—probably bothers her most. Write a letter, and I'll deliver it."

He snorted humorlessly. "A band-aid for a mortal wound? I need to see her."

Cam expected her to argue. After the day's conflict, a trip to Destry's school—trespassing on faerie land to slip into a girl's dorm room—was a terrible idea. Aunt Val would kill them if she found out. Kill them, revive their dead bodies to flay with a switch, then kill them again. He'd be lucky if it ended there.

But Tyla just said, "Flying you there is no harder than delivering a letter. I'll meet you in the library after dark."

He spun around. When had she realized? Tyla rolled her eyes. "I know you're going to look for some law to mitigate that sentence. What else would you do?" She started for the door. "But first, eat the dinner I send up. Last thing I need tonight is you fainting from lack of food. You'd fall off, fifty feet in the air, and then where would we be?"

Cam laughed softly. Tyla could make him smile even when his mood was dark. "You'd have a squished goblin king."

"Exactly. Eat your dinner. I'll be back in a couple hours."

Flying with Tyla was the best part of Cam's day. The height didn't bother him, and Tyla could hold his human weight easily in her largest goblin form. Finding a way that was mutually comfortable had taken practice, but they'd worked it out over the years. Now, the wind rushing through his hair and the occasional rocking of her vast wings were pure pleasure.

Stars blinked in and out, and the moon cast a glossy shine on Tyla's feathers. She'd grumbled about the bright night; she had to fly higher to avoid being spotted. It was still smarter than walking, however, where Cam was liable to encounter faeries who might take exception to goblin presence on their land.

Tyla circled the school, looking for the correct balcony, making sure no one was around. Apparently satisfied that it was clear, she went into a steep dive. Cam barely suppressed a whoop of surprise. He could sense Tyla's malicious grin.

She landed, and Cam leapt off. Tyla eyed him with one gold orb. "I suppose you want me to be a lookout too."

"If you wouldn't mind. And perhaps knock on Destry's window on your way to the roof."

Tyla's bird eyes rolled as easily as her human ones. "Those vines will hold you. I've seen plenty of faerie kids use them. Climb up and knock yourself."

Cam's smile slid from his face. "No. She has every reason to hate me right now. I'll make sure I'm welcome first."

Another eye roll. Tyla launched herself from the ground, shrinking to a normal-sized raven as she flew to the balcony. She tapped at the glass-paned door with her beak. Cam waited, heart in his throat.

It took four tries before Destry opened her door, eyebrows creased in confusion. Tyla immediately took flight for the roof. Destry looked around, frowning. She hardly reacted when she saw Cam on the lawn. "What are you doing here...Your Majesty?"

"Can I come up?"

Her face resembled a white marble statue in the moonlight. "You're the goblin king. You can do whatever you want."

"No, Des. I'm so sorry for today...tonight. I'll explain. But I won't come up unless it's okay with you."

She turned away from the balcony with a shrug, but she left the door open. Cam took that as consent. He clambered up the sturdy vines. Des was sitting on her bed when he came in, her back stiff. He knelt before her. "Des, I didn't mean any of it, I swear. I never wanted to say those things to you."

She didn't meet his gaze. "You aren't a puppet. No one forced you to say them."

"I was trying to protect you. Dessie, the entire goblin world thought you might have slashed a willa. If I'd acted friendly, no one would have believed your innocence. They'd have thought I was covering for a friend, and you'd have been voted guilty and subjected to goblin punishment."

"What about after? Or were you just keeping up the act?"

His mouth twisted, bitterness strong as lemon juice on his tongue. "After, I knew your people—sweet faeriekind—intended to have their way with you. They'd have given you a worse sentence if there was any inkling we're friends. Like I said before, the goblin king has enemies in the faerie court."

Destry twisted her nightgown between her fingers. "That's all it was? You aren't...you weren't..."

"Angry at you over Wings? Of course not. I know you'd never hurt her."

"No. Yes. I mean the forest too. For going in when I said I wouldn't. For breaking a promise—a real one. Will you forgive me for that?"

He reached to tug her hair, the way he sometimes did when she was being ridiculous, and found he couldn't do it. Cam chafed her bare arms instead, her skin soft beneath his fingers. "Tyla explained. If I'd known the whole story...yes, I still would've been mad. But I would have stayed and listened. And I wouldn't have made you cry."

She dropped her head into her hands, a violent shudder running through her body, and began to do exactly that. Cam sat on the bed next to her. "I'm so sorry, Dessie."

She sniffled, wiping tears away with her palms. "Don't be. I'm just...just relieved. I thought I'd lost my best friend."

He pulled her into his arms and rocked her. Guilt gnawed at him. An explanation, a simple apology, and he was forgiven. But he couldn't—wouldn't—let himself off the hook that easily. "I'm figuring out what to do about your sentence. I think there's a law somewhere—one giving me the right to mete out half the punishment, whatever way I see fit. We'd lie, say I did something terrible to you for the other half. It would cut your strikes to five."

"What if people figure out the truth?" She shook her head. "If they realize we're friends, our secrecy would be pointless."

He pulled away to look in her face. "Des, I'm expected to watch. And faerie punishment is harsh."

She laughed nervously. "They're not cutting my wings off. They said ten strikes with a golden rod. That can't...it can't be that bad, right?"

Cam wanted to argue, but the law was an old one, and he hadn't found it yet. If he was wrong, no point making her dread the Striking even more. He stacked her pillows up, then leaned back on them, pulling Destry with him. She nestled close, head on his shoulder. Her hair smelled of a summer storm. She said, "What happens next? After tomorrow night?"

He stared at the painting on her ceiling. "I'm not sure. The lesson thing could be problematic now."

Destry snorted. "You think? Everyone in Rí Kobold hates me."

"No. A lot of them believed you, or they wouldn't have voted 'not guilty,' no matter what Aunt Val and I said. And seeing your people's harshness won you some support. That's why I didn't clear the court-room." He stopped, because that was the extent of his good news.

"But I still won't be welcome there, as long as people think I could've done it." Destry's voice was small. "Cam? What's a *felindeamhan*?"

His stomach hollowed, but he kept his answer light. "New word, huh? Where'd you learn that one?"

She shrugged, and Cam knew he wouldn't get specifics...which was a shame, because he needed a target for the impotent fury building in his chest. The single word told him too much about how she'd been treated after leaving the willa grove. The way she'd been treated *in* the forest still gutted him.

He held her tighter. "It's a particularly insulting way to say 'she-dem on'... the sort of word that gets someone punched in the face."

She nodded, but her shoulders hitched with suppressed tears. Cam stroked her hair. "Once Wings is okay, when the willas are communicating again, I can exonerate you. That was another reason for tonight. The other goblins will believe my testimony about the willas' memories. They won't think I'm lying just so we can see each other."

"How long before she's better?"

"Dante says at least two months. With all the delays, she's lucky to be alive. That fire was a smart move. I 'heard' Wings, but we were at the other end of the castle. By the time I got there, the willas were in a frenzy. It was like listening to twenty people screaming at once. The smoke led us to the right place."

"It wasn't smart. It was desperate." She yawned, rubbing her eyes. "Cam? Did someone else really send me that knife? Or were you afraid admitting you'd sent it would make things worse?"

"No. Besides the fact that it's a willa slayer—" he repressed an instinc-tive shudder—"I'd have worried you'd impale yourself, no matter how well you're doing in Combat."

Destry laughed harder than the comment deserved. But she shook her head when he asked why. "Then where did the dagger come from?"

"I'm not sure. But we're going to find out."

"*We* sounds good." She hesitated. "I love you, Cam. You know that, right? I couldn't have asked for a better brother or friend."

He heard the nervous shake in her voice. Cam had learned a long time ago that Destry didn't say those words. His family expressed affection openly, but he'd never pushed that on her. They both knew how they felt, and it was enough.

His heart squeezed. "I love you, too, Des. Always have."

She curled into him, breathing getting deep and regular. Cam wasn't willing to move and ruin what little peace she had. He lay there for a long time, staring at the storm rolling across her ceiling.

"Camden Darkwater, you idiot! What is wrong with you?"

Several painful yanks on his hair jerked Cam awake. He grabbed for the assailant, but Tyla had already moved. He sat up, pulling a bleary-eyed Destry with him.

Cam glared at his personal assistant. "What was that for?"

"Stupidity! I dropped you here for a short visit, not to take a nap. You missed my warning whistle. And now Destry's magic partner is heading to the balcony, to climb up and surprise her with brownies."

Destry's eyes flew open all the way. "Tristan?"

Cam rubbed his stinging scalp. "For this you ripped out a fistful of hair? The guy knows me and Des have been friends for years."

Tyla propped her hands on her hips. "And don't you think today's events might have engendered some animosity in him? He may take exception to finding you in bed with his intended."

Destry's flush could be seen even in the dim moonlight. "I'm Tristan's magic partner, not his 'intended.' And Cam and me weren't doing anything."

The goblin girl rolled her eyes. "I couldn't care less if you were. But it's too late for Cam to climb down without being seen. He'd better hide, or you'd better get outside."

Destry frowned. "How do you know Tristan is coming *here*?"

"Because when no one listened to my warning, I flew down to stall him. He recognized me from your description—I suppose you don't know many shapeshifting raven-girls—but my assurance you'd gone to bed didn't deter your Tristan. He said, and I quote, 'Des never locks her balcony door. If she's asleep, I'll leave these in her room.'"

Destry flung a pillow across the room, temper-tantrum style. "Those better be some good brownies." She dashed out the door, closing it behind her.

Cam looked at Tyla. In unstated agreement, they crept to the wall behind the door, where their sensitive goblin ears would easily pick up the conversation. Cam heard the boy hoist himself over the railing, heard Destry's quiet, "What are you doing here?"

"Why do you sound surprised?" Tristan asked. "It's not exactly a new thing."

Tyla quirked an eyebrow at Cam. Destry said, "You just didn't mention it earlier."

"Hard to do with our headmistress standing there. 'Hey, Fey Elena. I sneak up to Destry's room after curfew most nights.' That'd go over well."

Destry laughed weakly; she probably knew Cam was listening. Her magic partner didn't pick up on her tension, or else he attributed it to the crummy day. "I brought you some serious stress relief—better than a plain brownie. Dark chocolate caramel pecan brownies from Mellie's. I snuck down there during your trial, since I couldn't do anything else."

A short gasp, followed by sounds of culinary appreciation; clearly, Destry had taken one. Tristan commented, "I met your friend Tyla on the way here." No reply. Destry probably had a mouthful of brownie. "She seemed nice. Way nicer than that monster goblin king."

Destry finally came up for air. "You've never met the goblin king."

"Don't need to. He let them put you in jail and take you to trial. He ought to know you better after months of dragging you over for lessons—why, no one knows. He should have stood up for you."

"Sometimes things aren't that simple."

The boy didn't argue, though Cam bet he wanted to—especially since Destry seemed to have left him in the dark about their friendship. In an obvious attempt at easing things, he said, "I know you'll miss the magic lessons. And the willa trees."

"Yeah. It'll be a few months before the willas can exonerate me. But at least it's not forever."

Sudden stillness. Then: "You want to go back?"

"Of...of course."

"After what they did to you?"

Destry sounded stiff. "The goblins aren't the ones who found me guilty. They're not the ones who'll hurt me tomorrow." Her voice broke. "That's our people, Tristan."

Prolonged silence, broken only by the sound of feet shuffling and muffled sniffles from Destry, like her face was pressed into the boy's chest.

Fantastic. Now they were *hugging*.

Tristan said, "I'm setting the record for screwing up today. I just thought... Well, never mind what I thought. I'm an idiot, okay?"

Cam rolled his eyes—and noticed Tyla smiling gently, like she thought the self-proclaimed idiot was sweet. Destry sniffled again. "It's alright, Tris. I've been glad for you today."

He laughed harshly. "Yeah. Like when I hurt your feelings so bad, you go running to the woods. Or when I misunderstand everything you say or make assumptions about what you want. There's a lot to appreciate."

"How about when you checked on me every chance you got? Or wanted to come with me to a place that scares your wings off? Or bought brownies to drown my sorrows? Those are pretty good."

The boy sighed. "I'll do another good deed and let you rest. But Destry? I'm on your side, wherever that is, whatever you want. Remember it."

At least he didn't sneak a kiss; Des returned too quickly for that. She slipped inside, a small box in her hands, expression self-conscious. "You didn't tell him," Cam said flatly. "Your magic partner has no idea who I am."

Destry flushed, but she met his eyes. "No. Are you gonna lecture me about honesty tonight?"

Tyla took the box, popped it open, and snagged a brownie. "I'm going to wait out there while you two have an uncomfortable conversation." She plopped the box onto a dresser and sauntered out the balcony door.

Cam sighed. "Des, are you and that guy serious?"

She pulled a cross between a pout and a scowl. "Someday, we've got to do that whole binding-ceremony thing. Right now, we're not even committed."

"But you're friends." She didn't answer, and he said gently, "No lectures tonight. I'm just saying you ought to clue him in before someone else does."

She folded onto the bed. "You sure are considerate of Tristan."

Cam snorted. "I'm thinking of you, not him. Truthfully, I think he's a bad influence."

Destry gave him a look that questioned his intelligence. "What?"

He pointed at the box on her dresser. "Sneaking into your room—which he does regularly—to bring you the faerie equivalent of wine coolers. Not exactly responsible behavior."

"For the record, you snuck into my room, too."

"But I didn't bring brownies." Cam smiled to let her know he was playing—mostly. He pushed Destry over, so she was lying down, and pulled her blanket up to her chin. She just watched him, looking dazed. Cam slid the box of brownies further away. She didn't need more. "Des? Was that kid right? Do you always leave your room unlocked?"

She yawned. "You said no lectures."

"Just a question."

Destry shrugged. "That door, I guess."

"Who all knows that?"

She yawned again. "I'm not sure."

Cam crouched in front of her, closer to eye level. "Think."

"I'm too tired. I don't want to think right now, about any of it. I want to sleep. Please."

He hated it when she did that, the please and sad chocolate eyes. Scary goblin or not, he could never say no. "Make me one promise, and I'll let you."

"Anything," she groaned.

"Lock your doors from now on—both of them. And don't go out after dark with Tristan until we figure out who sent you that knife."

"That's two." She half-smiled. "But I promise. And I'll never break those promises. Ever. Eeevvv-er."

The last couple words sounded extremely loopy. He made a mental note to throw the brownies out a window before he left. "Okay. Go to sleep now."

"Cam?"

"What?"

"Will you sing me a song? Like you were singing to Wings? I heard some faerie singing to his plants tonight..." She trailed off, eyes closing.

Frowning, Cam shook her. "A faerie singing my kind of music? The kind I sang in the forest?"

She opened her eyes begrudgingly. "Think so. Will you sing for me?"

The music he'd been using in the forest required power. Cam was too drained to sing a healing song, and he had other concerns. "Tomorrow, Des. Get through tomorrow, and I'll sing for you."

A glistening tear slipped out, making a salty track across her temple into her hair. "Okay."

"And if that guy shows up again, don't talk to him. Just stay with people you know."

"Three promises," she pointed out carefully. "I'm going to sleep now, before you come up with four." She rolled over, turning her back on him. He chuckled.

Tyla came in a few minutes later. She raised her eyebrows at Cam, still sitting on the floor. "I don't know about you royal goblin types, but this goblin girl could use some sleep. Especially since I still have to haul your heavy butt across hill and vale."

He pressed a kiss to Destry's temple, then stood, stretching muscles wound tight from worry and stress. "Sorry, Ty. I was just thinking."

"About the gardener?"

"Eavesdropping?"

"I always do." She took another brownie from the box. "Do you know any faeries who grow plants using goblin songs?"

"No. Destry might, if she knew them, but she's..."

"Destry," Tyla finished around a mouthful of chocolate and caramel. She swallowed. "Your girl's a little off, for a faerie. But I like her."

Cam ran a finger over the gold stripe on Destry's arm, visible in the moonlight pouring through the open door. "They call us monsters and barbarians. Yet they branded her like cattle."

She sniffed. "Typical faerie culture. You know that pretty gold band will burn through Destry's skin and muscle if she tries to run away? And those rods...they draw her magic, Cam. Her life force. They're no different than goblin fangs or talons. But it's beautiful, so it can't be barbaric."

Cam's teeth clenched. "I'd rather be my kind of monster than theirs. Let's go...while I still can."

JUSTICE

"Camden Darkwater, would you be still?" Tyla sounded exasperated. Tyla *was* exasperated.

Cam didn't care. He grabbed the cloak she was forcing on him and tossed it on the bed. "No, I won't. I don't have time." He was due at the faerie justice building in an hour and a half. Cam had spent every spare minute, and some that weren't spare, searching for that law.

He remembered his law tutor mentioning it during one of his earliest lessons at the castle. But it was an obscure, unused clause—the type only a scholar would know about—and the man who'd taught him had died three years before. Neither Brumal nor his aunt recalled that particular loophole, and Cam couldn't chance asking someone he didn't trust.

Tyla picked up the cloak. "You still have to be dressed. And you punched your valet in the nose."

"I told that insufferable bigot I didn't want to wear red."

They both knew clothing color hadn't been the real problem. The real problem had started when Cam interviewed the delinquent forest guards. They claimed Brumal had relieved them of duty to deliver a message to the fey palace. When Cam confronted Brumal in the private audience chambers, the man blustered, "It was a personal matter."

"The guards are *not* to be used as your personal errand boys, especially when removing them endangers the willa forest!" Cam fumed. "What could be *that* important?"

Brumal's lips thinned. "Is the forest truly what you're concerned about? Or that fey girl?"

A voice spoke from the doorway. "Surely, His Majesty would never care for some worthless fey more than the sacred willas."

Cam looked around. His valet stood there, holding a burgundy vest. "This is a private interview."

"My apologies, Your Majesty. The door was open. And I wanted your preference on clothing colors for tonight. Perhaps red, to represent—"

Cam spoke through gritted teeth. "Just pick something you deem appropriate. As you frequently remind me, that is your specialty."

"You're certainly good for little else," Brumal added, glowering at the valet. He turned back to Cam. "This incompetent fool was pressed into service as a messenger yesterday when one of our usual messengers fell ill. He delivered what I was led to believe was an urgent missive from an old acquaintance at the palace—the very reason I utilized the forest guards. But it's since proven to be a simple misunderstanding, due to this moron bumbling the message."

The valet drew himself up, face mutinous. "I did my best, High Chancellor Brumal. As you say, wardrobe is my specialty—not words. Now, Your Majesty, about your clothing—"

"For the second time, I do not care," Cam growled. "Pick something and leave me be. I have more important—"

"Red," the valet interrupted determinedly, "could symbolize blood. Fey blood in payment for the willa blood that was spilled."

"No," Cam bit out. "I don't want to symbolize an open artery."

"Perhaps black, then, to symbolize death? A pity the fey are punishing that faerie slut, instead of the goblins. She won't get half what she deserv—"

Which was the point Cam snapped and punched him.

He immediately regretted it, but he was still too angry to go after the quickly-retreating valet. Brumal had bustled away to do damage control, leaving Cam without answers regarding his chancellor's decision to relieve the forest guards.

And leaving Tyla to act as his valet now. Of course, he'd never actually wanted a valet. And the sum total of two hours sleep, caught here and there, wasn't helping Cam's disposition. He turned back to the open book on his dresser. "Quit fussing over me, Tyla."

At first, he thought his terse statement had bought some peace—until pain seared through his right leg. Tyla stepped away, glaring. He'd forgotten how adept she was at giving a perfect charley-horse. Cam rubbed his thigh. "What was that for?"

"You!" she flared. "I'm your friend, oh exalted King of the Goblins, for five years now! You don't get to dismiss me like some servant!"

Were those tears in her eyes? Cam closed the book carefully. Gripping Tyla's shoulders, he dropped a gentle kiss on her cheek. "I know, Ty. I'm sorry."

She blinked the tears away. "If you're sorry, put on this stupid cloak."

"There are more important things. I have to attend the Striking to satisfy those faerie fools. I don't have to get prissed up for them."

Aunt Val strode in, skirts swirling. "Yes, you do. You're a king, Camden, which carries certain expectations. You will meet them or answer to me."

He gave a humorless bark of laughter. "Are you going to cut a switch?" His aunt had threatened him often enough when he was younger, though she'd rarely followed through.

Aunt Val eyed him narrowly. "Do you think something changed because you're seventeen? Perhaps you could best most here in the castle. But the same blood runs through our veins, and I just heard you assaulted one of our employees. Do not press your luck."

Two women, both extremely capable and moderately irritated. Cam chose the smart route and backed down. "I'll make reparations after the trial, even though that idiot doesn't deserve them."

"Good." She held out two letters. "In that case, I may have good news for you. These were delivered a short time ago."

Cam read them, one after another; his heart leapt into his throat. Was this what he thought? He wrapped his aunt and Tyla in crushing bear hugs, then dashed to the door. "Meet me in the library, Tyla. Bring parchment, quills, and seals." She didn't answer right away. Mindful of her tears earlier, Cam forced himself to stop. He bowed low. "Please, friend of mine. Your assistance would be much appreciated."

Tyla grinned. Cam took that as a yes. He rushed from the room, boots thudding loudly on the wooden floor.

Cam hated the justice building. No matter that its architecture was the most appealing he'd seen in Si'fliegen. He wanted to rip down the stone trees, the carefully wrought mosaic. Most of all, he wanted to demolish the golden podium that had been erected in the middle of the aria—the recessed room where Destry would shortly be led in, and where she would suffer faerie justice.

A few steps led to the top of the podium, where two poles held golden shackles. The person was clearly meant to kneel at the top, wrists imprisoned. In two slots stood a couple of thin rods, each about a yard long. They, too, gleamed bright gold.

Several people nearby shot him questioning looks, uncertain who the tall young man was. They sidled away from the enormous black wolf at his side. Cam smiled grimly. He'd won this argument with Brumal. His chancellor had warned most strenuously against coming in human form. But Cam refused to take the shape that scared Destry, no matter how she tried to hide it.

He fingered the rolled papers in his belt pouch. One was the official document he and Tyla had drawn up, showing the law that did indeed exist. Both the letters he'd received contained the same information—one a note of exactly which book and chapter to look in, the other a familiar feminine hand with a brief lesson on that particular law and its creator. At the bottom of the last was a postscript: *Just in case.*

The second item in the pouch was a letter from Destry; it had arrived shortly before he left. Cam had read it, and re-read it, and still
didn't know if he could do what it asked. Because Destry wanted him to
do...nothing. She didn't want the executor to gain a victory over either
of them, the letter said. She'd rather take the punishment. Besides, if the
goblins thought their king was partial to Destry, he might not be able to
exonerate her later. She couldn't stand the thought of losing access to the
willas and Cam because she'd been scared. Her note ended with: *Do you
respect me? Or am I still the little girl next door?*

He'd brought the note to give him strength. Because he did respect
Destry, because he admired who she was, then and now. He knew her
arguments, his aunt's arguments, Brumal's arguments, were sound. But
the legal document was also there—just in case.

The deputy headmaster for Destry's school paced over and bowed.
"Riamon Windwings, at your service. Might I stand here?" He didn't
even look nervous at the sight of Brumal.

Cam raised one eyebrow; the other faeries had given them wide berth.
But he nodded. Riamon faced the aria with a brief smile of thanks.

That advisor, Alissa, strode in through a basement level door in the
aria. Destry followed, face pale. Cam noticed that the gold band on her
arm had been removed, leaving a red stripe instead. Big surprise. Faeries
reacted badly to gold; that's why they used it for negative magic, such as
this.

Headmistress Elena followed. The presence of a guardian was required in underage cases. A youth—Destry's magic partner, presumably—came with her. He must have been allowed because of their relationship. The boy's jaw was set, his arms crossed tight, like he was
restraining himself. Executor Faris swaggered out last, in trailing yellow
robes. A guard positioned himself at the doorway as if Destry was a
criminal who might break for it.

A murmur swept through the balconies. Some faeries looked surprised. Had they not known how young she was? Cam wondered bitterly
how many showed up only because their court duties required it. One
man—a middle-aged faerie with long, silver-streaked blonde hair—stood
apart from the others. His lips twisted contemptuously as he looked

over the crowd, but when Destry approached the podium, he turned his intent gaze on her instead.

Her wings weren't even out. Cam watched her kneel on the podium, ankle-length white dress puddling around her. Had Destry's headmistress chosen that dress as an indication of innocence? She slid her wrists into the shackles, palms down. The official sketched a circular motion around them, making the shackles tighten.

The executor read a formal speech about why they were there, then glanced up, eyes seeking out Cam. "We're ready to proceed. Is the goblin king here?" He clearly thought Cam was some representative of the court. Unsurprising, since Cam always met officials in goblin form.

Cam smiled. The muffled squeals of the crowd as he transformed were immensely satisfying. His smile grew wider, exposing his fangs. "He is." He gave a satirical bow to the executor, then slid back to human shape seamlessly. He thought he saw Destry smile too.

The man looked unsettled, but he turned to the podium, withdrawing the golden poles. "Then let there be no delays." His eyes sparked with vindictiveness; he'd seen Destry's brief grin.

She closed her eyes, Cam saw her lips form the silent words: *Accept it.* What did that mean?

Executor Faris lowered the rods.

The instant they touched Destry's hands, her shoulders stiffened; her jaw tightened. She breathed slowly and deeply, the careful breaths obvious even from a distance. Shimmering red and silver mist rose around her and spun away—visual evidence of her magic being drawn. Destry's hands fisted. Ten seconds...twenty seconds...thirty...forty...fifty...sixty. The rods gave off a bright crystalline sound, incongruous in the tense courtroom. The executor lifted the rods.

"The first strike has been dealt."

Destry kept her eyes closed, though her body sagged in relief. The executor set the rods against her skin again. Destry did as she had before, her magic leaching out in swirls of color. Tyla's ironic comment came to mind: *It's beautiful, so it can't be barbaric.* Another full minute, during which Cam breathed as carefully as Destry. The ringing noise.

"The second strike has been dealt."

Destry sucked in a shuddering breath; a tremor shook her body. The executor raised the rods again. Riamon murmured, "She's doing well." Was the reassurance for Cam or himself?

Cam slid a hand into his pouch. Doing well or not, Destry was obviously in pain. And there were eight more to go. Brumal saw his gesture and growled. The warning—meant for Cam—carried into the aria. Destry's eyes flew open, searching for the source of the sound. Her gaze fell on Brumal, and she swallowed.

The rods fell.

Her gasp carried to everyone watching. Her shoulders jerked. Destry bit down on her lip, body trembling visibly. Thirty seconds...fifty...seventy... She whimpered, tears welling in her eyes. "Why is he taking longer?" Cam whispered between tight lips to Riamon. It didn't matter that the man was faerie. At the moment, he was an ally.

"The more she fights, the harder it is to draw her magic, and the longer it will take," Riamon said.

Another muffled whimper from Destry. The rods rang out, and the executor lifted them. "The third strike has been dealt."

The fourth was worse. Tears raced down Destry's cheeks, her shoulders hitching with suppressed sobs. Halfway through, her magic partner started forward, restrained by the headmistress's hand on his shoulder. The guard at the door shot the boy a warning look; he stepped back, hands clenched and shaking.

Cam was copying him. He reminded himself that he could do nothing until they finished five. A little voice in his head—something like Destry's—reminded him that long-term thinking was necessary. Cam squashed the voice mercilessly. Destry hadn't realized what she was facing.

It took ninety seconds before the rods rang out. Advisor Alissa frowned pointedly at the executor. Looking annoyed, he waited for Destry to suck in a few shuddering breaths. She unclenched her fists, fingers trembling. The executor touched the rods to her skin again.

Destry jerked back against the metal bracelets, hands fisting, metal digging into her skin. Her breath came too fast. Whimpers forced their way past clenched teeth. And Cam clenched the railing, willing himself to remain human. He reminded himself that he was not allowed to rip the executor or any of the useless faerie officials limb from limb. He counted to seventy...eighty...ninety...ninety-five...

Destry cried out—once, twice, three times, her voice falling into sobs on the last.

Cam broke.

The sound obliterated the control he'd been exerting, the thin veneer of civility. Without conscious intent, his legs crouched, gathered for the spring. His body shuddered, shoulders broadening, teeth elongating and sharpening, hair rippling along his skin like blades of grass in a windstorm. He loosed one outraged growl. His cloak billowed behind him as he launched into the air, vaulting to the aria below.

Pain. It pooled around Destry like water, lapping at her fingers and toes, cresting over her body in waves. She tried to stop the sobs working their way up her throat, but the overwhelming tidal wave couldn't be handled in silence.

Five more...there are still five more.

I can't do this.

A heavy thud shook the podium, breaking the contact between the rods and Destry's skin. The pain rushed away, and she gasped for air. Her vision was clouded. She could barely see the executor stumble back, but she heard Cam's goblin growl. "Enough!"

Destry blinked the tears from her eyes. Cam was straightening from a crouch, an imposing sentinel looming between her and the executor. Had he *jumped* into the aria? Faris was on his butt on the floor, tangled in his fancy robes. He scrambled to his feet, wings quivering and chest puffed out. "The sentence was for ten strikes, Goblin King. Not five. Surely you wish to see justice done."

A low rumble echoed behind Cam's words. "I have seen it. Now I claim the right of equal retribution." He reached into a leather pouch at his waist and withdrew a scroll, flinging it at the executor's feet.

The right of equal retribution? Her head felt fuzzy. Was he talking about that law...the one she'd asked him to ignore?

The little man scowled, but—with a nervous glance at Cam—he picked up the scroll and scanned it, face growing ever redder. Alissa read over his shoulder. The executor looked up. "This is highly irregular. There are proper channels, forms that are generally observed—"

Cam took one menacing half-step towards the officiator. "Generally. But not today. Nothing in the law stipulates a time. I may claim my right whenever I wish. Since half the chosen justice has been meted out, you can make no argument."

Alissa caught the executor's eye. "Irregular, but not improper. Would you violate the treaty between us and the goblins?"

The faerie looked like someone had put a swelling spell on him. With one poisonous glare, he threw down the rods and stalked from the aria. Alissa turned towards the podium, Cam at her heels. She made the circular motion in reverse, and the shackles released Destry. She was shaking too badly to stay up. As she sagged to the podium floor, Cam caught her.

She leaned her forehead against his shoulder, shuddering. "Why did you do it, Cam?"

"I'm a goblin, not a monster." He glanced up, and Destry followed his line of sight. Dozens of curious and disapproving faerie faces stared down into the aria. Cam swept her into his arms. "In for a penny, in for a pound." He headed for the lower-level door. The guard started to intercept them, and Cam growled, an angry, full-throated sound that rolled through the room. The guard jumped out of the way.

Tristan and Headmistress Elena followed them into the dim hallway that led outside. The fey woman said sternly, "Goblin King! I demand to know what you plan to do with my ward."

Cam's voice was an easier growl this time. "What I came prepared to do. 'Just in case.'"

Color rose on the headmistress's cheekbones, but she stepped away with an ironic smile.

"Wait," Tristan snapped. "You're letting him take her?"

"Better she's subject to me than to your people." Cam bent a pointed look on Destry. "Or do you disagree?"

Tristan's wings hummed rapidly, but he came closer, gripping Destry's hand. "That depends. Des...do you trust him? Do you want this?"

She tossed one look at the golden podium, visible through the open aria door. Remembered pain swept her body, ghosts of the original, and her fingers clenched Tristan's. New sobs rose in her throat. "I can't go back in there. I can't. This is better."

His jaw worked. "Okay. Okay." He glared at Cam. "Look, I don't care that you're a king. I don't care that you could tear me apart. You'd better not hurt her."

Cam hesitated, like he was uncertain how to respond. And Destry knew she should still her raspy crying, should tell Tristan what she ought to have told him long ago. But she could only blubber. Cam took matters into his own hands. "Your magic partner will return to you in better shape than she leaves. I promise by willa and by earth."

Tristan examined Destry; his brows were furrowed, like when he worked out a math problem. He gave a stiff nod. Cam turned, striding out of the gloomy hallway into the gauzy evening light.

MARKED

✦

Like the night before, dark hadn't fallen yet. There was a definite nip in the air—that opposite-weather phenomenon, turning late April into fall. Shivers seized Destry, an avalanche of shaking chills. Cam phased human. "Maybe this will help."

She was shivering too hard to explain that his goblin shape or even the weather had little to do with it. The rods, however... This bone-deep cold had gotten worse with each removal of her magic, like someone was leeching the fire out of her. Cam pulled her closer.

A raven swooped down and melded seamlessly into Tyla, alighting on the grass. "I guess respecting Destry's wishes didn't go too well."

Cam gave a bark of laughter. "No. And we have a new problem: how do I get her to the castle? You flew me here. Brumal ran. We have no transportation."

"I'll just fly her instead."

Destry choked. "Fl-fl-flying?" Her chattering teeth broke the word into four syllables.

"Not an option," Cam said. "She'd fall off, shaking like this."

At least he'd kept her secret.

"I believe I can help." They all turned; Alissa strode around the building, Riamon at her side. She pointed to a small hill. "There's a wagon over that rise, parked on a dirt road. It's only used for delivering things from market. Ri can drive you to the castle." She glanced at Destry. "If that's what you want."

"She has little choice," Cam said in his best royal tones.

"Should Destry ask to stay, I'm relatively sure you'd honor it," Alissa said. "I deal in both politics and friendship, and love, if it comes to that. Ri's been bending my ear with gossip for a while now."

Cam's face hardened. "Then you'd be wrong. No matter what she said, I wouldn't leave her for your people to finish meting out justice. I'm a barbaric goblin, after all."

Alissa didn't *quite* roll her eyes. She turned to her brother. "The horse is in the shed. Get that wagon, and yourself, back here before dark."

"Perhaps. And perhaps I'll stay with my student. Never fear, Liss, I will return your cart by morning. I shall not even allow the goblins to eat the horse. Could you inform Elena where I have gone—or am going, to be more precise?"

She poked him in the shoulder. "You and your precision. Fine." She added, "Make sure it rings true, Goblin King." And with that cryptic statement, she hurried off around the building.

Tyla sighed. "I'm sure Brumal is taking care of the official details. Which leaves me with the hard part: telling your aunt." She leapt and transformed midair, taking flight effortlessly into the setting sun.

Riamon stared after her, smiling. "What a very impressive sort of magic you goblins have. Shall we go?"

No one talked much as they trekked up the hill. Destry offered to walk; Cam gave her a black look and kept going.

The cart was exactly where Alissa said, a small vehicle with a bench up front and a seatless rear box. Cam set Destry on her feet and pulled off his cloak, wrapping it around her. He boosted her to sit in the box. "Stay here while we hook up the horse."

Destry grabbed his arm. "Cam...what did I just do? Now you can't exonerate me. I can't ever come back after tonight. And your kingdom will hate you. All I had to do was keep my mouth shut, not show how bad it was. Instead, I ruined everything!"

"Actually, the goblin king ruined everything, if we wish to be accurate," said Riamon equably, leading the horse over. "And you're resourceful young people. Surely this evening may be salvaged. You must simply find a way to, as my sister put it, make things ring true."

Not until they were on their way—Riamon driving them along the most deserted route, Cam holding Destry in the box—did the fey man add, "You were doing well, the first two strikes. How did you manage it?"

"A faerie I met last night gave me some advice." She explained the gardener's suggestion. "I tried, I really did. And it made the first couple bearable. But then I saw Brumal's wolf form and thought of everything out there—the scorione, the hobgoblins—and I just couldn't."

Riamon nodded. "Given the type of your magic...fire faeries are born to fight. I doubt giving up was ever an option for you."

The wheels crunched over small rocks and sticks. Cam steadied Destry as the wagon jolted them. He pulled her more snugly into his arms, then said to Riamon, "You're Deputy Headmaster at the fey school, aren't you? Headmistress Elena's assistant?"

"Indeed."

"How much do you know about law?"

Riamon laughed. "I, very little. Elena, however, was a law professor before she took the post of headmistress. But I believe you already knew that—or suspected it, to be exact."

"True. But two people sent me information, and I didn't recognize the other handwriting."

Riamon shook his head. "To that, I plead not guilty. Your anonymous benefactor must be particularly knowledgeable about mutual law, and unafraid to challenge the system, yet someone who could not openly reveal themselves. Unless you know such a person, I expect it will remain a mystery."

Destry didn't ask what they were talking about. She was too exhausted. The buzzing of insects and chirping birds returning home for the night acted like a lullaby. Despite the bumping wagon, she kept dozing off in Cam's arms, then jerking awake. He pressed her head to his chest. "Rest, Dessie."

She didn't wake until the wagon bounced to a stop. Destry looked around, confused. "This isn't the main entrance to the castle."

"I think we should stay under the radar," Cam said. "We're taking the private passageways."

Destry refused to be carried this time. The shaking had stopped, and the weariness, according to Riamon, came from missing her magic. The narrow stone halls were dark, despite the faerie light Riamon summoned. Destry stared at the glowing ball in his palm. Being bereft of magical ability made her feel unexpectedly vulnerable.

They approached the last turn in the passage, right before the door hidden under the tapestry. A light flickered around the corner. Cam grimaced. "Better prepare yourself, Des."

Her grip on his fingers tightened. What else could happen tonight? "Why?"

"Because you're probably about to see me get switched."

Cam's aunt waited at the door, a lantern at her feet. She took one look at them and said, "Camden." The single word held everything from irritation to admiration.

He made another face. "I know. Believe me, I have every understanding of the headache I created."

"Do you? We worked quite hard during the trial to show your impartiality. Leaping into the aria and running off with Destry seem to contradict that."

"You've been present as the goblin rep before, Aunt Val. Could you have sat through ten?"

"Whether I could have or not has little bearing on the issue. Neither does whether I agree with your actions. The decision we now face is how to present this without losing face with your constituents and exposing Destry to further unpleasantness from her people."

"My people aren't much of a concern," Destry said.

Lady Val sighed. "All due respect, my dear, but I doubt you understand the ins and outs of our politics or yours."

Riamon patted Destry's shoulder. "She's correct in this instance. Executor Faris had many reasons for his actions. The potential negatives for your kingdom were merely a side benefit. And this evening, played correctly, might work to Destry's advantage." He added dryly, "You weren't privileged to see the show, but I assure you: what most of the faerie world saw was a goblin—a monstrous goblin, to be accurate—leaping into the aria and abducting a vulnerable young girl."

"Nonetheless, my nephew's public display necessitates public retribution on our part. Proof. Otherwise, it will be seen as a rescue and nothing more."

Riamon said delicately, "One could simply choose an action and allow the well-oiled gossip mill to do its work. Were he seen as putting his brand on her, for example... I believe both kingdoms might draw their own conclusions as to what that means."

Val's gaze sharpened. "A goblin mark?"

Cam frowned. "I don't like that idea."

"What would you prefer, Camden?" Lady Val sounded exasperated. "Throwing her in jail for a month? Doling out physical punishment, as if she's a recalcitrant apprentice? Handing her back to her people to finish the job? A goblin mark is an excellent piece of politics." She looked at Riamon with new respect.

"Consider the story playing in most faerie heads right now," Riamon said. He'd begun cleaning his glasses, but used them to gesticulate instead. "A lovely heroine. A rough hero, who watched her endure hardship with stoic determination. When he sees her efforts to withstand the pain of the rods, he's impressed in spite of himself and impulsively leaps into the aria to claim her. As for the goblin public, none of whom were present, they may assume you thirsted for a personal sort of revenge."

Cam said grudgingly, "I'll give it some thought."

Glaring, Lady Val pressed her hands to her hips. "Give it more than that. If you don't have a better idea, take our suggestion. And take her to your room, where she can recover. I'll house Deputy Headmaster Riamon myself. Best we not advertise their presence."

"Here we are." Cam pushed open a polished wooden door banded with coppery metal. He waved Destry into a small antechamber. Embers burned in a stone fireplace, their gentle glow reflecting off a carved wooden side table and a couch. It was welcoming—but Destry ached for that fireplace to crackle with warmth.

Cam led her through the first room, into his bedroom. She'd expected a formal-looking chamber the size of a ballroom—he was king, after all—but this reminded her of Cam's room back home. Though it was larger and the items goblin-made, his preferences showed in the warm earth tones of the décor, the simple lines of his furniture...and the mess typical of any space he inhabited.

Cam opened a set of doors on the wall opposite the antechamber. "C'mere, Des. You'll like this."

She followed him onto a balcony. Next to it, close enough to touch, grew a slender willa. Destry's eyes widened. "I thought they only grew in the forest."

"You can transplant them in certain conditions. But they have to be young for it to take, and willas don't often reproduce. This is the only willa with the right personality in decades." He reached over the railing, and the tree leaned toward him. "He isn't connected to the others' lifeblood and doesn't share their memories. A completely independent entity. That's why he's still awake."

Destry clutched the railing, but the chance to meet another willa was too tempting. She leaned over the edge to stroke the branches. "Oh! He *feels* different from the others. Like he doesn't mind being alone, even enjoys it."

Cam's eyebrows slid upward. "You do understand them."

She straightened and shoved her hair out of her face. "Did you think I was lying?"

"Wouldn't be the first time. But no. I just thought you might have misinterpreted what you felt. Why didn't you tell me?"

How did she explain? "Because you're you. Cam. The amazing goblin king. The guy who does everything right. And I'm me. It would have been so embarrassing to find out I was wrong."

He shook his head. "It's time to leave the hero-worship behind. I'm human, same as you. Sort of."

Destry had more important things on her mind. She paced back inside, settling on his russet bedspread. "What's this goblin mark your aunt was talking about?"

Cam sat beside her, looking solemn. "It's my personal mark—not too large, smaller than your faerie tattoos. Put on your shoulder, it wouldn't even show when you're dressed. To a goblin, it would be an honor. But faeries regard it as an insult—a disfigurement."

"I wouldn't see it that way."

He nodded, but his face remained grave.

"Then what's the problem?"

He gripped her hand, calloused thumb rubbing circles on it. "I don't want to hurt you. Not after tonight, not ever."

"The mark...the mark hurts?"

His expression turned pleading. "Some. Not as bad as those rods. And just once, I promise."

Destry searched his face, then turned and slipped her dress off her right shoulder. "Go ahead." Cam still hesitated, and she said, "We have to do *something*. I'd rather get this over with. Please don't make me wait."

He sighed. "Again with the please and the sad eyes. Give me one minute." He marched to the balcony, beckoning the willa until it extended a branch over the sill. Cam took a knife from his pocket and sliced off a thin twig.

Her mouth fell open. "Cam!"

"It's a small thing, Destry." His voice was rough. "The willa blood is useful, and the tree will be good as new by morning."

Cam strode over and set the branch nearby. He placed one palm on her shoulder blade and began murmuring the words of ancient magic. A pinprick of pain blossomed, spiraling out until it felt like someone was pressing a hot iron to her skin. Tears flooded her eyes. Destry gasped and bit her lip, but she refused to make any more sound. Cam felt bad enough already.

Then he was squeezing willa blood onto her burning skin, smoothing it with his fingers. The pain softened and died as if it had never been. Cam dropped a gentle kiss on top of her head. "I'm sorry, Dessie. Forgive me?"

His words were barely audible. Destry blinked away tears and faced him. "There's nothing to forgive. Believe me, if I had a choice between this and five more strikes with those rods... There's no contest." She gave him as convincing a smile as she could manage. "How does it look?"

Cam chuckled darkly. "It's the most beautiful pain I've ever inflicted on an innocent." He pulled her to her feet, to his mirror. "See for yourself."

She peered over her shoulder at the silvery circle, several inches in diameter, that twisted in a pattern reminiscent of willa branches. She brushed one hand over it, then withdrew her fingers when it smarted. "It *is* beautiful, Cam. Thank you."

"Don't thank me for hurting you." He squeezed another drop onto her shoulder. "It's ironic."

"What?"

He pulled her arm out, rubbing willa blood over the red mark where the band had been. "I was angry with the faeries for branding you, but I just did the same thing. And mine can't be removed."

Destry glanced again at the silvery circle on her shoulder. "There's a difference, Cam. I wanted this one."

He sighed softly. "Alright. Dinner and bed. I'm not sending you back until morning." When she opened her mouth, he said, "No arguments. I'm a barbaric goblin who does as he pleases."

Hours later, she lay curled up on his couch in a blanket and one of Cam's tunics, a fire crackling in the fireplace. The flickering flames were comforting, but despite her bone-deep exhaustion, Destry couldn't sleep. She shifted for the tenth time in as many minutes and readjusted her pillow.

Cam appeared in the doorway, shirtless, wearing the loose pants he liked for sleeping. "Still awake?" She sat up to make room for him. He dropped onto the couch and snuggled her into his side. "Maybe you need to take my bed."

She laughed at the thought of Cam squeezing onto the couch—fine for a faerie girl, not a hulking goblin. "I told you, the fire feels good. That's not it."

"Worried?"

Destry shrugged. "Too much on my mind. And someone broke his promise. I distinctly recall a promise to sing to me."

"You were half-lit at the time. I'm not sure you want to hear my version of an ancient lullaby."

"You won't do it anyway. Goblins are notoriously untrustworthy."

"Sassy brat. Be quiet." He began to sing, low and soothing. The words rushed over her like water; Destry felt herself sinking deeper and deeper. She fell asleep with the sound of Cam's bass rumbling in her ears.

Ruined

❖

In the darkness of a hidden room, Shadow paced. Back and forth, back and forth, breathing fast in time to the metronome of his fury. He slammed his hand into the edge of a rough-hewn table; the chemicals on it, in their glass beakers and bowls, crashed to the floor. Acrid fumes mixed with the scent of stone and damp. He kicked one dish and sent it spinning across the flagstones.

The loss of so much of his work—delving deeper into chemicals than goblins generally dared go—didn't matter. Nothing mattered. The plan had been perfect. Flawless. And that bumble-handed oaf had barreled in and ruined it all.

When Shadow had seen the fool leap into the aria, he'd barely restrained himself from leaping in after and ending his incessant interference. Any other goblin king would have been capable of observing the necessary deed, but not this one. Now, Shadow had to rethink the entire plan. He sent another round of chemicals smashing into the wall.

His shoulder twanged, heavy with pain. It had hurt since the girl double-blasted him, and his efforts to heal the injury himself were useless.

Shadow stopped, leaning on the wall. Calm, he reminded himself. All was not lost. He simply had to change his time frame. Challenging, but not impossible.

Her soul was a fiery one. That thought comforted him. It would be worth the trouble in the end. For now, he must think. He must plan. Shadow set to gathering his chemicals again, bent over his painstaking work long into the night.

36

CONFESSION

✦

The ride to school the next morning was quiet, though not uncomfortable. Destry's conversation with Riamon revolved around her goblin mark. "At least you won't mind wearing that one," he said. "Rather better than fang marks on your neck."

The cart bumped over a rough patch. Destry checked the map Cam had drawn them—a route skirting the most populated areas. Lady Val had quashed Cam's plans to go with them, asserting that he needed to do damage control. She threatened to whip him if he went, and Destry if she allowed him to.

Tyla volunteered to fly overhead and make sure their return to the Academy went smoothly. Cam reluctantly acquiesced, but he'd pulled Destry aside. "I want to know if you have problems today. If the rumors get bad, if your professors are being difficult, whatever. I'll help you deal with it."

"How? By going full-goblin on them, like you did to Jared and Mom's pervert boyfriends?"

Cam's chuckle was more a pleased growl in his throat. "How did you know?"

"Wasn't hard to figure out, once I learned the truth. You can't do that to my teachers, Cam. You can't fight all my battles."

"I don't intend to fight your battles, Dessie." His voice sounded oddly tender. He pulled her into one of his rough hugs. "But you need someone to turn to, and I'd rather be that someone."

She breathed in his scent—soap and leather and fresh-turned earth. "I can't send you a message. The school might not deliver it after last night."

"Can you get out of classes by four? I'll meet you at the edge of the forest."

"I can be there."

"Then go. And be careful." He opened the door, almost slamming it into a slender young man. Cam hissed in exasperation. "What are you doing here? I told you I don't need help dressing."

The guy held out a stack of folded shirts, swallowing nervously. "Just delivering these, Your Majesty. Nothing more." He handed over the clothes and fled.

Cam looked so satisfied that Destry asked, "What was that about?"

"Success. And to think, it just took one tiny punch in the nose."

Lady Val, standing nearby, began scolding Cam for unfitting behavior, and Destry left before she came under fire too. It was a good start to the day, but the closer they got to the faerie realm, the more nervous Destry felt. She asked Riamon, "Do you think it will work?"

He frowned. "The goblin mark? I fail to see why not. At the very least, proof of goblin retribution will keep you safe from the executor. And I believe the goblins will either find Camden's actions satisfying to their sense of vengeance or to their sense of romance. You must not mind their belief that he branded you like cattle."

They came to the bridge manned by goblin guards, and Destry tensed. Cam had said to use her mark to gain safe passage; the story of his revenge-slash-romance needed to spread. She met the guards' hard eyes, then slipped her dress off her shoulder to display the silvery circle. With a mockingly courteous sweep of his arm, the reddish wolf man allowed Riamon to drive over the bridge. Flushing, Destry adjusted her dress.

The vindictive pleasure in his eyes made her feel, for the first time, like there was some shame in the mark Cam had given her.

When Riamon rolled to a stop outside the school, Destry stared up at the building, shoulders tight. Would her classmates ask about her experiences? And how should she answer? Riamon seemed to read her hesitation. "Following your regular routine would serve you best. You have enough time to change before breakfast." He tapped the scars on his neck. "I have experience with the pain of unfortunate celebrity. Act as though everything is normal, and most of your peers will follow suit."

If nothing else, Destry wanted to get out of the white dress and burn it. She gathered the delicate material and slid off the wagon awkwardly. Inches from the ground, something jerked at her clothing, and a loud ripping sound rent the air. Destry staggered as she landed.

Riamon leapt down beside her, a leather-clad grasshopper. "Don't move. I'm afraid you caught your dress on a bit of splintered wood. It's damaged. Torn, to be specific."

Destry moaned, but she stood still as Riamon disentangled her gown. Luckily, the dress had split straight up and down, though the rip went to mid-thigh. Destry clutched it together, wincing. This would be *so* helpful with squelching any rumors about her and Cam. Mumbling thanks to Riamon, she hurried into the foyer.

Students were trickling down for breakfast. A few girls eyed her but didn't say anything. One of her failed magic-partner candidates waved. Destry forced herself to wave back before bolting for the staircase. Halfway up, someone called her name. Destry turned, fighting a scowl when she saw Julya. She didn't feel like listening to the girl crow over her disgrace. "What?"

Julya eyed her torn dress. "Will you be in Gardening today?"

Destry remembered Riamon's advice. "Why wouldn't I?"

Julya shrugged. "I'm having trouble with that last growing spell. Thought we might partner."

Partner? Surely Julya knew she couldn't do any magic in class. Why would she want to work together, especially in Gardening, where she did better than Destry? The other girl's face was carefully normal, and it dawned on Destry that she wasn't looking for a chance to gloat or humiliate her. Julya turned away. "You don't have to."

"No," Destry said. "I...that would be good."

"Bring a pen. You're taking the notes today."

Tristan was sitting at the fountains, a textbook in his hands, by the time Destry worked up the nerve to leave her bedroom and head downstairs. He met her halfway, eyes oddly diffident. "You're still in one piece."

She nodded.

He gestured towards the dining hall, but he didn't take her hand or throw an arm around her shoulders, like he usually did. "Want some breakfast?"

Destry just stood there. After an entire night at the goblin castle, she'd expected an exuberant hug, an exclamation of pleasure. She'd expected Tristan to be waiting anxiously, not act as if they'd simply separated for classes. Partway to the dining hall, he noticed she wasn't with him and turned.

She met his eyes uncertainly. He walked back to her, a frown creasing his forehead. "Des?"

"Are you mad at me?"

He looked surprised. "For what?"

"Going to the goblin castle. Not staying to let the executor finish." It was the only explanation she could think of.

"Destry, watching that was one of the worst experiences of my life. How could I be mad that you chose not to suffer?" His face softened. "You are okay, right?"

"I'm fine." She said it like it was true.

Tristan glanced at the dining hall. "Are you afraid to go in there?" She shook her head. "Then what?"

How could she say *he* was the problem? That, whatever else she'd expected from the other students, Destry had expected normalcy, stability, from Tristan. Or at least hoped for it. The fear that he now saw her differently left her feeling alone.

But fear and confirmation were two different things...and she might not like his answer. "Nerves, I guess. Let's go."

There weren't enough people eating for a hush to fall over the room. Still, more than one conversation paused when she and Tristan walked in. Sara—sitting with David—waved. As Destry and Tristan slid into chairs at her table, the redhead sighed dramatically. "Finally! I've been waiting for *hours*!"

"For what?"

"Well, the entire school knows what happened at the Striking. Fey Elena wanted it kept quiet, but one of the girls has a sister who works in the palace, and she heard the gossip and told her sister, who told some friends... Anyway, everybody says the goblin king leapt into the aria, ripped the gold podium apart, hit the executor with it, and carried you off over his shoulder. And no one could do anything about it."

Destry grimaced. "That's not quite right."

"Oh, I know." Sara spread jam on a piece of toast. "I made Tristan tell me the truth. Got to say, it's almost as good as the first story. But why'd he do it?"

Cam and Destry had gone over her side of things before she left. She was prepared for this. But she hadn't been prepared to say it in front of Tristan, too. Somehow, she'd expected a private talk over brownies before she had to face the entire student body.

A flush crept along her cheekbones. "After all those lessons at the castle, I guess I made an impression on the goblin king. He saw me in the aria and realized that I wouldn't have slashed up a willa tree. He felt terrible for prosecuting me, and it was obvious the executor didn't like me, so King Darkwater saved me from him."

Sara's eyes were round behind her purple glasses. "But Tristan said the goblins are still going to punish you. What'll happen?"

"It already did. The king said if I was rescued by a goblin, I had to wear the mark of a goblin. He made his personal symbol on my shoulder."

David made a face. "Kind of prehistoric, isn't it? Like bonking you in the head with a club and dragging you to his cave. Those marks don't come off."

Destry rubbed the reddish band on her arm, fainter after the willa blood but still there. "He's not the only one who marked me."

Sara groaned. "Fire and wings! I'm sorry. You probably don't want to talk about this. You just looked so normal this morning, I figured nothing too awful had happened."

Destry stifled hysterical laughter. Last night had been the epitome of awful, even if it had ended okay. She couldn't think of those rods without shuddering, and she'd woken up from nightmares of being imprisoned alone with the executor, who slowly drained her magic and turned her into a withered husk.

The rest of breakfast was either silent or stilted; Destry ate quickly. When she stood, Tristan did too, though his food was only half-finished. He followed her to the foyer. "Do you want to work inside or out?"

No offers of sweets, no reminder that they had the perfect excuse for skipping class? Something definitely wasn't right. The bright sunshine seemed more reassuring than a dim classroom. "Outside."

As they walked to their usual spot, Destry said, "It'll be hard to do much, since I can't use magic until tonight."

He held up the textbook. "We can work on theory. And I want to ask you a question." His noncommittal tone told her nothing.

Destry slipped under the shade of their tree. "I need to talk to you also."

Silence stretched between them, tripwire-tight. Finally, Tristan said, "Guess I'll go first." He stared fixedly at the ground. "I just want to know...how much do I need to worry?"

This tension was all about her well-being? Destry breathed a silent sigh of relief. "I told you, I'm fine. My magic will come back soon, and the goblin mark...getting it *did* hurt, but not now." Not too much, anyway. Cam said it would be tender for several days.

"That's not what I meant. I'll worry about that no matter what you say. I meant, do I have to worry about you and him?"

The relief dissipated. "Him who?" Tristan looked up, half-impatient. With a sense of dreadful certainty, Destry said, "The goblin king? Tristan, he just felt—"

"I heard that line of bull you fed the others. And I'm not concerned with *his* reasons or *his* reaction. I'm remembering yours, the way you looked at him when he carried you out of the aria. That wasn't the face of someone who's taken a few lessons, Destry."

She searched for the right words, a good answer. Tristan added tightly, "We aren't committed. I don't have any right to ask what you do or who you do it with. But I do deserve the truth, and what you've been telling me about you and the goblin king isn't it."

It was Destry's turn to stare at the ground. "It's not what you think." Her explanation tumbled out, everything from moving next door to Cam to finding out he was the goblin king to Cam's request to keep their friendship secret.

When she finished, another long silence stretched between them. Tristan's face was stiff. "Why didn't you tell me?"

"We barely knew each other when I found out! I didn't know if you were trustworthy enough to keep it to yourself."

"But you've known better for a while. Why didn't you tell me later?"

She flushed. "I just...didn't know how. I was afraid to hurt you, once you realized I hadn't trusted you from the first."

He laughed humorlessly. "Yeah, this was definitely better."

Destry hung her head. She didn't realize she was chewing on a hangnail until Tristan tugged her finger loose. "Destry, will you look at me? I'm not gonna yell at you or anything."

She met his eyes, hesitant. He sighed. "Look, we're magic partners. We ought to have a little trust between us, but the goblin king knows more about you than you'll probably ever share with me." He snorted. "Wish I *had* known about you and him. Would've saved me some serious worry last night."

"I'm sorry." Destry couldn't think what else to say. Nothing sounded right.

Tristan shrugged. "At least I know now. Want to review for that metalworking test?" He folded to the ground and opened the textbook.

She sat beside him and pulled her knees up, wrapping her arms around them. "Don't you want to talk about it?"

"What do you want me to say? That it's okay you don't trust me? That I don't care? I do, and I don't lie to you."

"I want you to tell me how to fix this. I know you're angry, and I deserve it. But there has to be something I can do."

Tristan ran one hand through his hair. "You don't get it, Des. I'm not mad. I'm scared. My magic, my life, is tied to yours. In a few years, I have to count on you to give a commitment, or we both lose a huge part of what makes us. And I don't know if you can do that. I think your heart's tied somewhere else."

She didn't have an answer. She couldn't say she had no other ties, not without lying. She couldn't even say she was ready to commit to him.

He stood. "Look, I need time to process this. Maybe we should skip tutoring this morning."

Destry bit her lip, but she didn't protest; she had no right to.

Tristan nodded, more to himself than to her. "Okay, then." He started across the grounds. After a few steps, he turned back. "I really am glad you're alright." He turned away again, and this time he didn't stop.

As soon as he was out of sight, Destry dropped her face into her knees and cried. How had she screwed up so badly? Why hadn't she listened to Cam, the time upon time upon time he'd lectured her on honesty? She'd hurt her magic partner because she didn't want to deal with the unpleasantness of confessing her lie. But confession would have been so much better than this.

Destry went to her room and spent the morning studying goblin magic, but even that left a sour taste in her mouth. Without the ability to control magic, she couldn't put anything into practice. The weariness, the frustration, the chill that lingered no matter how warmly she dressed...they were all unwelcome reminders. She could sentence Tristan and herself to such a life with her unwillingness to make a commitment.

Classes were a relief, despite the discomfort of being around other students. At least they took her out of her own head. Still, she watched the clock eagerly as the afternoon wore on. When her gardening class released at ten minutes until four, Destry thanked Julya (who hadn't been snide once) and bolted for the door. She stashed her books in her room and hurried downstairs, out into the bright sunlight and onto the road leading to the river.

As she approached the dorms for older students, someone with fiery hair bounded down the front stairs. Destry swore inwardly when Sara skidded to a stop. "Hey, Destry. Whatcha doing here?"

"Just...taking a walk. How about you? Deserting me for the fancy independent dorms?"

Sara grinned. "Next year, you'll be old enough for them yourself. I wanted to see if there are free rooms where we could bunk up."

She wanted to be roommates? Even after the last couple days? Destry didn't have to fake a smile.

Sara looked down the road toward the river. She added slyly, "You're taking a walk, huh? Maybe meeting a blue-eyed faerie boy?"

Destry breathed a sigh of relief; she'd forgotten that couples who wanted to be alone often hid on the riverbank. Better for the redhead to assume she was making out with Tristan than to join Destry on her "walk."

Sara took her silence as confirmation and smiled wider. "Okay, I never saw you here. Have fun."

Yeah. Fun was exactly what she had in mind, with a magic partner who couldn't stand her and a goblin king with worries of his own. Destry stifled the sarcastic thought and headed for the forest.

Into the Woods

Destry hurried the rest of the way to the woods. Her legs felt shaky by the time she reached the tree line. The lack of magic made her tire easily. She searched the white trunks and found Cam, leaning against a willa. He straightened when he saw her. "You made it. I was afraid I'd have to storm your school."

She laughed. "Good thing you don't need to." Cam nodded, but his expression was grave. As she came closer, Destry noticed his eyes were red-rimmed. "You've been crying."

"It's nothing." He looked away, jaw clenching.

Her stomach hollowed. What else could have happened in the few hours she'd been gone? "Cam, what's wrong?"

"I can't..." He shook his head, then trailed off, throat working like he was trying to swallow tears. "Wings died today."

"But...she can't have. You said she was out of danger!"

His voice came out husky. "Some kind of infection set in, maybe from the scorione venom. She started going downhill last night while I was at the justice building. By this morning, there was nothing I could do."

Tears brimmed in Destry's eyes. She swiped at them, but more just took their place. "I'm so sorry, Cam. Will the rest of the forest be okay?"

"Eventually. Willas grieve, just like you or me."

"Will they be alright by the time I can visit again?"

He didn't meet her gaze. "Hard to say."

She desperately needed to know that the white trees would move again, would still trail their branches on her shoulder in friendliness. "You must have some idea."

He took a deep breath, released it. "I don't think you *can* come back. Not after this, not with a willa dead."

"What? Can't the willas still exonerate me? I know it may take longer, but—"

"The death of a willa is different than an injury to one," Cam said. "It will affect our magic for months. People can never forget it. No matter what the willas tell me, your faerie magic will always seem like a threat to the other goblins."

Destry sank numbly to the ground. This couldn't be happening. Everything they'd done—the rods, the mark, the secrecy that had hurt her magic partner—had been pointless. Her grief for Wings made the other pain resonate deeper, an echo of what might have been.

Cam crouched next to her. "I'm sorry. I'm so sorry. If there was anything I could do, I would."

The words were definite, but a barely-there hesitancy in his voice made them sound less sure. As if he was hiding something... "What aren't you telling me?" she asked.

"Nothing. There's no good solution."

"But there is a solution."

"Not one I'd allow you to do." He cut her off when she started to argue. "No, Destry. We tried to make this work, and it didn't. Just go back to school and work with your magic partner and live your life. We'll see each other once in a while, and that will have to be enough—for both of us."

Destry laughed, thin and humorless. "Tristan can barely stand to do lessons with me. I messed up, and I'm not sure I can fix it. I'm not even sure I should. Committing to Tristan means committing to the fey world—where I'm supposed to hate goblins and be terrified of willa trees, work faerie magic and follow the rules. I can't live at home again unless I lose my magic, which means condemning Tristan too. And the things that make this whole mess bearable—you, the willas, the goblin world—won't be part of my life anymore. What else can I lose?"

Cam stroked her hair. "You'll find a way to work it out. You have to. My solution isn't feasible."

"And you can't let me decide for myself? You should trust me, even if no one else does!"

"It's not a matter of trust, it's a matter of friendship. You'd have to leave everything behind, you'd have to leave your magic behind, you'd be bound to me forever! That's not a solution, taking away the life you're supposed to have."

"The life I'm *supposed* to have?" She snorted. "That life involves a type of magic I can't work and a partner who doesn't want me! Please, Cam. Let me decide what I need, instead of choosing for me."

He sat silent for a long, long moment. Destry balled her fists up until the nails dug into her palms and tried to stay quiet. If he hadn't answered yet, Cam was considering. He met her eyes with an air of desperate finality. "It's a goblin spell—an old one. It's how my dad released his magic to keep it from harming Mom. The magic goes to the intended recipient instead of dispersing, like Dad's went back to my grandfather until I was ready."

Her heart started thumping. "But if it's a goblin spell..."

"It's supposed to work on faeries, too, though no one has ever tried it."

"You mean my magic could go to Tristan, and I'd be normal? Why do they tell us there's no alternative? I can't be the only faerie who's had doubts about this magic partner thing."

"Because giving up your magic affects you for the rest of your life, and how you feel now is nothing compared to giving it up completely. Those rods only inhibit your ability to use magic for a short time. The effects would be ten times worse if you gave it up forever."

Destry frowned. "Your dad seems fine."

"That's because another goblin strengthens him. Those 'father-son camping trips'—our visits to the castle—were necessary for more than one reason. My grandfather worked a spell every time we came here, to strengthen Dad and nullify the side effects. Now that he's gone, my aunt does it."

That sounded better than she could have hoped. "Can't faeries do the same?"

"Your magic is too unstable to support each other. Only a goblin can do that part, which eliminates it as a viable solution. A faerie has to stay with the goblin host, day in and day out, because magic doesn't hold well in interspecies spells. How many goblins are going to take on a faerie for life? And how many faeries would be willing?"

She looked down, feeling inexplicably shy. "This faerie would, with the right goblin. But I can't come back to your kingdom, so 'day in, day out' living might be a problem."

"That's not an issue if you have no magic," he said slowly. "It's what you can do that scares people. But would you really want that? You and me, for life?"

Destry hesitated. Losing her powers would hurt, no denying that. But she'd had magic for less than six months. Surely she could adjust. And she could visit Beverly without causing her harm; she could spend her days with the willas and a lifetime as Cam's friend. Those things mattered more than any magic ability.

She lifted her chin. "Yes."

Cam sighed. "You agreed without even a full moment's thought. I realize this sounds good right now, when everything is a mess. But it's a huge part of yourself to give up, and you may change your mind once things calm down." He stood and offered her a hand up. "I can't encourage you to choose this out of my own selfish desire to have you with me. Let's sleep on it, okay?"

She let him pull her to her feet, the burn of reckless excitement heating her cheeks. If they worked this spell, she could go back to the school—not to stay, but to tell Tristan he was free. He could pick any girl he wanted, instead of choosing Destry because he had to. And he and Cam would understand that she was their friend despite her screw-ups and her lies. "There's no reason to sleep on it. I know what I want. If you respect me, you'll respect this."

"Des, I...I don't know." She'd never seen him so uncertain.

"Please, Cam. Please."

He closed his eyes. "You're sure?"

"Yes."

Cam sucked in a deep breath and took her hand. He turned towards the pale forest. "Fine. Let's go before I change my mind."

They walked through the forest in silence. Destry was afraid to say anything, afraid Cam might change his mind...maybe even afraid she would. *I wondered if this was possible months ago, on the bus to school. Giving up my magic and being normal sounded good then. Why am I scared to get what I wanted?*

A wind blew through the trees, chilling her. She snuggled close to Cam. He winced and pulled away, guarding his shoulder like it was uncomfortable. Destry frowned. "Are you okay?"

His smile seemed forced. "My efforts to heal Wings this morning were painful to her. She caught me in the shoulder. Got Tyla too. Just a bruise, better in no time."

"I really am sorry about Wings."

Cam gestured towards the center of the forest. "The spell has to be worked in the willa grove. Would you like to do it in her clearing?"

That seemed like a fitting place to start her new life. Destry nodded.

The sun was getting lower in the sky by the time they reached Wings' spot. Destry's eyes fell on the tree. She'd been apprehensive about seeing a dead willa, but Wings looked the same as always, aside from a three foot section of trunk swathed in silvery gauze. Cam followed her gaze. "We'll remove her before she turns black. A dead willa is bad for the forest. The other trees will keep trying to support her, no matter what."

He seated her at the base of a second willa, across from the great tree. Butterflies swarmed in Destry's stomach, and she chewed at a hangnail—the same one that had been bothering her earlier—as Cam sat, close enough that their knees touched. For once, he neither scolded her about biting her cuticles nor pulled her finger from her teeth.

"Let's go over the process," he said. "We don't want mistakes on something this important. The spell is fairly simple. You'll repeat a long incantation about releasing your magic. Then I'll do some special things to make the spell take, and I'll have to pierce your tattoos with my fangs, to give you my magic and lend you strength."

Her shoulder blades burned. "You have to bite me? Like a vampire?"

"You'll hardly feel it. Since you aren't goblin, it's a necessary part of the process."

"But won't that take away from your magic?"

He shook his head. "I can draw strength from the willas. That's why we do this in the forest."

"And you're sure my magic will go to Tristan?"

"Certain."

Destry's gaze strayed to Wings, wrapped in her funeral gauze. Whether it made sense to her (or anyone else), she couldn't lose her relationship with the willa trees through cowardice. "Let's do it."

Cam nodded. "Repeat what I say, exactly how I say it."

The spell truly was long. Thanks to her study, Destry recognized some of the words: things about returning magic, and goblins, and fire faeries. Cam translated line by line, so she knew what she was saying.

Finally he said, "Almost done. One more line, that says you give up your magic to me. It allows me to direct the magic to the right person." He spoke the ancient words slowly—*Imé schennar sie mir anamsel*—and waited for Destry to repeat them.

Partway through the phrase, she faltered; something seemed wrong. The word for magic was nowhere in it. "Cam...are you sure this is right?"

"Do you think I'd do this if I wasn't absolutely certain I knew how?"

She managed a weak smile. "No. Guess I'm nervous."

"We'll have to redo a couple lines." He spoke the words, with Destry mimicking doggedly. But when they got to the last phrase, she paused again. Cam repeated it a third time. Still, she hesitated. He said, "The spell will take all night if you keep this up."

"It's just...something doesn't feel right."

He took her hand. "You're a magic being who's giving up your magic. It's not going to feel right."

"Maybe I'm not ready. Maybe we should wait."

Cam sighed. "Destry, I won't repeat this game every time you have a spat with your magic partner. You and Tristan argued, so you came running to me. Now, you want to tell Tristan how self-sacrificing you'd have been, so he'll forgive you."

She stilled. "How'd you know I fought with Tristan? We didn't talk about that."

"Tyla saw you. She flies over for me all the time."

"You said she was with you this morning, working on Wings."

Impatience sharpened his voice. "Des, helping you do this will have repercussions for me in the fey kingdom...repercussions I'm willing to deal with, as long as you're happy. Yet you're interrogating me about minutia. This boils down to trust. Do you trust me enough, or don't you?"

She stared into his slate green eyes—eyes she knew more completely than her own. Cam's words from two years ago whispered through her remembrance: *No matter what, he had no right to take something you didn't want to give.* The Cam she knew would never pressure her about a decision this big. She shook her head slowly. "I guess I don't. Not enough."

He looked down at their entwined hands; his grip on her wrist tightened. "I wish you hadn't said that, Destry. I truly do." Cam raised his other hand, murmuring rapid-fire words that blurred into an incomprehensible mess. She didn't have time to pull away before red light flashed across her vision. Then she was falling, falling, falling into darkness.

38

SOUL NECESSITY

✦

Cam stretched and glanced discreetly at the clock on the wall of his private audience chamber. His aunt shot him a warning look, which he understood well enough. He had to stay until Executor Faris was done airing his grievance. The man had shown up at four—over an hour ago—and was taking his sweet time finishing the official business.

He'd brought papers to be filled out, signed, and duly witnessed, attesting to the administration of a suitable punishment for Destry Firewings on the part of the goblins. He'd accepted Aunt Val's witness that they'd utilized a goblin mark as retribution. He'd brought the scroll Cam flung at him in the aria and asked to view the actual law in the actual law book—which was idiotic, since the same statute could be found in faerie law books.

After that, the executor went into a discourse on how there had been error on both sides, part of which centered around his humiliation at the goblin king's hands. Was the man kissing up, or was he angling for an apology? Hard to tell. But he seemed to be winding down.

Cam stifled a sigh of relief. He'd sent Tyla to meet Destry at the edge of the woods; she shouldn't wait there alone. The goblin girl was supposed to send Destry back to school if Cam didn't arrive by 5:30. If he could get rid of this self-indulgent politician, he might still make it in time.

A heavy knock on the door interrupted the executor's monologue. Cam barely kept from going full-goblin and gouging the arms of his wooden chair. One more interruption, one more delay. "Come," he growled.

Faris's eyes flickered nervously to him, confirming Cam's suspicions. Powerful enemy or not, he'd impressed upon the executor that he, too, was no one to trifle with. He'd outwitted him, a move the faerie man probably held in higher regard than brute strength. It was one small victory.

The servant manning the front door stepped inside. "Sorry to interrupt, Your Majesty, but there's someone asking to see you. He says it's urgent."

Aunt Val smiled, perhaps to make up for Cam's surly tone. "That's fine, Marla. We're nearly finished. Executor Faris, would you like to sample some of our fine goblin delicacies while we complete this paperwork?"

The executor's eyes wavered between Aunt Val—also in human form—and Cam. A lovely woman and rare foods must seem more appealing than Cam, who'd been civil but stony-faced the entire visit.

Faris bowed. "A pleasant end to a visit of unfortunate necessity. But if I might clarify one thing before we disperse... Am I to take it, Goblin King, that the faerie Destry is now under your protection, as she bears your mark?"

So this was a fishing expedition. Cam stood, but he didn't bow. "Take it as you wish, Executor Faris. I hope we will not have cause to meet again soon."

The executor looked unsatisfied, but he didn't protest, and Aunt Val gestured for him to precede her from the room. Cam turned to the servant. "Bring him in, Marla."

"Your Majesty, he's—"

"Just show him in, please." Cam curbed his impulse to banish all castle employees to the four corners of the Fold, or at least from his castle. Besides this interruption, there'd been an argument in the kitchens between the head cooks (who wouldn't be satisfied without Val's or Cam's judgment), plus a guard who referred to Destry by a variety of obscene names, clearly assuming his monarch would approve. Then when Cam had actually needed the hovering valet, because some of his preferred attire was missing, the man was nowhere to be found.

Marla hurried out. His visitor must have been impatient; in less than a minute, the door swung open. The faerie boy Tristan stood there, wings out and jaw set. Cam frowned. "What are you doing here?"

"Looking for Destry." Tristan's eyes swept the room. "She'll miss curfew if she doesn't get back to the Academy."

"I'm aware of your school's restrictions." The Academy set curfew a good hour before the sun went down—unsurprising for a night-blind society that operated on a sunrise to sunset timetable, but still inconvenient. Cam circled around his desk. "You didn't need to come here."

"I'm trying to keep Des out of trouble."

"That would be a pleasant change," Cam said coolly. "Considering your habit of teaching her to break the rules."

"We got detention one time," Tristan huffed. "Besides, *I'm* not the reason she ended up in the justice center, getting her magic drawn."

That obnoxious, self-righteous faerie-boy! "I took numerous precautions to keep your magic partner safe. And as I understand it, she went to the willa forest yesterday because *you* couldn't accept her decision to study goblin magic."

Flushing, Tristan opened his mouth, then closed it again. His shoulders drooped, and his expression melted from indignation to misery. "You're right," he said, looking away. "That was my fault. Just like it's my fault she came here today."

Satisfaction rushed Cam, but guilt wiggled in and ruined it. Though Tristan might not be the best influence, he clearly cared about Destry. He'd been brave enough to challenge Cam the previous day, even in goblin form. Blaming this entire mess on a kid no older than Des herself was unfair.

He gestured for Tristan to come into the room. The faerie complied warily. Cam slid onto a stool at the tall table and offered the other to Tristan. "Actually, *I* asked Des to meet me at the edge of the willa forest today. Your conscience can rest easy."

"Wish it could." Tristan folded to the seat, eyes downcast. "She told me...about you and her. I was upset that she'd lied to me, I walked off. When classes were over, I looked for her—to make up, you know—but she's not at the school. Then I ran into Sara, and she asked why I wasn't at the river. Destry told her she was meeting me there." He thumped his heel repeatedly against one of his stool legs, a nervous human metronome. "If I'd reacted better this morning, maybe Des would've told me where she was going tonight."

Cam grimaced. "Give yourself a break. I've got experience with Destry's tendency to avoid the truth."

Tristan shrugged, face noncommittal. "So, where is she?"

"Des never made it here. The executor showed up and kept me from meeting her on time. I sent Tyla to wait with her at the edge of the willa forest. You should have passed them on your way in."

"They weren't there." The boy crossed his arms. "And Destry's magic trail led to this castle. It's how I figured out where she went."

"Her what?"

Tristan said reluctantly, "Faerie magic. You kind of yank the right energy strands, and they light up and show where someone went. I'm not very good yet—still learning. But there was a strong fire trail from the edge of the woods to here."

"And this magic trail is specific to the individual?"

"It's specific to the element. How many other fire faeries are wandering through your woods?"

"You're certain she wasn't by the river or at the school?" Tristan's baleful look was answer enough. Cam sighed. "Then Tyla must have brought Destry here." Though he couldn't imagine why his otherwise capable assistant would do anything so idiotic. Without Cam's protection, with Wings injured, the castle was no safe place for a faerie.

But saying that would panic the fey boy. Cam forced a reassuring smile. "We just need to find my assistant."

That proved simpler to say than to do. Tyla hadn't been seen since she left for the willa forest, and a search of likely places around the castle turned up neither girl. A half hour later, they ended up back in the audience room. Cam turned to Tristan. "This magic trail you followed...did it go anywhere else?"

Tristan gestured toward the open door. "Down that hall...in and out the main entryway. And it branched off some in the forest. I just thought she'd be here, with you."

"Show me." Cam followed Tristan along the halls. The boy stopped periodically to do a twist-then-yank hand motion.

"This is it," Tristan said, halting outside a familiar door.

Cam pinched the bridge of his nose. "My room. The trail is probably from this morning." He didn't miss the sharp glance Tristan gave him.

"Magic impressions don't last that long. What about your assistant? Is she a fire goblin?"

"You said the spell only detects faeries."

"I said it was a faerie spell, which means you goblins couldn't use it. It detects specific elemental trails. Any creature that uses fire as their element would show up."

"Tyla is an earth sign," Cam said, "like me and three-fourths of our race. But the other fourth are fire signs, which means the trail in here might not even be Destry's. We'd better check the woods."

Tristan's wings hummed. "I'll go to the school, get a few friends to help. If we have to search every branching trail I saw—just the two of us—it could take hours."

"So could a trip to the school and back to the forest." Cam waved for the boy to follow him into the hall. "We can find help here."

"More goblins?" Tristan's lips thinned. "Why don't you just kill Des yourself and save some time?"

A pinprick of anger burned in Cam's chest, all the worse because Tristan's accusations —spoken and unspoken—held some truth. Maybe Cam hadn't caused the mess in the willa forest; maybe he wasn't to blame for the faerie court's actions or the goblin world's attitudes. But he'd allowed Des to be a part of his life again, knowing the potential for disaster.

Oh, Cam could say he'd been respecting Destry's choices. That she had the right to decide whether seeing him was worth the dangers. It would even be true. But the biggest truth was that he needed her. And his selfish need conflicted with his duty to keep her safe.

No sense dwelling on that now. It was done and too late to change. "I didn't intend to call my guards to search the forest." Cam turned towards the healing wing. "There are a few people I can still trust."

"This is becoming ridiculous, Your Majesty."

Cam turned to his chancellor, who had stopped just feet into the willa forest. It took every ounce of self-restraint not to throat-punch him. "What is?"

"This faerie girl, and the trouble she creates everywhere she goes. We shouldn't be in the woods right now. Old friends or not, sometimes one must accept that a friendship has turned into a disadvantage."

Cam felt Tristan tense beside him. Dante patted the boy's shoulder. "Since when have goblins feared these woods? Perhaps we should concentrate upon finding the missing girls, one of whom is a goblin subject."

Brumal lifted his chin but fell into step with the rest of them. He'd been coming in the front door of the castle as Cam, Tristan, and Dante headed out, and another person had seemed like a good idea. Despite his hulking half-bear goblin form, Dante was no fighter, and the more people they had to follow the branching magic trails, the better.

Or so Cam had thought.

They were nearly to the center of the forest when Tristan stopped. "One of the trails goes off that way, in a diagonal through the trees." He pointed left. "Another goes straight along the path I took here."

Cam eyed the lowering sun. "Brumal, why don't you and Dante explore that direction? Tristan and I will take the main path. If you don't see anyone, double back and meet us on the faerie side of the wood."

The chancellor's brows pinched, a line forming between them. "Surely, I should come with Your Majesty. Evil may walk the woods after dark."

"I'm equal to dealing with it," Cam said. Brumal stood there as if undecided. Cam snapped, "If there *is* a problem, we're wasting time. Am I your king or not?"

Brumal pressed his lips together. "Indeed, Your Majesty. My wish to stay with you was simply an indication of my loyalty." He stalked in the direction Tristan had pointed, Dante at his heels.

Cam pulled a knife from his boot and grasped the bottom of his cloak. He cut a strip of cloth and tied it around the tree at the head of the trail. "No one else can see your magic strands," he explained to Tristan. "This marker will show where we've been."

They jogged along the main path. When they were nearly two-thirds of the way to the faerie realm, Tristan said, "It skews off again here." He pointed right.

"You're pointing towards Wings' clearing. Tyla wouldn't have brought Destry to visit the willa."

"Are you sure?"

"No." Cam sighed, tying another strip of cloth to the nearest tree. "But if she did, I'm going to beat them up one side of the Fold and down the other."

A dark laugh edged from Tristan. "Normally, I would point out how barbaric that sounds. But tonight...I agree."

On that rare note of goblin/faerie accord, they strode towards Wings' clearing, racing the lowering sun.

When Destry opened her eyes, she thought night had fallen. It took a minute to realize that she was surrounded by a tent of dense fabric. The air had a closed-in, oppressive feel.

She lay on her back, spread-eagled. Destry tried to sit up, but something thick and unyielding dug into her wrists and legs; she was bound to the ground. She twisted her head, hoping to see what pinned her.

"Willa roots seemed fitting," said a guttural voice.

Destry's heart sped. She'd thought she was alone. Her faerie vision made it hard to discern shapes in the shadowy tent. She squinted into the gloom. A cloaked and hooded figure sat against one fabric wall. "What?" Her question came out wobbly.

"Willa roots. They seem appropriate for what we're doing together. After all, the willas make this evening possible."

That voice. The one from her dream. Destry's wings stung her shoulder blades, but they had no room to come out, with her back pressed tight against the hard-packed earth. She tried to marshal her confused thoughts. She remembered walking with Cam, coming to Wings' clearing. "What did you do to Cam?" she rasped.

He—whoever he was—chuckled quietly. "Nothing. Taking his shape was a kindness to you. Or would have been, had you cooperated."

"I don't even know you." The memories came back in a jumbled rush: Cam, pressing her to say the line that felt wrong, performing a spell that thrust her into darkness. "Why would you do something kind for me?"

"I considered it a gesture of appreciation. Even hobgoblins occasionally observe the niceties."

Her breath hitched. He shifted to face her, and the fabric on one side of the tent parted slightly. A gleam of light slid along obsidian nails. "You've heard of my kind." An odd combination of bitterness and smugness coated his words.

Destry forced herself to speak. She didn't know what else to do, and instinct warned that she didn't want this creature to fall silent. "How can you be a hobgoblin? If you looked like Cam?"

"Magic and science work well together for those clever enough to combine them. Unlike the goblins, who care only for their green and growing things. Unlike the faeries, who wish to remain *pure*." The last was spat with such loathing contempt that Destry flinched. The hobgoblin either didn't notice or didn't care. "The pain of the transformations matters little. To go about unnoticed, unsuspected, is worth every heady drop of anguish."

Silence, broken only by the muted chirping of evening insects. Something scuttled in the dirt nearby. Seconds later, small barbed legs pricked their way up Destry's right arm, scurrying over her shoulder. A maroon centipede the length of her hand came into view, stopping inches from her face; a row of needle-like spines protruded along its back. Destry whimpered as the centipede's spines separated, fanning out into dozens of smaller ones. They shook, rattling against each other in warning.

A flash of movement, too fast to track, brought the hobgoblin to her side. Destry cried out as his hand flew towards her face.

Crunch.

The hobgoblin lifted one long finger. Skewered on his nail, the centipede writhed obscenely. "She must stay alive, little one. More's the pity," the monster crooned. He began pulling the spikes off. They separated from the body with small popping noises. The rattling ceased.

He slid the insect from his nail and tossed the pieces aside. "The scorione was a wise choice on my part."

An instinctive shiver—the realization of danger narrowly avoided—rolled along Destry's skin. Which was stupid, since the centipede, no matter how lethal, was far less dangerous than the hobgoblin. She forced herself to focus on his words. "That...that monster was you?"

"The monster *is* me. I am your unnamed fear, Destry Firewings—the machinator of your downfall. The knife, the note, the attack on the willa tree. Such creatures as you are predictable. You rushed to the rescue and put the final peg in my plans."

"But why? If you want to drain my magic, you could have caught me any time coming through the woods."

"You little understand what I want." Fury seethed beneath the hobgoblin's words. He turned away from her, edging the tent flap open a few more inches. "What I need."

Careful not to be obvious, Destry pulled against the willas binding her. Small rocks and clumps of dirt ground into her skin, but the willas held fast. She twisted her wrists, straining to get her hands on the roots. Her plant magic might...

"They will not release you." The monster spoke with detached amusement, though he never turned from his contemplation of the willa grove. "Without your ability to manipulate energy strands, you have no special control over plants. Without your magic, you have no defenses at all."

She made herself stop twisting, though her heart sped up. "Why did you let me live in the forest?"

"You refuse to ask the real question—the only one that matters." The hobgoblin stepped away from the light. "I let you live because that was my intent. I knew the executor would handle certain things for me, given adequate excuse. Your face betrays you, Destry Firewings—your face and your marks and your magic and your love of these trees. The executor would not let a potential usurper to the throne remain unsullied." He moved with frightening grace to kneel next to her. "Ask me what I need."

"First...first tell me why we're in this tent."

"You know why." He leaned closer, but the tent was still too dark to make out anything beneath the hood besides black fangs gleaming against pale skin. A chemical scent stung her nose. "The light burns me like fire. I must wait for dusk. Now—ask me what I need."

She hesitated.

The hobgoblin bared his fangs. "Ask."

Destry choked the words out. "What do you need from me?"

He laughed, rough and low and triumphant. "Do you know how my kind are made, sweet faerie? How I came to be?"

"Yes."

"We're beautiful creatures, talented in magic, intelligent beyond reckoning, swift and stealthy. We lack only one thing. What is it?"

Humility? Destry choked back a hysterical laugh, a bubble of frantic emotion held in check too long. Angering the hobgoblin would be a bad strategy, and the real answer lodged in her throat, suffocating.

The silence stretched into one, two, three heartbeats. The monster trailed one nail along her arm. "Tell me, Destry. What do I need?" When she still said nothing, he pressed the point down, punching through the skin and into tissue. Pain lit her nerves. He ignored her cry, lifting his nail to his lips. A granite-colored tongue snaked out, caught a single drop of blood. He pulled it into his mouth with a sound of pleasure and pressed his nail to her arm again, an inch above the previous place. "Answer."

Her reply was a mere thread of sound. "You have no soul."

"Indeed. Do you know that I remember all? Everything from the day I was born? I remember my mother's face after she birthed me. Her revulsion. She left me on the bed, her ebony hair still damp with the sweat of labor, and fled. She never returned. The only thing my mother bequeathed to me was a need for fire, for a soul that flames as hers does."

He leaned closer, breath icy against her cheek. "Ask me again what I need."

This time she shook her head, more afraid of his answer than the pain he threatened her with.

The hobgoblin's guttural chuckle echoed in her ear. "Refusal will not change it. Refusal will not stop me. My need is deep and ever-lasting. I *need* your soul."

39

ENOUGH

———————————✦———————————

C am stopped on the path and turned to Tristan. "This is the last magic trail?"

The boy looked frustrated. "Yeah. We've covered every single one."

They stood near the entrance to the faerie realm, where the forest left off and the rocky expanse leading to the river began. They'd found nothing in Wings' clearing, nothing along the multitude of paths they'd followed—and Tristan said the magic indicators were growing fainter.

The boy jerked his hand, twitching the magic. "The trail's almost gone here, but it was stronger in the forest. She never came back to the river."

Cam nodded slowly, staring into the white trees. Would Des really have wandered the willa forest that afternoon, taking branching path after branching path? Tyla would never have let her. "Tristan, can you check for an earth element?"

"You want to know if your assistant made it to this end of the forest?"

"Yes."

The faerie's shoulders rose in an uncertain shrug. "The spell should be the same as with the elements I'm used to. Problem is, you've been all over this forest with me. We won't be able to tell if the trail is yours or Tyla's."

"Shouldn't there be two?"

"Maybe not. Sometimes they overlap."

Cam scrubbed a hand along his face. "Which also means you can't tell if there was one fire sign wandering these woods—or more."

Tristan followed his logic just fine. "You think some fire goblin got Destry?"

"I hope not. But Des and Tyla wouldn't stay here after dark—not after the willa attack—and the sun has almost set. Let's follow that path again." He pointed in the direction of Wings' clearing, where Tristan said the trail was brightest.

They were about to turn off the main path when Cam heard voices. "Hold up. Someone's coming."

"I don't hear anything."

Cam made an impatient shushing motion. He led Tristan along the path. Moments later, Dante and Brumal came into view, Dante supporting Tyla. The healer saw them coming and stopped, helping the goblin girl sit on a patch of dried-out grass.

"Ty!" Cam hurried over and knelt in front of her. "Are you hurt? What happened?"

She shook her head. "I'm...not certain. I left to deliver your message, but I don't remember anything after you caught up to me in these woods."

"After I caught you in the woods? This is the first time we've seen each other since you left the castle."

She frowned. "No. About halfway through the forest, someone called my name. I turned and saw you jogging towards me. You said, 'I'm afraid your services are inconvenient this afternoon.' The next thing I remember is waking up on the forest floor with Dante and Brumal hovering over me."

Cam glanced at Dante. "Is she alright?"

"She will be. Whatever spell was used on her clearly muddled her memory. Otherwise—" The healer knelt by them, too, his hair a bright patch in the darkening forest. He indicated some marks on Tyla's arms.

"She was bound to the ground with willa roots. The intent was to incapacitate her."

Tristan said, "So she couldn't reach Destry with a message."

Cam's heart thudded roughly. "This confirms that it's a goblin. Few faeries have strong plant magic. Brumal, stay with Tyla. Dante, Tristan, and I will follow the trail to Wings' clearing."

Brumal stabbed a finger towards Dante. "Let the healer remain with her, while I stay at your side. You have no idea what might lie in wait, Your Majesty."

"Let's make this simple," Tyla said. "Help me up." She snapped her fingers at Tristan, who offered her his hand with a look of confusion. She pulled herself to her feet. "I'm coming with you. Destry is my friend, too."

"Ty, you could be a handicap—"

She snapped her fingers again, and a short burst of energy sizzled across them. "I'm not entirely useless. Stop wasting time."

Several hundred yards later, Tristan halted. "The trail splits here. We've followed these paths already. Don't they both lead to that willa?"

Cam nodded. "Brumal, you and Dante take the one furthest away. The beginning is marked. Look for a strip of my cloak tied around the willa. You'll see signs that we went through there. Follow our trail to the clearing." He started down the path with Tyla and Tristan.

As the forest got darker, Tristan began to stumble. Tyla said, "Come here before you kill yourself. Can't believe how night-blind faeries are." She pulled him close enough to lean on his arm and direct him. She still looked pale, but there was no point arguing with Tyla.

Tristan asked, "Who do you think is doing this? Some goblin who wants revenge for the willa tree?"

Cam peered through the grass, looking for anything they might have missed. "Maybe. And it may have nothing to do with Wings. Those other girls—"

"What girls?"

So Des hadn't told him about that, either. Cam gave him a quick summation. Tyla added, "There hasn't been an incident in months. If there ever was a threat, we hoped it had moved on."

"But now you think it was waiting," Tristan said. "Watching and waiting for another faerie...just like Destry."

I need your soul. Those words hissed in Destry's mind long after physical sound had faded. The hobgoblin turned away, facing the crack in the tent—watching it silently. Destry couldn't force herself to speak again. Fear shriveled her throat.

He had been the scorione. He'd done all of it: sent her the dagger, lured her into the woods, attacked Wings. He'd planned for the goblins to prosecute her. Yet he'd somehow known Cam wouldn't let the goblins hurt her, and he'd known the executor would.

He'd said pretending to be Cam was a kindness, but how? What would have happened if she'd said those words: *Imé schennar sie mir anamsel*? She'd thought he was Cam. Without a doubt, Destry would have allowed him to pierce her tattoos—except for the one word that sounded wrong: *anamsel*. She'd never run across it in her magic studies, but now...now, she could guess what it meant.

The hobgoblin pulled the tent flap back on one side, then the next, then the last two, fastening them open with shining pins. Destry caught a glimpse of silver gauze, and her stomach lurched. It was Wings' roots holding her.

The hobgoblin knelt at her side. "This ritual must be performed in the open air of the willa grove, which is inconvenient. But as you see, I planned even for this. The feeble rays of dusk are tolerable to a hobgoblin."

"Why don't we wait until night?" That sounded equally horrible, but stalling was better than doing nothing.

"Because I do not wish it," he said shortly. For the first time, Destry thought she heard something normal—something human—in his voice. Frustration.

He busied himself, using his nails to scratch ancient words in the roots binding her. Destry couldn't read most of them. Wings must have been deeply withdrawn; she didn't even flinch.

While the hobgoblin worked, Destry searched frantically for an avenue of escape. The monster's last statement seemed important. Surely, he would have preferred to work at night. Despite his boasting, he stuck to the remaining shadows whenever possible, avoiding the weak sunshine. So why hadn't he planned this ritual for later? What would be different in a few hours?

Someone at the school or the castle might realize she was missing...but the monster could have circumvented that problem by luring her out after curfew instead, disguised as Cam. He'd have less risk of being discovered. And she'd have gone with him easily, especially if Cam hadn't intervened at the justice building. After ten strikes, the comfort he offered would've been irresistible.

Except...

The executor hadn't administered all ten strikes. *That* was the variable the hobgoblin couldn't have foreseen. The strikes drained magic, and what had the hobgoblin said earlier? *Without your ability to manipulate energy strands, you have no special control over plants. Without your magic, you have no defenses at all.* Had he worried her magic would affect the willas? Or had he simply wanted to remove her ability to fight back?

Either way, he'd framed her for that specific crime so the punishment would be severe enough to drain her magic for a full two days and nights. Destry felt sure of it. But Cam had jumped in, and then carried her away for the first night. The hobgoblin had not intended this part of things.

And Destry's magic would return soon.

The creature pulled three vials of silvery liquid from his cloak. It looked like willa blood. "This is one of our connections, Destry Firewings. Few know of the Imperial family's fondness for growing things, and for these trees in particular. It is scandalous in fey society. But for the truest members, their blood runs in the willa veins. When exposed, they are irrevocably drawn to the trees."

"We're *not* connected."

The hobgoblin ignored her disgust. "To take someone's soul is an old magic. I searched many years to find it. There must be enough similarities for the soul to attach to the new form—one of which is blood. I needed a relation, not too distant. I needed a fire-seeking element. I needed someone in whose veins ran the willa need. I never thought, when I found the spell, to ever work it. And then I heard of you."

The creature took one vial and placed the others on the ground. He twisted his fingers around the cork, dark claws a creeping spider against the silvery tube. The hobgoblin hissed as he pulled the cork loose, as though the action caused him pain. Wasn't that the shoulder she'd blasted when he was a scorione? An injury could give her an advantage, however small.

She watched, hoping his motions would reveal more. How badly was he hurt? The hobgoblin poured willa blood over the roots, a little on each set of words. "You show a disappointing lack of interest, fire fey. Do you not wish to hear my tale?"

Destry searched for a useful response and came up empty. She wanted to keep him talking, yes...but why would the monster reveal so much? The likely answer—that he was certain of victory—left her stomach hollow.

The hobgoblin moved to another root. "It seems you don't. Which is reason enough to continue." He tipped blood from the vial over another set of carved words. "While hunting in Si'fliegen one night, I chanced upon two faerie men leaving a tavern. They carried the scent of strong magic. I followed, expecting an easy meal. As they walked the deserted roads leading to the palace, the first man commented on the second's unusual foray to the tavern. 'I can count on one hand the number of times you've been drunk,' said he. 'You must be thinking of her tonight.'

"Then they spoke of a long-lost daughter. The second man had searched the fey school year after year for her, but in vain. 'She's long past the age of discovery,' he said. 'I fear that my child has died.' Then—" a sneer crept into the hobgoblin's voice— "the man began crying. Does it make you happy, fire fey, that your father wept maudlin tears over you?"

Destry's hands curled into fists. "My father abandoned me. If you're looking for a girl whose father wanted her, you found the wrong person."

The hobgoblin made a noise between a scoff and a hiss. "The first man told the second not to despair. 'They bring in new students each semester. I'll search them for you.' He requested—and received—a description. Fair skin, pale blonde hair, brown eyes. Likely a storm type, based on the girl's heady love of thunderstorms. The father also insisted that during her childhood, she'd shown signs of being a fire fey—a family gift. 'Perhaps,' he sighed, 'this is better. She would have been marked as one of us. I wouldn't bring her into this life by choice.'"

The hobgoblin sat back, examining his handiwork. "By that time, I had no idea of feeding. I suspected who the second man was. I followed and was rewarded. He and his friend did not go to the palace, but to the separate lodgings accorded to the Imperial family. That was the beginning of my search. And you are the end of it."

"But what if I'm the wrong faerie?" Destry said.

"Then it will be unfortunate for you." He took another vial in hand. "But as compensation, you'll have the rare privilege of tasting willa blood before repeating the final line. You are among exalted company. Willa blood is the drink of goblin kings." He laughed roughly. "I could be a king of a different sort."

"Why are you telling me this?" Destry rasped. "It won't help. I won't drink the blood, I won't repeat that line." It took all her fortitude to say the words, pinned to the ground in front of him.

He stared at her—or she assumed he did, under his hood. "I tell you this because it pleases me to cause you fear. I tell you so you'll know: my desire is as desperate as your terror. In the end, you will do it all."

"I won't," she whispered.

She hoped it was true.

The last rays of the sun were fading. The monster undid his cloak fastenings, and it slid to the ground with a gentle susurration of fabric. The dusky evening light revealed a young man's body, shirtless and pale and perfect. Shining dark hair curled around the face of an avenging angel. Even the slender black fangs and the raw wound on one shoulder couldn't detract from that impossible beauty.

She met his eyes and started to shake. Though his eyelids were open, he had no eyes. A fathomless sea of black and gray nothingness swirled in his eye sockets. Foggy pits too deep to see bottom, they pulled her in until she was lost and gasping.

The hobgoblin smiled. "Am I not beautiful?" He drank the willa blood from his vial with relish, then held up the last. "Your turn."

The hobgoblin knelt beside her. Instinctively, Destry clamped her lips closed. He ranged the points of his nails along her right arm. "When I push through your skin, into your tendons and muscles, you will scream. And I'll pour this down your throat. Spit it out, and I slash another willa, refill my vials, and we drink again." He increased the pressure, pinprick warnings of coming pain, and his smile sharpened into vindictiveness. "Or you can cooperate, like a good little faerie, and get the same result with less pain. Choose, cousin."

Choose.

The word splashed over her, bringing a numbing sense of clarity.

How many times had someone taken away her choice over the years? Beverly's boyfriends, Jared...even Beverly, however unintentionally. All wanting cooperation, all taking too much and giving too little, leaving her with nothing but fury and fear and an aching sense of powerlessness.

Now this monster.

Well, maybe he'd manipulated the fey court into draining her magic. And maybe her magic would return in time, or maybe it wouldn't. Regardless, she had one power left—a bitter, hollow path to victory, but victory nonetheless. She would not give up the power left to her.

Choose.

Destry tried summoning magic to her palms but felt only a few tingles. She needed time—time she wouldn't get by allowing him to cut her like a steak. She met the hobgoblin's empty gaze and opened her mouth.

The thick willa blood oozed along her tongue and throat, coating it with nauseating sweetness. The hobgoblin leaned closer. "Wait," Destry gasped. "I did what you asked. Tell me something in return."

The expression on his face might have been surprise. "What else would you wish to know?"

"Will you change? Once you have a soul?"

The hobgoblin smiled again. "Are you asking if I will strive for heaven? If I will be 'good?' Child of faerie, I want one thing from a soul:

immortality. Life after my time on this earthly plane ends. I care not if I am numbered with the demons of Hell."

He stroked the willa root on her left wrist. "*Lassca.*" The root released her, but his hand closed around her arm instead. It felt as unyielding as the tree roots, and colder. "Do you know, Destry, that most beings claim to value their souls more than their lives? But their behavior tells a different tale. Few value their souls enough to save them at the cost of their lives."

He lifted her wrist to his mouth. "Here is what we shall do: I will sink my fangs into your wrist and draw your life force a bit at a time, until you finish the incantation we began in the clearing. It will be painful beyond reckoning. Once you give up your soul, I'll stop draining your life and complete the ritual. And you may exist as I now do: a soulless creature."

Destry felt frantically for her magic. The tingles in her hands were stronger, but not nearly strong enough. Time, more time. "What if I don't give you my soul?"

"Then you'll die, slowly and in exquisite anguish. For my fury would have no bounds."

She and the hobgoblin stared at each other. The sound of feet tromping through the woods broke their silent contest. On the other side of the trees, Cam strode into view, Tyla and Tristan behind him.

Destry's heart leapt. "*CAM!*"

Her long scream should have gotten his attention, should have angered the hobgoblin. But Cam just turned to Tristan. "You said the magic trail stops here. Let's spread out and search the area."

"I'll take him, since he's half-blind," Tyla said.

Why hadn't they heard? Destry screamed again, but Cam just nodded. "I'll circle around that way. Meet me back here."

Destry watched in disbelief as they moved in a circle through the trees fringing the clearing. The hobgoblin's guttural laugh filled the tent. "Do you think I would be in the woods without protection from that oaf?"

Protection? What protection could a simple tent offer? Four tall stakes and fabric, nothing more. And yet... Her first lesson with Cam tickled her memory. *If you wanted to soundproof a small area, it would make sense to cast the spell on cloth and tent stakes.* Nausea washed through her.

The hobgoblin bared his slender fangs. "Your screams will bring plea-sure to my ears alone." He lifted her wrist to his mouth. "Will you say the words?"

Destry closed her eyes. The price of delay would be high. By the time her magic was accessible, would she have enough life force left to use it? *Choose.*

"I won't," she whispered.

He sank his fangs into her wrist.

Anguish ricocheted from her arm through her body. It skittered along her limbs, down her back, up her throat and to her head. Pulsing hotter, colder, sharper. So many forms of agony. Her vision blurred, every nerve begging for the solace of unconsciousness.

Destry writhed and screamed, bucked and screamed, and after an eternity, the hobgoblin withdrew his teeth. Her wrist burned cold, but the pain ebbed. Destry's vision cleared enough to see the hobgoblin's pleased smile. *"Imé schennar sie mir anamsel,"* he said, and a deeper terror rushed Destry.

She wanted to comply.

Just say it. Just end it.

Who did she think she was?

She couldn't hold out against torture.

But...

She also wanted to live.

And the monster's vindictive smile left no doubt: she was dead the second that phrase escaped her lips. So when he hissed, "Say it!"...

She locked the words inside.

Desperate, determined.

Terrified.

My choice. Not his. My power. Not his.

Something flickered in her chest—whispers of magic, a fire strength she barely recognized—urging her to hold steady.

The hobgoblin slid his fangs into her again.

And Destry's world disappeared.

It dissolved into a timeless void of agony and screaming and sobbing and refusing.

Pain. Pain. Pain, pain, pain.

The withdrawal of fangs, the choking relief.

Her refusal to speak.

Back to agony.

Again and again and again.

When she wasn't screaming, Destry heard the others arguing, heard Tristan snap, "The strongest trail stops there, right by that big tree!" She heard Brumal and Dante join them. Their tense but quiet discussion sounded strange against her cries.

The hobgoblin leaned close to her ear. "You are lost, faerie. Listen."

Over her sobbing, angry voices rent the air: Cam yelling at Brumal, the chancellor's terse suggestion to search the castle again. The hobgoblin laughed. "They will leave, and you'll have nothing left to wait for. Give in. Give me your soul, and I'll give you your life—what little is left."

She tried to focus on him, but the world just spun. Destry closed her eyes. She could feel...what? What did she feel, what was that, working its way into her palm? It itched, it burned, it would not be ignored.

Choose.

She drew a shuddering breath. "No."

"Then you die," he said calmly. But rage roiled beneath.

This time, when he sank his fangs into her wrist, he sank them all the way in. It was not meant to spare her. And this time, Destry screamed as she hadn't before. She screamed for the agony and the terror, for what she was about to do and everything she was going to lose. And she sent all her pain and all her power into one place.

A bolt of magic blasted from her palm. She opened her eyes in time to see it burst against the side of the hobgoblin's face, wreathing it in flames. He jerked back, loosing a tormented roar, stumbling into the left corner of the tent. It fell along with him, burying them both in suffocating blackness.

The hobgoblin thrashed, jostling her and kicking her wrist—the one that now held his fangs, buried deep in skin and muscle. Their frigid poison sent waves of pain through her bones. Destry cried out again.

The monster stood, throwing off the tent. His hand strayed to his mouth. On his face, realization dawned: the understanding of what she'd just taken from him.

My power. My choice.

Across the clearing, five people swiveled around, faces etched in shock.

Cam's roar reverberated in her ears, even through the half-blackness she kept sinking in and out of. "*DESTRY!*"

The hobgoblin laughed, exultant, as if he felt nothing from the charred ruin of his face. "Dead, oh mighty Goblin King! Dead."

The blast from Tristan's palms hit the creature in the chest only seconds before Cam—fully goblin—pounced. Destry caught quick, confused glimpses of them fighting, the hobgoblin laughing wildly, slashing with his claws. Tristan bellowed in agony, but she didn't see why.

Tyla swooped past her field of vision, an enormous bird, catching the creature before it could escape. She flew high, shrinking against the darkening sky. Then the hobgoblin was falling, falling, his euphoric scream stabbing into Destry's ears. His body slammed against the ground with a sickening crunch. A blur of muscle and granite—Cam standing over the monster, arm raised. His claws raked the creature's neck in a final death blow.

Her vision fuzzed. Two hazy forms staggered over: Tristan, one wing hanging askew, dragging the tent off of her, and Cam, shouting words to make the roots clutching her give way. They were both alive. And the monster was dead. That had to be enough. Destry closed her eyes and sank into darkness.

A DELICATE BALANCE

C am's hands shook as he pushed the willa roots away from Destry. Her face was white, the hollows around her eyes blackened. Dante joined him, melding out of his half-bear goblin form. His eyes settled on the one arm that was unbound. "Oh, Camden. I'm sorry."

Tristan, on Cam's other side, was crying freely. "Why are you sorry? She's still breathing, you're a healer! Fix her!"

The healer pointed to the black spots in the wound on Destry's wrist. "Those are hobgoblin fangs—poison. Even if I could get them out, she'd never survive. He's drained too much life force. She has minutes, fifteen at best."

Cam stared numbly at Destry; he barely felt the tears on his goblin skin. His eyes fell on the phrases etched over and over into the willa roots. *Give of the willa...share of the soul...give of the willa...share of the soul...*

His head jerked up. "Get these fangs out. Now."

"I don't have the right equipment," Dante said. "Tweezers, a knife..."

Tyla shoved past Brumal, who looked ill. "My beak. Cam's claws. Show us what to do." She shrank into the raven and lit on Dante's hand.

Destry woke with a scream when Cam cut into her skin. Her sobbed pleading, "No, no, no more!" twisted his stomach and tore his heart. Beside him, Tristan wept as he helped hold her still. But within minutes, the black fangs sat on the forest floor.

Cam stood, gathering Destry into his arms. Brumal barred his way. "What are you going to do?"

"Magic is part of her life force. If I use the King's Strength spell to share magic with her, it'll keep her alive."

"How?" Brumal gestured around the clearing. "The willas are all asleep, Camden. You cannot draw their power when they sleep."

"The willa by my window. He's still awake."

Cam started past Brumal, but the older goblin grasped his shoulder. "This is too dangerous! Do it wrong, and you could both die!"

"Then I'd better do it right." He threw off Brumal's hand and ran, powerful legs eating up the distance through the forest.

Destry moaned as his gait jarred her; Cam forced himself to ignore it. Better she stay awake—even in pain—than fall unconscious again. But seconds in, her eyes slid closed. He jostled her, eliciting a whimper. "Des? Stay awake. I need to know what happened."

She mumbled something about the hobgoblin wanting her soul, words drifting away at the end like a renegade wisp of fog. He shook her again. "Dessie! Wake up!"

Another weak, whimpered sentence, fading into that ominous stillness.

Another rough shake from Cam, another question.

It was a hideous cycle. Never before had his willa forest felt like a place of nightmares. But now the silence pressed against him, leaving nothing but the rasp of his own breathing in his ears. A few times, he stopped to shake Destry awake. She cried, but she tried to obey his request for information. He got a garbled picture of how she'd come to be in the woods, what she'd thought the ritual would do, and what it really was.

The trees opened up, and the castle came into view, washed pale by the moonlight. Destry's head lolled against his shoulder. She'd fallen unconscious moments before, and Cam had been too afraid of losing time to stop and wake her again. Panting, he raced for the willa tree near his balcony.

He lay Destry on the roots, then fell to his knees and pressed his hand to the tree. Without the willa's agreement, he'd do no more than injure it. The second it acquiesced, Cam began speaking.

The words came haltingly. His perfect memorization felt far away, in this moment of panic and pressure. Brumal's words from days ago played—too loudly—in his head. *That spell requires a very delicate balance to do properly. Give too much magic to anyone besides a goblin—and the surplus of foreign magic will kill the person you wish to save.*

He completed the spell and waited, barely breathing. *Please let me have remembered the spell right.* Destry was paler by the minute, her breathing shallow. He didn't have time for another repetition. One heartbeat...two...

Willa energy rushed into him; Cam gasped at the enormity of it. Vast untapped reserves, limitless power heaving in the earth below—it set his senses ablaze, nerves screaming with awareness. Too much magic for him to hold. He broke contact with the tree and reached for Destry.

He couldn't use the wrist the hobgoblin had. With those bloody wounds, it might not conduct the magic. He lifted the other hand; Destry woke with a gasp. Her chocolate eyes roved over him, fangs poised above her wrist. She whimpered, and Cam tightened his grip. "It's okay, I'm just going to share my magic with you."

"Lies," she sobbed. "You want my soul, not me. No more, no more, no more."

Cam dropped her wrist, grasping her face tightly between his palms. "You're all I want, Des. Trust me." He dropped a gentle kiss on her lips, like he had that night after Jared.

Her eyes searched his. How reassuring would he seem in goblin form? But Destry nodded. He laid her on the willa roots. She wouldn't look as Cam sank his fangs into her wrist.

The difference between draining magic and giving magic was intent. Cam concentrated on images of Destry, healthy and smiling. Her hair shining in its messy braid, her chocolate eyes bright with laughter. He thought of everything he wanted her to have: happiness, love, safety. He remembered all the times they'd shared, every good emotion she roused in him. And somewhere in the middle of it, he was surprised to realize that the feeling of love was not as brotherly as he'd always thought.

Cam wasn't sure when to stop. He wasn't sure how to control the flow of magic. He might be killing himself. But Destry was dead if he didn't act, so the risk, however great, was worth it.

He began to shake, weakness spreading through his body. Lethargy dragged at his limbs. His brain moved sluggishly. Maybe that was enough. He eased his teeth from Destry's wrist. Her eyes were less bruised looking, and faint color brushed her cheeks. He pressed his ear to her chest.

Thump. Thump. Thump. Her heart still beat, steady if not strong.

A wide hand clasped his shoulder. Cam looked up. Dante. He hadn't noticed him arriving. The healer felt the pulse in Destry's neck. "You did well. Barring unforeseen complications, she should live."

Cam nodded wearily. Destry's eyes were closed, like she had fallen asleep. He preferred to think of it that way, instead of unconscious. Dante offered him a hand up.

He stumbled to his feet, weaving, and propped himself against the willa. In the distance, Brumal, Tyla, and Tristan emerged from the woods. Tristan leaned on Tyla. Brumal wore his wolf form and had a body—presumably the hobgoblin—slung across his back. When he reached the trio, Brumal tipped the creature off his back and morphed human.

Cam stared down at the body, and what part of him had any room left for surprise, was. In death, the ferocious, beautiful hobgoblin had turned into the unassuming man who'd been his valet in the castle.

"At least I can dress in peace now," Cam said. He took one step towards the body and crumpled to the ground. The last thing he saw, before blackness covered him, was Destry.

Cam woke in his bedroom with a throbbing headache and the sense that he wasn't alone. He caught sight of Tyla, sitting on the end of his bed and staring out his open balcony doors. The moon was high in the sky, and the chirp of nighttime insects drifted in, a lullaby that urged Cam to sleep again.

He pressed one hand to his head, noticing he wasn't in goblin form any longer. "Ty? What in the Fold are you doing in my bed?"

She twisted around, glaring. Her gold eyes were red-rimmed. "I'm not crying over your idiot self, that's for sure."

"Yeah, I know." He sat up, stifling a groan.

Tyla leapt to her feet. She dashed around the bed and pushed him down again. "Stay there, you earth-cursed fool. Dante and Lady Val will have my head if you're up gallivanting around. Trying to use the King's Strength spell when you've never done it before... You're lucky you didn't kill yourself and Destry both."

Cam gave up pitifully quick, sinking onto the fluffy pillows. "Wasn't much risk. She would've died if I didn't. Now, she's alive." Tyla turned her back on him and poured a glass of water from a pitcher on his bedside table. She tossed some of Dante's powdered herbs in and stirred silently. The bottom dropped out of Cam's stomach. "Tyla? She is alive, right?"

She turned, glass in hand. "Of course she's alive, though not entirely due to you. You overdid it with the magic. That's why you feel like a half-drowned dragon-mouse now."

"Then how—"

Tyla handed him the glass. "Drink, and I'll explain." She settled on the end of his bed. "Your valet—who was actually a hobgoblin—dropped some vials. We found them when we burned that enchanted fabric. There were traces of willa blood in them and on Destry's lips. Not sure what kind of spell he was doing, but he must have forced her to drink some. Dante thinks the willa blood prepped Destry's system. It kept the overdose of foreign magic from shocking her body and killing her."

Cam finished the water. He pulled a face. Dante's herbs were helpful but bitter. "Where is she?"

Tyla took the glass. "Dante moved her to the healing hall, along with Tristan. It's been five hours since you passed out. Destry hasn't woken up yet, but Dante said that's good. It means her body is accepting the goblin magic."

He frowned. "Des *and* Tristan? Is he—" Cam remembered the faerie boy's wing hanging askew. He'd stepped in front of the hobgoblin to keep it from attacking Tyla and gotten clawed for his trouble.

"Dante's been applying a salve to the injuries and drenching them in salt water every hour since we arrived. His wing will be okay—just not as pretty as before." Tyla shrugged. "Since he got the scars being 'heroic,' he probably won't care."

"You seem pretty blasé about someone who tried to save your life."

A blush graced her cheeks. "He's an idiot, too. I was more prepared to fight than he was."

Maybe he shouldn't tease her just now. "You were brilliant out there, Ty."

She grinned. "Why, thank you, my liege. But I'm still not helping you upstairs to see Destry."

He swung his legs over the side of the bed, clutching the headboard for stability. "I don't need your help to do that. I *do* need to see if the magic is holding. I need to talk to Brumal about that hobgoblin. I need...I need..." He stopped, dizzy.

Tyla pushed him down a second time. "Did I mention Dante included some sleeping herbs in there? You *need* to rest. Destry will be good for a few hours, thanks to the oversupply, and I'll take care of the other problems." She kicked at his calves until he gave up and dragged his legs onto the mattress. Tyla pulled the covers over him and kissed his cheek. "Glad you're alright, O Goblin King."

The next time Cam woke, bright sunlight shone through the window and his guard goblin was gone. He forced himself out of bed and into clean clothes, grimacing when a sudden movement set his head throbbing. "Great. The one time I could use a valet, and he's not only an evil hobgoblin but also dead."

He took enough time to draw energy from the willa tree and to express his thanks. The male seemed pleased, although not overly so; his independence wouldn't allow that. Cam strode out of his room feeling better than he had in hours.

He reached the staircase to the healing hall. Brumal was on his way down. He stopped and waited for Cam, face set in lines of reproof. "You ought not be up and about, Your Majesty. Your aunt will have our heads."

"I need to speak with you."

Brumal sighed. "Then I shall accompany you to the healing hall."

As they took the stairs—slowly—Cam explained what Destry had told him about the hobgoblin's spell to steal her soul. Brumal looked startled. "I don't think such a thing is possible."

"But the hobgoblin thought it was," Cam said. "Which is probably why he applied as my valet. All the information about faeries who need to use the firewell comes to me. Servants are expected to be underfoot. It wouldn't seem odd if a valet lingered in my chambers once I was gone. He could collect information with no one the wiser."

Brumal pressed his lips into a thin line. "He certainly used his knowledge to advantage. That message from the fey palace—he manipulated me into sending the guards. How that benefited him isn't clear, but I can hardly be blamed for falling prey to one of the most intelligent monsters in the Fold."

Cam bit back a response. Manipulated or not, his chancellor's decision rankled. Still, he had more pressing concerns. They stopped outside the entrance to the healing hall. "Brumal, has the school—"

The chancellor said, with forced patience, "The Academy has been notified, and I've squashed the rumors until we can choose the most advantageous story. Truly, Camden, I can handle this. Do not forget that I've been at court for decades—since before your father left for the human world."

Cam grinned. "I can't forget—not with Dad's penchant for storytelling. He especially loves the one about traveling with you to the human world. He starts the same way every time: 'Camden, *always* double check your knots. First day out on our trip, and Brumal was more concerned about lunch than tying his horse properly!' Then he complains how the horse ran away, and he had to sleep all night in a dwarfish bed because you returned to the castle for a new mount."

Brumal's chuckle was strained. "Indeed. All these years later, Gregor still teases me at every opportunity."

Cam smiled apologetically. Brumal never had liked the story, since it made him look foolish. "I'm staying in the healing hall until Destry wakes up. Send word if my attention is needed on anything."

Dante didn't look surprised to see his king. "I wondered how long Tyla could detain you." He gestured for Cam to follow him. The healing hall was peppered with windows and divided with folding panels, so the space retained a sense of airiness. In each section was a slim bed, a chair, a small table with a pitcher for water and a glass. None of the other cubicles were occupied.

At the end of the room, Dante had arranged the dividers to make room for three beds and several chairs. Tristan slept in one of the beds. Cam noticed the tears in his left wing and winced. Dante said, "They're much improved, I promise you. Since saltwater is his strengthener, I've been using a saline bath on them, which helps dramatically. He would benefit from the saltwater fountain at his school, but I doubt we can move him until Destry wakes. His refusal was adamant."

Cam's eyes had already moved to the next bed. Destry curled on her side there, sleeping, wrists bandaged. Her hair was still tangled, her face still smudged, but she looked peaceful and less pale. Dante followed his gaze. "I put a sleep spell on her when cleansing her wrists. The one with the hobgoblin fangs will be quite painful. I didn't remove the spell until recently, so she would be able to rest. She does well, Camden."

Cam smiled gratefully. Despite the political necessity of keeping Brumal as chancellor when he took the throne, he was easier with Dante and often wished the older man wanted to help run the kingdom. "Who's the third bed for?"

"You, of course. The faerie lad is not the only intractable person in this room. I'll bring more herbal tinctures—and no, none of them are sleeping draughts. I expect you to at least sit there if you refuse to sleep." He indicated a deep, thickly padded leather chair.

Cam still felt drained. He took the chair Dante had indicated—without complaint—and dragged it closer to Destry. The noise woke Tristan. He sat up with a hiss of pain. "Guess I should've paid more attention in combat class."

Cam—who might normally have voiced his agreement—didn't. A faerie's wings were important. Nearly losing one was a high price to pay for being inexperienced and stupid and brave. "Battle scars. They're good for impressing girls, anyway," he said lightly.

Tristan's eyes strayed toward Destry. "Wonder if they'll impress the right girl." The boy added, "Dante said it's okay she's sleeping this long, but I'm not sure."

"He knows what he's doing. Dante is versed in caring for all types of creatures." Cam refused to voice the fear that lingered in his mind.

Tristan shifted, adjusting his wings with a heavy grimace. "I guess. It's just...she left because of me. If something happens, this is my fault."

Dante strode past, arms full of dried herbs. "In point of fact, it is the hobgoblin's fault. Marvelously intelligent creatures without a shred of conscience. Perhaps we can leave the blame where it belongs: with the perpetrator." He didn't linger to see if they agreed.

Cam and Tristan exchanged grim smiles. The boy said stiffly, "Do you know anything else about what happened?"

They both knew his true meaning. Did Cam know what Destry had been thinking, why she'd willingly gone into the woods with a stranger? Cam sighed. "Just what I pieced together from things Des said last night. She wasn't very...coherent." Remembered fear turned his stomach and tightened his chest. Cam forced himself to breathe.

Tristan looked down at his hands. A strand of magic began glowing in them, wound over his fingers. He fiddled with it like some fidget toy. "I don't know how to thank you...for something that big. For saving Des's life. I...I couldn't have helped her, faeries can't share magic like that—not even magic partners." His voice cracked on the last word.

Cam couldn't say any of the things he wanted to. That he'd been saving his own life as much as Destry's in that reckless gamble last night...that Des was a part of him he couldn't imagine living without...that he didn't know a way forward if she was gone. They were all truthful, and they were all wrong to say to this boy who would have equal claim on Des's time— and probably affection—in the years to come.

His heart clenched a little tighter.

Cam managed an unsteady smile. "Thanks isn't necessary, Tristan."

The faerie boy held his gaze, mouth quirking into a resigned smile. "Thank you anyway." He tossed his glowing magic strand into the air. "Wanna tell me what Des *did* explain last night?"

As the magic strand faded into invisibility. they sat back to make stilted conversation and wait.

GROUP EFFORT

D estry woke up to not one, but two half-angry, half-relieved guys. They were sitting together, talking. Cam gestured decisively as he explained a combat technique. Their heads swiveled towards her when she struggled to sit up. "Destry!" It was Tristan who spoke, but Cam got to the bed first, pulling her into his arms.

He was growling, a low, restrained rumble. She started to laugh, then to cry, and came up with a hysterical whimper. But she clutched at Cam when he would have pulled away. "You found me."

"Of course I did. Finding you is the most necessary thing I've ever done." He whispered, so quietly she had to strain to hear it, "My roots begin and end with you, Destry Adams."

She didn't recognize the phrase—probably some goblin declaration of friendship—but the sound of a promise was unmistakable. She rested her head against Cam's broad shoulder. "*How* did you find me?"

"It was a group effort: me, Tristan, Sara, Tyla. We'd have been too late otherwise." Another growl rumbled through him. "What were you thinking, going into the forest with some stranger?"

His carefully checked anger made her stomach flip-flop. "I didn't know he was a stranger. He looked... Cam, he looked just like you."

He leaned away, as if startled, and peered into her face. "You're saying he took my form?"

"And your voice." A shudder raced through her, breaking the words into too many syllables.

Cam pulled her close again. "That explains some things." He rubbed soothing circles on her back. "You're still in trouble, though. Letting anyone—even me—drain your magic? I swear, I'm going full-goblin on you for the next month. I hope you're scared out of your wings every time you see me."

Despite the promises of retribution, Cam's arms were the safest place she'd ever known. Destry burrowed into his chest, inhaling the scent of soap and earth and freshly washed clothes. She felt him drop a kiss on top of her head.

"She *did* almost die," Tristan said. "Probably punishment enough—right?"

Destry pulled back, and Cam released her, his expression sliding into politeness. He stepped away, allowing Tristan to get closer. He sat on the edge of the bed, taking her hand as carefully as he'd handle a white-puffed dandelion. "Des, I'm so mad at you."

"I can tell," she said, because his face was gentle.

"I am. I'm just more relieved. The mad will come out later." His fingers trembled. "Don't ever—ever—do something like that again. Cam said you thought your magic would go to me?" She nodded, and his eyes darkened. "Even if that hobgoblin's promises were possible, you aren't giving up your magic, living a half-life, for something you *think* I want. Promise me, Destry."

Cam's bark of laughter broke the intense moment. "Won't do any good, Tristan."

A reluctant smile tugged at Tris's lips. "Probably not."

She flushed. "Giving up my magic wasn't supposed to ruin my life. It was supposed to fix things for both of us." She stared at her bandaged wrists, trying to sort out the details in her head. She had a fuzzy remembrance of Cam kissing her, but everything was too jumbled to be sure.

They spent the next half hour talking, while Destry gave a more co-
herent explanation of what had happened with the hobgoblin. She tried
to ignore her throbbing wrist. The one Cam had pierced wasn't bad, but
the one mauled by the hobgoblin ached bone deep. When tears started
in her eyes, Cam, Tristan, and Dante (who'd come to hear the story) all
noticed.

Dante stood. "Enough talking. Tristan must go to the bath I've set
up in the adjoining room. I replicated sea water as exactly as possible. A
long soak would be good for your wing." Tristan sighed but headed for
the door the healer indicated. Dante turned to Cam. "Please explain the
healing process to Destry while I gather items for cleansing her wounds.
Sleep spells are not foolproof, and we don't wish to frighten her, should
it wear off during the procedure."

Destry frowned at the retreating healer. "What's he talking about?"

Cam sat next to her again, his weight making her mattress dip and sliding her closer to him. "You have to stay here a few days. The hobgoblin
drained almost all your life force. Magic is sustaining you, keeping you
from slipping into a coma or worse. It'll compensate while your body
heals."

"I don't mind being here. But what procedure did he mean?"

"You remember how I shared my magic last night? We'll have to do the
same thing a couple times a day until you're close to normal." Cam took
her hand, sliding his calloused thumb across the back of it. "I wish there
were a better way, but this time the monster was truthful. Faeries don't
have the ability to share magic. Your people can't help."

Oh. She tried to control her facial expression, but it didn't work. All
Destry remembered about the previous night was pain—too much of it.
She blinked rapidly, willing herself not to cry. "That's...that's okay. Nice
of you to share."

Her joke fell flat. Cam stroked her tangled hair. "You won't feel it.
Dante or I'll put you to sleep, and when you wake up, it'll be over."

"No. I don't want that to be my memory of you: confusion and pain
under the willa tree. I want to stay awake."

Dante agreed to her request. The healer explained that the injection
of magic acted as a painkiller and should make the process comfortable.

When Cam first took goblin form and lifted her wrist to his mouth, Destry's heart sped up. But, as Dante predicted, the sharing wasn't painful. Cam used the fang marks already there; she barely felt it when he slid his teeth into them.

Dante stopped Cam when it was enough. He carefully removed his fangs and changed form, then slid one hand under her jaw. "Des? You okay?"

She was able to give him an honest smile, though it fell away when they cleaned her other wrist. The hobgoblin poison was hard to remove, which necessitated a painfully thorough cleansing of the wounds twice a day. After a minute of trying to be stoic, Destry buried her face in Cam's chest and cried while Dante worked on her.

She didn't argue about lying back down. Cam sat in the chair next to her bed, looking drained. He offered her his hand, and Destry took it with her less-injured one. For a moment, neither spoke. Then Cam said, "So you were willing to come here, and live like this—" he indicated the wrist that wasn't throbbing— "forever?"

She wouldn't lie to him. "Yes."

He squeezed her hand gently. Neither of them said the other half of the statement: that things had changed. Her willingness had been based on not having to ruin Tristan's life to get what she wanted. After a few minutes of silence, Destry said, "Cam? Something's been bothering me."

His chuckle was rough. "Just one thing?"

"It's something you couldn't figure out before. You sent several letters to the queen, hoping she'd protect faerie students from the hobgoblin. Except no one did anything."

He nodded. "No one would even acknowledge that they'd gone missing."

Destry thought back to the nightmare moments in the tent, to her conversation with the monster. "I think I understand why. And if I'm right, I need your help to do something about it."

They spent the rest of the day in an enforced waiting period. Neither Cam nor Destry was strong enough to traverse the castle, let alone trek through Si'fliegen. Instead, they sent Tyla on a scouting mission to the fey palace. She returned within hours, a scroll with a broken seal pinched in her beak. After examining the evidence, they sent a message to Riamon, asking him to contact his sister. If all went well (and Alissa was willing), she would meet them at the fey palace the following morning. But the day wore on with no response from either sibling.

Tristan returned (reluctantly) to the academy that afternoon, moved only by Dante's insistence that his wing would suffer permanent damage without the ministrations of fey healers. Destry suffered a guilty relief when he left. Had her magic partner known about her quest for justice, he would have insisted on helping. This way, if the confrontation went badly, Tristan wouldn't be involved.

The next morning, Destry, Cam, and Lady Val met in the hall outside of Cam's room. "The meeting has been arranged," Lady Val said as they started downstairs. "And Brumal waits for you in the entry hall."

Destry asked, "How did you convince the executor to set up the meeting?"

"We reminded him that the prudent man cultivates favor in more than one place. Because of the potential results of the hobgoblin's attack, he was willing."

Cam added, "That doesn't mean he'll be our ally. The executor will go with whichever side has the upper hand."

Cam's aunt paused on the last landing. They could see Brumal standing near the front doors, his bearing stiff. Lady Val met her nephew's eyes gravely. "Be careful how you handle this. A wrong move could land our kingdom in serious trouble."

He kissed her cheek. "I'll do my best not to start the next faerie-goblin war."

Brumal watched them descend the stairs. "I do not encourage this course of action, Your Majesty."

"You made that clear last night," Cam said coolly. The older man had spent the first half of dinner arguing against their plan, then stormed

from the table when they refused to budge. "It doesn't change my obligation."

"Your obligation towards whom? The faeries? Let them deal with
problems in their leadership. Do not put yourself in way of faerie anger."

Lady Val frowned. "My nephew is within his rights. The crime under
investigation affected both goblin and faerie subjects. Do you support
him or not?"

Brumal bowed deeply. "Of course. His well-being, this kingdom's
well-being, is all I am considering."

"Maybe that's the problem," Cam said. "Both kingdoms spend an
inordinate amount of time protecting their own and worry little, or not
at all, about the other. More cooperation could lend us both greater
strength."

Brumal's lips thinned. "I would not allow your subjects to hear such
statements, Camden. They're not ready for these revolutionary ideas."

They followed him out the doors and to the waiting horse. The dense
cloud cover was accompanied by an unseasonably warm day for the
current fall weather. Destry smiled her appreciation for both things, but
Cam grimaced at the overcast sky. "Sure hope that rain holds off. Soaked,
dripping dignitaries aren't impressive."

He vaulted onto the sleek black animal and lifted Destry up in front
of him. According to Cam, goblins usually converted to their stronger
goblin forms when covering an otherwise tiring distance. In the instances
requiring human form, no self-respecting goblin would be caught dead
in a carriage. Most were skilled bareback riders. Cam must be, because
the enormous animal wore no saddle. Destry had never been on a horse
in her life. Still, the other option was riding on Tyla the giant bird.

Brumal ran alongside them in wolf form; he kept up easily, nearly
as big as the horse. The fast pace was too uncomfortable to carry on
a conversation. Once they crossed into Si'fliegen, passed through the
countryside, and merged onto one of the smooth-cobbled streets, Cam
slowed the horse to a walk.

Destry looked up the winding road to the faerie palace, sitting atop its
hill in cool dominion. She shivered. She'd felt brave in the goblin realm,

fueled by righteous anger and her horrific experiences. But presented with hard evidence of the power she faced, Destry's courage withered.

Cam murmured, "Breathe. It's going to be okay."

"What if it isn't? What if we can't prove anything? They'll run me out of the fey kingdom."

"Then you'll come live with the goblins. You can have the room next to mine, and your magic partner can have the third one. And he can learn goblin magic, too, whether he likes it or not." She felt Cam laughing to himself.

Destry didn't respond. His arm tightened around her. "Seriously, Des. If you can save yourself from a hobgoblin, you can handle this, too."

"But I didn't," she choked out. "You did. You and Tyla and Tristan."

"Oh?" Cam's voice quieted, intensity without volume. "I must have forgotten the part where *I* defied a monster, where *I* held out against excruciating torture until help could arrive."

"That's not—"

He continued like she hadn't said anything, "I suppose it was Tristan who—knowing the cost was his life—blasted the creature, removing its fangs and its ability to feed on anyone else."

"I didn't mean—"

"And of course, *Tyla* must have been the person with enough sense to attack him when we were in the clearing, allowing us to finally locate you and finish the job."

Destry curled her hands into fists. "But I never would have survived if you hadn't come to the rescue! I couldn't have defeated the hobgoblin by myself!"

"Neither could we." Their horse trotted over a delicate marble bridge, hooves echoing against the stone. "No one could have taken that monster alone. You'd already weakened the hobgoblin, and the rest of us still barely managed to stop him."

They crossed a wide courtyard and drew up in front of the palace. Cam swung down, then lowered Destry to the ground. "Hobgoblins don't leave survivors—not willingly. He'd have killed you after that spell. You kept yourself alive against one of the most formidable predators in the Fold. Be proud of yourself." He brushed one calloused thumb along her jaw. "I am."

Destry flushed. Brumal loped up beside them, changing into human shape. Cam dropped his hand as a servant scurried over to take the horse's reins. Thunder rumbled, and they ascended the curving staircase and entered through the massive front doors.

A QUESTION OF HONOR

E xecutor Faris waited near a trio of fountains much like the ones at the academy. "Goblin King. High Chancellor Brumal. Faerie Destry. I trust the journey through our lands was uneventful. Have you need of refreshment?"

Brumal stepped forward. "A thoughtful offer, but no. The gravity of our visit forces us to business and hopefully a swift resolution."

The faerie official nodded. He motioned for them to follow, but Cam said, "I believe it's customary to have more than one witness from your kingdom, that the proceedings may be accepted as truthful and fair."

The executor stiffened. "I understood this to be an informal discussion of a concern on the part of Your Majesty."

"Among those of high rank, even the informal ought to be conducted with utmost care. We'll wait while you find a suitable witness."

"That won't be necessary." The statement came from Alissa, who hustled in from one of the many doors branching off the vast foyer. "I'm free of duty and carry the necessary rank for such a task." Destry breathed a silent sigh of relief.

Executor Faris looked less and less pleased, but he bowed to Cam. "Follow me."

He led them to an imposing door on the ground floor level. A servant bowed them into a throne room, more intimate than the one in the goblin castle. The queen sat reading a letter. She looked up as they approached. Her eyes flickered over Alissa, and a frown creased her brow. She smoothed it, descending the dais to meet them.

"Goblin King. I just reviewed your missive. I own myself both surprised and relieved. Hobgoblins haven't plagued these parts for years. I'm grateful that your letter was not to warn, but to inform that the problem was already dealt with."

Cam smiled. "That's always welcome news for those who feel the pressure of ruling. Though I'm surprised there was no suspicion in your kingdom. The monster has been here for some time, and his preferred victims were faeries. He must have been incredibly circumspect to arouse so little concern."

"Indeed," Liselle said coolly. "What will you do with the creature? Your letter said only that the threat was nullified."

"We won't need to do anything further. The monster had no interest in being captured. He's been dealt with on a permanent basis."

The queen's face paled. She turned to the window. "I must commend you on such decisive action."

"Is something amiss, Your Majesty?" Cam sounded solicitous, but his eyes never left the queen. "I expected this news to be met with jubilation."

"Of course Queen Liselle is pleased," the executor blustered. "Fey sensibilities are more refined than those of goblinkind. Such news must naturally be startling."

The queen turned back around. The muted light creeping in the windows gleamed on her ebony hair. "As you say, Executor Faris. It comes as a shock that this creature not only preyed upon our people, but also our students." She gestured to Destry.

Cam said, "He was able to access her because no one here paid attention to my warnings. I sent word several times about a threat in the forest and each time was assured there'd been no disappearances. I find that hard to believe, knowing now what was preying along the river."

"Yes, a regrettable lapse in communication. Had I realized, I would have ordered a closer inquiry into the matter. The problem will be dealt with."

Cam frowned. "A lapse in communication? I sent those letters to you directly."

The queen's eyebrows rose. "You intimate—what, precisely? That I knew what was happening and ignored it? Those are dangerous words, Goblin King, especially as they're not backed by proof."

"Actually..." Cam reached into his pocket. He pulled out a rolled scroll with a broken seal: the royal seal of Rí Kobold. He handed it to the executor. "A concerned citizen found this among your possessions, Your Majesty, and brought it to us."

The man scanned it, then handed it to her. The queen made a sound of dismissal. "I've never seen this. A scroll I supposedly saw, delivered by your hand, is inadequate proof of your accusations—no matter what it says."

"But magic leaves traces," Cam replied. He pulled out a leather sack of the powder Brumal had used at the trial. "If we sprinkle this across the letter..."

"A letter I just handled in your presence. You shall have to do better than that."

"I intend to." Cam turned to the little man. "Under mutual law, the ruler of one kingdom may challenge the ruler of another if there's adequate proof that improper or unwise actions have endangered the opposing side. The consistent refusal to acknowledge the disappearance of these girls, and likely other citizens, made identifying the hobgoblin's presence impossible—which was detrimental to my kingdom as well as your own. You're bound to accommodate me in a search for the truth."

Alissa said, "I'm afraid that's the law. Violation of it is considered violation of the treaty."

Cam indicated the scroll. "If you'll provide escort to the queen's private chambers, I'm certain we'll find more of these."

Liselle's palms began glowing. She curled her fingers around them. "Even were that scroll mine, it would have been obtained through a spy. Goblin King, your accusations will be met with retribution if they're not withdrawn."

Executor Faris watched her with thinly veiled curiosity. "With such a heavy charge laid, Your Majesty, it would be best to put this matter to rest—for the good of the kingdom."

"Simply prove the ridiculousness of the allegations," Brumal agreed. "Then we can walk away in peace."

Her gaze turned icy. "Do not talk peace to me, Brumal. You of all people know how that chance was destroyed."

The chancellor didn't respond. The queen turned to Destry. "And what say you? Did I not warn you to be careful in Rí Kobold? Does that seem like the action of a queen who cares little for her subjects?"

Destry met the woman's eyes. Despite the haughty expression, fear flickered there. "You did, Your Majesty. And you probably do care for your subjects. But I think there's someone you cared about more."

Liselle's face hardened. "It seems I have little choice, if even my subjects will level such accusations. Prepare to leave my kingdom, Destry Firewings. Once my innocence is proven, you'll no longer be welcome." She swept out the door.

They followed her up a flight of stairs to a set of apartments. The executor held out a restraining hand. "I should go first, Your Majesty, to circumvent any accusations of tampering on your part." Queen Liselle stood stone-faced as he opened the door.

The queen's chambers were immaculate. A fresh breeze wafted through the open double doors leading onto an elegant balcony. Destry stood beside Cam and the queen as Brumal, Alissa, and the executor conducted a thorough search, but they found nothing except personal correspondence and drafts of formal letters. "Are you satisfied?" Liselle asked.

Cam held up one hand. "If I could beg your indulgence... Like yourself, I'm aware of my vulnerability—a public official under constant scrutiny. My apartments have provisions to allow me privacy. Surely you possess similar accommodations."

He looked to the executor, who wavered for a second before saying, "I can't help you. The queen's privacy is her own."

Cam nodded. "It doesn't matter. Perhaps you recall that goblins excel in areas faeries find challenging? Such as our ability to create—and sense—hidden spaces. A legacy from our affinity with the Earth and the caverns beneath it."

He walked the room, trailing long fingers over the marble walls, pausing every so often...stopping at a corner. He ran his hand along the wall, pressed. A narrow block of marble slid out with a hiss.

Cam carried the drawer to the elegant writing desk. Several scrolls sat in the marble box, all with broken seals. Liselle's lips were pinched and white. "You had one. The rest could have been planted."

Cam scooped dust from the leather pouch and sprinkled it over the drawer. The scrolls glowed: silver, blue, and red. The silver vapor drifted toward Cam, hovering like his own personal cloud. The blue swept around the room and then out the door. The red vapor drifted toward the queen and wreathed her. Cam waved a hand to dispel his. "With your particular magic signature? At the very least, you handled these, broke them open. It's difficult to believe you never read them."

The queen turned towards her balcony. Executor Faris murmured, "If there is something that ought to be said, my queen, a private admission would be better than a public inquiry. The goblins may request that, since the incident involves both kingdoms."

Her hands clenched. "Ask Brumal."

"Your Majesty?"

She whirled back into the room. "Brumal knows what happened."

Cam glanced at his chancellor. "What does she mean?"

Brumal's jaw tightened. "Queen Liselle approached me after the third letter you sent. She feared the information might lead to worsening conflict between our races and wished to keep the situation quiet. She knew you wouldn't agree, so she requested my help."

Cam's face hardened. "And you agreed to it, or you would have told me this months ago. Why?"

Brumal scrubbed one hand from forehead to jaw. "I have experience you lack, my king. Preserving the tenuous peace between our peoples seemed best."

Liselle laughed harshly. "He agreed because he owed me a debt long overdue." Brumal started to speak, but she raised her palms, glowing bright. "No! You had personal reasons for agreeing, and I refuse to let you heap guilt on my shoulders alone."

The chancellor stepped back, stopped by Cam. The queen met his eyes. "When I was little older than Destry, I ran tame in the goblin castle. Your father and I and Brumal were friends. When Gregor left for the human world, Brumal went along as his traveling companion. I wished to continue my visits, eager to prove you weren't the monsters you'd been labeled. That changed the night after they left.

"I always used the private passageways to leave the castle. They appealed to my foolish sense of adventure, as did coming and going unescorted. Partway through the passages, I sensed some presence along the corridor. In seconds, the lights went out, plunging us into blackness. Before I could raise defenses, my assailant was on me. He countered every move I made. You can imagine what happened in the darkness." Her eyes were wide, fear and fury writ large on her face.

Hot, grasping hands...the press of a heavy body... Destry's stomach twisted.

The queen raised her chin. "I managed to do one thing. I gave him a faerie mark on his chest: the mark of my fire. So he would always remember his deed, so he could never truly escape it."

Cam's eyes were heavy with compassion. "Your Majesty, I can't express enough sorrow for what happened to you."

She laughed, but it was an ugly sound. "The *regret* of your race. I'm familiar with that. After it was over, after he fled, I didn't know what to do. I stumbled to the palace, immersed myself in the fountain. I cried myself to sleep and tried to forget.

"By the time Brumal returned, a month and a half later, it had become clear that I wouldn't be able to forget. I was with child. I went to my friend and begged him to find the goblin responsible and bring him to justice. He refused."

Camden turned to his chancellor. "Is that true? You refused to help someone whom the goblins had wronged?"

Brumal's face was pale. "Your Majesty, consider the circumstances. Your father was gone, and without him, I had no particular importance. Many disliked the way a possible faerie queen had been allowed to roam free in our domain. I would have lost much and gained nothing, including justice for her."

"You would have gained some self-respect," Cam said harshly.

"He never had much." Ice frosted Liselle's words. "Always wishing to be faerie, to be royalty, so he could pursue me. I'd turned him down before. If he and your father had not left for the human world, I'd have suspected Brumal—particularly since my assailant knew my defense tactics quite well."

Cam's frown deepened. "They left in the morning. I remember that from Dad's stories. And the attack happened that evening?"

"Yes."

He tapped one finger restlessly on the desktop. "Dad told me that he and Brumal rode horses on that first trip to the human world. They intended to tour the magical lands before crossing the Fold. But their first day on the road, when they stopped for lunch, Brumal tied his horse wrong. It escaped while they were in a dwarfish tavern.

"Not wishing to make the entire journey on foot, Brumal left my father at an inn and returned to the castle in wolf form. He came back late that evening—well after midnight—riding a broken-down nag. When Dad asked how our stables contained anything so inferior, Brumal confessed: he'd been too embarrassed to return to the castle. Instead, he purchased a plow horse from a farmer. The horse rarely moved faster than a walk. Dad still teases him about it."

Brumal gave him a sickly smile. "Your Majesty, you've mistaken the timing. It was several days into our journey before I lost my mount."

"No. Dad loves using that story as an example of something good that began poorly. I've heard it at least fifteen times."

Liselle's breathing quickened, audible in the suddenly silent room. "You. All this time, I thought you were covering for some noble—leveraging the knowledge in exchange for power. All these years, it was you."

Her palms glowed white-hot. Power blasted from them, wreathing Brumal. Cam jerked Destry away from the scorch of heat.

Brumal raised his own hands, but his cloak, his vest, his shirt were already burning away, leaving him bare from the waist up. A shimmering black pattern of rising flames gleamed on his left pectoral.

Cam said, "So, this is why you kept silent. Not because of guilt over betraying a friend, but because you were afraid that if the hobgoblin were captured, the story might come out and your evil discovered."

Red suffused Brumal's cheeks and neck. "My evil? *My evil*? It's her fault—that faerie tart who rules the kingdom! I cautioned your father not to allow fey women in, with their bewitching ways and magic temptations. He ignored me! I'd only returned for the horse. I chose the private corridor to accomplish the deed with less embarrassment. And there she was in her red gown, perfume wafting down the hall, taunting me the way she always did. I showed her—showed her that I was as much a man as her faerie lover, not some beast to be spurned." He met Cam's gaze, half-angry, half-beseeching. "You know how they see us, Camden...as little more than intelligent animals."

"You're not an animal," Cam said. "No animal would've hidden its bestiality. You did. That's why you didn't take a horse from the stables, so no one could place you in the castle. In fact..." A look of comprehension swept over his face. "You used the same tactic to avoid record of your communications with Queen Liselle. The forest guards aren't official messengers—they don't follow their protocols. Using them meant your letter deliveries were never recorded on the master list." He turned to the executor. "Executor Faris, I'm remanding this goblin to faerie custody. His justice is handed over to the fey, to deal with in whatever way you deem fit."

"What?" Brumal's eyes widened. "After everything I've done—everything I've given your kingdom—"

"You did everything to protect yourself. You endangered our *willas* to protect yourself. Loyalty is one of our deepest tenets, yet you betrayed the trust of allies and friends. I wash my hands of you and your fate."

Brumal seemed to swell. His jaw elongated, fur rippled along his skin, his teeth lengthened into fangs, and seconds later, the enormous wolf crouched where he had stood. "Move," Brumal growled at the queen, who blocked the way onto the balcony.

She didn't. Power gathered in her hands, a ball of flame and energy. The wolf barked out a dark laugh. "Your power won't breach my fur. Not fast enough." His legs bent, ready to spring; Destry's wings shot out. The queen's, the executor's, and Alissa's did the same. Brumal leapt for Liselle.

Something barreled into the wolf mid-air: an enormous goblin with granite-like skin and obsidian claws.

"Cam!" Destry cried. He and Brumal landed with a thud, then morphed into a fearsome blur, growling and snapping and rolling. Cam loosed a roar of pain, but Destry couldn't see what had happened. The three older faeries edged closer, but there was no way to separate the mass of teeth and claws, no way to use the power building white-hot in their hands.

Destry couldn't help at all. The hobgoblin's attack left her unable to manage a single bolt of power. She watched Cam and Brumal somersault, the wolf landing on top, huge paws pinning him, claws biting into his skin. Blood flowed from a gash along Cam's cheekbone.

Brumal bared his teeth.

43

BATTLE-CHOSEN

◆

D estry's breath lodged in her chest, heavy as molten iron.

Cam wasn't throwing Brumal off.

His arms trembled as he pressed against the wolf's shoulders, his own claws gouging into Brumal's fur and muscle. The monster's blood dripped down Cam's hands and arms. He strained closer to Cam's throat, mere inches separating teeth from flesh. Saliva dripped onto the hollow at the base of his neck, slick against granite skin.

The fey released their palmed power, flinging it at Brumal's exposed side in a mass of blinding light. The smell of singed fur filled the room, and the wolf snarled more viciously, but he didn't release Cam...

Who couldn't throw him off. Not at partial strength, drained from continued sharing with Destry.

The faeries palmed more power.

Brumal's teeth snapped in a frenzy, slicing shallow gashes along Cam's neck. Cam jerked his head sideways to avoid having his throat ripped out. The movement weakened Cam's blood-slicked grip. He grasped frantically at fur, at skin, but Brumal was free.

He lunged.

In a blast of fiery vision, Destry saw what would happen.

Brumal's teeth, closing around Cam's neck.

The clamp of jaws, the jerk, the tearing.

The gush of red, the wolf's muzzle slicked with gore.

And Cam—too still, depthless black eyes gone sightless.

A fire of rebellion seared Destry's body. She would *not* let this happen—not her, battle-chosen of the fey. She was flame, she was purpose. Her body moved of its own accord, the heat seizing her limbs and pulling them into motion.

Brumal's side was to her, jaws inches from Cam's throat. She took several running steps and threw herself in a rolling dive between his front and rear legs, barreling into Cam, pushing her wings as wide as they could spread. The sharp edges caught Brumal's stomach, legs, ribs. He howled and leapt back.

Destry kept rolling. She tucked her wings, gripped Cam with all her strength, and heaved. He rolled with her, and they landed in a heap in the floor. Power blasted around them, the deafening boom of up-close fireworks. Cam shielded Destry with his body as the room shook. Another agonized howl... Destry looked up.

Fire bloomed from Liselle's hands. Brumal dodged it, blood trailing from his wounds, vivid against the white marble floor. He crouched. A third bolt from Liselle caught him in the flank, but he was already airborne. He sprang for Executor Faris, who stumbled back, tripped up by his robes. Brumal soared over his head and through the window. A shower of tinkling crystal shards rained down on the floor.

And then silence, broken only by their gasping, shuddering breaths.

Alissa ran to the window. "He's going for the countryside. I'll send out search parties." She pelted from the room.

The executor shambled to his feet. "I must speak to the tailor about these robes," he said dryly.

Cam grabbed Destry's face between his palms. His skin felt slick, and there was probably blood on her face now, and she didn't care. He was alive—*alive*—obsidian eyes still shining bright. The all-consuming heat rushed out of her as suddenly as it had come, leaving Destry limp.

Cam growled—loudly—but his hands trembled. "He could have torn your wings off."

"Better than tearing your throat out."

He pressed a kiss to her forehead, with another rumbling growl for good measure. "I *am* very attached to that particular body part." Cam stood and pulled Destry to her feet; she groaned. Her acrobatic feat had caused some serious re-injury in her wrists, and her body ached from slamming into the unforgiving marble floor.

Executor Faris righted a chair for Liselle, then turned to them. "Queen Liselle has been quite overset by these events, and I must oversee search parties, as I assume will you. Surely any other matters can be taken up later."

"No." Cam sounded exhausted, but he stood straight. "Your Majesty, we never finished discussing your part in this. Why did you do it? Why, when you knew girls were dying, would you ignore my warnings?"

The queen sank into the chair, face wan and tear-streaked. "After Brumal refused to help, I left and spent my pregnancy living among humans. When the baby was born, I barely looked at him. I left him on the motel room bed and returned to the faerie world."

She swiped a few tears. "I told my parents that being the potential ruler of our race had frightened me. They were pleased to have me back and never delved deeper into my reasons for leaving. Mother, afraid I might run again, arranged for the magic ceremony to happen in private rather than traditionally. I took up my duties as if nothing had changed. I married my faerie prince and thought the worst of my life was over."

She pressed a hand to her abdomen. "It was only years later—when I knew the joy of loving my other children—that my choice began to haunt me. He was my son as much as they were, yet I ran away from him."

Cam frowned. "He was a hobgoblin. A creature without a soul."

"Would he be without a soul if I had taken him with me? If I'd cared for and loved him rather than leaving him alone, naked and cold and crying? No, I have lived to bitterly regret my choice that night. Why else would I keep those letters, incriminating as they were? They were one of my only links to the son I never watched grow up."

"How did he know who you were?" Destry asked.

The queen slid aside her outer robes to reveal a silver pin on her dress. It looked like Destry's goblin mark. "Camden's father gave me this—a symbol of friendship. When I left the Fold, I took it, planning to sell it if my funds ran low. But I never did. After the child was born, I left my few belongings at the motel. Whoever took him in must have passed on what I left."

She sighed. "I heard the rumors of a hobgoblin in the area and supposed it couldn't be my son...until he sent me this pin, rolled in a copy of the spell he tried to use on you. I'm sorry, Destry, but I couldn't deny him. If my son had a chance to gain a soul, I had to let him try—even at your expense."

Destry couldn't answer. She simultaneously had too little and too much to say. Hearing Liselle's story hadn't banished her anger, her fear, but it provided context—a context she understood too well. She groped for Cam's hand, squeezing it tightly.

The executor looked between them and the queen. His shoulders sagged. "It would be best to handle this quietly, Goblin King. Perhaps you would allow us to deal with the situation, rather than formally bringing charges against our kingdom."

"Perhaps. Provided I'm satisfied with your solution." Executor Faris nodded, and Cam added, "It would, however, be unwise to renege on our agreement."

The queen laughed bitterly. "Worry not, Goblin King. My influence will be stripped as soon as possible. You should be more concerned over who will inherit it." She stood. "You can see yourselves out."

The corridors buzzed with activity, courtesy of Alissa's efforts. She stood in the center of it all, directing grim-faced guards and organizing search parties. Cam and Destry slipped through the melee and outside, where a gentle rain misted down. While Cam retrieved their horse, Destry reveled in the cool drops soaking into her thirsty skin and—hopefully—washing away some gore. Cam led the horse over. He glanced at Destry's wings. "Think you can furl those razor-bladed beauties?"

She bent a pointed look on his goblin form. Sighing, Cam melded to human shape. Destry half-regretted it. The cut on his cheek looked worse like that, the wounds on his neck and shoulders more obvious. But she turned so he could see her back, allowing her wings to furl with a whoosh of red mist.

"Show-off." Cam pulled himself onto the horse with a groan, then helped Destry up. "This is the second time in three days we've been in battle. Another time, and I'm locking you in my castle for good."

She lifted her face to the rain. "Yeah, except the bad guys—two of them, anyway—lived in your castle too." Cam pulled her close, and Destry didn't worry how it would look to anyone, fey or goblin. "Do you think they'll catch Brumal?"

"No." He urged the horse to a trot. "Brumal knows the area well, and those injuries won't slow him much. But he'll be too busy evading search parties to come after us, and he can never return to these kingdoms."

"What do you think Liselle meant...that you wouldn't like the new ruler?"

His arm tightened on her waist. "I'm not certain. And right now, I'd rather not think about it. How about for five minutes, we just be plain old Cam and Destry?"

Thunder rumbled. The sound lifted her spirits, and she laughed. "Plain old Cam and Destry, bloody and battle-scarred, riding a horse in a thunderstorm in an enchanted kingdom? Sounds plausible to me."

Cam chuckled. "Me too."

So they rode to the goblin castle, while the rain poured down around them and turned the world to silver.

Destry spent the next week at the castle. The storm had healed some of the damage to her wrist, but it still needed the attention of a healer, and Destry needed Cam's goblin magic. Fey Elena sent word for her to stay as long as necessary; the message had an inexplicable undertone of relief.

The story of the hobgoblin and Brumal spread quickly. Destry went from being reviled by the majority of the people in Rí Kobold to being admired. It was a pleasant change, especially once word leaked out about her fondness for sweets. More than one sugary treat made its way into Destry's hands, courtesy of a penitent goblin.

She had little idea what was happening in the faerie world. With finals only a week away, Tristan came to the castle each morning to study and bring her news, but the information was sparse. There were rumors that the faerie queen was stepping down. The supposed reasons varied: Liselle's health was failing, she'd been traumatized by a savage goblin attack, the confirmation of hobgoblin deaths in Si'fliegen had undermined the queen's faith in her ability to rule. None named the real reason.

Cam was gone most days, heading a manhunt for Brumal; he made several trips to the faerie palace too. One afternoon, he returned with a legal document from the fey government. The provisional officials offered Destry a chance to press charges against the queen. She couldn't bring herself to do it. She just wanted the fey kingdom to have a trustworthy leader. Cam delivered her answer to Executor Faris: the document would be returned—unsigned—after Liselle's removal from office.

Cam and Destry spent their evenings together. Sometimes, Destry studied while Cam worked on kingly-type paperwork or letters. Other times, they explored the castle, visited his aunt, played goblin board games, or hung out with Tyla and a few other congenial goblins. One night, they donned hooded cloaks and walked to Mellie's, who apparently knew Cam almost as well as she knew Tristan. He explained that no goblins possessed Mellie's special ability. He'd been using the café to keep in touch with Destry since he first left for "school."

On the day finals started, Tristan came to walk her to the academy. Destry's wrists had healed, and she no longer needed Cam's magic, so she rose early to pack her clothes and little gifts she'd accumulated from the goblins. She was about to pack the last item—a miniature willa tree one of the journeyman students had carved—when Tristan knocked on the open door. "Ready?"

"Almost."

He strolled over. "Can I see?" Reluctantly, Destry handed him the tiny willa. He examined it, eyes intent. "This is pretty."

She shrugged. "The guy who carved it was mean to me after the willa attack. He wanted to make up for it."

"Yeah, but it means more to you than that."

Destry met his eyes. On the surface, everything seemed fine between them: no awkwardness or discomfort. But she'd just spent the last week and a half in the goblin castle...with Cam. Surely Tris had some conflict about that.

He smiled gently. "There's something I need to say...something I should have said a long time ago. It's okay that you love this place, Des. I don't want you to pretend to be somebody different for me."

"I don't want you to pretend, either."

"I'm not. Look, you needed someone when you were younger, and Cam was there. He's your home. I shouldn't take that away."

"That doesn't change who *we* are. Magic partners. Friends."

Tristan grinned wider. "I know that, too. You planned to let a goblin drain your magic and give it to me. That's a good litmus test for friendship." She must have looked doubtful; his face slipped into seriousness again. "I realize it's not that simple. But we have several more years. I can do the things Cam did for you. I can be home for you too."

"I don't want a second Cam. I want you: Tristan." She took a deep breath. "The person I'm committing to."

The words were hard to say. Destry had given serious thought over the past week to what she wanted and what she was willing to pay for it. Her friendship with Cam was inviolable, but she couldn't abandon Tristan. Time to accept her life in the faerie kingdom.

Tristan shook his head. "You made a good point, that night at Mellie's. Our relationship will be shaky if we make promises too soon. Plus, I'm not sure either of us knows what sort of relationship it ought to be. Commit to me as a friend—even as a magic partner. I think that's all we're ready for." He offered her the tiny willa tree. "We both screwed up. We'll both do better. Good enough?"

"You'll both fail your exams and have to live here permanently if you don't move it." They twisted around. A glossy raven perched on Destry's windowsill. Tyla took flight and transformed midair, dropping lightly to the floor. "I came to see what was taking so long."

How much had Tyla heard? Probably most of it. Tristan didn't seem bothered, though. In fact, his eyes glinted with admiration. He tossed

Destry's bag over his shoulder. "We're deciding whether I leave Destry behind as a snack for Cam, or if I take her back to the academy. Took a lot of pleading, but she won me over."

Tyla raised an eyebrow. "Tough sell. I'll walk you out." As they headed down the hall, she added, "I've been looking into your little mystery."

"Mystery?" Tristan looked askance at both girls.

Destry nodded. "Remember that gardener I mentioned? Cam wants to know who he is."

"Why? What difference does it make?"

Tyla ticked points off on her fingers. "He went out of his way to help Destry, though they'd never met. He sings goblin songs to grow plants. And he showed up at Destry's Striking. Cam and Destry realized it was the same person when they compared descriptions. Taken together, those things seem significant."

Tristan frowned. "What did you find out?"

"Nothing. Absolutely nothing." Tyla sounded miffed. "I haven't found a single gardener matching their description. Haven't seen the man around Si'fliegen or in the palace. And I can't give his description to our fey allies, because we don't know why he's so interested in Destry. Might be information better kept private."

Destry had been sure that Tyla, spy extraordinaire, would find some answers. Uncertainty and relief jumbled into a confusing mess in her chest. Answers might mean yet another problem —one she wasn't ready to deal with. But ignorance hadn't kept her safe, either.

Tyla started down the stairs to the entrance hall. "Don't worry. Might take longer than expected, but I always accomplish my missions. You just head to the school like good little faeries and pass those exams."

Good little faeries? Too bad Tyla wasn't in raven form. Destry could've pulled out a few feathers to retaliate.

Tristan grinned. "I always ace my finals. But I need a substantial incentive to behave."

Tyla said dryly, "Angling for desserts to sneak into school?"

"Not exactly. Still, if you're offering, we can detour by the kitchens while Destry tells Cam goodbye."

Destry elbowed him in the ribs. "No one's getting sugared up this morning. I already said bye to Cam." She was acutely aware that she might never return to his castle like this and hadn't wanted to be teary-eyed on the way to school.

Tyla smirked. "Poor Tristan. I'll eat a second cookie at lunch, just for you. Good luck on those exams."

Mr. Perfect-Grades-Tristan doesn't need luck, Destry thought morosely. *Send it my way instead.* But finals were shockingly tolerable. There was one benefit to the hobgoblin's attack: with so much goblin energy in her, Destry had a plausible excuse for using spoken magic during her tests. For her Combat final, Fey Renalt asked her to explain the defense techniques she'd utilized with the scorione, the hobgoblin, and Brumal. She told him about everything, including that strange moment of fire and heat when her fey instincts had taken charge and directed her movements. He listened—with occasional compliments or reprimands—then said that since she was still alive, she must have learned something.

Grades were given out at the farewell banquet on Friday night. Destry was surprised that she'd passed, and passed well, in more than just Combat. On the way out of the dining hall, a slender boy with close-cropped black hair approached her. "You're Destry, right?" He rubbed his neck as if uncomfortable, a set of water tattoos gleaming against his deep brown skin.

"Ye-e-s..." She shot a questioning look at Sara, whose eyes widened in dismay.

Sara collected herself. "This is Adam. Becca Tommin was his magic partner."

"Oh." She wasn't sure what to say. Like the other girls, Becca had lost her magic—and her life—to the monster, leaving their partners forever bereft of their missing halves.

Adam's eyes fell on Destry's wrist, on the dark scars on its underside. The hobgoblin attack had become common knowledge at school. "You probably don't want to talk about what happened. But I just wondered...did the hobgoblin say anything about...is it for sure Becca's gone?"

Destry said, "Hobgoblins don't spare anyone. He'd have killed me, too, if he could. I'm sorry."

"Yeah. Yeah, me too." He scuffed one foot on the floor.

Sara patted his shoulder awkwardly. "Are you coming back to school next year?"

"Not sure yet." Adam shrugged. "Not much point, if I'm gonna lose my magic. But maybe I'll enjoy it as long as I can." He scuffed his shoe along the floor again. "Okay, I gotta...I gotta pack. Thanks, Destry." He walked away, swiping at his eyes. She watched him, wishing there was something to do besides giving up.

CHANGED

---◆---

T he next morning, Destry met Tristan on the front steps of the school. The bus rumbled in the background as students loaded their bags to leave for the first flight home. Smirking, he handed her a box of Mellie's brownies. "Be sure your guard goblin doesn't confiscate these." Cam would be home for the summer, and in the interest of being more open, she'd shared that news with her magic partner.

He tapped the phone number jotted on the lid. "Be nice to have a little faerie communion over the summer, right?"

Destry propped the box on one hip and her hand on the other. "So any faerie would do?"

"Nah." Tristan kissed her cheek, his eyes bright with mischief. "Just one."

Over by the bus, Arnie hollered, "Enough smooching, Windwings! You'll see her next semester! C'mon, bus is leaving."

Tristan grinned. He pressed an equally mischievous kiss to Destry's other cheek, then darted to the bus. Seconds later, he appeared at a window, waving. With a hydraulic whoosh, the doors swung closed, and the bus pulled away. Destry waved until it was out of sight.

She ate a brownie and climbed the hill for a last firewell visit and a final look at the willa forest. Every time she remembered that Wings would be well by the next school year, relief rushed through her. As the sun climbed the sky, she turned back to the academy, an ache stirring in her chest. Time to go home...or to leave home. Maybe she was doing both.

The headmistress stood in the great hall when Destry made it inside. She waved her over. "I need to speak to you, child." She seated herself on a bench near the front door, and Destry joined her.

"I have both pleasant and unpleasant news," Fey Elena said. "You'll be pleased to know that the goblin king is coming here within the next half hour. He intends to escort you to the human world."

"And you'll let me go? I thought you didn't like the goblins."

"After the debacles of the last few weeks, my opinions have altered somewhat. The goblin king acted selflessly after the attack in the forest. Attempting to share his magic with you—trying to use the willas' strength when he'd never done so—was dangerous. He could have died or faced the wrath of the faerie world had you died. Instead, King Darkwater saved your life."

Destry asked the question she'd been hesitant to voice. "Will it change things for me and Tristan?"

"Impossible to say. Your magic will continue to return, but as far as we know, the goblin magic will always linger. I can't predict how that will affect your bond with your magic partner. We'll deal with problems as they arise." The headmistress continued, "To my less-pleasant news... You heard the queen was officially deposed?"

Destry nodded. "Do they know who the next queen will be?"

"The queen will be chosen from a group of selected individuals, and I'm afraid the officials wish to include you in that group."

"What? Why would they do that? I'm a half-faerie who lived in the human world most of my life. I don't even know who my father is."

Fey Elena said, "And yet there are indicators, ones that the politicians are now aware of. The creature chose you, Destry. He was the son of the queen—a queen who could trace her lineage to the Imperials—and needed a relative. Add in the reasons your heritage was suspect in the first place, and you've become a person of interest for factions who want the Imperials returned to the throne, particularly those who desire a half-blood."

Destry frowned. "But if my father never claimed me, they can't be sure—"

"The political leaders are calling for a test of parentage. That would find your father, no matter if he stepped forward to acknowledge you."

Destry had spent the last few weeks contemplating her feelings about that exact person. According to the hobgoblin, her father had searched for her. But first he'd abandoned her, leaving Beverly to deal with something she was incapable of dealing with. "Can't I refuse?"

"You could. But it would be unwise, unless you plan to leave our world altogether. The politicos, even the general public, would assume you had something to hide."

"So I have to find out who my father is, whether I want to or not."

"Essentially." Fey Elena sighed. "The officials wanted to speak to you today, but I said you've already left for home. And the arguments and picking candidates will take months. You have the summer. I can promise little else."

Destry considered that as she collected her backpack from her room, as she paced through the great hall and past the burbling fountains. The summer didn't sound like a long time compared to her entire future.

She swung the front door open. Cam stood on the porch, rumpled chestnut hair gleaming. The new scar on his face accentuated the sculpted cheekbones, the smile that always meant safety to her. "Where's Rupert?" Destry teased, eying the lone bag slung across Cam's back. "He'll be devastated if you leave him behind."

A flush crept over his cheeks. "Don't tell Dad...but I gave him to one of Dante's apprentices. The kid is new to the castle and lonely. He kept sneaking into the audience chamber to visit Rupert. I figured, why not make them both happy?"

She lifted one hand to her lips, making the motion of locking them and pocketing the key. "I won't tell. But I thought you wanted that mangy bird to like you."

Cam shrugged. "After the last few weeks, it seems less important. I think holding on to Rupert was more about holding on to my old life—the one where I took care of animals and they liked me, where I took care of you and was able to keep you safe, where my largest choices still had relatively small consequences." He looked away, voice turning gruff. "Growing up is hard, even for a goblin king."

Destry closed the door and took his hand. "At least we get to do it together."

"There is that." His fingers twined with hers. "Ready for a trip through the Fold?"

"As long as I don't have to ride on Tyla's back."

Cam laughed, and, hand in hand, they started down the steps.

It was a rainy day in Vicker, Texas, but that didn't discourage the students who packed Andy's Restaurant, celebrating the first week of summer vacation. Destry swung her feet, thumping the booth with her heels as she stuffed another chili-topped cheese fry in her mouth.

"You plan to leave any of those for me?" Cam slid into the seat across from her and snagged a fry off the plate.

She smirked. "Don't take forever getting here next time. I had to sneak out of my house, so your mom wouldn't see me, then walk the whole way, and I still beat you."

"Walking wasn't necessary, you know. You could give in and let me buy you a bike. Call it a thank you gift for saving my life."

"Call it expensive," Destry said. "I can deal with this myself."

He leaned back against the red vinyl seat, propping his feet on Destry's bench. "Never said you can't. Just that you don't have to."

"What if I want to?"

A lazy grin spread across his face. "Faeries are notoriously stubborn. It's your choice."

She kicked him but smiled, lifting her arms above her head for a long stretch. A few people—former classmates—eyed her fey marks. How did she seem to them? After all, she'd left for a new school and come back with tattoos on both arms and legs. More importantly, she'd come back with experiences that had changed her forever.

"Things okay with Beverly?" Cam asked.

Destry made a face. "Besides being grounded for getting 'tattoos?'" Her mom's anger hadn't been a complete surprise, but getting in trouble for something Destry couldn't change (and hadn't actually done) sucked. Especially since Bev had specifically curtailed Destry's time with Cam...and informed his mom. So sneaking around was now on the agenda. Destry refused to miss a chunk of her summer holiday with Cam through unjust imprisonment.

He looked like he was suppressing a smile. "At least she's being a real mom again."

Destry nodded. The improvement in Bev's drinking had led to improvement in other areas. For once, she was without a boyfriend, kept her bills paid, and seemed reasonably happy. "She didn't go out all weekend. I think her job keeps us apart enough to let me visit without sending Mom into drinking mode."

The bell above the door jangled. Destry glanced at the newcomers. Her breath caught. Jared strode in, a petite blonde on his arm. He didn't notice their booth, tucked away in a corner. The girl found a table while Jared rushed toward the bathroom, holding his stomach.

Cam hadn't seen Jared, either—his back was to the door—but he must have noticed Destry's change in mood. "Dessie? You okay?"

She nodded, then shook her head. "Can you do something for me?"

"Probably..."

Destry took a deep breath. "Jared's here. With his new girlfriend."

Anger lit Cam's eyes, and he half rose. "Good. I never got to deal with him before we left last holiday. When we're finished, he'll be too scared to bother you again."

She pulled him down. "I'm not asking you to deal with him. I'm asking you to stay out of it while I handle things." Her hands fisted on the scarred formica tabletop. "I need to, Cam." She couldn't spend every vacation worrying that she'd run into Jared. She couldn't keep feeling like his helpless victim.

He searched her face. "Okay. But you have backup if you need it."

Destry squeezed his hand and stood. Legs shaky, she marched over to the blonde girl, who looked up with a quizzical smile. "We're not ready to order. My boyfriend will be back in a minute."

"I'm not your waitress." She sank into the seat across from the girl. "My name is Destry Adams."

The girl's eyes widened, then narrowed. "I've heard about you."

Destry pressed her lips into a line, but she couldn't stop the heat crawling up her cheeks. "I'm sure Jared told you a great story, but whatever he said, it wasn't the truth."

The girl rolled her eyes. "He dumped you. Why would I believe anything you have to say?"

"Because guys like Jared don't change. He forced himself on me. I doubt he's treated you better."

A flush crept up the blonde's cheeks now, and her eyes darted towards the bathroom. "What girl would be stupid enough to stay with a guy who doesn't understand the word 'no?'"

Destry spoke gently. "Maybe a girl who thinks it's her fault. Who believes Jared when he says she gave the wrong signals. Who doesn't have a good friend to set her straight, to remind her that 'no' means no, even if someone else wants her to say yes."

The girl's chin trembled, but she crossed her arms. "You need to go. Before he comes back."

Destry gave her a regretful smile. "Actually, that's what *you* need to do."

They sat in silence for several long moments. The blonde closed her eyes, and a tear crept out of one corner. "He really hurt you?"

"Yes."

Another tear joined the first. "He kept telling me how bitter his ex-girlfriends were, that I shouldn't talk to them. I was dumb enough to believe him."

Destry glanced at the men's room. The door was still closed, but for how long? "You don't have to take my word for it. Ask the other girls he dated. I bet you'll hear the same story." She listed several names.

"Maybe. And maybe you just want to break us up so you can have him back."

Destry snorted. "I've got better options than Jared."

The blonde shot a glance at Cam, sitting in the booth, trying to act unconcerned. He wasn't, of course, but Destry appreciated the effort. Jared's girlfriend hesitated, then took out her phone. She composed a quick text. Destry caught a glimpse of the words 'going home early' before she sent it and stood. "I'd say it's been nice talking to you, but it hasn't."

Movement startled them both: the bathroom door, creaking open. The girl jumped. She hurried towards the exit. Jared came out in time to hear the bell on the door jangle as it closed behind her. He looked confused. Then he saw Destry sitting at the table, and anger clouded his face.

He strode over. "What are you doing here? Where's Rachel?"

Destry's heart sped up, but she feigned nonchalance. "She decided to eat someplace where the company is better."

He leaned down, forearms on the table, back to the room—cutting off everyone's line of sight to Destry. To an observer, it would look like Jared was leaning closer to chat. "What did you tell her?"

"The truth."

His fists clenched until tendons stood out on his arms. "Look, I tried to play nice over Christmas break. You were too stupid to cooperate. And now—"

Destry placed her hands on the table within inches of his. She snapped her fingers; a tiny flame danced over her left hand. Jared's eyes widened. She cupped her fingers, and the flame grew into a small fireball that nestled in her palm.

He stumbled back. Destry closed her fist, smothering the fire before anyone else could see. She stood and stepped closer, until they were less than a foot apart. "Now...what? Do I look like the thirteen-year-old girl you molested, Jared? Do you think I care about your threats?" She bent a meaningful look on his clenched fists. "If you think the burns from the doorknob were painful, just mess with me again."

His jaw hung. "You...you and Waters. You're both freaks."

"You say that like it's an insult." Destry held out one hand expectantly. "We have some settling up to do."

"Settling up?"

"You trashed my bike. You owe me money for a new one."

"I'm not giving you money." The numbness was seeping out of his voice, replaced again by anger. But this time, fear tempered it.

She met his stare evenly. "A hundred should cover it."

"For that heap of scrap metal?" He pulled out his wallet and shoved a couple bills into her hand with swaggering bravado. "Because I'm nice, I'll give you $25."

Destry snagged the wallet, examining its contents. "That bike had a lot of sentimental value. So we should make it $200 to cover my pain and suffering." Jared glared, but he didn't object as Destry pulled more cash out. She handed the wallet back. "Now we're even. Leave me alone, and it'll stay that way."

They could never truly be even. Neither money nor revenge could restore what Jared had taken from her or make up for the moments of fear. But she wanted to put him where he belonged—in her past.

He glanced at her hands again. Without another word, Jared turned and left.

Destry loosed a long, shaky breath. Straightened her shoulders. And realized something: her wings weren't pressing against her shoulder blades, screaming for release. She hadn't needed to hold them back a single time during the confrontation with Jared.

Changed, indeed.

She sauntered to the booth, where Cam's shoulders were relaxing and his hands unknotting. She plunked the cash in front of him. "Still want to find me a bike?"

He grinned up at her. She perched on the edge of Cam's bench, nudging him with her hip. He scooted over, and Destry slid across the seat until their shoulders nestled perfectly together. Contentment curled in her chest, warm as embers waiting to be stoked into a fire. She kicked her feet onto the opposite bench and grinned back at Cam. "This is gonna be a good summer."

ACKNOWLEDGEMENTS

$\blacklozenge$

While writing tends to be a solitary act, the process of bringing a book to life is a true group effort, and I'm blessed to have an amazing group in my corner. I owe so much gratitude to:

My husband: You showed me firsthand that broken people can mend, leaps of faith are worth taking, and love and laughter will vanquish so many challenges. My roots begin and end with you, Nathan.

My kids—Sara, Colton, Sam, Cate, Sean, and Cam: You changed my world in the best of ways. Everything I create carries little pieces of you. Thank you for being patient when I was lost in the Fold (many, *many* times) and for helping out so I could make publishing a reality. You guys are my wings.

My mom, Carolyn Churchwell: You ignited my love of words with the Berenstain Bears, multitudes of fairy tales, and so many readings of The Velveteen Rabbit that the book fell apart. Thank you for giving me a creative heart, creative hands, and the love to make those things matter. I'm the person I am because of you.

My stepdad, Chuck Churchwell: I'll always treasure your belief in me (and your certainty that I was destined for a completely unrealistic level of literary success). I wish you were here to hold this book in your hands. Instead, this story carries you in its heart.

My sisters, Selena Wilson and Diana Bales:

Selena, thank you loving this story *almost* as much as you love me, and for the endless goblin king fan art, character discussions, and fiction-based shenanigans.

Diana, thank you for hours and *hours* of graphic design advice, "how does *this* look?" texts, and for a listening ear and practical help when I was tearing my hair out over images, printing, and more.

I can't imagine life without you two in my corner.

Toni Suzuki of Edits by Toni: Thank you for understanding the heart of this book and its characters, and for handling my work with both passion and dedication. *These Tangled Roots* shines more brightly because of you.

My critique partners, Hannah Hounshell and Lexis Coen:

Hannah, thank for helping me carry this dream when I'd grown weary. I couldn't have kept going without our late-night texts, commiserations, and your faith that this story needed to be told.

Lexis, thank you for being an amazing (and suspicious) beta reader, proofreader, and formatter...and for sharing my dorky sense of humor. Our laughter over ridiculous things kept my heart light.

The Power Triad—Allisa White, Adelaide Thorne, and Adrienne Quintana: You may not all know each other, and you may have carried the name 'beta readers,' but your contributions went well beyond that title. Thank you for offering feedback that enhanced characters, brought out themes, revealed weaknesses, and generally made this book what it is today.

My beta readers—Becky Moynihan, Tyffany Hackett, Baj Goodson, Indigo Woods, Rebecca McCoy, Cassie Oveson, Erica Nadvornik, Rhye Di Marco, Stevie Rae Causey, Rosie Talbot, Grace K, Virginia See, Lorraine Starks, and Sheridan Sharp: Whether you read an early version or a later one, your comments and enthusiasm shaped this story. It wouldn't be a tenth of the book it is without you.

Charlie Holmberg and the authors of LitService podcast: Your first chapter critique offered pro direction when I needed it most. Thank you for giving me the confidence that this book might be good enough for a broader audience to enjoy.

Erin, Ava, Eden, and Vivian Fisher: I'll always carry your enthusiasm, friendship, and support in my heart. Special thanks goes to Ava Fisher for writing my first piece of fan mail. You gave me a "why" that helped carry this book to publication..

Early readers Amanda Carter, Nicole Vowels, Ashley Juergens, Jennifer McDonald, Trisha Willard, Maddy Egbert, Vanessa Byers, Christine and Breana Manning, Sharon and Erika Faragher, and Olivia and Kit Burbank, along with the (former) teens of Open Minds Homeschool Co-op (you know who you are):

Thank you for loving this story in its infancy. Your support encouraged me to share my words with a wider world.

Heather Christenson: 'Early reader' is an inadequate title for your contributions to this book. Thank you for pushing me to converse with a published author when I was scared, reminding me that my writing was worth reading, and cheering me on with the best of hearts.

Koby and Trevor Young: Thank you for offering rides, visits, and (most importantly) chocolate during my first few times attending Storymakers writing conference. Who needs found family when I have family like y'all?

Speaking of family...a great big thank you to my (great big) extended family, many of whom have cheered me on since my initial awkward, way-too-long, not-so-great stories. Whether you're part of my life by marriage or by blood, your support is an incomparable blessing. And my never-ending gratitude to the friends who saw worth in those not-so-great stories. Your enthusiasm encouraged me to create something I felt worthy of sharing with the world.

I can't forget the gratitude owed to my Heavenly Father. All good things ultimately come from Him, and I'll be ever-grateful that He gifted me with a screwy brain that makes up stories without my permission. If my books spread even a fraction of His love through the world, I'll be satisfied.

And last but not least—I'm forever grateful to each reader who's given this story a chance. Thank you for letting Destry, Camden, and all the denizens of the Fold live in hearts besides mine. I may write the words, but readers bring them to life.

TO MY READERS

---◆---

I t's been said that an author begins a story, but the reader finishes it. I believe that to be true.

Thank you for being part of *this* story.

Enthusiastic readers will always be essential to an author's journey. No marketing plan can replace word of mouth, so if you enjoyed *These Tangled Roots*, please recommend it to others!

And if you want to manifest some serious main character energy:

- leave a review on Amazon, Goodreads, or other review sites (short or long, I love them all)

- snap a book pic and share on social media (feel free to tag me)

- request this book at your local library

I'd love to have you join me on this author adventure! I'm always eager to hear from my readers. Find me on Instagram at @daphnetatum and at my website: daphnetatum.com.

May your bookish journeys always bring you joy,

Daphne Tatum

Content Warnings

I love it when a reader wants to explore the magical world of the Fold with me! However, I always want to be transparent about potentially upsetting events within these pages. Readers should exercise their best judgment if sensitive to the following:

- attempted sexual assault (one character pins another character down, kisses her several times without consent, and tries to grope under her shirt; he's stopped before he can do anything further)

- fantasy peril and death (non-graphic: some blood but no gore)

- magical torture (non-graphic: an antagonist causes magically-induced pain to a character)

- mention of past sexual assault of a side character (vaguely described, no details)

ABOUT THE AUTHOR

Daphne Tatum grew up in the wild forests of her imagination, befriending mythical creatures and riding dragons. As an adult, she hoped to become a library troll and live among the stacks of books, but the position was already filled. Instead, Daphne spends her days homeschooling her kids, writing books about magical places, and pretending that cooking and taxes don't exist.

She lives in Texas with her husband, too many cats, and the perfect number of kids. Daphne hopes her books will create portals for a new generation of readers to get lost in.